Praise for *Stone and a Hard Place*

"The magic is believable, the characters could be people you know, and the twists, turns and mysteries to be solved glue your eyes to the page. You will never forget these characters or their world."
—*Jacqueline Lichtenberg, Hugo-nominated author of the* Sime~Gen *series and* Star Trek Lives!

"Somewhat reminiscent of the Dresden Files but with its own distinct style."
—*John W. Ranken, Amazon reviewer*

"I am reminded of Jim Butcher here...Darker than most Urban Fantasy, not quite horror, but with a touch of Lovecraftian."
—*Wulfstan, Amazon Top 500 reviewer*

"Dramatic protagonist sucked me right in...I instantly wanted to spend more time with Alastair Stone...I definitely want to see more from this author!"
—*Shawna Reppert, award-winning author of* The Stolen Luck, Ravensblood, *and* Raven's Wing

"Fast-moving fun!...[t]he book is full of the things I like in a book, and they are presented in a clean, brisk style. This is a book well worth checking out.."
—*Jason M. Hardy, author of* Hell on Water, Drops of Corruption, *and* The Last Prophecies

"Stone is a completely believable protagonist, and, frankly, damned likeable. We all wish we had college profs as engaging as he is!"
—*Silas Sparkhammer, Amazon reviewer*

ALSO BY R. L. KING

THE ALASTAIR STONE CHRONICLES

Stone and a Hard Place
The Forgotten
The Threshold
The Source
Core of Stone
Shadows and Stone (novella)

SHADOWRUN

Shadowrun: Borrowed Time
Shadowrun: Wolf and Buffalo
Shadowrun: Veiled Extraction (coming in 2017)
(published by Catalyst Game Labs)

ALASTAIR STONE CHRONICLES: BOOK SIX

BLOOD
AND
STONE

R.L. KING

MAGESPACE
PRESS

To my mom, Cheryl King (1933-2011),
who instilled in me a love of spooky things

ACKNOWLEDGMENTS

For some of these, I should just cut and paste from the previous books, because they're almost always going to include the same cast of characters: Dan, my ever-understanding spouse, for inspiration and support; John Helfers, my editor, for making my stuff better (and for the great snarky comments he puts in the manuscript); Mike Brodu, my Picky Beta Reader (you should see the dozens of pages worth of discussions we got into about bits of this book); and Glendon at Streetlight Graphics for another fantastic cover.

Thanks also to Mike Murphy, a longtime friend, gaming buddy, and retired California law enforcement officer, who gave me some pointers about the cops and their behavior.

And hey, thanks to the Ojai Valley for being such a great place to grow up. I'm pretty sure all those cool spooky urban legends I heard as a kid just sat there in the back of my brain for years until they could be inspirations for my books.

| CHAPTER ONE

I'm getting too damn old for this.

The thought hit Jason Thayer's befuddled brain half a second before he doubled over and threw up into the gutter.

It was somewhere on the far side of two a.m., and he was seriously regretting his decision to walk back to his motel room instead of accepting Ed's offer to call him a cab.

"It's not far," he'd said. "The night air will do me good," he'd said.

God, he was an idiot.

The only thing worse than an idiot was a *lost* idiot.

The party had been fantastic: Ed's parents had a big spread, complete with bar, swimming pool, tree-filled back yard, and big-screen TV on which to watch the impressive collection of porno-graphic movies the guys had procured, and they'd kindly agreed to clear out for the night in order to allow their son's friends to drink too much and get sick all over the deck. After all, Ed was only going to get married once, right?

There weren't supposed to be strippers—Ed had put up a token protest, complaining that if his fiancée found out about them he'd be spending his wedding night in the doghouse instead of the honeymoon suite. But they'd gotten a few shots into him, and be-fore long he was cheering along with the crowd as the two eerily limber women had done things to each other that didn't seem anatomically possible.

Yeah, it didn't get much better than this.

Or at least it hadn't before things finally started to wind down. One by one the guests tottered off, either to cabs called for them or to crash on one of the many couches or beds scattered throughout the house. Things were still going when Jason left, but he could see that the party maybe had another hour of life left and even through his alcohol-soaked haze he knew he wanted to get at least some sleep before tomorrow—preferably in his own bed, not surrounded by a bunch of snoring drunks.

Throwing up at the bachelor party was one thing. Throwing up on the bride in the receiving line would be something else entirely.

Now, weaving along a winding, rock-lined street that looked like all the other winding, rock-lined streets in this godforsaken excuse for a neighborhood, Jason was beginning to re-evaluate the whole cab thing. Ojai, a few miles north of his native Ventura, was a small town, and nothing was very far from anything else. But even the couple of miles he had to cover seemed like an interminable hike when his head was pounding, his stomach was doing the cha-cha, and his shirt reeked of sweat, nachos, cheap beer, and the not-so-subtle hint of whatever perfume the blonde stripper had been wearing way too much of.

She'd been one fine-looking lady, though. Tall, tanned all over (and he meant *all* over), and built like a brick shithouse—whatever the hell that was supposed to even mean. He had vague memories of trying to coax her into one of the bedrooms with him as she ground herself on his lap in time with the driving beat of the music, and of her laughing cheerfully and calling him a "naughty boy" before sashaying off to rejoin her fellow performer in the front room. Ah, well. He'd tried. Nobody could say he hadn't tried.

High school had been less than ten years ago, but despite the good time he'd had at the party, he'd gotten a good headful of the reason why clichés got to *be* clichés: because they contained at least a little bit of truth. You really couldn't go home again—not like the way things used to be, anyway. The guys—chubby party animal

Shane, athletic ladies' man Kurt, and longhaired wannabe jock Chris, who everybody called "Cramp" for reasons best left in the past—had been his best buds through high school in Ventura. They'd hung out together, dated the same girls and never committed to one, played on the same sports teams, and got into trouble on weekends. Not too much trouble, since Jason already had his mind set on the police academy even at that point, but enough that high school overall was a pretty good time in his life. A time before a lot of things had gone, as his friend Alastair Stone would say, "pear-shaped."

Now, though, with his stomach roiling and his head feeling like somebody had used it for home base, high school seemed another lifetime ago. None of the others had left the area: Shane sold shoes at the mall in Ventura; Kurt, after losing his dream to play pro ball to a bad throwing-arm break in his senior year of college, worked at his dad's landscape supply company; and Cramp, who'd never seemed to know quite *what* he wanted to do with his life, still lived at home and held down a dead-end job at a local hardware store. When the four of them had gotten together for dinner in Ojai prior to tonight's party, Jason had a hard time joining in with their conversations, and even as great as the party had been, some small corner of his mind just wanted the night to be over. Even though he'd only lived in the Bay Area a year, the apartment he shared with his sister in Mountain View already felt more like home than this did.

Swaying back and forth, he grabbed onto a street sign for balance and glanced up at white letters that swam across it: Foothill. He was on Foothill Road. Assuming he was facing the right direction, he should be able to keep going for another quarter mile or so and he'd be close to Ojai Avenue, the town's main drag. His motel was there, maybe another mile up the road. But once he got to Ojai Avenue, he was home free.

First he'd have to get walking, though.

He rolled his head back and stared up into the black carpet of stars peeking through the canopy of ancient oak trees, one hand clutching the street sign to keep him from falling over backward. You could actually see them here, since there weren't too many streetlights and most of the houses, set far back from the street, were dark by now. He almost never got up to Ojai when he'd lived down here; back then, he and his friends considered it nothing but a boring little bedroom town full of rich people, old hippies who hadn't quite figured out the Sixties were long gone, and artsy-fartsy weirdos. Still, a little slow-down and back-to-nature wasn't altogether horrible after the faster pace of the Bay Area. He'd go crazy if he had to stay here long, but a few days wouldn't be so bad.

Come on, dummy. You can gawk at the stars all night, but it's not gonna get you back to the motel any faster.

He pushed himself off the sign so hard he almost fell over, lurched back to a mostly standing position, and started off in the direction of Ojai Avenue again. It couldn't be much farther, right?

Then he spotted the shadowy figure up ahead.

He stopped, blinking, trying to decide whether what he was seeing was really there, or if it was just another illusion brought on by too much booze. But no, it sure looked real: a tall, slim form climbing over the low wall separating the packed-dirt sidewalk from a leafy, tree-filled vacant lot.

"Hey," Jason called amiably, waving a hand. He wondered if the figure was drunk too. Maybe they'd climbed over the wall to puke discreetly in the leaves, and was now coming back to the road to do exactly what he himself was doing: trying to walk back to wherever they were staying.

The figure stopped at the sound of his voice and stood in the middle of the path, staring at him. It didn't return his greeting. Jason frowned, his brain trying to get itself around whatever odd cues this person—he couldn't even tell if it was a man or a woman—was putting out.

Cautiously, he moved closer. "Hey," he said again. "Nice night, huh?" His voice sounded very slurred, and he almost laughed.

The figure tilted its head to one side. "Nice...night," it agreed. Its voice was creaky and oddly inflected, as if it were unfamiliar with using it. It sort of sounded like a male voice, but it was still impossible to be certain.

"You sound drunker than I am," Jason observed. "You—"

Then he got a look at the figure's eyes.

He shouldn't have been able to do that, since there were no streetlights in the vicinity and very little light from the moon. But there they were anyway—

—and they were glowing.

I have got *to be plastered.* Jason shook his head a couple of times, figuring it would drive off the weird vision and make the world make sense again.

But no, the figure's eyes still glowed faintly, in a most disquieting shade of red-orange.

"What the hell—?" he began, but the figure merely turned and disappeared back over the wall. Jason could hear it rustling through the leaves.

He stood there for a few more moments, listening to the sound of the stranger recede until it was gone, wondering if he'd really heard or seen it at all. That had been fucking freaky, was what that had been.

Naturally, the first thought that followed "fucking freaky" was *I gotta tell Al about this.*

Somehow (he'd never be quite sure how, but God had a reputation for looking out for drunken idiots), Jason made it back to his motel. It was right on Ojai Avenue, and in an even better stroke of good fortune, all the rooms were on the ground floor. God might be looking out for drunks, but even he had limits, and Jason suspected stairs were probably among them.

He fumbled his key into the lock and stumbled into the room. Blearily, he noticed the digital clock on the nightstand read *2:57.*

That was way too early to call Al, who would flay him alive if he called at three in the morning. And he could do it, too. Flaying was something Alastair Stone was really good at. The thought made him giggle, for no apparent reason.

"Okay, then," he muttered. "Lemme just sleep for a while. Need to sleep anyway. I'll call him in the morning."

Yeah, that was a good idea. Just get some nice sleep, and call in the morning.

That was the best idea he'd had all night.

| CHAPTER TWO

I t was ten a.m. on a late-summer Saturday morning, and Alastair Stone was only just now getting home.

He hummed an old Zombies tune as he came in through the garage, still mulling over the previous night. The show, a new local band at a little hole-in-the-wall club on Castro Street in Mountain View, had been excellent, and what had happened afterward had been even better. Her name was Kelly, she was a paralegal, and she'd even fixed him breakfast before seeing him off. Not just perfunctory coffee and toast, either. She'd made *eggs*. They both knew it wouldn't go any further, and that was quite all right. He didn't make a habit of that sort of thing, but sometimes an enjoyable night was just an enjoyable night.

Stone tossed his keys on the counter, threw his overcoat over a nearby chair, and glanced at his answering machine. As usual, its red light was flashing. He punched the button almost idly, only half-listening. Whoever it was, they could wait.

The first two messages were typical: old Hubbard up at Stanford wanting to discuss something about his syllabus, and some survey monkey trying to solicit his opinion about vacuum cleaners. He picked up his coat and was heading out of the kitchen when a familiar voice issued from the speaker: "Hey, Al? It's Jason. Call me back when you get a chance. Think I found something weird going on down here that looks like it's right up your alley."

Stone paused in the doorway. Jason had left a couple of days ago to attend an old friend's wedding and recapture the nostalgia of his youth (or something—that second part was mere speculation). He was due back in a day or two; Stone hadn't really paid that much attention to the details. But—'something weird' that might be 'right up his alley'? Interesting. He leaned on the counter and played through the messages again (erasing the survey monkey), listening more carefully this time. He could hear a hint of something odd in Jason's voice, like he was trying to sound flippant, but wasn't completely hiding the fact that something had spooked him.

That wasn't unusual: a *lot* of things spooked Jason Thayer. He was a good friend, and a good guy to have around if you were planning to be in a bar fight, but even after all this time he still did everything he could to avoid playing in the same sandbox with things that went bump in the night. Only problem was, when your two most frequent companions were a mage who moonlighted as an Occult Studies professor and a sister who had recently discovered her own fledgling magical abilities and who snarfed up anything weird and freaky like it was catnip, that could pose more than a bit of a problem. The end result was that Jason's version of 'weird' could be anything from a few unexplained knocks in a dark room all the way up to a full-blown extradimensional portal in the walk-in fridge of the local McDonald's. You never could tell with him.

And of course he hadn't left a phone number. Stone hunted around in the untidy pile of papers and old mail on his breakfast bar until he found the scrap where he'd jotted down the name of the motel, just in case there was some emergency.

Nest Motel, Ojai. Ojai—he vaguely remembered hearing something about it. Artsy little tourist town somewhere near Ventura, which was where Jason and his sister Verity were originally from. He picked up the phone, got the number for the motel, and asked the bored-sounding clerk to ring Jason's room.

There was no response. A generic answering-machine voice picked up and told him to leave a message, which he did.

He then proceeded to get caught up in his latest magical re-search and forget about the whole business until late the following morning. In the middle of hunting for some books he needed, it occurred to him that Jason hadn't called back yet, and that was odd. Even if he was sleeping off a hangover (which was entirely possible, given his reasons for the trip), it seemed strange that he hadn't at least checked in to explain his previous cryptic message. Stone shoved aside a stack of books on his desk and picked up the phone.

Once again, the clerk (a different one this time) put him through to the room, and once again, he got voicemail. Stone frowned. Normally this wouldn't have even tripped his suspicions: Jason had gone down to Ojai to hang out with a bunch of old high-school friends and attend a wedding, which meant he'd probably just had too much to drink and decided to sleep it off at a friend's house instead of driving back to his motel.

However...

Stone's mind kept going back over 'something weird' and 'right up your alley.' That last part practically screamed that what-ever Jason had found, it was from Stone's side of the street—or at least he thought it was. And even considering Jason's level of (dis)comfort with the supernatural, Stone doubted that he'd have taken time out of his busy weekend of debauchery and school-days sentimentality to call if it hadn't been something worth calling about.

"Jason, if you can rouse yourself from your sybaritic stupor long enough to call me, I'd appreciate it. You've got me curious now, and you know how rude it is to get me curious and then leave me hanging. So call me." As he hung up he realized he'd sounded a little too grumpy, but he wasn't kidding about the curiosity thing. When it had any connection to the supernatural, Stone half-expected cats to start coming up to him on the street any day now to say, "Dude, dial it back a bit."

He sighed. It was probably nothing. Just Jason overreacting again, and probably embarrassed to admit it. Stone would have a good time teasing him about it when he came back home.

The phone remained stubbornly silent for the rest of the day, which made Stone even more annoyed because the anticipation was making it impossible to devote his full concentration to his spell research. This stuff wasn't the sort of thing you wanted to be distracted while you worked on—slip a variable or transpose two symbols in a spell formula, and all kinds of nasty consequences could occur. Some of them were merely amusing, while others (admittedly requiring a *major* error in the formula) could take out entire city blocks. The only certain thing was that whatever happened wouldn't be pleasant.

Finally, Stone ran a frustrated hand through his hair and tossed his notebook aside. Maybe it was time to go out and find something to eat. He couldn't remember if he'd bothered to stop working to grab something for lunch. *I really need to see about finding a new housekeeper,* he thought while heading downstairs. *Another one who can cook. And preferably who isn't possessed by an extradimensional hitchhiker.* He wished Verity were around, but she'd left town before Jason had to go on a camping retreat with friends back east. She was off in the middle of nowhere for a couple of weeks at least.

He was heading out toward the garage when the phone rang. He strode across the kitchen and snatched it up. "Yes?"

"Who is this, please?" A male voice. Not Jason.

Stone narrowed his eyes. "What do you mean, 'who is this?' You called *me*. Who are *you?*"

"My name is Lieutenant Peter Casner, sir. I'm with the Ventura County Sheriff's Department."

Stone froze, momentarily speechless.

"I'm calling in connection with Mr. Jason Thayer. Do you know him?"

"Of course I do. Is he all right?"

There was a pause. "Can you please tell me who you are, and how you know Mr. Thayer?"

The chill grew stronger. He leaned forward, propping himself against the counter. "I'm Alastair Stone. I'm a friend of his. What's happened?"

"He's—missing, Mr. Stone. We found two messages from you on the voicemail at his motel room, and we were hoping you might be able to provide us with some information about where he might be."

"If I knew where he was, I wouldn't have left two messages on his voicemail," Stone said. He took a deep breath, gathering his thoughts. "How do you know he's disappeared? He was supposed to be down there to visit some friends and attend a wedding. Perhaps he just decided to stay with them instead of coming back to his room."

"We've spoken to his friends, sir. None of them saw him since the night before last." There was the sound of papers shuffling. "On one of your messages, you said he'd made you curious about something. Can you tell me what that is?"

Stone considered. He couldn't exactly tell the cop that Jason had found something supernatural afoot in sleepy Ojai. That was a one-way ticket to a tasteful room with bouncy walls. Or at the very least to being regarded from this point forward as a crackpot in the official police records.

Hmm...or was it?

"I don't know, precisely. That's why I was trying to contact him. I teach Occult Studies up here at Stanford, so likely he found some interesting local legend or ghost story he wanted to pass along." Nothing like the truth—or at least some part of it—to save himself from being entangled in a big mess of lies later on. Not to mention getting that academic credential from a top-level university out there on the table. At least if he was going to be a crackpot, he'd be a *respectable* crackpot.

"Is there anything else you can tell us about where he might be, Mr. Stone?"

"*Dr.* Stone, actually." Yeah, okay, pretentious as hell. But if he had to go down there and investigate—which was looking increasingly likely—he'd need all the frontloaded 'I'm not a raving nutter' cred he could muster to offset some of the questions he'd probably have to ask once he got there. "Sorry, but no. He didn't tell me anything more than the name of his motel." He frowned. "So you're saying he just—didn't turn up where he was supposed to be? He didn't attend the wedding?"

"I'm not at liberty to give details about the case, sir. Do you mind if I leave my phone number with you, and if you hear from him or hear anything about his possible whereabouts, could you let us know?"

"Of course." Stone's voice trailed off, his mind already spinning. He jotted down Casner's number on a nearby notepad. "Lieutenant?"

"Yes, sir?"

"There's more to this than you're telling me, isn't there?"

"I can't say, sir. I'm sorry. But please let us know if you hear from him."

An hour later, Stone was on the road heading south. He could have performed a tracking ritual from his home, but finding someone that far away could get tricky, not to mention inaccurate. Even if he was able to pinpoint Jason's location, what could he do with the information? Call up the local authorities and pass it along to them? He could see that working well: "Yes, officer. I'm—er—a psychic. And I got a vision of my friend who's missing, in his car off the side of the road somewhere near a lot of trees." Yeah, they'd pay all *kinds* of attention to that.

So, road trip it was.

It would have been faster if there'd been a portal nearby, but there wasn't. Sometimes the mundane way was best anyway. Especially since he wanted to have his own car available.

He settled for weaving a small 'disregard me' spell around his big black BMW during the long dull stretches of 101 between Gilroy and Santa Barbara where there was very little traffic, cranking his favorite Queen CD to eleven, and opening up the car to somewhere north of a hundred miles per hour whenever he could get away with it. You didn't do that when any other cars were around, because invariably the only other driver within ten miles of you on the freeway would suddenly decide he *had* to drift into your lane just as you came screaming up on him at nearly twice the speed limit (Stone thought it might be one of those things that highlighted magic's twisted sense of humor), but if the road was clear, it made long trips go by a lot faster.

As he drove, he thought about what might be going on with Jason. What had he seen that had made him call Stone in the first place? Teasing about his skittishness around the supernatural notwithstanding, Jason had a pretty strong constitution when it came to dealing with the stranger end of the spectrum, once he'd allowed himself to admit it existed. He was also, thanks to the magical heritage he'd gotten from his mother, quite a bit tougher in the face of threats from the magical world than your garden-variety mundane. Magical powers got passed from same-sex parent to child, so Jason's sister Verity ended up with the mojo, but Stone was becoming increasingly more convinced (especially given Jason's odd ability to serve as a magical power battery) that the opposite-sex children weren't quite as left out of the party as was commonly believed. That was part of what his current research was examining, and Jason had been serving as his favorite (and so far only) guinea pig.

He went over what he knew about the situation: Jason had driven down to Ojai a few days ago and checked into the Nest

Motel. His friends had seen him two nights ago, after which he'd disappeared.

Had he returned to his room at all? Had something happened to him on the way back to the motel? Had he perhaps met a woman and gone off with her? *No, that's speculation. Stick to the facts.* There was no point in indulging in flights of fancy, at least not until he had more data. The only other thing he could be sure of was that there was more going on here than a simple disappearance. Lieutenant Casner had clearly been trying to keep his voice even and give nothing away, but Stone was good enough at picking up conversational nuances that it had come through like a beacon that the cop was holding something back. What could it be?

The answer was: it could be anything. When you were dealing with the magical world, you weren't limited by the normal restrictions of mundane life: things like drunken auto accidents, bar fights, and seduction by women rendered smoking hot by beer goggles. If only it were that easy, Stone wouldn't be so apprehensive about what he was going to find. When you brought the spooky stuff into the equation, you could be dealing with anything from poltergeists to extradimensional abduction. And everything in between.

Slow down, Stone admonished himself, temporarily dropping the BMW's camouflage magic as he blew past an ancient VW Beetle chugging along in the slow lane. *It's probably something perfectly mundane. In fact, you'll probably get down there only to find he's already shown up at his motel room, wanting to know what all the fuss was about.* His mind drifted back to an old episode of *The Twilight Zone* he'd seen when he was younger, about a little girl who'd disappeared from her home. Her father's friend, some sort of scientist, had immediately started poking around in search of portals to other dimensions instead of simply looking under the bed or in the closet. *Of course,* you *thought it was perfectly normal to look for her in the other dimension...*

None of this was doing him any good. He swapped out the Queen CD for Pink Floyd and settled back to cover the rest of the distance. He wouldn't get any more information until he arrived in Ojai, and no amount of speculation was going to change that.

Even with magical assistance and only one brief stop in San Luis Obispo, it was still nearly ten p.m. when Stone arrived in Ojai. Traffic was quite sparse as he cruised up the main road into town. Since there wasn't much he'd be able to do tonight, he pulled in to a 24-hour restaurant, sat down at the counter, ordered a cup of coffee, and gave the middle-aged waitress his best charming smile. "I'm looking for a place called the Nest Motel. Can you help me?"

She smiled back (of course she did—Stone had long ago found that, at least in this country, the combination of his accent and an engaging grin was nearly foolproof against women of a certain age) and placed a steaming mug in front of him. "Sure. You're not far. Just keep going toward town, and you'll see it on the right in about half a mile." She glanced around as if expecting to see someone with him. "Are you on vacation? Ojai's beautiful this time of year."

"No, just down here to—er—look up an old friend."

"Well, I hope you enjoy yourself," she said, smiling and moving off to greet a couple who'd just come in.

Stone sipped his coffee, thinking about how he would proceed tomorrow. It was probably too much to hope that he'd be able to get into Jason's room at the Nest—even if he could talk the desk clerk or a maid into letting him in, he'd arouse too much suspicion if he was caught poking around the motel room of a guy who'd recently disappeared. He supposed the best place to start was to talk to Jason's friends, assuming he could find them. Jason had never mentioned any of their names.

His gaze fell on a folded newspaper someone had left on the stool next to him. Idly he picked it up and spread it in front of him, glancing over the headlines. He expected to see typical small-town stuff: politics, high school sports, maybe a profile of some local philanthropist's latest venture. Instead, a headline stretched over a photograph of a smiling teenage girl: *Police Have Few Clues in Murder of Local Student.*

Eyebrow raised, Stone unfolded the paper and skimmed the article. The sixteen-year-old girl's body had been found just off someplace called Foothill Road by a pair of elderly dog-walkers early yesterday morning. Her throat had been cut, and it was estimated she had only been dead for a few hours before she was found.

"Terrible thing," said a soft voice in front of him. He looked up to see the waitress refilling his cup. Her eyes cut down to the paper, and then back up to Stone. "Just terrible. She was a lovely girl. Lived here all her life."

"I'm sorry," Stone said.

"Everybody's a little on edge," she continued. "We just don't have that kind of thing around here. But please—don't let it upset your stay. I'm sure the police will find whoever did it soon."

"I'm sure they will," he murmured. The waitress moved off again and he continued leafing through the paper. He didn't doubt that murders around here were rare, but especially in these times it was nearly inevitable that even a peaceful town like this would win the grim lottery at some point. Another thing you learned fast when you rubbed shoulders with the world of the supernatural was that it was often the sleepiest, most idyllic little towns that harbored the most horrific secrets. Even if that wasn't true here (and he hadn't heard anything on the mystical grapevine to indicate that it was), there were plenty of threats out there that were completely mundane in nature. All it took was for one of them to drift through town and cross paths with a target of opportunity.

The rest of the paper was more of what he'd expected, and his gaze slid over it without really taking in the ads, football scores, local news, and columns of classifieds. He was finishing his coffee and contemplating whether he wanted another refill when a thought occurred to him. He pulled the paper back over and leafed through it until he found what passed for the society page. It was full of small photos, each accompanied by a brief wedding, birth, anniversary, or funeral announcement, along with a short piece on the local high school's twenty-five year reunion that had taken place the previous weekend.

Glancing over the wedding announcements, Stone soon nodded in triumph. Of the four on the page, only one featured a couple that was the correct age to have been Jason's classmates: Edward Novak and Anneliese Nelson.

Checking to make sure the chatty waitress was occupied, he pulled out a small notebook and jotted down their names, along with their best man and maid of honor. He folded up the paper, tossed it on the counter, and motioned for his check.

It didn't take him long to find the Nest Motel: it was right off the main drag, a meandering, single-story place that looked old but well maintained. Stone checked in without asking the clerk any questions about Jason, and soon found himself in a small room tastefully decorated with framed photos of the local mountains.

On a whim, he sat down on the bed, closed his eyes, and reached out with his magical senses. The motel didn't have that many rooms, but the odds that he had been given the same one that Jason had occupied were still fairly low. He was neither surprised nor terribly disappointed when he got nothing more than faint bits of random emotion, nothing different than he would have gotten in any similar place. If Jason had been here, he hadn't done anything remarkable while in the room.

He unpacked and decided to make it an early night. With any luck at all, he'd call the police tomorrow and they'd tell him that Jason had turned up, all was well, and he could head home and finish up his spell research before the new quarter started in a couple of weeks.

Unfortunately, that was the kind of luck he didn't often have.

He slept badly, haunted by uneasy dreams. Jason kept calling desperately to him for help, but he was unable to reach his friend, no matter how hard he tried. When Stone awoke early the next morning, he could barely remember the dreams.

| CHAPTER THREE

A phone call to the local police department confirmed what Stone had all but known to be true: Jason was still missing. He didn't tell them he was in town; they'd find out soon enough, but he didn't want to get called in to answer a bunch of questions—at least not until after he'd had a chance to chat with one or more of Jason's friends.

He got a copy of the local phone book and located the names he'd found in the paper. As he suspected, neither Edward Novak nor the former Anneliese Nelson answered their phones: they were probably off enjoying the sights (or more likely, each other) on some balmy Hawaiian beach. He had better luck with the best man, a guy named Chris Merrill. The woman who answered the phone told Stone that he worked at one of the local hardware stores, and should be there now.

Merrill turned out to be a skinny young man of medium height, with longish brown hair and the tanned complexion of someone who spent a lot of time in the sun. Stone waited patiently while he helped an old woman pick out a bag of nails, then moved up. "Excuse me. Chris Merrill?"

Merrill turned. "Yeah, that's me. What can I do for you?"

"I'd like to chat with you for a few minutes, if you can spare them."

"About what?" Brief suspicion drifted over the young man's face.

"About your friend Jason Thayer."

Merrill took a deep breath. "Are you a policeman, Mr.—"

"Stone. Alastair Stone. No. I'm a friend of Jason's from up north. I understand he's gone missing."

Merrill nodded, frowning. "Yeah." He tilted his head, looking troubled. "You're from up north? You mean up in the Bay Area?"

"Yes."

"And you came all the way down here? He's only been missing for a couple of days…" He seemed to be trying to work that out.

Stone had to admit that the whole thing probably did look pretty odd from Merrill's perspective: here was some strange British dude at least ten years older than Jason, claiming to be a good enough friend that he'd drive all the way down from the Bay Area to look for him. His reasons were none of Merrill's business, though. "Yes," he said. Sometimes the minimalist answer was the best. "So—do you have a few minutes to chat with me?"

"Uh—sure. Hold on, let me tell the boss I need a break, and we can go outside."

He emerged a couple of minutes later and joined Stone, who was leaning against a column outside the store watching the traffic going by. "So what do you want to know?"

"Jason came down here to attend a wedding, right?"

"Yeah."

"Can you tell me what he was doing the night he disappeared? Were you with him then?"

"We all were," Merrill said. "Well, all the guys, anyway. We were all at Eddie's bachelor party."

"Was that here in town?"

Merrill nodded. "Yeah. Anneliese—she's the bride—woulda killed us all if we got strippers, so we just had a party—you know, barbecue, pornos, music, lots of booze. And a couple strippers," he added with a sly chuckle. "But don't tell Anneliese that. One of the guys' parents has a nice spread up in the Arbolada with a pool, and they cleared out and let us have it for the night." He grinned, remembering, but it was fleeting and quickly faded.

"The Arbolada?" Stone raised an eyebrow, noting Merrill's change of mood.

Merrill waved vaguely. "Yeah, it's a part of town. Lots of nice houses there."

"How long was Jason there?"

"I dunno," he said, shrugging. "I was a little out of it by that time, you know?"

"I suppose Jason was as well?"

"Everybody was. The booze was flowing free."

"When he left—did he take his car?"

"Nah. The cops came to get it yesterday morning, Eddie said. That's the guy whose parents own the house."

"So he left without his car? That seems odd."

"Not really. Eddie's parents insisted everybody hand over their keys before we got started. Said they didn't want to be responsible for anybody gettin' hurt. Lotta guys slept it off at the house and left in the morning. Plus Jason's always been kind of a straight arrow about stuff like that."

"I see." Stone pondered for a moment. "Did anyone see him leave? Did you talk with the others at all about this, after it was determined he was missing?"

Merrill nodded. "Yeah. We even went out a little bit yesterday and checked a few places we thought he might be, but he wasn't there. We thought maybe he mighta gone off with one of the strippers or something."

"But he didn't?"

"No. Kurt called 'em, and they both said they left around two a.m. and went home. The cops came the next day to talk to all of us, but nobody could remember seeing Jase leave."

This wasn't helping at all. If nobody had seen him leave, that meant he hadn't talked with anybody. And if he'd been as drunk as Merrill had implied, it was quite possible that whatever "weird thing" he'd seen had been entirely in his head. People called friends with all sorts of strange declarations when they were smashed off their asses.

Except...

Stone's mind went back to the message on his machine. Jason had sounded odd, but he hadn't sounded drunk. A little freaked out, maybe. Nervous. But not drunk. He took a deep breath. "All right, Mr. Merrill. Thank you for your time."

Merrill nodded. "Yeah, no problem." He looked like he was about to say something else, but instead stared at the ground. "I'd better get back to work."

Stone started back toward his car, wondering where he was going to look next for answers. Maybe he'd have to bribe the desk clerk at the Nest to let him into Jason's old room, to see if he could get any readings from—

"Mr. Stone?" Merrill's tone was strange, tentative.

He stopped, turning back. "Yes?"

Merrill came closer. He glanced around like he wanted to make sure nobody was watching, then said quietly, "There is one other thing...maybe."

Stone raised an eyebrow and leaned in closer. "What other thing?"

He glanced around again. "When the cops came to talk to us— they didn't say anything about it to us, but I overheard a couple of 'em talking when they didn't think I noticed." He paused, and his next words came from him as if he didn't want to say them. "I don't know if you know this, but they found a girl murdered in that area the day after the party. I think...maybe they might think Jason killed her."

| CHAPTER FOUR

S tone barely remembered the drive from the hardware store back to the motel. He dropped into the room's single chair and scrubbed at his hair, his mind whirling. Chris Merrill's words had rocked him hard; he was still recovering enough to think clearly.

Merrill hadn't had anything else to offer regarding the speculation—he said the two policemen had noticed him right after that and glared at him hard enough that he made himself scarce. The only other thing he'd told Stone was that he hadn't shared what he'd heard with anyone else. "I don't know why," he mumbled when asked, not meeting Stone's gaze. "But I know there's no way he killed anybody. No fucking way."

"Well, we're in agreement on that," Stone had said, and left after giving Merrill the phone number of his room and asking him to call if he learned anything else or if Jason turned up.

The only thing was, Stone realized as he sat there staring at a framed print of a local mountain range tinged with eerie pink, he couldn't be sure that they *were* in agreement on that, and that was what had hit him so hard. Of course, he knew Jason would never kill anyone—let alone slit the throat of a sixteen-year-old girl—if he was in control of himself. That kind of act would be so contrary to his core nature as a protector and defender of the weak as to be unthinkable.

But there was the matter of the "weird thing." That was the variable that made everything much less cut and dried, and much more potentially horrific. There were plenty of "weird things" out there capable of controlling an unsuspecting human's mind, or taking over their body and wearing them like a cheap suit. Stone, Jason, and Verity had just spent the better part of the previous year dealing with just such a thing: the extradimensional creatures dubbed "the Evil," who possessed usually willing hosts and fed on negative emotion. Still, even though the Evil were mostly under control at this point, with only the scattered remnants of their invasion force left leaderless and adrift all over the country with no way to reproduce or supplement their number, that didn't mean there weren't at least five other things capable of similar possession or control that Stone could think of without even trying hard. And that was just the relatively "common" ones. His years of experience dealing with the spirit world had taught him long ago that even the "common" entities didn't have that much in common, and the more esoteric varieties were all unique, mostly powerful, and always dangerous.

What the hell had Jason gotten himself into?

Stone took out his notebook and began jotting down a timeline to help him keep everything straight in his mind. Jason had arrived in Ojai on Thursday afternoon, attended the bachelor party on Friday night, and walked back to the Nest Motel (or at least started to) sometime in the wee hours of Saturday morning. The message he'd left on Stone's phone had been timestamped a little before seven a.m. on Saturday, which meant he must have disappeared sometime between then and when the police had called Stone late Sunday afternoon.

Grabbing the local phone book again, he opened it to the back and was pleased to find a map of Ojai taking up two of the last few pages. He studied it carefully but could find no street labeled "Arbolada." Chris Merrill had said it was a part of town, but the map didn't list it. He tossed the book back on the bed, gathered up his overcoat, and headed to the motel office.

The clerk nodded when Stone mentioned the name and asked where it might be found. He dug a map out of his desk drawer, spread it on the counter, and pointed out a jumble of streets not far to the northwest of the motel, on the other side of the main drag.

"Hmm..." Stone mused. "So it wouldn't be at all odd for someone to walk back here from there, say if he'd had a bit too much to drink and didn't want to drive?"

"Nah, it's not far. Although if he was really drunk, he might get lost. It's kind of a maze over there if you aren't familiar with the area." He tilted his head. "Hey, can I ask you something?"

"Of course."

"Do you—uh—know somebody else who was staying here?" His voice was carefully noncommittal.

Stone crossed his arms over his chest. "You mean the man who's gone missing?"

The clerk looked relieved. "Yeah."

"What makes you think I do?"

He shrugged. "Well, that's your Beemer in the lot, right?"

Stone nodded.

"It's got a Stanford license plate frame, and he was from the Bay Area too. I mean, we get a lot of folks in here from up that way, but—"

"—but usually not odd single Englishmen who don't act like tourists?" Stone asked, raising an eyebrow.

"Well—yeah. I mean, my other guess would have been you're up from Hollywood scouting locations for a picture or something, but the license plate—"

"I do know him, yes. He's a friend of mine. I was concerned after the police called me, so I came down to see if I could help find him." He tilted his head. "I trust the police have already gone through his room?"

The clerk nodded. "Yeah. They took his stuff and did a pretty thorough search. They released the room, though. There's somebody else in there now."

"Thank you," Stone said. "I appreciate your help. I'm trying to get a sense of where he might have gone after he left the party he attended on Friday night. Hence my question about walking back here from the Arbolada. You don't know whether he came back here, do you?"

"No, sorry. We don't keep tabs on our guests' comings and goings. We're not modern enough to have those fancy electronic key cards. Just regular normal keys here."

Stone nodded and thanked him for his help.

He considered his next steps: clearly he needed to conduct a ritual to find Jason's whereabouts, and he needed to do it soon. The problem was that his motel room was far too small for even a rudimentary circle—and he wanted something more than rudimentary for this spell. Even if he pushed all the movable furniture (which didn't include the bed) up against the wall, it barely left enough room for a circle he could stand comfortably in and stretch out his arms. That meant he was going to have to find a bigger space.

Mundanes never had to worry about problems like this. If he was home, he had a large open space in the attic of his townhouse that had been set up for just this sort of ritual. But down here, he was limited by a tiny motel room, of all things. And since every hotel room he was likely to find around here was probably not much bigger, that meant looking for something larger he could rent.

He procured the current issue of the local paper, located a coffee shop downtown, got a respectably sized infusion of caffeine, and settled into a back corner to look over the real estate ads. It took him a while to find a couple of places that looked like possibilities, as it wasn't that easy to find rentals by anything less than a month. With the new quarter starting in two weeks, he sincerely hoped he'd be able to wrap this up a lot faster than that. Possibly today with any luck at all, assuming he could secure the premises that fast. His ritual to track people was a good one, and there was no reason it shouldn't zero in on Jason's location with little fuss and bother.

Assuming, of course, that he was still alive.

No. Not going there. He's alive, and I'm going to find him. He circled the ads he'd found, tore out that portion of the page, and left the rest of the paper for the next customer.

The real estate agency, it turned out, wasn't far from the coffee shop (Stone was beginning to suspect that nothing in this town was very far from anything else), so he left the car where it was and walked over. He found the place amid a collection of artsy little shops that comprised most of Ojai's picturesque downtown area.

The woman behind one of the two desks looked up as he came in. She smiled, rising to come to the counter. "Good morning. May I help you?" She was a little younger than he was, her trim frame clad in a suit that somehow managed to simultaneously pull off "businesslike" and "bohemian."

He returned her smile. "I hope so. I'm looking for a short-term rental, and this one seems to fit the bill nicely." He slid the ad across the counter and indicated his preference.

She glanced at it and frowned a little. "Oh, I'm sorry," she said, and sounded like she actually meant it. "That one was just rented yesterday. If you tell me what you're looking for, though, I might be able to help you. We have a few new listings in today."

He shrugged. "I'm not terribly picky. I just need something for a few days while I'm here. I'm—not fond of motel rooms."

Her eyes twinkled. "I don't blame you," she said. "There are some nice places here in town, but they're not cheap." She offered him her hand, grinning. "I'm Lindsey Cole, by the way. And you're not from around here."

"What was your first clue?" he asked, chuckling, as he shook her hand. Her grip was firm and warm. "Alastair Stone."

"Nice to meet you, Alastair Stone. And my first clue was that if I'd seen you around here before, I'd remember it." She met his gaze with cheerful forthrightness. Her eyes were a warm brown. "Now, let's find you a rental, shall we?" Turning, she grabbed a sheaf of papers from her desk and riffled through them, then pulled out two and brought them back. "These should fit your needs. They're both detached houses—a one-bedroom cottage and a small two-bedroom home. Do you have a preference, or would you like to take a look at both of them?"

Stone considered. He wanted to get started with the ritual as quickly as possible, but it wouldn't do him any good if he picked one at random and it didn't have the space he needed. He couldn't exactly tell her he needed something appropriate for setting up a magical circle. Better if he saw it for himself. "Suppose I take a look at both? Just to be sure."

"You got it," she said, and looked pleased about it. "C'mon. Do you have a little time? Business is slow this time of day, so I can take you out there now if you want."

"Er—sure." He was surprised, figuring she'd just give him the addresses and turn him loose on his own. "Let's go, then."

She jotted a note for the door, picked up her purse, and motioned for him to follow her.

The first house, the one-bedroom, was less than half a mile away, up one of the side streets that crossed Ojai Avenue. It was a guest cottage behind a larger home, and Stone knew immediately it wasn't going to be big enough.

"I'm terribly sorry," he said, shaking his head as soon as they entered. "This won't do for what I need. It's got to be a bit larger."

"That's all right," she said briskly. "The other one's bigger. Farther out, though. It's almost out to the East End. Is that okay?"

Stone shrugged. "Since I've next to no familiarity with this area, I haven't the faintest idea. Let's find out."

They headed back to her car and soon they were cruising back up Ojai Avenue. "So what brings you to Ojai, Mr. Stone?" Lindsey Cole asked. "On vacation?"

"Not exactly. I'm meeting up with a friend down here." That wasn't *technically* a lie. Maybe if he played this right, he could get a little free information along with a rental recommendation. "I noticed in the paper that you've had a bit of unpleasantness here recently."

She glanced over. "Oh, you mean the murder?" she asked. "Terrible thing. We haven't had a murder around here in as long as I can remember. I just hope the police catch whoever did it soon. Everybody's a little on edge. You don't have to worry, though," she added quickly. "It really is quite safe here."

"Oh, I'm not worried," he assured her. "Besides, I'm sure it didn't occur anywhere near the house we're looking at, right?"

"No, nowhere close. They found her just off Foothill, in the Arbolada. The police haven't released any information yet, but everybody knows. Small town and all. Some of the high-school kids have already even started a little memorial up there."

Stone had stopped listening when she said "Arbolada." He forced himself back to awareness, replaying what she'd said until he caught up. "And—they've no idea who might have done it?"

"Not that they've said, but that doesn't mean anything, I suppose. I'm sure it wasn't anyone from around here." She shook her head. "Anyway, as I said, I'm sure it won't affect your stay in town."

They both fell silent for a couple of minutes, then she asked, "So, what do you do, wherever you are normally?"

"I—teach," he said, watching the scenery roll by without really seeing it.

"Really? That's great! What grade?"

He chuckled. "No, no. My students are a bit further along than that. I'm a professor at Stanford."

"Oh!" She grinned. "Well, I have to admit I was having a hard time picturing you shepherding a herd of kindergartners around."

"No, I'm allergic to children, actually."

That got her to look over in surprise, and then she laughed. She took a left and drove about half a mile up another road, then turned into a short driveway and parked in front of a small, neat house with a FOR RENT sign staked into the yard. "Well, here we are," she said, getting out.

This time, he knew he'd found a place he could work with. The house was fairly generic as befitted its rental status, a small, tan, stucco-sided affair with a shake roof and windows covered with the same standard-issue blinds that graced every cheap rental property in the western world. It wouldn't win any prizes for aesthetics, but it was furnished with more taste than Stone expected and it featured a large, wooden-floored living room that would be easily big enough for his ritual needs. He took a cursory look around to verify that the rest of the place was acceptable, then nodded. "This will do nicely."

"It's not too far out of town for you?"

He raised an eyebrow. "I've come from the Bay Area. We routinely drive half an hour for take-away. No, this isn't too far." Moving toward the door, he added, "I'd like to get settled in as soon as possible, if that's all right. Shall we go back and finish up whatever paperwork is necessary?"

She seemed surprised that he was in such a hurry, but nodded. "Of course."

Once they got back to the office, it took only a few minutes for Stone to sign the required papers and hand over the requisite funds. He collected the keys, thanked Lindsey Cole and started to leave, already plotting out the circle he'd need to build for the ritual to ensure that it went off without any unexpected surprises.

"Mr. Stone?" Her voice sounded a little different.

"Yes?"

She smiled. "Since—you're new in town, there's a wonderful Mexican restaurant downtown here that just opened. Would you be interested in having dinner with me tonight?"

His eyebrow crept up again. "Ms. Cole, are you asking me out?"

She shrugged, grinning impishly. "I know, it's forward, but all you can say is no, right? I'm a realtor. We get told no all the time. I'm used to it. And the yeses make it worth all the rejections."

He thought about it. Finding Jason was without doubt his number-one priority, but the ritual would only take an hour or so, after which if all went well he should be able to pinpoint his friend's location and track him down. And if not— "I'd like that," he said. "On two conditions."

"Yes?"

"I might need to cancel at the last minute, depending on what my friend has planned. So you'll have to promise you'll not take that personally."

"Fair enough. And the other one?"

"Even though you've asked me out, you must let me buy you dinner. I'm a bit old fashioned that way, at least on the first date."

She smiled. "You're on, Mr. Stone. Or should that be Dr. Stone?"

"Alastair will do fine. I'll pick you up here at seven o'clock." He waved as he closed the door behind him.

CHAPTER FIVE

Stone hadn't even unpacked properly at the Nest Motel, so in less than half an hour he'd gathered his gear, checked out, and driven back up to the new house.

As he drove, he thought about Lindsey Cole and wondered what had possessed him to accept her invitation. Sure, she was attractive, intelligent, and had a good sense of humor—all things he prized highly in women. But he didn't have *time* for this right now. Whatever had happened to Jason, it was almost certain it was connected with the "weird thing" he'd left the message about, which meant things were probably going to take a sharp turn into Deep Strange any time now. Taking uninitiated hitchhikers along into *that* particular territory could only end in ways he'd rather not think about.

Ah, well. Ritual first, then whatever came after second. If he ended up having to cancel dinner, then so be it.

After shoving all the furniture in the living room up against the walls and making sure the blinds were all drawn tight, he took his time setting up the circle, using materials from the black leather duffel bag he hadn't even bothered to take out of the trunk at the motel. When he had everything the way he thought it should be, he paused to check it against one of his books, despite the fact that he'd done this particular ritual dozens of times and could no doubt write his *own* book about it at this point. He'd been called arrogant more times than he could count (and sometimes it was even deserved), but he wasn't arrogant enough to take chances with a friend's life.

Since he knew Jason well he didn't strictly need a focus object, but he used one anyway: an old baseball cap Jason had left at Stone's townhouse a few weeks ago when he and Verity had been over for dinner. Taking the cap, Stone settled himself carefully into the center of the circle, lit the candles around it with a flick of his power, and took several deep breaths to center his mind. He closed his eyes and willed magical energy into the circle, focusing on the cap and the thread connecting it to its owner. To this he added his own connection to Jason, the friendship they had developed over the last couple years, the shared adventures, and their mutual association with Verity. All of these strands wove themselves into the sending, forming a slim but powerful cord that reached out into the magical realm and sought its match. If Jason was alive and not somehow hidden behind magical protections, this spell would find him. All it would take was patience, and time.

The minutes stretched on. Stone willed himself to remain calm, to keep his breathing steady, to remain vigilant as he followed the slender cord on its search.

Something was odd.

Something was wrong.

In all the times Stone had performed this tracking ritual, it had ended in one of two ways: either the ritual had located the person it sought, allowing him to magically mark the spot so he could find it in the mundane world, or else the searching cord had ranged out for a few minutes and then collapsed back in on itself, ending the ritual. If the latter occurred, it indicated that the subject of the search was either dead or outside the ritual's effective range, or that they were behind wards or other magical methods of obfuscation. Stone was a powerful mage and his range was extensive, which meant that the spell could take as long as half an hour to determine that it wasn't going to find anything. He could even sometimes get a glimpse of a target behind a ward, assuming that the ward's caster was significantly less adept with the Art than he was. Either way, the spell would give him *something*.

This time, though, what he got back was something he couldn't make sense of. A couple of times he seemed to get a quick bead on what looked like Jason's essence, but that essence was wrong somehow. Weak. Fluctuating. Stone couldn't come up with the right words to describe it, because he'd never experienced it before. And every time he tried to home in on it, to direct the searching cord to pin it down, it danced away like it was never there. It was like trying to grab a handful of smoke. Frustrated, he gritted his teeth and tried to tighten his focus, increase his power, and narrow the beam of his search down to punch through whatever force was blocking him.

The next time he picked up a quick impression of Jason, he was ready. He gathered his power and forged it into a metaphorical blade, using his will to wrap the searching cord around it and drive it into the middle of the dissipating cloud of smoke. Dimly, he could feel his body beginning to sag: he knew he'd only get one shot at this before he'd have to stop and renew his energy.

And then, suddenly, something else was there, reaching out for him, grasping at his mind. He pulled back, startled, struggling to shore up his mental defenses. He routinely built a certain baseline level of protections around his mind even during his everyday mundane life, since there were all sorts of things out there that would take advantage of an unprotected wielder of the Talent, but he hadn't expected anything like this.

He knew he couldn't stay long—it was too risky to take the offensive against whatever this thing was without a lot more preparation. Still, Jason was out there somewhere, and he wasn't going to let this attempt at locating him go without one last effort. He could do the ritual again, sure, but it would be harder without the tether object adding to the search's potency. He took a deep breath, focused harder, and sent out a call: *"Jason!"*

The—thing, whatever it was, seemed to perk up at the sound. It moved closer to him—if you could even call it that. It had no form,

R. L. KING

not even a shifting mist in the astral world. It was nothing more than a series of fleeting impressions, and a growing sense of malevolence. Stone fought to keep his defenses up and forced himself to "listen" for any response from his friend.

A growing sense of dread began to seep into his consciousness: an overwhelming compulsion to get out, to flee, to *run*. He did his best to ignore it, devoting a corner of his mind to keeping his defenses strong but otherwise reaching out, trying to catch any impression that Jason might have heard his call.

And then, suddenly, there it was.

"...Al...?"

It was weak, so weak. He wasn't even sure he'd actually heard it, or whether it was simply the wishful thinking of a tired brain. He stiffened, trying to pinpoint which direction—as much as that concept meant anything in the shifting geography of the astral world—the voice had come from.

It was not repeated.

Meanwhile, the formless thing flowed around him, testing his mental shields, its impression radiating unwholesome curiosity along with the dread.

It wants to know what I am.

Despite all his efforts, Stone couldn't maintain the link any longer. He felt his ethereal presence beginning to fade as the slender cord of his spell tugged itself, and him along with it, back toward his body. Since there was nothing he could do to stop this, he instead chose to hasten it. Severing the connection instantly rather than letting it fade in a more natural manner would be harder on him and would probably give him a hell of a headache, but it also meant that whatever was so interested in him wouldn't have a direct line back to his body.

It didn't mean it still couldn't find him—just that it would have a harder job of it, and maybe that would buy him enough time to track Jason down before it came calling.

With a flick of his mind, he cut the cord. Immediately, it shimmered and disappeared. His mind slammed back into his body and he felt himself reeling backward, his head lighting up like he'd just been beaned by a fastball.

He hit the floor in a crash of flailing limbs, knocking over one of the candles that fortunately had already gone out when the ritual died.

For several long moments he lay on his back, staring up at the room's ugly wrought-iron light fixture and letting his heartbeat and breathing return to something close to normal. His head throbbed and cold sweat soaked his shirt and his hair.

That was not the way he liked to end rituals.

He sat up, probably before he was ready, setting off new blossoms of pain inside his skull. It didn't matter, though: he didn't have time to coddle himself. If he hadn't gotten anything else out of that ritual, he'd gotten the most important thing: Jason was alive. And if he was alive, that meant two other things:

First, whoever (or whatever) had him wanted him that way, because it would have been laughably easy for it to kill him if that was what it intended.

Second, as long as he remained alive, Stone could find him.

That "as long as he remained alive" part was the sticky bit, though. Since he had no idea *why* this—whatever it was—had taken Jason, he likewise had no idea how important it considered keeping him alive to be. Now that it knew there was a mage on the scene who was strong enough to threaten it, it might just decide to cut its losses and eliminate any way, no matter how tenuous, it could be tracked.

That meant Stone had to hurry.

He dragged himself to his feet, leaning on a nearby chair for balance, and blinked several times. The circle lay smudged and inert before him; he'd clean it up later, after he got back. Grabbing a bottle of Advil from his bag (every mage worth the title would agree that ibuprofen was a vital, if unsung, addition to one's magical kit-bag), he tossed a couple back with some water and headed to the shower.

As he let the hot water roll over him, he realized his next steps were not quite as mapped out as he'd hoped they would be: he'd expected to find Jason's whereabouts and thus be able to track him down. Finding out he was alive but currently untrackable had not even occurred to him, so he hadn't made any contingency plans to deal with it. Where could he start looking if he had no idea where Jason was?

It didn't take Stone long to answer that question.

| CHAPTER SIX

It was a little before four o'clock when Stone found the place off Foothill Road in the twisting, oak-strewn maze of upscale homes the locals called the Arbolada. The road was narrow, bounded on either side by decorative rocks, and he had to drive almost a quarter-mile past the small makeshift memorial before he could find a place to pull off and park. He tossed his overcoat in the back seat and hiked back along a narrow dirt path, with the road on his right side and a low wall of light-colored stone on his left, sparing only a brief glance for the few cars that passed slowly by.

He continued working through possibilities as he walked, considering and discarding several astral or ethereal entities that could potentially be responsible for abducting Jason—but none of them fit. It didn't help that his head still throbbed as if someone was riding on his back and whacking him periodically with a mallet. The ibuprofen had taken care of the worst of it, but the rest would take time. Lost in thought, he reached the memorial almost before he knew it.

He approached it slowly, stopping to examine it from a respectful distance. The memorial had been constructed against the same low wall facing the road: a collection of wilting flowers, greeting cards, teddy bears, spent candles in holders, photos, and other memorabilia carefully piled around a white wooden cross with ASHLEY written across the horizontal bar in black block letters, and two hearts in red drawn below it on the vertical. On the other side of the wall stretched a small vacant lot dotted with mature oak trees. The ground there was covered by a thick carpet of dead leaves, and showed evidence of having been recently disturbed.

Stone sat down on the wall with his back to the field. After making sure his defenses were up, he bowed his head and closed his eyes, reaching out with his magical senses. Anyone who saw him would probably assume he was merely reflecting or praying; he didn't think that would arouse any suspicion near such a place.

The first thing he noticed was that the location of the girl's murder was not where the memorial had been constructed. The astral world practically roiled with emotion here, the normal calm tranquility that would no doubt suffuse such a peaceful residential area shattered by leftover traces of terror and pain. Stone shook his head, letting his breath out slowly. This kind of thing was always hard on the observer, and the more violent the energy, the tougher it was. Ashley had not died slowly, or easily.

All this emotional pain was not doing the vestiges of his headache any good at all, but it had to be done. He adjusted his mental shields to filter out most of it, dimming the scene from a bright riot of reds and jagged shapes into something more muted. He concentrated on finding any traces of Jason, since at this point nothing he did would bring the unfortunate Ashley back from the dead.

The specific site of the murder was easy to spot: it was a flaring knot of ugly reds beneath a large oak tree about halfway back on the right side of the vacant lot. Without letting his focus slip, Stone carefully rose, climbed over the wall, and headed toward the spot. Whatever investigations the police had conducted in the field appeared to be completed, as he saw no sign of crime-scene tape or anything else that indicated he shouldn't be here.

Approaching slowly, he stopped several feet from the site, appearing to be interested in something in a completely different direction. If there *were* any police lurking around here waiting for the murderer to return to the scene of the crime, it wouldn't do for them to find him carefully examining a spot that they probably hadn't even publicized. Closer now, he reached out again.

And there it was.

Jason had been here.

Stone shut his eyes tighter, trying to more precisely locate where his friend had been, and what kinds of emotions he'd been experiencing while he was here. Had he come upon the scene of the murder and tried to help? That seemed very much like him—even stumbling drunk, there was no way he'd ignore the desperate pleas of a terrified teenage girl from somewhere off in the darkness. But if whatever had killed her had been supernatural in origin—

But—no.

Without consciously realizing what he was doing, Stone retraced his route back to the wall, hopping over it and back to the narrow path that passed for a sidewalk here. The sense of Jason was stronger here than it had been closer to the scene of the murder. And—

It seemed...*unaffected.*

Stone frowned. It had already been long enough since Jason had been here that the emotional residue was beginning to fade, especially when it had to compete with the relative excess radiating from the murder site. But what little Stone was able to get puzzled him. Jason had been here, and had been...unfocused, a little frustrated, but mostly just—

—well, for lack of a better word, *normal.*

The way he would have been if he'd done exactly what his friend Chris Merrill had said he'd done: walked back to his motel from a party after having too much to drink.

Could it be that he had walked past here, but not encountered anything to do with the murder? Perhaps the girl had already been dead by the time he came by, or hadn't been killed yet. There was nothing in the traces that indicated to Stone that Jason had been disturbed, angry, or in any way affected by the experience of a teenage girl having her throat cut in close proximity to him.

Wait...wait...

He moved a bit up the street, following Jason's likely footsteps until he was fifty feet or so past the memorial. He walked slowly, careful not to trip as most of his awareness was not currently in the real world. As he continued to trace Jason's path, the unfocused, unremarkable quality of Jason's essence began to change. He stopped, relaxing, letting the impressions wash over him, taking them in.

There it was. Still not fright, exactly: certainly not terror. But a definite sense of *wrongness,* as if something had happened that was out of the ordinary. It still couldn't have been the murder, not unless Jason or his unseen abductor had taken special pains to obscure the indignation, protectiveness, and outright *rage* that Stone knew would be pouring off his friend in waves if he were confronted with such a scene. But something about it was definitely not right.

The "weird thing" that Jason had called about? Maybe he'd found it right here.

Not that that gave Stone any idea what the hell it *was.*

And nor, for that matter, did it give him any idea where Jason was now.

He paused, sitting back down on the wall, and closed his eyes. His headache protested against this level of concentration, but mages didn't get very far into their training if they gave up at the first hint of pain. This time, instead of looking at the spot where Jason had experienced the incongruous emotions, he looked back the way he'd come, back toward the murder site.

This time, from this angle, it was clearer. A tendril of reddish energy, originating somewhere near the scene of the murder, twisting and undulating against the peaceful backdrop of oak trees and meandering lane, hovered in the air. Stone turned slowly, following it outward with his magical senses. It reached the spot where Jason had stopped and then changed directions, moving in a generally southerly direction. He couldn't see an end to it.

He paused, considering. He'd seen this sort of thing before: usually when there was a tendril like this, it meant there was some connection between its point of origin and wherever it reached. Already it was fading: he doubted it would last the remainder of the day. He didn't have much time. Whether it ended at wherever Jason was being held or where the murderer was hiding, it didn't matter. Either way he would find answers.

He hurried back to the BMW, taking the risk that the tiny tendril wouldn't collapse on itself during the time it took him to get to the car and return here. As it was, he'd have to do something he didn't like doing: drive while his magical senses were active. Wherever the tendril reached, he was fairly sure it wasn't within walking distance, and he didn't have time to take the chance that it was close enough to reach before it faded.

The tendril was still there when he slowed down next to the spot where he'd last seen it. He shifted his vision over and drove as slowly as he dared, hoping it didn't leave the road and force him to exit the car and set out overland. With a corner of his mind he activated one of the focus objects he wore, a ring with a blocky purple stone, and fed some of its stored power into keeping a lock on the tiny red thread. It was somewhat like trying to follow a glowing laser beam at twilight, with only the faintest of clouds to delineate its path.

It took him back out of the Arbolada and toward Ojai Avenue, surprisingly keeping mostly to the road. That suggested to Stone that he was following a person rather than a supernatural entity. Things like spirits and other summoned beings rarely followed roads—in fact, most of them didn't even acknowledge their existence. But humans—even those possessed or otherwise controlled by these spirits and beings—did.

Quite likely, he was following the murderer.

He couldn't get a sense of Jason anymore; that required too much concentration, and there would be no way he could keep enough of his mind on the road to avoid running into parked cars or being pulled over for erratic driving. So he continued on, taking a right and continuing to the southwest.

There was a fair bit of traffic on Ojai Avenue, since by now it was getting to the beginning of what laughably passed for an evening commute around here. He eased the car onto the main drag, keeping the tendril in his peripheral vision while he readjusted most of his attention to the mundane world. It meandered out and then moved southwest again in a short time, so he took the first left to continue down a road called Country Club Drive.

He couldn't look too closely because he had to re-establish the tendril's position, but the road looked about like he'd have expected something called "Country Club Drive" to look: the BMW cruised past pricey homes, open fields, and the entrance to what was apparently a major local resort. Trees lined both sides of the road, obscuring all but the most fleeting glimpse of the opulent houses, most of them set far back from the road behind tall gates.

Another several minutes of careful driving brought him to the end of Country Club Drive, to a T intersection with Creek Road. He paused, grateful that there was very little traffic on side roads in this town, and then made a right turn, still following the tendril.

It led him for another mile or so, snaking along a narrow, twisty road heavily flanked by trees on both sides, before veering abruptly to the left and disappearing into the forest. Stone found a place to pull off, locked the car, shrugged into his coat, and followed it.

He walked slowly through the trees, the carpet of leaves crackling under his feet. Ahead, the tendril drifted along in a still mostly southwest direction. It was stronger here. He was getting close.

He paused at that realization, thinking fast. He couldn't just blunder into whatever was up ahead. He had no idea whether anyone was there, whether they were watching or waiting. Did they know he was coming? His mental defenses hadn't pinged any attempts to breach them, which meant that whatever had touched him back during the ritual either hadn't found him yet, or was intelligent enough not to try a direct confrontation.

Or it was strong enough to do it without him noticing. Which was not a thought he wanted to have right now.

It could be nothing—a dead trail, or a deliberate wild-goose chase. If the thing had tracked him back to his body fast, it would have had plenty of time to set up something while he'd located the memorial and examined the area. He didn't think that was the case, though. Paranoia was definitely a good thing when you were dealing with the supernatural realm, but too much of it could get you killed just as fast as not enough. He had to press on and see what he'd find.

So, he compromised. He couldn't keep an invisibility spell up long enough for it to do any good—that was not one of his strongest areas magic-wise, and a few minutes was all he could manage without exhausting himself. His "don't notice me" spell, however— the one he'd used on the BMW as he violated several speed limits on his way down here—came as second nature. It might not protect him from any powerful beings from the spirit world, but if there were any live humans here it should hide him well enough that he could do a bit of recon from a safe distance and then decide his next move once he'd gathered more useful information about what he was facing.

He put up the spell, gave it a bit of power from his ring to maintain it, and continued forward.

Step by step, the twisting red tendril grew brighter. Stone broke through the trees into a dusty area about the size of a small parking lot. The only thing he could see was a weed-strewn paddock surrounded by a wooden fence, the sort where a horse might be kept, and on the paddock's far side, a ramshackle building that could have been a large shed or a small barn. Its doors, closed now, looked as if they would swing out into the field when opened.

The whole place had a deserted, unkempt feel to it: the dusty field showed neither horse droppings nor any sign that human beings had been here recently, and the weeds had nearly taken over the area around the barn itself.

The red tendril snaked through the paddock and disappeared, as Stone knew it would, into the barn.

He glanced around to make sure no one was approaching from behind him, then took a deep breath. This could be a big mistake, but he didn't have a choice: if Jason was in there, then he had to find him. He faded back behind a tree and spent a moment not only reinforcing his concealing spell, but also adding more power to his mental and physical shield spells. At the very least, it was unlikely that something would catch him completely unaware and get a full-strength shot off against him. He wished he'd brought more focus items with him: all he had right now was a pair of rings, and he was holding one of them in reserve in case of emergency.

As prepared as he was going to get, he stepped back out into the light (it was a good thing it was summertime: at least he didn't have to do this in the dark) and moved along the fence toward the barn.

It was grandiose to call it a "barn": a single-story structure, it was about the size of a two-car garage, its wooden sides faded and cracked under what might at one time (probably before Stone was born) have been a coat of vibrant red paint. The double doors in the front were fastened with a hasp through which a rusty lock dangled, its shaft hanging open. The sense of isolation was strong: Stone was sure even without his magical senses that there were no living beings inside that barn, human or otherwise.

If that were true, then either Jason wasn't here, or—

But no, that kind of thinking wouldn't do him any good. He didn't have time for it. He stepped forward.

The smell hit him with almost palpable force before he made it all the way to the barn. Fetid, rotten, with a barely discernible coppery tang overlaying it, the odor rolled out of the many openings between the slats of the building. It wasn't a physical cloud, but it might as well have been. Stone paused, taking a slow, deep breath.

This was not good.

This was not good at all.

Still, as bad as the physical smell was, the sheer psychic taint bathing the area was worse. Stone took a step back, pausing to adjust his mental barriers to block most of it out, but even his formidable defenses couldn't turn all of it aside. Something horrific had occurred inside this humble building.

Something—or someone—had suffered torment behind those weathered doors.

For a few seconds, he thought about just leaving now: going back to town and alerting the police that he'd found something they needed to see. But two things made that impossible for him: first, that whatever was dead in there could be nothing but a horse, cow, or other large animal. The smell was too strong to be a small one, but this place *was* a barn. Maybe someone had left an animal in there to die, or killed it for whatever reason and left the carcass. It would be pretty embarrassing if the big-city Englishman brought a squad of cops up here only to show them the last mortal remains of Bessie the Cow. Sure, it wasn't likely—that kind of crushing psychic residue would require a level of conscious suffering he didn't think an animal had the capacity to experience—but it was possible.

That wasn't the main reason he didn't leave, though. With the teenage Ashley's murder having happened so recently, he honestly didn't think the police would have a problem with citizens reporting potential repeat performances, even if they *did* turn out to be false alarms. *Especially* if they turned out to be false alarms.

No, the main reason why he remained here—why he steeled his will, squared his shoulders, and moved to climb over the fence, slide the lock off the hasp, and push open the barn door—was that he had to know what was in there.

He had to know it wasn't Jason.

He winced as the door swung open a bit, creaking, catching against the dirt and weeds on the ground. With more room to get out now, the stench was nearly unbearable. Stone pulled a handkerchief from the inner pocket of his overcoat and pressed it to his mouth and nose; it helped a bit, but not much.

Even with the numerous chinks and holes piercing the barn's wooden skin, it was still quite dim inside. The sliver of light let in by the open door illuminated a dusty floor with a few stray bits of hay clinging to it, but the rest of the interior space on either side and the rear was lost in dappled shadow. Leaving the door open, Stone summoned a small light spell and shone it around.

He stared, an electric ripple running up his spine and stiffening his body.

Whoever had created the scene inside, they had taken no pains to conceal their handiwork. On the side farthest away from where Stone stood in shocked immobility, a dark form lay on the dirt floor, its limbs splayed out as if it had been deliberately arranged that way. He had to move in closer to see the details; when he did, reluctantly, the form resolved itself into a human body.

He closed his eyes for a moment, taking a deep breath, and then forced himself to hold his light spell higher and examine the scene more closely.

It wasn't Jason.

Nothing else was immediately obvious except that it had been, at one time, probably male. All that remained now was a collection of blood-soaked limbs, matted hair, filmy staring eyes, and a messy clump of internal organs spilling from the body's abdominal cavity. It was more obvious at close range that the corpse's arms and legs had been purposely arranged, spread-eagled and arms extended like it was trying to create some kind of macabre snow angel. Insects, both flying and crawling, hovered and writhed in and around the body, and gobbets of dark blood stained the ground everywhere around the immediate vicinity. Stone glanced down to make sure he hadn't tracked through it on his way in, but it seemed to be confined to the area just around the body.

In fact, he realized, "confined" was a very good word to describe what he was seeing. It was as if the body and the area around it had been somehow enshrouded within an invisible dome that limited the spread of blood to a carefully delineated area.

His eyes widened as the implications of that sunk in.

What he was seeing here was not just an area, but a crude yet carefully constructed *circle*.

That was all he was able to take in before something slammed into him from behind.

| CHAPTER SEVEN

S tone staggered forward, barely catching himself before he pitched headlong into the gory tableau on the ground. He flung himself sideways, recovering his balance against the barn's side wall and wheeled, readying himself for another attack.

There was nothing there.

Breathing hard, he hurried to the door but did not poke his head out yet. Whatever had hit him had put a lot of force behind it: even through his shield, it still felt like someone had whacked him between the shoulder blades with a large, pillow-covered hammer.

What the hell—?

And then he felt it again: the same terrorized impulse that had gripped him during the ritual. The near-overwhelming compulsion to flee, to run, to put as much distance between himself and this scene as he possibly could.

"All right, you bastard," he growled under his breath. "Big mistake, trying to play that game with me."

He stepped out into the paddock, and once again something slammed into him, from the front this time. The force drove him backward into the wall of the barn, but his shield, still at full strength, took up the brunt of the impact. Something shimmered in front of him, dancing away. Without conscious thought he gathered energy and flung a blast of pure arcane power in the direction of the shimmering thing, and was rewarded by a flare of red in the air several feet in front of him.

Something else hit him from the side, throwing him into the fence. He rolled, panting. *There's more than one of them?* This was *not* good. He could already feel his shield losing a bit of potency—it would hold for a while yet, but if he had to take too many more of those hits, he was going to be in trouble. Not to mention the fact that he wouldn't be able to fling those blasts of energy many more times either. Diverting more power from his ring to supplement the shield, he dragged himself back to his feet. "Who the hell are you?" he yelled. "What do you want?"

He didn't think he would get an answer, but it couldn't hurt to take a shot. The terror was trying to worm its way into his head again: sweat beaded on his forehead and his heart raced, but he clamped down his mental defenses and forced himself to ignore it. His gaze darted around, trying to pick the shimmering figures—at least two of them—out of the dusty afternoon sunlight.

Another one hit him, from behind again. He pitched forward and went down on his face. *Three?*

Maybe getting the hell out of here wasn't a bad idea, actually. He had no idea what he was up against, and trying to fight three (or more?) of them, whatever they were, on his own might be a Very Bad Plan.

He scrabbled up to a sitting position, paused to reinforce the shield again (it didn't work quite as well this time—he could feel its energy fading even more with each successive impact) and raised both hands, this time sending out a crackling wall of force that, with any luck, would hit at least one of them. It wouldn't hurt much, but it might drive anything it hit back far enough that Stone could put some distance between himself and them.

His trick worked. Two more red spots flared about six feet off the ground, shoved backward by Stone's magical bulldozer. They darted around and faded back to near-invisible shimmers, but didn't approach.

Stone's mind continued spinning out plans and possibilities as he got himself upright and began backing off in the direction he'd come. Had these things been here all along? Were they watching the barn, and only triggered or summoned when someone entered it? Would they have appeared for anyone, or were they tuned to only attack those who might threaten them? Even though they were strong, Stone didn't think they were the murderers—or at least not the masterminds of whatever this operation was. "You're here somewhere, aren't you?" he murmured, eyes flashing. "The host of this little party, I mean, not your lackeys. Show yourself."

There was a ripple of something almost like mocking laughter inside his head, but nothing more. One of the little shimmering figures struck him again as he was climbing over the fence. He fell awkwardly, landing on his side, his breath knocked from him.

Two of them came down to pummel him this time, taking turns, ramming him into the fence like a series of one-two punches from a heavyweight boxer. Stone rolled into a ball and activated his second ring, pouring more power into his shield. Clearly, they could keep this up longer than he could resist it.

I need to get out of here.

Closing his eyes, he lashed out with an undirected blast of force, risking more power than he wanted to. His headache, which by this point had mostly faded, spiked into his forehead again. The satisfaction of seeing one of the shimmering forms flare brighter red and fly to pieces in front of him didn't make up for the growing fear that he was in deep trouble.

Fast, brutal combat spells were not something he, as a white mage, was adept with. He could use them, sure—in fact he'd gotten rather good with them, his more frequent use of them than was strictly proper for "respectable" white mages contributing to the slight darkening of his "pale gray" status, and his ongoing study of the powerful methods used by the mysterious and unconventional gray mage Harrison had made them come more easily than they used to—but even then, they weren't something he went out of his way to cast if he had other options. Especially not since he didn't dare to use Harrison's magic and risk burning out his own.

Right now, he wasn't coming up with too many options.

He rolled back up, his heart doing its best imitation of a heavy-metal drummer. The two remaining shimmers had backed off, flitting to and fro a few feet away. Stone took another step back toward the tree line, keeping the two of them in sight. They remained still. Were they going to let him go?

The strange laughter sounded in his head again. He got a brief image of Jason, too brief for anything but mere identification, and then yet another impact struck him, this time down low. It took his legs out from under him; as he hit the ground, two more took their turns from behind him and rolled him over and over, back toward the barn. His shield shrieked in protest, its smooth surface glowing red in the spots where they'd hit it. Normally invisible, it began taking on the pinkish tinge that told Stone it wouldn't hold against too many more of those attacks.

More than a bit of desperation drove his actions now. He got back to his feet more quickly than he thought possible and staggered toward the tree line as a thought poked itself into his mind from somewhere: maybe the things had been summoned from the crude circle around the corpse, and were tied to that location. If he could get far enough away from them, maybe they wouldn't be able to follow—or at least maybe their power would wane to the point where he could deal more effectively with them.

He had no idea whether it was true, or whether it would even work. He didn't have time to consider it. Instead, ignoring the pain from the multiple impacts, the thudding in his chest, and the stabbing spike in his head, he jogged away from the barn.

One last shimmering fist slammed him from behind. It was the last straw for his shield. It flared and faded in a haze of psychic feedback, blunting most of the impact Stone took from being propelled into the trunk of a large oak tree. He sank to his knees against it, steeling himself to take the blows he knew were coming—

But they didn't come.

He raised his head, looking back toward the barn, shifting to his magical senses.

Nothing.

Had he been right? Had the things, whatever they were, been attached to the barn, and couldn't range out past their metaphorical tethers?

He took a deep breath and slowly, ever so slowly, hauled himself back to his feet. For a moment he just stood there, listening to his harsh breathing and the thumping of his heart. He'd been luckier than he ever had any reasonable expectation of being. But now he knew he was alone against something unknown, quite probably out of his power league, and able to call in friends.

For the moment, though, none of that mattered. All that mattered was that, against all odds, he'd gotten away. At least for now he was safe.

And then a voice boomed at him from off to his right:

"Don't move! Put your hands against the tree and remain still. This is the police!"

| CHAPTER EIGHT

S tone spun, his adrenaline from the fight with the shimmering things still cranked up to the point where reacting to additional threats was instinctual.

Two guns were pointing at him from two different directions.

"I said, put your hands on that tree *now!*" a sharp male voice barked. "This is your last warning!"

For about a half second, Stone thought about making a break for it, but the thought died before it even took full form. Getting shot by the police would not be a pleasant end to an already unpleasant day. Instead, he did as directed, turning slowly with his hands up and pressing them against the tree.

Two cops, one large and imposing-looking, the other smaller and younger, hurried up to him, guns still drawn. The younger one stood back and kept his weapon trained on Stone while the larger one patted him down. "He's clean."

"It's not me you want to be dealing with," Stone said, fighting to keep his voice even and calm. "It's what's in that barn over there."

The large cop grabbed his arm and pulled him back from the tree. "Take off the coat," he ordered. "Slowly, and hand it over here."

Stone kept his gaze on the cop as, with careful deliberateness, he slid out of his overcoat and held it out. The cop, whose nametag above his badge identified him as *Aguirre*, took it and draped it over a nearby tree branch. "Okay, hands behind you, please."

This was getting ridiculous. "Officer, I—"

"Behind you," Aguirre repeated, clamping a meaty hand on one of his wrists and twisting it around behind him. Not hard, just inexorably. He removed a set of handcuffs from his belt and snapped them around Stone's wrists.

"Am I under arrest, then?" he asked.

"Not yet. If that changes, you'll be the first to know." He hooked a thumb toward the barn. "What were you saying about what's over there?"

Stone took a deep breath. This was not going to look good, no matter how he spun it. "I think I've found another victim of your murderer," he said quietly. "Have a care—it's not pretty in there."

The two cops exchanged glances. Some unspoken communication passed between them; the younger one backed off, gun still pointed in Stone's general direction, and began speaking into the mic clipped to his uniform shoulder.

Stone remained silent, his gaze moving between the two cops and back toward the barn. He hoped he'd been right about the shimmering guardians: that they'd be uninterested in anything that wasn't magically potent. Otherwise, these policemen might be in for some trouble and there was nothing he could do about it with his hands locked behind his back and a gun aimed at him.

The two cops, obviously waiting for backup before they investigated the barn, remained near Stone. "Let's have you just sit down there against the tree while we wait," the younger one, whose nametag read *Farrell*, said. He and Aguirre took hold of Stone's arms and lowered him to a seated position. Stone gritted his teeth; he didn't think he'd taken any serious injury from being battered by the shimmering forms, but his body felt like he'd just done five rounds with Ali and this wasn't helping at all.

"Do you have any identification?" Aguirre asked.

Stone knew the whole "anything you say can and will be used against you" bit, and that he should probably keep his mouth shut, but he had nothing to hide. "My wallet is in my coat," he said, nodding toward the tree where they'd put it.

Farrell retrieved it and glanced inside. "Says your name's Alastair Stone. Resident of Palo Alto."

Stone nodded. "That's right."

"What are you doing down here in Ojai, Mr. Stone?" Aguirre asked.

"Looking for a friend." Stone shifted his arms behind him. The position they'd put him in was not at all comfortable.

"Out here?"

"He's gone missing," Stone said. "I had reason to believe he might be here."

They were spared further conversation by the sound of someone crunching through the carpet of dead leaves. In a moment, two more cops emerged: a man and a woman. They both had their guns drawn as well, though they were currently pointed at the ground.

"What's the situation?" the male half of the pair demanded.

"Picked this guy up out here after some kid reported hearing something weird in the woods, sir," Aguirre said, pointing at Stone. "He says there's another murder victim in the barn up there."

"Does he?" This cop was older than Aguirre, with a square, open face and thinning hair. "All right, let's check it out. You two keep an eye on him. Come on, Wu."

Stone sat silently against the tree, focusing his magical senses toward the barn and the two new cops disappearing behind some trees. If the entities in the barn attacked them, he'd have to decide whether he wanted to do things that would end up making him have to answer a lot of uncomfortable questions—assuming he didn't get killed outright by a skittish Aguirre and Farrell before he could do anything useful.

It was only five minutes before the other cops returned. Wu's face was ashen, and even the older cop looked like he was trying hard not to throw up. "Dear God..." he murmured.

Aguirre looked alarmed. "He was right? You found something?" He glanced at Stone and then back at the cop.

The older cop nodded, eyes haunted. "Yeah, and it's bad. Get on the radio and call it in. Get the crime-scene guys up here, and tell 'em not to make any plans to go home tonight."

Wu hurried off, clearly relieved to get away from the scene, and the male cop turned back to face Stone, his face growing hard. "You," he said. "What do you know about this?"

"I told you—I was searching for a friend and came upon it. I was about to head back to call you gentlemen when—" he indicated them all with a head movement "—I found I didn't have to."

The cop's eyes narrowed. "Really. You just *happened* upon this abandoned barn out in the middle of nowhere, that just *happened* to have a messy murder victim inside."

Stone sighed. "Officer, please. Surely you don't think I killed him? I've no experience with forensics, but even the brief look I got before I left told me that whoever your victim is, he's been dead for several days at least. I only just arrived in town yesterday."

The cop ignored his tone. "Okay," he told Aguirre instead. "You and Farrell take him back to the station for questioning. We're gonna be here a while."

Aguirre and Farrell nodded, hauling Stone up to his feet. Again, they weren't rough with him, but didn't seem particularly fazed by his wince of pain. They prodded him along and he walked in silence back up out of the trees. Two squad cars were parked just off the road.

Stone paused as they reached them. " My car's up the road a bit. Black BMW. The keys are in my coat pocket. If you'd be so kind as to see it gets back, I'd appreciate it."

"Don't you worry, Mr. Stone. We'll take care of it." They loaded him into one of the squad cars, still handcuffed, and drove off.

They took him back to the police station, a small, neat building not far from downtown, ushered him into a featureless room with a table and two chairs, and left him there, telling him someone would be along to talk to him in just a few minutes.

He shifted in the uncomfortable chair, acutely aware of the camera high up in the corner of the opposite wall. He was sure they were watching his every move, so he had no reasonable choice but to sit here and wait for them. He was sure he could get away if he needed to, but they had his wallet so they knew who he was and where he lived (and if they looked through it in any more depth, they'd also know where he worked), meaning that he'd cause more problems than he'd solve by doing anything but cooperating. It wasn't like they had anything on him, nor that he didn't want to cooperate with them. They were trying to find Jason too.

The door opened and another man came in, this one dressed in a suit rather than a police uniform, his badge in a holder clipped to his breast pocket. He was tall and balding, one of those sorts who had probably been athletic twenty years ago but had let himself go to seed a bit in the intervening time. He carried a file folder in one hand and a cup of coffee in the other, and put both of them down on the table.

"Dr. Stone," he said, nodding. "I'm Lieutenant Casner. We spoke on the phone recently, do you remember?"

Stone's eyebrow rose. This was unexpected, though he supposed it shouldn't have been. "Of course I do."

"Would you like something to drink? Water? Coffee?"

"What I'd like, Lieutenant, is for you to let me out of these handcuffs. It's not as if I'm planning to escape."

Casner considered, then nodded. He came around behind Stone, pulled a set of keys from his pocket, and removed the cuffs. "Better?"

"Yes, much better. Thank you." Stone shook his arms, making rather more of a show of rubbing his wrists and rolling his shoulders than was truly necessary, then settled back in the chair. "Am I under arrest?"

The detective shook his head. "No, Dr. Stone. But I do have some questions for you before we let you go, if you're willing to answer them. You don't have to, of course, and if you'd like to consult an attorney and have one present, we can arrange for you to do that before we talk."

Stone shrugged. "I have nothing to hide, Lieutenant. Ask your questions."

Casner opened his file folder, extracted a sheet of yellow legal-pad paper with a few scribbles on it that Stone couldn't read from where he was, and pulled out a pen from his inner jacket pocket. "Why did you come to Ojai?"

"That should be obvious. To look for my friend Jason Thayer."

Casner wrote something on his piece of paper. "Why? Do you have some reason to believe that you'd have a better chance of finding him than we would?"

"No." The lie came easily. "Other than the fact that I know him better than you do, so I might think of avenues to follow that your men might miss. Also, I'm sure the police are quite busy—I don't know how it is here in Ojai, but where I'm from they're usually so overwhelmed by murder and other violent crime investigations that they don't have as much time as they'd like to pursue these kinds of cases." A diplomatic response: it was better than saying, "I really didn't think you lot would waste your time trying to locate a grown man who's been missing for less than three days."

Casner wrote something else down. "How long have you been friends with Mr. Thayer?"

"About two years."

"Mmm-hmm." Some more jotting on the page. "Have you had any luck finding leads to his whereabouts since you arrived in town? When was that, by the way?"

"Yesterday afternoon. And no, not much. Although I understand that the police suspect that he might have something to do with the murder of the girl who was found in the Arbolada."

Casner looked up at him, surprised. "Where did you hear that, Dr. Stone?"

"Not at liberty to say. It's true, then? Was that what you weren't saying on the phone when we spoke last?"

"We're—looking at many possible persons of interest. Naturally, because Mr. Thayer was placed in the area close to where the murder occurred during the same time frame, we'd like to have a chance to talk with him. He might have seen or heard something."

Stone raised an eyebrow. "Lieutenant, please."

"It's true. I won't lie to you: he's definitely among those we'd like to talk to due to the suspicious circumstances and timing of his disappearance, but there's also another potential reason: he might have stumbled onto the crime scene and the murderer took him to keep him from talking."

"Not likely, though: if the murderer was capable of slitting the throat of a sixteen-year-old girl, then surely he'd have no compunctions about killing another person to preserve his secret?"

"Those are all excellent questions, Dr. Stone. But please: may I continue?" At Stone's nod, he tapped his paper with his pen. "Let's talk about what you were doing at an abandoned barn off Creek Road this afternoon. That seems like a very odd place for you to have even located, given that you're not familiar with the town and have been here such a short time."

Stone took a deep breath. This was where things could start getting sticky if he didn't tread carefully. He *didn't* have any mundane reason why he'd know about the location of the second murder. He couldn't exactly say, "I examined the scene of the first murder using my magical senses and followed an astral cord connecting the two sites." Even if he were foolhardy enough to make such a statement, he knew Casner's response would be either to accuse him of being a smart-ass or to assume he wasn't firing on all mental cylinders. Neither of which would help his chances of getting out of here and back to his search for Jason any time soon. He decided to go with a variation of the truth. He'd still look a bit unhinged, but that couldn't be helped. At least he could back it up with his credentials. "I know you won't believe this, Lieutenant, but—I had a dream that led me to that location."

"A dream." Casner's tone was politely dubious, and he wrote something else on his paper.

Stone nodded. "You've still got my wallet—did you look through it at all?"

"No. We just looked at your identification. Your personal items will be returned to you when you leave."

"Well, if you had, you'd see that my place of employment is Stanford University. I'm a professor of Occult Studies there. I believe I mentioned that when we spoke as well."

Casner stared at him, forgetting to write anything down. "A professor of what?"

"Occult Studies. You know—magical rituals, witches, ghosts, ley lines, paranormal occurrences, psychic phenomena, that sort of thing."

Casner simply continued staring at him for several more seconds, and then he said carefully, "I...see."

Stone shrugged. "You don't believe it. I'm not surprised—most people wouldn't."

"You can't blame me for being skeptical, Dr. Stone. And—you say they teach this kind of stuff at *college?*"

"It's a small program and we're not exactly a big draw, but for the sort of people who appreciate that sort of thing, it's a legitimate discipline."

Casner paused, jotted something else down on his paper, then looked up. "So, you're telling me you're psychic."

"I have...flashes. It's not a speciality, and I can't do it at will. But sometimes I have dreams that end up being—well—useful."

"And this dream told you—what? Where to find a murder victim that nobody else had found yet?"

"It told me that I'd find something of interest in a place that looked like that, and the general vicinity where it might be. Naturally, since I'm searching for Jason, I thought it might have been referring to him."

Casner let out a long, slow exhalation, tapping his pen on the table. "Let's get back to the—um—non-supernatural for a minute, if we can. I'm assuming you can account for your whereabouts for the past few days?"

"Of course. I was home, in Palo Alto. You know I was there when you called me. Before that, I can give you the names and phone numbers of at least four people who can vouch for my whereabouts." He leaned forward, meeting Casner's eyes with his own focused blue gaze. "Lieutenant, you don't think I killed those people, do you?"

The cop shook his head. "No, Dr. Stone, I don't. If I did, you'd be under arrest already. But I do think you know more about something—and I'm not even sure what, exactly—than you're telling. I don't know how much of this 'I had a dream' stuff you're feeding me that I should believe. I know there's a lot of that kind of thing around here: Ojai's got a lot of harmless weirdos. It's part of what brings the tourists in. But that doesn't mean I believe any of it."

"Nor do you need to, if you don't plan on arresting me," Stone said. "Am I free to go, then?"

"You're free to go whenever you like," Casner said. "But I will ask you to tell me where you're staying, and be reachable in case I come up with any other questions. I'm assuming that our crime-scene guys won't find anything you wouldn't want us to know about?"

"I was in the barn," Stone said. "I didn't get more than a few feet from the body, and of course I didn't touch it or anything near it. You might also find witnesses or evidence that I was at the scene of the other murder, earlier today. I wanted to see the place, given that my friend is under suspicion. I also wanted to see if I could find any evidence that *he* was there." He considered not mentioning the circle, since it probably wouldn't be obvious to anyone unfamiliar with the occult that it *was* a circle, but then reconsidered. "One thing, though..."

"Yes?"

"I think your killer might have some connection to the occult."

Casner's gaze sharpened. "What makes you think so?"

"Your crime scene examiners might notice that the pattern of blood around the body is bounded by a large circular area. It's hard to spot because it's quite crude, but if you look carefully, you'll see it."

Now the cop was staring at him with frank disbelief. "What the hell—"

Stone shrugged. "I don't know what it means. I didn't get a close enough look at it to tell for sure."

"So you're saying that—what—Satanists or something did this?"

"I don't know, Lieutenant. As I said, I'd have to examine the scene more closely, and I doubt you're going to let me do that. But rest assured, my expertise is at your disposal should you need it. May I?" he asked, reaching for Casner's pen.

When he handed it over, along with a strip torn off the bottom of his sheet of paper, Stone jotted down the address of the house he'd rented. "That's where I'm staying while I'm in town. I don't know the phone number—just settled in earlier today, and I haven't memorized it yet. I'll get it from my wallet when you give it back to me."

Casner took the slip of paper and his pen back, looking at Stone like the conversation had gone in a completely different direction than he'd planned. "All right, Dr. Stone," he said slowly. "Thank you. I appreciate your cooperation."

Stone stood. "Anything else, Lieutenant?"

"Just one thing. I know you're trying hard to find your friend and I'm not going to tell you to stop doing that. But please remember: impeding or interfering with police work in any way is a crime, as is trespassing."

"In other words: stay out of your way, and don't be found near any more murder victims."

"Essentially, yes. I don't want to see you in here again, Dr. Stone, unless you need help with something or—" he nodded at the slip of paper "—the department decides to...er...consult with you about the crime. Though if I were you, I wouldn't hold my breath waiting for that, honestly."

"Of course not. Thank you, Lieutenant."

Casner showed him out of the interrogation room and gave him back his overcoat and wallet. "I think somebody brought your car up here. You might have to pay to get it out of impound, but they might not have had a chance to get it in there yet so you might be lucky."

That would make one *thing I've been lucky with today*, Stone thought sourly. He handed the policeman one of his business cards after he located his phone number and jotted it down on the back, and soon after he was standing outside the police station.

He retrieved his car—which he didn't, in fact, have to pay for— and drove back to his rented house, finally allowing the last of the day's adrenaline to drain from him. He'd never been arrested before (all right, technically this didn't count as arrested, but being handcuffed and having two cops aiming guns at him made it about as close as he ever wanted to get). Add that to the scene in the barn and the battle with the shimmering entities, and all he wanted to do to get home, take a long hot shower, and get several hours of uninterrupted sleep. There was so much he still needed to do: figure out what those things that attacked him were, and what was directing them; determine what the connection was between the murders and Jason; figure out if the murders were the main component of the thing's plan, or only a side effect.

And, of course, figure out what had become of Jason. He knew he was out there somewhere, but he also knew that he wouldn't be any help to his friend if he made stupid mistakes due to physical and mental exhaustion. Furthermore, if he was wise he'd still need to put up at least a simple ward around the house before he could let himself rest, and that was about all he'd have the juice to manage tonight.

By the time he checked the place out for lurking magical threats, finished the ward, and trudged inside, it was after eight o'clock. He was asleep before nine.

It wasn't until the next morning that he remembered he was supposed to meet Lindsey Cole for dinner last night.

| CHAPTER NINE

Stone took a deep breath and opened the door to the tiny real-estate office.

Lindsey Cole looked up from her desk. When she spotted him, her expression grew cool. "Good morning, Dr. Stone." Her voice was inflectionless, dead steady. "I hope everything is all right with your rental property."

Across from her, the older woman at the other desk looked between the two of them with quizzical confusion.

Stone stood at the counter. "Can you spare a moment?" he asked. "I haven't had coffee yet this morning—perhaps you might join me?" He, too, kept his voice neutral.

She considered. "I don't know—I've got things I need to—"

"Please," he said softly. "Just hear me out. Only a few minutes."

She glanced over at the other woman, then nodded and picked up her purse. "I'll be back soon, Florence," she said.

Florence was eyeing Stone with an appraising—and approving—gleam. "Take all the time you need, honey. I'll hold the fort."

"I wanted to apologize for last night," Stone said as they walked past the art galleries and clothing boutiques toward the coffee shop. "And to explain."

"You don't owe me any explanation, Dr. Stone," she said. She hadn't looked at him, and her expression still hadn't thawed.

"Of course I do. I promised to meet you, and I didn't. That was frightfully rude. I just wanted to tell you why. If you want nothing more to do with me after you've heard my explanation, I'll certainly understand and I won't bother you again. Fair enough?"

After a moment she nodded. "All right, fair enough." Then, almost reluctantly: "Was it something about your friend?"

"Indirectly, yes." They reached the coffee shop and he opened the door for her. As he followed behind her, he spotted a few copies of the local paper in a rack. The headline, in large letters, read: *Murder victim discovered near Creek Road.* He took a deep breath and continued into the shop.

When they were seated at a table near the window with their mugs, he leaned back in his chair and decided to go for the direct approach. "The truth is, I couldn't meet you because I was being questioned by the police."

Her head came up, her eyes wide. "What?"

He nodded. "By the time they'd finished with me, I'd frankly forgotten about our date. I do apologize for that. All I can say in my defense is that I've never had anything like that happen to me before, and it was a bit—er—unsettling. The whole afternoon was unsettling, honestly."

She was staring at him. "Questioned about—what?"

"I happened upon something when I was searching for my friend. There was a bit of a misunderstanding."

"Happened...upon something? I don't understand."

He nodded toward the rack of newspapers. "I—found the site of the second murder."

She gasped, nearly dropping her mug. "You—" Glancing around, she dropped her voice to a murmur. "You found—"

"Down on—I think it was called Creek Road, yes. In a barn."

"And the police—"

"They showed up shortly after. Apparently someone spotted me wandering about down there and called them. Can't blame them for that, really—I know people are on edge after the first killing."

Lindsey swallowed. She set her mug down on the table, looked up at him, then back down into her coffee. "I—I don't know what to say."

He gave her a gentle smile. "I completely understand if you want to just get up and go back to your office now. I won't trouble you anymore. I'm sure this is a shock for you, and my being a stranger, you—"

"No, no." She looked up again, shaking her head. "No, that isn't it. It's just—wow. That must have been horrible for you. And the police—did they arrest you?"

"No. It quickly became apparent that I was just at the wrong place at the wrong time—I have people who can vouch for the fact that I was in Palo Alto up until two days ago, so I couldn't possibly have committed the murders. But I'm afraid—well, all of that rather drove the idea of a lovely Mexican dinner right out of my mind. I hope you'll forgive me."

She paused, smiled faintly. "Well—you did say you might have to cancel at the last minute if something came up with your—wait." She frowned. "You said you were 'searching' for your friend? I thought you said you were meeting him."

Stone sighed. "I didn't tell you quite the whole truth there. That's why I'm down here, actually: my friend's gone missing, and I'm trying to find him."

"Missing?"

"He was down here to attend an old friend's wedding. He called me sometime early Saturday morning, but by the time I was able to return his call, he'd disappeared."

She took a slow deep breath and another sip of her coffee, and said nothing.

Stone regarded her for a moment. When he spoke, his voice was soft: "Ms. Cole—truly, I understand. You thought you were going to have a pleasant evening over dinner with a newcomer to town, not get involved with someone who comes complete with a whole bagful of difficult issues." He started to rise. "I'll walk you back to your office if you like, or—"

"No," she said suddenly, as if coming to a decision. "Please, Dr. Stone—Alastair—sit down." When he hesitated, she added: "I might be able to help you, if you'll let me."

He shook his head. "The last thing I want to do is get you involved." That was true. Getting *anyone* involved in this was something he wanted to avoid with extreme prejudice. People who got bound up in his particular brand of supernatural adventures tended to have unpleasant things happen to them. Especially when they had no idea what they were getting themselves into.

"Why not? Do you think it's dangerous, somehow?" She smiled. "I didn't say I'd go tramping around out on Creek Road with you or anything. I *did* just meet you, after all. I might be an optimist, but I'm not an idiot. I just thought if you had any questions about getting around Ojai or anything else that might help you look for your friend, you could ask me. I've lived in town all my life, and anything I can't answer, I can probably find somebody who can."

Stone considered. It was an offer he hadn't expected, but it *did* make a certain amount of sense. He wasn't familiar with how to get around in Ojai, relying on maps and guesses. Asking Lindsey a few questions about specific aspects of the town wouldn't put her in danger, and having a local around could be a big help in his search. "Are you sure you want to?" he asked. "Not that I don't appreciate the offer, but—"

"Sure I want to," she said. "On one condition."

"Yes?"

"I'd still like to have that dinner with you," she said, smiling. "It could be lunch, if you want."

"Tell you what," he said. "I think it's best we play things by ear now, since I've no idea where my search will take me or what I'll be needing to follow up on. If we don't manage to find a time to do it before I find what's become of my friend, I promise you we'll absolutely do it before I go back home. Deal?"

"Deal," she said with a brisk nod. She reached in her purse and handed him a business card. "The first number is my office. The second one is my cellular phone. I always have it with me."

Stone raised an eyebrow. "Ah, you've got one of those things, do you? A couple of my colleagues have them, but I'm not sure I'd want to be constantly reachable. Seems it could be rather inconvenient."

"They're a godsend for my line of work," she said. "People have to be able to get hold of you if you want to get the sales."

"All right, then." He stowed the card in his coat and gave her one of his with the number at the house written on the back. "I'd best be getting on with my search, but—" He tilted his head. "What?"

She was staring at his card. "Department of Occult Studies?" Looking him up and down, she said, "That's—unexpected." She smiled, adding, "You don't bite heads off chickens or sacrifice goats or anything, do you?"

"Certainly not," he assured her, indignant. "Chickens taste dreadful raw. The only thing I bite the head off is the occasional chocolate rabbit."

She laughed. "Well, that's good to know. You've come to the right place, anyway. Ojai's full of all kinds of things like that."

"Indeed? You'll have to tell me about it over that dinner." He'd heard occasional things about Ojai—it was home to a few minor talents, along with a whole lot of people who liked to think they had connections to the supernatural, but who really just liked to dress up in flowy caftans and play eerie music for the tourists.

"That's a promise," she said, also standing. "I hope you find your friend soon, Alastair. And not just because I'm looking forward to seeing you again."

| CHAPTER TEN

S tone didn't want to go back to the house after Lindsey left, so he got another cup of coffee to go and set off to walk for a while.

He was glad he'd been able to straighten things out with Lindsey: he had no illusions that his acquaintance with her would grow beyond maybe a nice evening or two before he headed back to the Bay Area, but he didn't like being rude to anyone who didn't deserve it. And, in a purely Machiavellian sense, having a knowledgeable local contact who was favorably disposed toward him wasn't something he was going to turn down. It wasn't his fault that so many women seemed to go for black overcoats and British accents—he had accepted many years ago that despite the fact that he thought of himself as more than a bit skinny and geeky-looking, he seemed to have something that appealed to many women. When the women were smart and attractive and had a sense of humor—well, he went with it. If they wanted to be deluded, who was he to complain about it? It wouldn't be gentlemanly.

What troubled him far more was that he was no closer to finding Jason. In fact, he might be farther away now than he'd been before. He had been so tired last night that he hadn't even had time to go over what had occurred that day, and this morning he'd been focused on meeting Lindsey.

He sat down on a picnic table to idly watch a mother and her two children toss a ball between them across a wide expanse of grass and let his mind wander.

So now there were two murders, and the tendrils of residual arcane energy that connected them indicated strongly that they'd been committed by the same person. Or thing. Or astral entity.

Or combination of the three. There was a thought to keep him up at night.

He wished he had his magical library here with him. He'd managed to replace much of what had been lost when his old house had been destroyed in an explosion a couple of years ago, but none of that would do him any good down here. He could go home, of course, but even if he drove like a maniac and took minimal rest breaks, that would still take up the better part of a day. Even longer, since he'd be forced to rest once he got back to Ojai. So realistically he was limited by his own knowledge and anything he could gather down here. He didn't think he'd have any luck finding magical tomes at the local library.

He also wished his apprentice were here. Verity Thayer, Jason's younger sister, had been studying with him for almost as long as he'd known her and Jason, and had proven to be both a quick study and a talented mage in the making. If nothing else, since she grew up in the area, he could send her out searching for research materials while he went on the offensive looking for the things from the abandoned barn and their boss.

Unfortunately, that wasn't possible. Verity was currently in Vermont, attending some sort of retreat with her friend and fellow mage Sharra and a group of other women out in the middle of nowhere. When she'd presented the idea to Stone and asked if he minded if she took some time off from her studies to go, she'd told him it was being held at a remote camping area at least a day's drive from civilization, and it would last the better part of a week. She hadn't been crazy about the "camping" part, but she and Sharra had settled into being good friends after a brief relationship a year ago, and she was happy for the chance to spend some time with her.

Stone had sent her off through the portal in Sunnyvale (which she was pleased she could use now, as the Evil were no longer plaguing the Overworld) the same day Jason had left for Ojai. He couldn't even contact her—which he felt he should do, magic not-withstanding, because it was her brother who was missing—because he had no idea exactly where she'd gone.

So, I'm on my own. Stone got up from the table and continuing his wandering path through the park. He smiled a bitter little smile: up until he'd met Jason and Verity, he was usually on his own, and he'd preferred it that way. Aside from his periodic temporary rela-tionships, which always ended when the women got the eventual and inevitable taste of the weirdness that suffused his life, he had a reputation for not being the easiest man in the world to get along with. It wasn't that he was unpleasant in some way, or undesirable company—it was simply that he could only take being around peo-ple for so long before his natural dry sarcasm and tendency toward moodiness took over and started him looking for the nearest exit before he ended up saying something he would later regret. Verity was, oddly, the only person he'd met in a long time that he enjoyed being around for more than a few hours before he had to recharge. He chuckled at that: it was probably a good thing that Verity mostly preferred women, and had shown no romantic interest in him (nor he in her), since otherwise Jason's protective brotherly instincts would have long ago taken over and caused problems with their working relationship.

He left the park and headed down Ojai Avenue, walking under the arches of the Spanish pergola that ran along the opposite side of the street from the Arcade and past the town's iconic post-office tower. A banner strung across the street at the intersection adver-tised a concert at an outdoor amphitheater called Libbey Bowl on the upcoming Sunday night.

Ojai really was a beautiful little town, but his mind was so pre-occupied that he barely saw any of it, his long strides taking him past a single-screen theater, several more boutique shops, and the library. With some amusement he thought about going in, just to see if they *did* have a 'magical tomes' section. The only thing that stopped him was that he didn't feel like dealing with another of Ojai's relentlessly polite and cheerful service people. When he was feeling moody, polite and cheerful people tended to get on his nerves.

He realized that this wandering, while undoubtedly pictur-esque, was doing him no good. It wasn't helping him find Jason; it wasn't even helping him get his own thoughts together. He might as well just go back to the house; if nothing else, he could rest for a bit. He had a feeling he'd better take his rest when he could get it.

He tossed his overcoat over a nearby chair and nearly missed the flashing red light next to the phone. It hadn't even occurred to him that this rental house *had* an answering machine. He stabbed the button without giving it much thought, figuring it was probably a message for the house's owners or the previous tenant.

The voice that spoke was male and sounded older. "Yeah, uh, I'm looking for Alastair Stone. My name's Stan Lopez—I'm with the Ventura Sheriff's Department. Could you give me a call if you get this? I'd like to talk to you about Jason Thayer. Thanks." He left a number and then the machine beeped. It was the only message.

Stone's eyebrows crept up. Had they found out something about Jason? Had they found him? He picked up the phone and punched in the number, waiting impatiently. After a few moments he was connected. "Sergeant Lopez," said the familiar voice.

"Good afternoon, Sergeant," Stone said. "Alastair Stone. You wanted to speak with me?"

"Ah. Yeah. Thanks for getting back to me so fast. Yeah, I want-ed to talk to you about Jason Thayer."

"So you said. Has there been a development? Have you found out something about where he's gone?"

"No. That's what I hoped to talk to you about. You're a friend of his, right, from up north?"

"Yes..." This conversation was going in an odd direction. Wouldn't the police already know that?

"I guess he hasn't mentioned me. I'm an old friend of Jason's family. His dad and I were on the force together. I've watched that kid grow up, him and his sister. I heard you were down here looking for him, and I just thought maybe we could compare notes if you have time."

Then it clicked in Stone's mind: he remembered Jason mentioning "Stan" a couple of times in the past, when he and Verity had gone down to Ventura to visit their old haunts. "Right. Of course I do. Just tell me where to meet you. Shall I come to the station?"

"No—I have lunch coming up in a bit. Can you come to Ventura and meet me at Fratelli's? It's a little place on Main, downtown. Do you know where it is?"

"No, but I can find it."

"Okay, then I'll see you there. And thanks."

It took Stone about half an hour and a couple glances at the foldout map on his passenger seat to find the little restaurant. It was an old place that looked like it had been owned by the same family for at least two or three generations, sandwiched between a thrift store and a walk-up rooming house. He went inside and paused for a moment in the doorway; the place was bustling.

"Over here!" a voice called, and Stone glanced toward the back to see a figure beckoning him toward a table.

He threaded his way through the crowds and approached. "Sergeant Lopez?"

The man stood up and offered his hand. "Good to finally meet you, Dr. Stone. Jason's told me a lot about you." He was maybe fifty or a little older, with close-cropped salt-and-pepper hair, a tanned, weathered face, and a solid frame a couple inches shorter than Stone. He wore a crisp, dark blue uniform and looked like the kind of classic, no-nonsense police officer who could put the fear of God into the hearts of criminals and errant kids alike.

"Yes, I remembered after we hung up that he's mentioned you as well." Stone sat down across from him at the little red-and-white-covered table. "How did you know how to find me? Did someone at the Ojai department tell you?"

"Yeah. Ever since Jason turned up missing, I've naturally been following the case, doing what I can on my off hours. Pete Casner mentioned you were down."

"Did he also mention that he nearly arrested me yesterday?" The waitress came by and dropped off water, a basket of bread sticks, and menus, but Stone kept his gaze focused on Lopez.

"Yeah. He did. He also told me that they're looking at Jason as a person of interest for the murder the other day. Which is bull-shit."

"Indeed it is," Stone said. He leaned forward. "Sergeant, did you see Jason at all when he was down here? Did he say anything to you?"

Lopez shook his head. "Nah. We were gonna get together on Sunday, day after the wedding, and catch up. First I heard he was missing was when he didn't show up. Did he say anything to you before he left to come down? Mention anywhere he might be going?"

"Just the wedding," Stone said. "Honestly I didn't pay that much attention. We haven't been getting together that often these days—both been busy with our own things. But I'm sure I'd have remembered if he mentioned anything odd he planned to do."

"Yeah." Lopez sighed. "Pete said something about him calling you early Saturday morning?"

"He did. I didn't get home until Saturday morning around ten, and the message was waiting for me. It was timestamped at around seven a.m., which is about the earliest he'd think he could get away with calling me." He gave a wry smile. "He knows I get a bit cross when I'm awakened too early."

The waitress came by again to take their orders. After she left, Lopez regarded Stone soberly. "I hear you stumbled on a murder scene yesterday."

Stone nodded.

"That's gotta be rough. I hear it wasn't a clean one, either. If you don't mind my asking, what were you doing out there? I know that part of Creek Road—there's not much there but trees and dust and the occasional junkie."

"Casner didn't tell you that part, then?"

He shook his head.

"Sergeant, did Jason ever tell you what I do?"

"Not exactly. He said you taught up at Stanford, but that's about it."

Stone took a deep breath. "My subject is the occult."

Lopez stared. "So, like ghosts and tea leaves and that kind of sh—er—stuff?"

"Yes."

"What's that got to do with finding the body?"

"I had a sort of vision that showed me that location. I—thought I might find Jason there."

Lopez didn't answer. He took a sip of his water and ate half a bread stick, never taking his eyes off Stone. Stone could almost see the wheels running in the man's head: *This guy is Jason's friend. I can't come right out and call him a freakin' loon.*

"Look," Stone said, saving him the trouble, "whether you believe it or not is irrelevant, really. What matters is that we've both got an interest in finding Jason. You called me because you wanted to compare notes. Shall we do that?"

Lopez took another bite of his bread stick. "Yeah," he said at last. "Let's do that."

Stone told the man what he knew, starting with Jason's phone message. He didn't say anything about his suspicion that his friend was being held by some sort of supernatural force; if the guy couldn't handle a garden-variety psychic vision, things from other planes of existence were going to be right off the table.

"Yeah, that sounds about right," Lopez said after he'd finished. "Jason's usually pretty straight, but if he was getting together with that pack of crazies he used to hang around with in high school, I'm not surprised he got himself falling-down drunk. I'm also not surprised he decided to walk back instead of driving."

Stone raised an eyebrow. "You said 'crazies.' You don't think any of his friends—" He let it trail off.

"Nah, they're all okay." he said, shaking his head. "They can get a little wild, but they're all good kids. Most of 'em still live around here. Jason was one of the few who left, after that business with Verity. You know Verity, right?"

Stone nodded. "Yes. I helped Jason when he was dealing with her issues a couple of years ago."

"Yeah, he said something about how that was how he met you. I don't get that whole thing, really, but it's none of my business who he hangs around with. How's she doing, by the way? I'm surprised she's not here too."

"She's away," he told him. "Back east, on a retreat with some friends. I'll call her as soon as she returns to civilization in a few days."

Lopez shook his head again and scratched at the back of his neck. "Man, that family's had some heavy shit to deal with, I'll tell you. First their mom getting sick, then Verity going off the deep end, then their dad getting killed in a stakeout, and now Jason turning up missing like this. You'd think God'd leave 'em the hell alone for a while, you know?" He sighed. "Well, anyway, thanks for coming, Dr. Stone. I wanted to meet you and give you my number, so you can give me a call if anything does come up. I'll drop whatever I'm doing and come up there if it'll help."

"I appreciate that, Sergeant."

"Call me Stan. Like I said, I'm not exactly acting in an official capacity here, but that doesn't mean I don't plan to do everything I can to find Jason. I'll keep an eye on the hospitals and—that kind of thing—in case he turns up. I'm sure the Ojai guys are putting out bulletins, too. We'll find him."

"We will," Stone said, nodding, wishing it were as simple as circulating some photographs and watching for unidentified injured or dead men. Because wherever Jason was right now, he doubted any mundane means would have a prayer of locating him.

This was one of those times when he really wished there were more mages in the world.

| CHAPTER ELEVEN

B ack in Ojai after finishing his lunch with Stan Lopez, Stone considered his next moves. He knew he'd have to go on the offensive as soon as possible: he didn't think for a moment that whatever was holding Jason would just let him go when it finished with him. Not alive, anyway. And since he had no idea why it was keeping Jason alive in the first place, he had to assume the worst: that it wasn't going to hold him for much longer.

That was, if it hadn't already disposed of him.

Sitting at the kitchen table in his rented house, he glanced at the copy of the local paper he'd picked up on his way back. The story about the second murder hadn't been very informative: it only provided minimal details about the specific location, and said nothing about the odd, primitive circle surrounding the body. The only bit of information it contained that Stone didn't already know was that the as-yet-unidentified victim was a man in his thirties and likely a drifter—apparently the area where he'd been found was popular with both drifters and locals as a place to take and sell drugs. The article also hadn't mentioned Stone at all, which was good.

He set the paper aside. The way he saw it, he had two options: he could either do another ritual to try to pinpoint Jason's location, or he could focus on trying to figure out what was behind the abduction—and probably the murders as well. Both had their disadvantages: since he knew Jason was being concealed by something with magical power, trying to find him without a tether object would be extremely difficult, if not impossible—and that didn't even include the possibility that since the thing holding him now knew Stone was out there looking, it might very well be lying in wait for him to try again. And as for figuring out what the thing *was*—he didn't have a clue where to start. As experienced as he was—and he had no false modesty, he was good—there were still more things out in the world that nobody knew a damn thing about than things they did. If this was one of the former, then all the magical libraries in the world wouldn't help him figure it out.

He scrubbed at his hair with both hands. It had been a long time since he'd felt this helpless. Unprepared, away from his familiar surroundings, and unable to shake the persistent thought that Jason was already dead somewhere, he felt his mind spin uselessly, like wheels trying to find purchase in loose dirt.

"Damn you, *think*," he snarled aloud. Without his two favorite sounding boards, he was reduced to talking to himself, and he didn't like it. This town was supposed to be full of odd people—surely there had to be *some* magical presence.

He flung himself out of the chair and began pacing the living room, staring out the window at the quiet, tranquil street. Then he spun, stalked over to the phone, snatched up the book next to it, and paged through it with frustrated speed.

Just as he expected, the yellow pages contained nothing listed under *Magic*.

Feeling very stupid and like he was just wasting time, he flipped past the *M*s to the *O*s.

Occult Bookstores.

"You've got to be bloody kidding," he whispered.

But no, there it was: *The Third Eye Bookshop and Mystic Emporium.* The listing was accompanied by a small display ad featuring typical occult symbology: pentagram, alchemical symbols, and a pyramid with an eye hovering above it. *Come in and explore your* magical *side!* it exhorted in appropriately flowery script. *Palm readings by appointment.* It was right there on Ojai Avenue; he'd probably passed right by it on his wanderings without seeing it.

Well, he wasn't getting far with any of his other avenues. If he couldn't find anything else to aid his investigations, he'd have to risk doing the ritual again. It couldn't hurt to check the place out on the off chance he might find something useful. He'd found useful things in stranger places.

The reason, it turned out, that he hadn't spotted the Third Eye Bookstore and Mystic Emporium was that it wasn't visible from the street. It was a little further up Ojai Avenue from where he'd been walking this morning, but he had to descend a flight of stairs into a hidden courtyard to get to it. The only thing that marked its existence from the street was a small sign, purple with golden lettering, on the side of the building near the stairs.

The courtyard was tiny and secluded, its neat lawn bisected by an equally neat little cobbled path with two whimsical stone benches along one side. The path ended in a single shop, the top half of its purple, two-piece door standing invitingly open. The display in the window contained the usual collection of things Stone had seen at countless other such shops: draped tapestries, candles, crystal balls, figurines of dragons and wizards, and a large stuffed black cat wearing a witch's hat cocked at a jaunty angle. Hanging from the ceiling so they caught the light were stained-glass images featuring fantastic creatures, a few crystal prisms, and a half-dozen fancy wind-chimes. A golden eye with rays emanating from it was painted on the front of the display window.

Stone pushed open the lower half of the door and stepped inside; a bell on the inside of the knob gave a cheerful tinkle. Stopping just inside, he switched to his magical senses and scanned the interior of the shop.

It was every bit as busy and cluttered as the window: its small confines were filled with tiny tables covered with dark lacy tablecloths, shelving units packed with books, decks of tarot cards, incense, and similar items. Every inch of the space was occupied, giving it the claustrophobic but somehow comforting aura of a crazy old auntie's favorite parlor. An earthy, sweet aroma wafted through the air, so strong it made Stone's eyes water a bit. The place certainly *looked* the part of a magical emporium, at least as far as the layman was concerned.

Unfortunately for Stone, he wasn't a layman. Equally unfortunately, this shop was about as magical as the local supermarket. Disappointed, he let his gaze linger over the shelves, paying particular attention to the books. Perhaps somewhere amid the stacks he might find one or two that might be—

"Good afternoon!" A pleasant voice from somewhere off to his left interrupted his examination.

He turned to find a well-padded woman in her late forties coming out from the other side of a counter that had been mostly concealed behind a rack of flowing, colorful robes and caftans. Dressed in a loose, multi-hued tunic and wide-legged white slacks, she had long, gray-shot reddish hair, a big smile, sparkling eyes, and wore far too much makeup and jewelry. "May I help you find something?"

"I'm just browsing," he told her. "I saw your sign as I was walking by and thought I'd see what a 'Mystic Emporium' might look like."

Her smile widened. Score another one for the accent. "Well, welcome, then. Browse all you like. I'll be right over there if you need anything." She waved a ring-bedecked hand in the general vicinity of where she'd come from.

"Thank you. I'll certainly do that."

True to his word, Stone spent the next ten minutes wandering the store. He devoted the most time to the bookshelves, crouching down next to a large one and scanning the titles for anything that might have a shred of magic. Most of the books were of the new-agey variety, more concerned with crystals and yoga than the actual practice of magic. He was about to stand back up when he spotted one that looked interesting: *Ojai: Lore and Legends*. It looked older than some of the others, its dull buff-colored cover marking it as possibly being printed locally. He slipped it off the shelf and leafed through it. It was short, only a little over a hundred pages, and contained chapters with tantalizing names like "Legend of the Char Man," "The Headless Motorcyclist," and "Magic of the Chumash." Deciding it couldn't hurt to read up on the occult happenings in the area even if they were all urban legends, he kept the book with him as he continued his browsing. He picked up a few mundane things that were useful in magical rituals such as candles and incense sticks, and carried them all to the counter.

The proprietress looked up from the scarf she was knitting. "Ah! Found some things, I see." She rang up his purchases, pausing over the book. "This is a good one," she confided, pointing at it. "I think it's my last copy, too. You're not from this area, are you?"

"No, this is my first visit here."

"Well, Ojai has all sorts of interesting history when it comes to the occult," she said. "Do you have an interest in the subject, or just curious in general?"

"I—dabble," he admitted. "I've heard a bit about Ojai's legends. I was hoping to find more research material, actually."

"Oh, I know," she said sympathetically. "There aren't that many books around, and I can't keep them in stock. You might try Bart's. Never the same thing twice, but sometimes you can dig up some real finds there if you're willing to get a little dusty."

He raised an eyebrow. "Bart's?"

Before she could answer, the door jingled again. "Oh, hi, Suzanne," the proprietress called over Stone's shoulder. "Be with you as soon as I'm done here."

Stone turned. The woman who'd come in was a few years younger than the proprietress, dressed in the style of bohemian elegance that he'd begun to identify as popular among the wealthier of Ojai's female population. Her chestnut hair (not a sign of gray this time) was swept back in a chic scarf, her makeup understated. "No hurry," the newcomer said, waving an airy hand. "I'll just see what you've got in this week."

The proprietress returned her attention to Stone with a conspiratorial nod toward the woman. "Suzanne's one of my best local customers. Very nice lady. Now—where were we? Oh, yes, Bart's! I'm surprised you haven't heard of it: it's one of the things the town's famous for. Open-air used bookshop. It's this huge, rambling place that probably has books nobody's looked at in twenty years, if you go back far enough into the stacks." She giggled. "I don't go often, because every time I do, I end up spending hours." She wrapped up his purchases and put them in a purple bag with the shop's golden-eye logo on it. "Check it out, if you have the time. It's worth a trip, especially if you like old books."

"She's right," Suzanne said, coming up behind them. "I've made some real finds there over the years."

"I'll be sure and take a look," Stone assured them. "Thank you both so much."

Well, that was something, at least, he thought as he headed back to his car with his purchases. He supposed he shouldn't have hoped he'd find anything genuinely magical at the shop: he wasn't by any means familiar with every arcane supply store and bookshop in California since he'd only come over from England a few years ago and the magical community wasn't known for being particularly chummy, but he was aware of a number of them, and hadn't heard of any in this area. He'd taken a shot and it hadn't panned out. At least he'd restocked some of his ritual supplies, and he might need those soon.

This Bart's place, though, sounded like it might have possibility. If it truly was as large and eclectic as the two ladies from the Emporium had implied, then it would be worth a look. One thing he *had* seen on numerous occasions were "diamonds in the rough" found amid moldering stacks of used books in out-of-the-way shops. Especially when elderly mages living alone passed away, their heirs would sell or donate their collections without having any idea what they had. More than a bit of Stone's recently replaced library had come from haunting obscure used bookstores in the San Francisco and Berkeley areas.

He glanced at his watch: it was a little after two. He could spare an hour or so to check it out, and then he couldn't wait anymore: he was going to have to try the ritual to find Jason again.

Bart's Books was only about five minutes away, on the corner of two residential streets a block off of Ojai Avenue. Stone wasn't sure what he expected to see, but this wasn't it: the place didn't look anything like any bookstore he'd ever visited. Shelves full of mostly well-used paperbacks lined the walls along the outside, and as he approached the entrance proper he spotted a sign instructing visitors to toss the money for anything they purchased from these shelves into the courtyard during non-business hours. He wondered how many people actually did it.

Stepping inside, he immediately understood what the proprietress of the Third Eye had meant when she said she avoided Bart's when she didn't have the time to spend hours among the stacks. Shelves full to bursting with books were arranged with haphazard exuberance in every direction he looked—there were little nooks with sitting areas, large wall-sized shelves packed with hardbound tomes, small tables scattered around the courtyard for readers, and passageways leading off into dim areas that promised even more books. A few customers drifted from one shelf to the next, occasionally pulling something out to look at. Across the courtyard was a table surrounded by more books. Seated behind it, a cheerful thirtyish man with long hair and round glasses waved a welcome at Stone as he approached. "Looking for anything in particular, or just browsing?"

As much as he would have liked to spend the rest of the day moving among the stacks searching for treasures, Stone knew he'd have to forego that particular temptation for now. "Do you have an occult section?" he asked.

"Sure. We have two, actually: the more valuable stuff is in there—" he pointed toward the doorway to a room off to his left "—inside, down the hall, and turn right into the first room you find." Then he pointed to his right. "The other stuff is down that hall all the way to the end—make a right and it's at the end of the row on the left. You can't miss it."

"Thank you." Deciding to check the "valuable" books first, he headed into the room and followed the man's directions until he stood inside another room, this one much smaller, with all four of its walls lined with bookshelves. A couple of the shelf sections were enclosed as locked glass cabinets. The hand-inked *OCCULT & MAGICK* sign was tacked up the top of the intersection of one open shelf and one locked one. The only light filtered in through a sky-light in the middle of the ceiling.

Glancing behind him to make sure no one else was in the room, Stone first examined the titles of the books, starting at the top of the open shelf and working his way to the bottom, then repeating for the locked one. Already he could see that this visit was going to be more profitable than the Third Eye. He hadn't yet spotted anything that would help him in his search for Jason, but several of the books were titles that interested him, and a couple would serve as replacements for some of his destroyed library. He pulled three off the open shelf and noted the positions of the ones he wanted in the locked cabinet so he could point them out to the man out front when he was ready to leave.

Next, he shifted his magical senses on and studied the books again. This time he didn't need to scan the shelves: indeed, he couldn't easily read any of the titles this way. He wasn't interested in the titles now, though. Immediately, two of the books lit up with glowing auras that marked them as more than mere mundane tomes.

Both of them were on the open shelf, surprisingly. Stone shifted back to mundane sight and realized why: they were both very dull-looking volumes, less than a hundred years old, their bindings unremarkable and unadorned. He slid them off the shelves and examined their front covers. The first one, titled *Ancient Occult Symbology,* had a faint yellowish aura. The second, *The Power and the Will,* glowed more brightly in a mottled brick red. Stone's hand tingled a bit as he held it. Whatever this book's title suggested, it was not a wholesome tome. Not entirely evil, but definitely deep into the territory trodden by mages at the dark gray end of the spectrum.

Still, it was magical, and Stone was nothing if not curious, so he added both it and the other one to the pile, picked them all up, and headed back out to the front. As he passed by the table where the proprietor sat, he held them up. "I'll be taking these," he said. "May I leave them here while I check the other section?"

"Sure, no problem." The man indicated a cleared space to his left. "I'll start an invoice for you."

Past the desk was a series of passageways, each one lined from ceiling to near the ground with packed bookshelves. These were interspersed periodically with inset alcoves like tiny rooms that allowed for even more books. There were sections on everything from sports to history to psychology, each one marked by another hand-inked sign, and a quick look as he moved by showed Stone that the bookstore's owners were not at all picky about what they sold. He suspected that they got much of their stock from people dropping off boxes of unwanted tomes gleaned from spring cleaning or taken from the homes of deceased relatives, which meant that many of them were probably worthless—unless that one person out there who was seeking that particular book managed to find his or her way here and brave the mazelike layout of the place long enough to find it. Stone found it all fascinating, and far preferable to the sterile modern bookstores that were steadily driving the smaller family-owned shops out of business. He made a mental note to return to Ojai some time and spend some serious hours perusing the place in detail.

For now, though, he moved briskly through the narrow rows in the direction the man had pointed him. He only passed one other customer, a beefy teenage football player type in a blue hoodie with *RANGERS* across the front, who was surreptitiously examining a book of artistic nudes. He ducked into a nearby nook to make room for Stone to slip past.

The second Occult section was larger than the first, tucked away in yet another niche topped with a sign reading *OCCULT, MAGICK, & ESOTERICA*. Stone moved inside and once again began a slow examination of the books starting at the left side of the alcove and working his way around it clockwise. It was harder this time because many of the books were piled haphazardly on little bench outcroppings in front of the shelves, and he had to sift through these as he went. When he found a book that interested him, he pulled it out and stacked it to the side. By the time he finished his mundane check he had found three possibilities.

His arcane senses immediately revealed the two of his three choices were indeed interesting in a magical sense. On the shelves three others lit up, all of them in the center portion of the nook. He was pleased: this visit was proving quite fruitful. He looked forward to taking the books back to his house and mining them for anything he could use to help him find Jason.

He never even saw the figure coming up behind him as he leaned in to take a closer look at one of the books. Something slipped around his neck and yanked him back, hard.

| CHAPTER TWELVE

S tone reacted instantly, instinctively flinging his body forward as the grip around his neck tightened, but it did no good. Whoever was strangling him was strong—a lot stronger than he was. He flailed, reaching up to try to free his airway, and his hands touched what felt like a leather belt. It was pulled too tight to get his fingers under it. He tried to cry out, but couldn't get enough breath to do it.

Getting a spell off was out of the question—white lights already danced in front of his vision, and he could barely form a coherent thought through his rising panic. *I'm going to get strangled right here in broad daylight!* was the only thing that got through. Potentially true, but hardly useful. The brain was perverse like that sometimes.

The pressure tightened, pulling him back into the figure. Stone got a glimpse of blue as he whipped his head to the side, and for the barest second his magical senses caught sight of some sort of strange, greenish aura hovering around the figure before he couldn't maintain them any longer.

Desperately he lifted one foot and tried to mule-kick his assailant, but his coordination was as shot as his mental processes, and the figure easily avoided the weak attack. Stone felt blackness begin to settle over him, and fought to drive it back. He couldn't pass out or he was dead for sure. He couldn't—

"Hey!" A garbled voice pierced the muddled soup engulfing his brain. "What the hell are you—"

Stone must have blacked out at that point, because when he opened his eyes he was lying on the ground, staring up at the concerned, half-panicked face of the long-haired bookseller.

"Oh, man," the guy breathed. "Oh, man—thank God. Just stay still. It's gonna be okay. The ambulance is coming."

Stone blinked. "Ambulance?"

"Yeah, man. That guy tried to strangle you! If I hadn't—"

Stone swallowed, taking stock. His neck hurt, his breath felt ragged in his aching throat, and his head was throbbing. Experimentally, he tried to sit up.

"You sure you want to—" the man started, but when he saw it was doing no good he took careful hold of Stone's shoulder and helped him to a sitting position.

"It's—it's all right," Stone said faintly, doing his best imitation of a three-pack-a-day smoker. "I—don't need an ambulance."

"He tried to *strangle* you, man! They're already coming. Cops, too. That was a bad scene."

Slowly, Stone realized he and the man had an audience. Several other people stood in the narrow walkway, trying to get a glimpse of what was happening and muttering among themselves. Then he realized that something was missing. "Where—who tried to—" He gently probed at his neck again and winced. He was going to have bruises there, he could tell.

"The kid who attacked you? He's over there." The guy looked angry and puzzled. "It was weird. As soon as I grabbed him and tried to pull him off you, he just—stopped. Didn't fight me, or even struggle at all. Just dropped his hands and stood there, like he had no idea where he was. We're holding him for the cops."

Stone raised his head a bit more. Just past the small knot of onlookers, he could see the blond brush-cut and blue hoodie of the teenager he'd passed in the aisle on his way to the Occult section. He stared. "Him?"

The guy nodded. "Yeah. Fucking freaky, if you'll pardon my French. He's a local kid. Can't be more than sixteen or so. I've seen him in here before, lots of times. It's like he just—snapped or something."

"Step back, folks, please." An authoritative voice cut through the crowd's muttering. They parted to let two uniformed police officers through. Stone recognized them as Aguirre and Farrell, two of the cops who'd picked him up at the scene of the second murder. They all regarded each other with varying degrees of surprise. Behind them came two uniformed EMTs who pushed past them and hurried over to Stone.

"That's the guy you want," the bookseller said to the cops, pointing at the kid. "He's the one who tried to strangle this guy here. I saw it."

Aguirre said something Stone couldn't hear to Farrell, and the younger cop headed off to deal with the young assailant. Aguirre came back over to Stone, who was now trying to wave the EMTs away. "Dr. Stone. You do seem to be in the middle of things around here." He sounded more concerned than annoyed, though. "Are you all right?"

Stone shrugged. "Aside from some bruises, I think I'll be fine. Just a bit shaken up." He sighed and gave up, letting the EMTs check him out. He noticed Farrell had shooed off the rest of the crowd so they had relative privacy.

"Mind telling me what happened?" He pulled out a notebook.

Stone began to describe the attack. The bookseller, who'd gone off with Farrell, came back with a bottle of water; he accepted it gratefully. It did hurt to talk.

"So you're saying," Aguirre said after he finished, "that you walked right past the kid, and he seemed fine then?"

"Yes. He was just browsing the books, same as I was. I didn't get any sense of threat from him at all."

"He didn't seem drugged or drunk?"

Stone shook his head. "I doubt I'd even have noticed him if the walkways here weren't so narrow. He had to duck into an opening to make room for me to get past him." He glanced over in the direction they'd taken the kid, suddenly remembering something. "Would it be all right if I talked to him for a moment before you take him away?"

"Why would you want to do that?" Aguirre looked suspicious.

"No particular reason. But I'd like to, if I may."

"I'm sorry, Dr. Stone. I can't let you do that. He's a minor, and we're not allowed to question him without his parents present."

"Fine, then." He turned to the EMT, who had raised his black T-shirt and was poking at his chest with a stethoscope while the other one checked his blood pressure. "Really—I'm fine. Just shaken up and a little sore, but nothing permanent. I need to be getting on my way."

"It would be better if you'd let us take you back to the hospital so a doctor can look you over," said the one with the stethoscope.

"I doubt that," Stone said. "Please—I appreciate what you're doing and your quick response, but if you could just finish up and let me know if I'm in danger of imminent death—"

The other EMT pulled off the blood pressure cuff and stowed it in his gear box. "Your BP's high, but that's consistent with the scare you took. We can't make you go back with us, but—"

"Well, good, then," Stone said, pulling his shirt down and starting to rise. Aguirre offered him a hand, and he took it. Once on his feet, he swayed for a moment, making the two EMTs look at him in concern, but he held up a hand. "I promise, if I feel worse later I'll come in and get checked out. Fair enough?"

They nodded, conceding. After making him sign a series of forms stating that he refused treatment and wouldn't sue them if he took a turn for the worse later, they gathered their gear and departed. Stone waited a moment longer to make sure he wasn't going to fall on his face if he moved, then motioned toward the front of the courtyard and followed Aguirre out.

By now they'd ushered all the customers out onto the sidewalk in front of Bart's; the only people who remained inside were the two cops, the EMTs, the bookseller, Stone, and the teenage boy. Farrell had handcuffed him, and he sat at one of the small tables looking confused and miserable. As Stone and Aguirre approached, Farrell said, "I called it in, and they called his parents—they'll meet us at the station."

"*Please* listen to me," the boy begged. He was a tall, muscular kid with clear blue eyes, a pug nose, and a strong jaw, and he looked like he was about to burst into tears. His eyes met Stone's and he leaned forward, raising up a bit in his chair. "Please, mister. I didn't mean to do it. I don't even *remember* doing it! I was just standing there looking at that book. You went past and the next thing I knew—"

Stone looked at him, startled by his words. He shifted easily to magical senses, his eyes going blank for a moment as he looked at the boy with new perception.

Whatever odd aura he'd seen around him before was nowhere in evidence. Either he hadn't seen it properly before—which was certainly possible, given that he had been in the process of blacking out at the time—or else it had been there before and was now gone.

The boy looked at Farrell and then back at Stone. "Please, you *have* to believe me!" His voice pitched higher. The hint of hysteria sounded utterly out of place in a voice that was probably much more used to calling football plays and chatting up teenage girls than to terrified pleading.

Despite his bruised neck and the residual numbing fear that came with nearly getting murdered, Stone felt nothing but sympathy for the boy. He *did* believe him. It was very clear to him now that something had taken the kid over and had departed as soon as the bookseller had come on the scene.

Something that could apparently hop in and out of bodies as easily as he himself would change a set of clothes.

Something that wanted him dead.

Stone let out a long, slow breath.

This changed a lot of things.

He looked at the boy. "I do believe you," he said softly.

The two cops stared at him, dumbfounded, as did the boy. "What the—?" Aguirre began.

Stone held up a hand. "You do what you need to do, officer. But I won't be pressing charges."

The boy's shocked expression suggested that everything that made sense in the world had all gotten together and boarded an outbound train for someplace far away. "You—believe me?" he whispered.

Aguirre grabbed his arm and pulled him up. "He might, kid, but I don't. Not yet. C'mon, we need to get you down to the station." He turned back to Stone. "Dr. Stone, I know you probably don't feel up to it right now, but we'll need to talk to you more about this later—"

"I'm not going anywhere, Officer," he said. "Not for a few days, at least. You know where to find me."

In less than fifteen minutes the police were gone with the boy, the EMTs were gone, and the curious customers, supplemented by a few more passersby who'd noticed the commotion and stopped to find out what was going on, had filtered back in. Several of them kept snatching glances at Stone while trying not to be obvious about it; he could feel their gazes on him, their interest an almost palpable thing. He needed to get out of here.

Stone was not a coward—far from it, in fact. In just the last couple of years he'd stood against more than one powerful magical entity and come out on top against some long odds. Still, he took a moment to gather himself sufficiently to go back down the narrow passage to the Occult section and retrieve the small pile of books he'd left there, along with the three on the shelves that had glowed to his magical senses. He didn't waste a moment and kept his shield up the whole time.

The bookseller, who was back behind his table but who still appeared nervous and shaken, gave Stone a worried, questioning look, as if he expected him to keel over any second. "You sure you're okay?"

"Fine." All this attention was starting to grate on Stone's nerves. He dropped the stack of books next to the others he'd picked out. "I'll take those as well—and there are a couple in the locked case I want."

Five minutes later he left with his purchases (which the bookseller had given him a substantial discount on, in light of events). His walk to the exit was through a gauntlet of customers' stares. It wasn't until he was back behind the wheel of the BMW with the bag of books tossed on the passenger seat that he finally allowed himself to relax. He sat there for a few minutes, then started the car and drove off.

From across the street, an old lady walking a dog paused to watch him leave, smiling a most unwholesome smile.

| CHAPTER THIRTEEN

B y the time Stone made it back to his house, checked his wards, and dragged himself inside, the events of the last two days had begun to catch up with him in a big way. He flung his coat over the chair and himself onto the couch, staring at the ceiling.

He was exhausted. He hadn't slept all that well the previous night: even though the entities that had tossed him around at the barn hadn't seriously hurt him—thanks to his shield—his body still felt stiff and achy and generally out of sorts. And now that the adrenaline of the afternoon had finally drained away, both his neck and his head were starting to hurt a lot.

He waved a hand and his bottle of ibuprofen sailed across the room; he tossed three back, swallowing them dry and wincing as they scraped down his raw throat. Right now, he decided, it would be quite nice to have something stronger. The temptation was powerful enough that he actually considered dropping by the hospital to let them check him out in hopes that they might give him a prescription, but two things stopped him: his deep and abiding dislike of hospitals, and the fact that he couldn't afford to dull his senses too much right now. Something out there was after him, and he had no idea what it was, or why. The only thing he'd dealt with personally that even slightly resembled this was the Evil, and despite the possession angle it wasn't acting at all consistent with them. That left him fresh out of good guesses.

Regardless of any of this, he knew there was no way he'd be doing any rituals tonight. In his present state it would be foolish at best and suicidal at worst. Either way, it also wouldn't do Jason any good. Reluctant as he was to admit it, he had to acknowledge that whatever had Jason either still had him and that wasn't likely to change today, or else Jason was already dead and there was nothing he could do about it.

He tried not to think about what the thing might be doing to his friend. He could deal with the guilt about that later, if it was called for.

Still, much as he wanted to just curl up and sleep for the next two days or so (assuming his various aches and pains would let him), he knew he wasn't going to get the luxury of that kind of idleness until after he found out what had happened to Jason. He hauled himself up off the couch, retrieved the bag with all the books he'd bought, and settled down to look through them. Maybe one of them would have something he could use.

He realized almost immediately that this wouldn't be productive. His concentration was shot. Tossing the book aside, he leaned back on the couch and sighed. He didn't quite understand it: he hadn't reacted this strongly to some of the serious magical threats he'd dealt with in the last couple of years, and some of them had injured him far worse than a few bruises. Why was *this* one bothering him so much?

He thought he knew, actually. Ever since he'd met Jason and Verity and they'd gotten him embroiled in the whole affair with the Evil, he'd had someone around to talk to. Someone to bounce ideas off, to poke him when he started getting too full of himself, to give him a metaphorical slap when his dark moods started creeping in and taking him over. It had never occurred to him that he'd grown *accustomed* to having them—or somebody—around. He couldn't even fall back on one of his short-lived serial relationships, giving her a call just to chat for a few moments and reconnect with a world where people didn't even believe magic existed.

R. L. KING

He realized that he was pretty much alone, and right now alone was not something he wanted to be.

He got up again and headed to the kitchen. This was not a wise thing he was about to do. There were other things he should be doing tonight. He couldn't afford to take the time.

But right at that moment, he didn't give a damn.

He pulled a card from his pocket, picked up the phone, and made a call.

"I must admit I was surprised to hear from you tonight," Lindsey Cole said, smiling. "Pleased, but surprised."

They sat at a candlelit table in the patio of Don Armando's downtown, sipping drinks and waiting for their orders to arrive. Stone returned her smile. "I hadn't expected to call either," he admitted. "But I needed a bit of a break, and since I was so rude to you yesterday—"

"Standing me up because you were at the police station isn't rude," she pointed out. She wore a green blouse that complemented the sparkle in her brown eyes, and had pulled her long hair back into a loose ponytail. "How's the house working out, by the way?"

"Very well." She hadn't noticed the bruises on his neck yet—he supposed they wouldn't be at their most obvious until tomorrow sometime—but he'd suggested they sit in the patio just the same. He didn't feel like answering questions about this afternoon; he just wanted to have a pleasant evening and forget about everything else for a few hours. "Much nicer than a motel room."

"Do you know how long you'll be staying in town?"

"Not really. The new quarter at Stanford starts in a couple of weeks, and I'll need to be back for that, of course, but I'm hoping it won't take that long to locate my friend."

"You don't think he might have just—left for somewhere, do you?" she asked. "I mean, people do that sometimes, without even telling their closest friends."

"It's possible," Stone said, even though he knew otherwise. "If I don't find any leads in the next few days, I might have to consider that he's done just that. If so, then there's not much I can do about it. He's a grown man and can go where he pleases, of course. But I've never known him to do anything like that, and it does seem particularly odd that he missed the very wedding he came down here to attend in the first place, don't you think?"

"Good point," she said, nodding. "Well, like I said, if there's anything I can do to help you—"

"There is one thing, actually," Stone said. "It may seem a bit odd, but it might be useful."

She tilted her head. "What's that?"

Stone sipped his Guinness. "I'm looking for information about local history. Particularly legends, stories, strange occurrences—that sort of thing. You mentioned before that there was a fair bit of that around Ojai."

Lindsey looked confused. "This is going to help you find your friend?"

"Well—when he called me, he told me he'd found something strange that he thought might interest me. I assume that means it's got something to do with the supernatural. I picked up some books on local history today, but I was hoping to get more of a personal account, if possible."

Their entrees arrived, and Lindsey arranged her napkin on her lap before answering. "Well—yes, there are quite a few stories. Mostly the sorts of things kids tell at sleepovers, to scare each other. Is that the kind of thing you want?"

"Anything you think I might find interesting," he said. He waved his fork. "You're right, by the way—the food here is excellent."

She smiled. "I'm glad. My friends give this place rave reviews." She took a bite, thinking. "Well, let's see. There's Char Man, of course. He's pretty famous around here."

"Char Man?" He raised a questioning eyebrow. He remembered seeing that name in the book he'd gotten at the Third Eye.

"Yes, he's probably the most well-known of the legends. Kids, and even some adults, have been scaring each other with him since before I was born. He's supposed to be some guy who got horribly burned in an accident many years ago, and he's been haunting the area down by Creek Road ever since."

"Creek Road?" he asked, surprised.

"Yes, the same place where—the body was found. But it's a long road, so probably nowhere near the same area." Pausing, she mused, "You know, a lot of the local legends center around that area, now that I think of it."

"Indeed?" He leaned forward.

"I'm not really that familiar with all of them, but the ones I remember hearing about are a headless motorcyclist, a couple of little kids on a bridge, and—I think there was supposed to be a vampire down there somewhere for a while, too."

"And all of these were near Creek Road?" He pondered. "Are there any stories you're aware of that *aren't* associated with it?"

"Well…there might be a couple haunted-house stories, but I'm not sure exactly. Char Man is definitely the most famous one I know of."

"Interesting." He sipped his drink. "In one of the books I picked up today but haven't had the chance to look at yet, it mentioned something about the Chumash. Is that a local Indian tribe?"

She nodded. "They were the main tribe in the area. A lot of things around here, like the Topa Topa Mountains and Ojai itself, are named from Chumash words."

"Any secret burial grounds, legends of evil demons, that sort of thing?"

"Not…really. The Chumash were a pretty peaceful bunch. I don't remember ever hearing anything about them being into the whole 'vengeance against the white man' thing, or anything like that. They've even got a casino somewhere up by Santa Barbara, I think."

He chuckled. "Yes, well, they don't sound very frightening then, do they? At any rate, I appreciate the information. I'll have to take a closer look at some of those books. It sounds like another trip down to Creek Road might be in order, though. I'll just have to make sure to avoid the police from now on."

"Always a good idea," she agreed.

"So," he said after a moment and another sip of his drink (it was doing wonders for his aches—he was going to need to order another one soon), "In the interest of not monopolizing the conversation with my odd interests—perhaps you might tell me a bit more about yourself. How did you come to sell real estate in this lovely little town?"

She laughed. "It's not much of a story. I did grow up here, and the housing market is good. A lot of people like to get out of the rat race of Los Angeles and live here. Some of them even commute down there, which amazes me. But Ojai's—different. Quieter. In a lot of ways, it's like the Little Town that Time Forgot. Some would say it's slightly more interesting than watching paint dry—mostly the kids, who can't wait to get out—but it kind of gets under your skin after a while. You'd be surprised at how many of them come back." Her eyes twinkled. "We also have a lot of celebrities who live around the area. It's not at all uncommon to run into one of them at the grocery store dressed in grubby shorts and an old T-shirt."

"When I first got here," Stone said, "the clerk at the motel where I was staying said he thought I might be up from Los Angeles scouting film locations."

She eyed him critically, with an impish smile. "Well, you do have that look. You definitely look—distinctive."

"By which you mean—a bit daft," he said, amused.

"You don't exactly fit in, but I like that. It's why I took a chance on asking you to dinner, actually. I like people who don't fit in. I thought sure you'd be married, or seeing someone, though."

"Or gay," he suggested. "I get that occasionally too. But no, none of the above. Honestly, I was surprised you were even interested. If you'll forgive my own forwardness, you hardly strike me as the type who would need to resort to asking odd strangers to dinner. Surely your social calendar is full to brimming."

She smiled. "You'd be surprised. I'm not exactly lacking for dates, but most of them have come from going to clubs with some girlfriends in Ventura. A surprising number of the men around my age in town are already taken. As much as I love it here, it does skew a bit older. Don't even ask me how many guys old enough to be my dad have asked me out. Most of them were very charming, but—well—I'm not really into that, you know?" She gave him a slightly wistful look. "And what about you? Nobody back home in the Bay Area?"

He shook his head. "Not for quite some time, actually. I tend to get rather caught up in my work and go for months without remembering that I haven't had a date."

"It must be interesting, teaching about the occult. I didn't even know that was an actual subject that people studied. Are your students psychic or something?"

"I suppose some of them might be," he said. "Mostly, to be honest, they're horror writers and goths and Wiccans. The Wiccans are the only ones who take it seriously. The writers are looking for material, and the goths are mostly looking for other goths of their preferred gender. And band names," he added.

She laughed at that. "I must say you seem a lot more—um—*normal* than I'd picture for a guy who teaches Occult Studies."

"Well, I did decide to leave my black robes and wooden staff at home. Sounds like I made the right choice."

"Probably," she agreed. "Though I'd like to see you in your black robes. You probably look quite dashing."

"I suppose this isn't the proper time to tell you it's actually an old bathrobe, then?"

"Depends on what kind of bathrobe," she said with a twinkle in her eye. "And what you wear underneath it." She smiled. "You know, that reminds me of when I was a little kid. There was an older girl who used to babysit me, and she and her friends had some kind of secret 'witch club' they belonged to. You know, all fairies and flowing gowns and magic wands and that kind of thing, and they got together and cast spells and made love potions and stuff. I used to look forward to her coming over because she'd let me try on her witchy robe. It was the prettiest shade of green. I wanted her to make me one, but she never did." She giggled. "Her family was Japanese. I forget her name, but everybody called her 'Mickey.' I used to call her Mickey Mouse." She paused for a sip of her drink. "Wow, I hadn't thought of that in years. See? You're good for me."

"Well, I hope so," he murmured.

They spent the next hour or so lingering over dinner and chatting about various subjects that had nothing to do with the supernatural, the murders, or Stone's search for Jason. He felt guilty when he realized that he'd enjoyed it more than he'd expected to. It might have been at least partly the couple of drinks taking the edge off the worst of his pain, but Lindsey was every bit as intelligent and charming as he thought she was, and he found himself regretting that she didn't live in the Bay Area. Maybe he might have been able to pursue something with her if she did. *Ah, well,* he thought. *Enjoy it while it lasts, at least. Tomorrow it's back to work.*

By the time they left the restaurant and strolled back to his car it was a little after ten. He drove her to her house, a neat single-story place on a quiet street a couple of miles from the restaurant. As he pulled into the driveway and came around to open the door for her, he made an amused little bow. "Thank you for a lovely evening."

She smiled almost shyly. "You—wouldn't want to come in, would you?" she asked.

He smiled too. "Actually, I'd like that very much."

Her living room was a lot like she was: neat and a little bohemian with a hint of whimsy. Her bedroom, a short while later, was even more so. "I'm glad I cleaned up in here," she said with a little laugh. "You should have seen it yesterday: clothes strewn all over everything."

"That's all right," he said. "You should see mine."

"Maybe I will sometime." She put up her hands and pushed his coat down off his shoulders. "Now why don't we get you out of that coat and I'll get us some drinks?"

"Brilliant," he agreed.

An hour later, after she'd succeeded in getting him out of considerably more than his coat (and he'd returned the favor with pleasure), he lay next to her, looking out the window into her backyard with a lazy, satisfied smile. Her head was nestled in the crook of his shoulder, his hand gently stroking her hair. Whatever aches and pains he'd been feeling before had long since been banished by the drinks they'd had and the pleasurable time they'd shared.

"Mmm," Lindsey murmured, her hand on his chest. "I think I might need to come up with a way to sell you a house, so I can keep you here. You can commute to Stanford, right?"

"Absolutely," he said in the same tone. "It's only—what—three hundred miles? No problem at all. Or perhaps you could come and sell houses in Palo Alto. The market is quite hot, I hear."

She chuckled. "Oh, really? Well, we'll just have to see how things go, won't we?"

"Indeed..." His voice was slurring a bit as the drinks and the exhaustion of the day began finally to catch up with him, but it was a good kind of exhaustion. As he drifted off, still stroking Lindsey's hair, he knew he would sleep well.

He wasn't sure what awakened him. Perhaps it was some vestigial bit of the low-grade defenses he kept running at minimal power even when he wasn't concentrating on them, or perhaps it was the sudden movement next to him in the bed.

Whatever it was, when his eyes flickered open sometime in the early hours of the morning, the first thing he saw was Lindsey looming over him, her arm raised above her head. "What—?" he started, confused.

The next two things his foggy brain registered were simultaneous: Lindsey's eyes were glowing with a faint reddish orange color, and her arm, holding something, was plunging down toward his chest.

He flung himself sideways, and whatever she had in her hand sunk into the bed where he'd been. Still reacting purely on instinct, he rolled back over and gripped her wrist. Something fell from her hand and dropped with a tiny *thump* to the mattress. "Lindsey!" he snapped. "What are you doing?"

Enough light streamed in from the window that he could see her face. Her expression was twisted into a chilling grin, her eyes still glowing with that odd light. "*Go back where you came from, mageling,*" she whispered. Her voice didn't sound like Lindsey: it had a rough, rasping quality that suggested something unfamiliar was using it.

"What?" Stone, still gripping her wrist, threw her over on her back and took hold of her other wrist as well, holding her down. "Lindsey, what the *hell* are you on about?"

"*Go while you still can,*" the voice that was not Lindsey's whispered. "*You cannot stop us. Your friend is ours now. Get out and we will spare you. Remain and we will use everyone in this town to destroy you.*"

Stone stared, heart pounding. The half-sleepy fuzziness in his brain burning off, he thought fast. Shifting to magical senses, he took a good look at Lindsey and was not at all surprised to see the same faint aura he thought he'd spotted on the boy who'd tried to

　　　　　　　　　　　　　　　　　　　　R. L. KING

strangle him yesterday. "Let her go," he growled. "Get out of her *now,* you bastard. Face me in your true form. And what do you mean, my friend is yours?"

She chuckled, an unwholesome sound entirely incongruous with her normally pleasant tones. *"Give up, mageling. You don't have the power to turn us away. Your friend is lost to you. Go now, or bear the guilt of what will come."*

And then, as suddenly as it had come, the eerie expression left her face and the glow left her eyes. Lindsey looked up at Stone, bewildered. "A-Alastair? What's going on?"

Stone released her wrists and spun, trying to spot whatever had just vacated her body, but all traces of it were gone. He sat upright, puffing, teeth gritted in frustration.

"Alastair?" She touched his shoulder. "Is something wrong?"

He lowered his head into his hands, shoving his hair up into untidy spikes. "No..." he whispered.

Lindsey sat up next to him. "What's going on? Are you all right?"

As he stared at her, the shocked realization came: *she doesn't have any idea why I'm agitated. She doesn't remember any of it.* She had no idea what had just occurred, that she had very likely just tried to murder him in bed.

Just like the kid at Bart's.

He felt around next to him until his hand fell on the hard smooth form of what she'd dropped: it was a slender letter opener, its blade now bent to the side where the mattress had turned it. He looked at it in disbelief for a moment, then back at her. The thing might not have been enough to kill him, but if she'd managed to drive it into his chest in the right place it definitely could have made a good try at it. "I—" he began. He was shaking. Already his mind was putting together the implications of what the thing that had taken over Lindsey had said.

Bloody hell.

"Alastair, you're scaring me."

You and me both. He struggled to get himself together. "It's— all right," he said, concentrating on keeping his voice even. "I— must have had a bad dream or something." Surreptitiously he dropped the letter opener over the edge of his side of the bed. She'd wonder in the morning what had caused the rip in the sheet, but right now that didn't even rate on his scale of things to be concerned about.

He had much bigger problems than that.

Lindsey looked dubious, reaching over to switch on the light. Her eyes widened. "You're pale as a ghost! And what happened to your neck?"

For a moment he didn't understand what she meant, but then it came to him: *ah, the bruises are finally making their appearance.* He shook his head. "It's all right," he said again. "I'm fine. I'm sorry I frightened you."

Still looking confused she raised her arms, rolling her wrists around. "My arms hurt," she said. "Like somebody grabbed me or something." She glanced sideways at him but said nothing. Instead, she pulled up the sheet to cover herself. "What *did* happen to your neck? You've got bruises. I—don't understand."

Stone took a deep breath. Right now, all he wanted to do was get out of here, get back to his rented house where he could try to figure out what the hell was going on and how he was going to locate whatever that thing was that had slipped into Lindsey's body with indecent ease. Still—none of this was her fault. He owed her at least some minimal explanation. "I didn't want to tell you," he said, his tone dull. "We were having such a lovely evening, I didn't want to upset you."

"What—do you mean?" she whispered.

"You'll see it in the paper tomorrow, no doubt." Speaking in the same colorless monotone, he gave her the highlights of the attack at Bart's. He left out the part about the boy's confusion after it was over.

She gaped at him. "You're—*kidding*. A teenage boy tried to *strangle* you? At *Bart's*?" Her eyes narrowed. "And you didn't *tell* me?"

"What good would it have done?" he asked, shrugging. He propped a pillow against the headboard and sat up the rest of the way. "All it would have done was worry you. It's not as if he's still at large—as far as I know they've got him in custody."

Lindsey gazed into her sheet-covered lap. She said nothing.

Stone reached out to gently touch her shoulder, and felt it stiffen under his hand. "Lindsey, I'm sorry. Really. I knew this was a mistake, but—I wanted to see you tonight. I didn't mean to cause you any distress. I should go."

He expected her to try to stop him—part of him wanted her to—but she didn't. She just nodded once, her expression half-miserable, half-frightened.

He dressed quickly and stood for a moment next to her side of the bed. "I truly am sorry, Lindsey," he murmured, then turned and left the room.

She said nothing as he departed.

CHAPTER FOURTEEN

Nobody pulled Stone over as he drove back to his house, which was something of a wonder, all things considered. He didn't feel the least bit tipsy anymore—the events of the last half hour had driven any remnants of that from his mind—but what he did feel was a bone-deep exhaustion that forced him to use every ounce of his strength and concentration to keep the big car on the road. Every one of his aches and pains from the past two days had returned, and from the way his body was protesting right now, they'd invited a few friends over to join the party.

All he wanted to do was sleep, but that wasn't possible. He checked the wards again to make sure nothing had tried to get in, took a fast cold shower, put some coffee on to keep himself awake, and gathered up the stack of books he'd bought along with a notebook. All of this he carried to the kitchen table and then dropped wearily into a chair.

The first thing he did was write down everything he could remember about the encounter with the thing that had taken over Lindsey: the glowing eyes, the raspy voice, the details of the aura, and everything he could remember about what it had said to him. Then, leaning on his elbow with one hand buried in his hair, he studied its words and wondered what Jason—and now he—had gotten themselves into.

"Right, then," he muttered, turning to a fresh page in the notebook. "Let's see what we know about you."

He wrote down his thoughts as they came to him, each on its own line:

> *More than one of them ("we")*
> *One leader and minions, or multiple equally powerful?*
> *They know what I am, and that I'm looking for my friend.*
> *They can apparently move in and out of mundanes at will. (mages? unknown)*
> *Jason is "lost" (imprisoned? dead? using him for something? hostage?)*
> *Guilt from "what is to come" (more murders?)*
> *Can attack when not possessing a person (see barn attack) (same creatures?)*
> *How many? At least three (from barn)*
> *Can they hide aura?*

He wrote the word "EVIL?" and circled it, then crossed it out. Whatever these things were, he was almost certain they weren't part of that group's scattered remaining force. For one thing, the Evil weren't indiscriminate body-hoppers, especially the weaker specimens that were, as far as he knew, the only ones remaining. Even the strong ones chose a body and possessed it with at least tacit permission, and couldn't vacate it except upon the death of the host. Although plenty of people existed out there whose goals aligned with the Evil, and thus they had never lacked for hosts, being forced to leave a host body killed all but the strongest Evil and diminished the others.

These things, on the other hand, seemed quite comfortable jumping from body to body while suffering no ill effects. In a way that made them more frightening, because they could be inside anyone, but both times Stone had encountered them, he'd seen the eerie greenish aura when he looked for it. If they couldn't hide that aura from those who could perceive such things, then at least from now on he could see them coming if he kept his guard up.

Except that, at least from what he'd seen at the barn on Creek Road, they had some ability to attack even when they *weren't* possessing a body. Unless the things that had attacked him at the barn were different from the ones that possessed mundanes.

How many different types of (quite probably related) things was he dealing with here?

Stone's other hand went to his hair, pressing on his forehead as he struggled to wrangle his tired thoughts into some semblance of order. Another thing that had been true of both the boy's possessor and Lindsey's was that the mundanes seemed to remember nothing of the possession after being vacated, and aside from whatever the thing might force the body to do while occupying it, seemed to suffer no ill effects from being under the control of a new driver. That was something, at least. Not much, but something. Having to deal with a bunch of mundanes driven insane as their brains tried to process what had happened to them would make this effort even more difficult than it was already was.

And what about Jason? Where was he in all of this? The thing had said that he was "theirs now." The most logical explanation for that statement was that they had possessed him, perhaps on a permanent basis, and hidden him somewhere. But if so, why?

Stone sighed and poured himself another cup of coffee. If Jason had blundered drunkenly into the scene of the first murder while walking back from the party, perhaps the entity had jumped from the murderer's body to Jason's. Why would it do that, though, instead of just killing him?

"Perhaps he was too formidable for it to cope with in its current body," he mused, jotting that down in his notebook with a question mark. He and Jason were about the same height—an inch or two over six feet—but while Stone was thin, Jason had an athlete's build and outweighed him by thirty or forty pounds, all of it muscle. Jason was also trained in martial arts and self-defense techniques. It would take a large or very strong man to be able to overpower him. *A lot stronger than would be needed to overpower a sixteen-year-old girl, especially if she were caught by surprise.*

Could that have been why he was able to get tantalizing glimpses of Jason's aura during the tracking ritual, but never anything long enough to lock on to? Because whatever had possessed him had submerged Jason's aura sufficiently enough to hide it?

And what of the fact that Jason was notoriously difficult to possess? At least that was true with regard to the Evil, but Stone had no idea if that quality extended to other extradimensional beings.

He threw his pen on the table in frustration. None of this was helping him find Jason. Even if any of his guesses were correct, what good did they do? Before he could confront this thing, whatever it was, he needed to find out what it was. He knew more now than he'd known yesterday, which was good, but still nowhere near enough.

Perhaps he could figure out a way to talk to the boy who'd tried to strangle him, or Lindsey herself once she'd had a chance to calm down. He wondered if she'd even want to see him again after what had happened. The way she'd looked at him—hurt, confused, and a little angry—he supposed he couldn't blame her. The whole thing had to be even more unsettling for her than for him.

He pushed the notebook aside and picked up one of the books: *Ojai Lore and Legends,* from the Third Eye Bookstore. Flipping through it, he found sections on some of the things Lindsey had told him about: Char Man, the ghost children who jumped off the bridge, and the decapitated motorcyclist all had their own sections, as did the vampire and a phantom bride she hadn't mentioned. There were other stories as well, including some Chumash legends related to the beginnings of the Ojai Valley and the alleged healing power of some of its hot springs, but what interested Stone most was the number of legends or ghost stories centered around Creek Road. That had to mean something. One of the first things you learned when you studied magic—*real* magic—was that a lot of those spooky stories that mundanes wrote off as urban legends so they could keep their sanity properly tethered had their bases in fact. Maybe not exactly as told, because stories like that had a tendency to "evolve" as they were passed from person to person, but when you traced them back to their origins, almost invariably magic had its thumb in the pie somewhere.

Stone took up his notebook again and began making a list for tomorrow: Talk to the boy if he could. Talk to Lindsey, if she'd see him. Check out Creek Road and see if he could pick up anything from the area. If it was some sort of mystic hot spot, maybe he could get a better feel for where Jason was, or where these creatures had come through. If there was some sort of breach in the fabric of the dimensions that had let them in, odds were good that was where it was.

He wanted to look through some of the remaining books, but as he reached for the next one he became conscious of a heaviness settling over his limbs, pressing down on his eyelids. He blinked and shook his head, trying to wake up, but it didn't help. Even the coffee wasn't helping. His body was telling him loud and clear, "I'm going to sleep *now*, you idiot. Do you have a problem with that?"

Well...he *was* tired. Perhaps he could spare just a few minutes...

He laid his head on the table, resting it on his folded arms. *Just for a few minutes...*

Loud, sharp pounding on his door jolted him awake.

"Dr. Stone, open the door, please!" a booming voice called. "This is the police!"

Stone blinked. Light streamed in through the window—how long had he been sleeping? Slumped over the table, his arm and neck bent at an awkward angle, his whole body felt stiff and unresponsive. His head was pounding, no doubt at least partially from last night's drinks. "Wha—?" he mumbled, running his hand through his hair. His voice sounded thick and muddy to his ears.

"This is the police, Dr. Stone! Open the door or we'll break it down!"

That got him to his feet. He gazed around uncomprehendingly for a moment, trying to figure out what was going on and why the police were yelling at him. "Just a minute, just a minute..." he said, though nowhere near loudly enough for them to hear him. "I'm coming..." Instinctively, he used a levitation spell to pick up the notebook and settle it on top of one of the ceiling beams, where it was invisible to anyone at floor level. Then, conscious of the fact that he must look like something dragged several miles behind a bus, he stumped over and flung open the door. "What is—"

He stopped. It wasn't just one policeman: it was two. He didn't recognize either of them. As he appeared in the doorway, both of them tensed, their hands going to their still-holstered guns.

Stone blinked again. Maybe he was still dreaming. A bizarre sense of *deja vu* wafted over him as he took in their hard, implacable faces. "What's this about?" he demanded.

"Alastair Stone, you're under arrest," said the older cop. Already the younger one was pushing forward past him.

Stone stood still, shocked, as the cop cuffed his hands behind his back. The *deja vu* was getting worse by the minute. "Wait a minute—for what?"

"Murder."

He stared. "Murder? But I thought we settled that—"

"The murder of Lindsey Cole," the cop said.

CHAPTER FIFTEEN

S tone sat numbly at the table in the interrogation room at the Ojai police department. Across from him, Lt. Peter Casner, his face a cold mask, leaned forward and clicked on a tape recorder.

"Let's start again, Dr. Stone," he said. "Tell me what happened last night."

Stone bowed his head. His brain felt pummeled. Shocked. Dead.

He hadn't put up any protest when the policemen led him to the car. He let them direct him into the back seat of the cruiser with broken docility.

Lindsey...

A lovely, vital young woman was dead, and it was his fault.

What the hell did any of this even matter anymore?

They'd taken him back to the police station in silence; unlike last time, they'd walked him in, fingerprinted him, and had him hold a board with his name and numbers on it while they snapped mug shots. The whole thing would have been surreal if Stone hadn't been so mentally stunned by the proceedings that he could barely form a coherent thought.

They took him into another room, gave him a set of orange scrubs, and told him to change into them and put his clothes in a bag. All of this they did with minimal conversation: the only words they said were directions on what to do. He followed them without question or argument. They wouldn't give him any other details about what had happened.

He glanced up through haunted, bloodshot eyes at Casner, his hair spiking everywhere at crazy angles, dark stubble shadowing his pale face. "I didn't kill her, Lieutenant," he said softly. He was alone; when they'd told him he had the right to call an attorney, he hadn't even responded. It was foolish, he knew. He didn't care.

"Just tell me what happened," Casner repeated.

This was the second time he'd told the story, but he didn't object. He simply told it again, his voice a monotone devoid of any kind of life. He described how he'd picked Lindsey up at her home and taken her to the restaurant, how they'd had dinner and drinks there and then he'd driven her home. How she'd invited him in, and he'd accepted.

"Did you sleep with her?" Casner asked.

Stone nodded, staring at the worn table again.

"And then what happened?"

"I—left, after."

"You left her house?"

"Yes."

"Why? Why didn't you spend the night?"

He shrugged. "I wasn't feeling well." He knew how inadequate that sounded, but he couldn't tell Casner the truth. In a way, though, it *was* a truth. Just not the relevant one.

"You weren't feeling well." The detective's tone suggested he didn't believe it. "She didn't ask you to leave?"

He shook his head. "No."

"She didn't ask you to leave and you refused?"

His gaze came up. This was new. "No. Why do you—"

"Dr. Stone, the ME's initial examination found bruising on Lindsey Cole's wrists, consistent with having hands wrapped around them. We don't have all the data yet, but are we going to find that those bruises are the same size as your hands?"

Stone closed his eyes and nodded.

"Please give verbal answers for the recording, Dr. Stone."

"Yes," he rasped.

"So you're admitting you grabbed her wrists? Maybe to hold her down?"

"No."

"No you're not admitting it? But you just said you—"

"I did grab her wrists. But not to hold her down." He hated this. He didn't want to reveal what had happened. Lindsey was dead—the last thing he wanted to do was cast her memory in a bad light, which is what he would have to do unless he wanted to try making them believe she was possessed. Even in his current less-than-optimal mental state, he didn't think that would go over well.

"Why, then?"

He took a deep breath. "She—something came over her." His voice was soft, still without inflection. "Perhaps a bad dream inter-acting with the drinks she'd had—I don't know. I awoke and—" He closed his eyes briefly, then opened them again. "I awoke and she was sitting over me, preparing to stab me with a letter opener."

Casner stared at him. "Dr. Stone, let me get this straight. You're saying that Ms. Cole tried to *stab* you?"

"Yes. I—don't think she realized what she was doing."

"Did either of you take any drugs last night?"

"No." For the first time since they'd brought him in, his voice took on a tinge of indignation.

"Are you sure?"

"I'm certain that I didn't," he said, his gaze dropping back down to the table. "And I don't think she did."

"Would you be willing to submit to a blood test to prove that?"

"If you like, yes."

"How many drinks did you have?"

"I had two at the restaurant, and another when we got back to her home. She had about the same."

"And you're saying that Ms. Cole tried to stab you with what, again?"

"A letter opener. It had a slender blade, about five inches long."
Forgive me, Lindsey. I hate having to do this to you. I know it wasn't your fault.

Casner opened a file folder in front of him and withdrew a photo, which he slid across the table in front of Stone. "Strange that you should say that. Take a look."

Stone's gaze flicked to the photo. He stiffened, his breath catching in his throat.

The color photo had been taken in Lindsey's bedroom. It showed a close-up view of Lindsey, sprawled half-seated against the headboard of her bed, propped up on a pillow. Her eyes were wide open, filmy, lifeless. She was naked, her lower body covered with a sheet, her upper body slicked with blood. Protruding from a wound on the left side of her chest was the same letter opener that Stone had dropped over the edge of the bed before he'd departed. He gripped the edges of the table with shaking hands and stared, unblinking, unable to take his eyes from the photo.

"So..." Casner said, "You don't think it's odd that the murder weapon was the very same thing that you claim she tried to stab you with?" He slipped the photo back in the file folder. "You know what I think, Dr. Stone? Try this on for size: you drove her home, just like you said. She invited you in. You had a few drinks, things got a little hot and heavy, you ended up in the bedroom. But somewhere in there maybe you tried something she didn't like, or she just decided that maybe she didn't want you around for whatever reason. She told you to leave. You refused. She tried to fend you off with the only weapon she had, and you took it away and stabbed her with it. Maybe it was an accident. That happens sometimes when people get emotional. Then you realized what you'd done, panicked, and took off."

Stone started shaking his head halfway through Casner's words. "No, no," he said. "Lieutenant. No." The image of Lindsey's staring, empty eyes had imprinted itself on his mind, and he couldn't drive it away. "I didn't kill her."

"Are you saying she stabbed *herself*?"

Stone bowed his head. If the thing had come back and taken residence in her body again after he left, he realized, it was entirely possible that that was exactly what *had* happened. If these things were powerful enough to make a stolen body cut a teenage girl's throat, then they were strong enough to override a human's powerful natural self-preservation instincts to force her to plunge a sharp object into her own heart. But there was no way in hell that Casner was going to believe that. He himself wouldn't have believed it if he hadn't seen the evidence with his own eyes.

"Dr. Stone? Answer the question, please."

"I don't know," he whispered. "All I know is that I didn't do it."

"Are we going to find your prints on that letter opener?"

"Probably. I took it away from her and threw it on the floor." Through the fog in his brain, something bubbled up. His voice took on a bit more life again. "Lieutenant, did your investigators find a small puncture or slash in the sheet and mattress on the side of the bed closest to the window?"

Casner frowned as he consulted his papers. "I don't have all the reports back yet. They're still working the scene. Why?"

Stone sighed. "It won't prove my story, obviously, but it might lend some credence to it. When Ms. Cole—attempted to stab me, I rolled to the side and she hit the bed with the blade. That was when I grabbed her wrists—just long enough to make her drop it." Remembering something else, he added: "And have them take a look at the opener itself. See if it was bent and then re-straightened. It was bent when I took it from her, so whoever—" the image flashed in his mind's eye again "—whoever killed her—would either have to have straightened it, or stabbed with it bent."

"I'll let them know," Casner said. "My guys are good, Dr. Stone. If there's anything to find, they'll find it."

Stone nodded. "I hope so, Lieutenant." He looked up. "What happens now? I assume you intend to charge me with Ms. Cole's murder."

"Not yet. But the law allows us to hold you for up to seventy-two hours before we have to charge you or let you go, and we're going to do that. What the investigators and the ME come up with will determine whether we pursue the case and charge you with the murder."

He frowned. "May I ask a question?"

"Go ahead."

"Why *aren't* you charging me? It sounds as if you're convinced that I'm guilty. Why risk allowing me to flee if you let me go?"

Casner sighed. "Because, Dr. Stone, this is a serious charge. You realize, if you're found guilty of this, it could mean life in prison. If they determine it was premeditated, you could get the needle. That's not something I take lightly. Especially because you're wrong: I'm *not* convinced you're guilty. Not yet."

"Why?" Stone's voice was dead again. He slumped in his chair.

"Call it my gut. There's been a hell of a lot of very strange stuff centering on you—and this friend you're searching for—ever since you arrived in Ojai. Before that, even, if the first murder is connected to the rest of this." He tapped his folder with his pen. "First, we find you at the scene of another murder you claim to have stumbled onto while following a—what you claim was a psychic vision. It looks suspicious, but you've got an alibi that places you nowhere near the victim when he died, and nowhere near the first victim, assuming they're connected. The very next day, a local kid you've never met before tries to strangle you in a public place, then claims he has no idea why and doesn't even remember doing it. A kid, I might add, who's lived in town all his life, has never been in trouble beyond the occasional school detention, never had any history of mental issues, and who passed drug and alcohol screens with flying colors."

He opened the folder and pulled out another sheet of paper. "Now, we get an anonymous call saying that a local woman—a woman you've been seen with just the previous night—has turned up murdered in her bed." He put that page back and picked up another one. "I've been doing some checking up on you, Dr. Stone: you've got a very interesting history. Professor at Stanford for about seven years, citizen of the United Kingdom, resident alien in the process of applying for dual citizenship, no criminal record in either country—but yet you were present when an elderly woman's mansion was destroyed by fire in Los Gatos shortly after you arrived in the U.S. You barely escaped with your life when your rented home in Palo Alto was destroyed by a gas explosion four years after that. You were injured in the explosion of an abandoned mine in West Virginia almost two years ago. And—" he studied the paper again, "—you were on the scene of that terrorist attack at Burning Man last summer where several dozen people were killed." He looked up, meeting Stone's gaze. "Trouble does seem to follow you, Dr. Stone, even if there's no way to connect you directly with it. Either that, or you're somehow seeking it out."

This was one of the things Stone had been dreading for years, ever since he got involved with Jason and Verity and the Evil: that someone would examine his life closely enough to put all the pieces together and figure out just how deeply buried in the unexplained he was. He scrubbed at his hair while searching for a plausible answer. "There isn't much I can say in my defense, Lieutenant, except to say that I do a bit of—investigation of potentially occult-related events in my spare time. I was working for the elderly woman in Los Gatos, and the West Virginia incident started out as another investigation, though the actual cause of the explosion had a perfectly mundane explanation. So did my home in Palo Alto."

"And Burning Man?"

Stone shook his head. "That one was—a case of being in the wrong place at the wrong time. I knew some of the people who died there. It's not something I'd prefer to dig up again unless absolutely necessary. The whole thing is still quite raw." He sipped from the bottle of water Casner had given him and his shoulders sagged back into a dejected slump.

The lieutenant leaned across the table. "If there's anything you want to tell me, Dr. Stone, now's the time to do it. Just because there's a lot of weird shit going down around Ojai right now and my gut tells me you're not the guy we're looking for doesn't mean the evidence won't show otherwise. And it doesn't mean I can do a damn thing for you if there's enough of it that I'll be forced to charge you. I'll tell you something you might not know: if the evidence convinces us that you didn't commit the murder, and we release you before that seventy-two-hour period is up, then the arrest won't go on your record. It just counts as you being 'detained,' which won't get you in any sort of trouble. But I can promise you this—and it's not a threat, it's simply the way things work—if you are charged with this murder, even if you go to trial and are eventually found not guilty, your life will never be the same again. It will be expensive, it'll put every aspect of your history, your personality, and your habits under a microscope, and it's possible you might even lose your job or be deported back to England. Like I said, I'm not saying this to scare you. I'm saying it because I want you to help us. If there's *anything* you're not telling us, don't wait too long."

He stood, gathering his files. "We've been talking for quite a while now, Dr. Stone. I'm going to give you some time to think things over. We'll meet again later. If you decide you want to talk before I get back to you, just tell one of the officers. Same if you decide you want a lawyer after all." He nodded to the uniformed cop standing by the door, who came over and motioned for Stone to get up.

❖

The cop took him to a small cell and waved him inside. He went without protest, lying on the narrow bed and turning away to face the wall. He closed his eyes as the steel door locked behind him.

He stayed in that position for over an hour, the image of Lindsey's bloody body playing on an endless loop in the theater of his mind, interspersed with flashes of her laughter, her sparkling brown eyes, her soft hands as they pulled him into an embrace and caressed his hair.

He hadn't loved Lindsey Cole: of course he hadn't. They'd only known each other for two days, whatever nascent relationship that might have been had barely grown into the initial stages of playful flirting and raw physical attraction. Could it have evolved into more? He had no idea. If history were any indication, odds were good that it would either have ended when he returned to Palo Alto, or else she'd have gotten a taste of the freak show that was his life and politely exited, stage left. That was the way it always happened. He was used to it. He didn't *like* it, but he was used to it.

But damn it, she hadn't even gotten the chance.

Someone—some*thing*—had killed her in cold blood. Or worse, so much worse: forced her to kill *herself*. What had she felt? If that was how it ended, had some part of her been conscious? Had the thing left her body once she'd moved past the point of no return? Had she bled out the last of her life in cold, unknowing terror?

All of it had been his fault.

Whatever this thing was, it wanted him. It had taken hold of Lindsey the first time to tell him so, after its attempt to murder him had failed. And if it wanted him, that meant anyone he was close to represented a potential avenue to get to him. If he hadn't succumbed to his baser instincts and asked her out, she'd be safe now, sitting in her office or driving her car around Ojai showing high-end houses to wealthy clients.

Instead, her body lay on a slab in a morgue somewhere. His mind's eye helpfully served up a full-color snapshot of what that might have looked like: her face bone-white, her lips cold, a

R. L. KING

Y-shaped line of rough stitching running from her chest down her abdomen—

Stop it. That isn't helping.

He knew it wasn't helping, but when did that ever matter? He couldn't stop it. For all his vaunted willpower and formidable mental strength, he was powerless to halt the images. He drew his knees up to his chest and wrapped his arms around them, his whole body shaking. He didn't cry—he wished he could, but his body stubbornly refused to cooperate. Eventually, his exhaustion finally catching up to him, he dropped off to uneasy sleep.

"Dr. Stone?"

Stone stirred.

A light knock on the bars. "Dr. Stone, you awake?"

He rolled over, wincing as every muscle and bone in his body protested against the thin mattress and the uncomfortable position. What time was it? How long had he been asleep? Slowly, he sat up.

Stan Lopez stood outside the cell. He wasn't wearing his police uniform; instead he wore faded jeans, battered brown cowboy boots, and a plaid shirt over a T-shirt advertising a recent interdepartmental chili cook-off.

Stone blinked. "Sergeant?" Jason's old friend was the last person he expected to see.

Lopez nodded. "Yeah, they said I could come talk to you for a few minutes. Privileges of knowing people around here, you know? Only if you want to, though."

For a moment, Stone didn't answer as he waited for his brain to emerge from its stupor. He sat on the edge of the bed, leaning over with his elbows braced on his knees.

"You okay?" Lopez asked.

Stone rolled his head back and forth. "No. I don't think I am." His gaze came up. "What can I do for you, Sergeant?"

"I just wanted to come by and see you," he said. "When I heard they were holding you for murder, I couldn't believe it. I still don't."

"I didn't do it," he said, staring back down at his hands. He rubbed his eyes, trailing his hand along his stubbled jawline. "I didn't kill her. But it seems they think I did, and it seems that the initial evidence supports their belief."

"I won't ask you about what happened," Lopez said. "I'm still a cop, and they can use whatever you'd tell me. Why didn't you get a lawyer?"

Stone shrugged without looking up.

"You really should, you know. This is a big deal, even if you didn't do it."

Stone didn't answer.

Lopez let out a sigh. "Okay. You do what you want. But like I said, I wanted to see you. Jason talks about you a lot—says you're a good guy and a good friend. I wanted to see if there was anything I could do to help you out—anything you need, that kind of thing."

"Thank you, Sergeant. I appreciate your kindness." Still, Stone didn't look up, and his voice was flat.

Lopez regarded him for a few moments. "Listen. I know this is hard on you. But lemme give you some advice, if I can."

Stone raised one hand in a 'go on' gesture.

"Fight," he said firmly. "If you didn't do it, fight it. Get yourself a lawyer. Work on remembering everything that you can about what happened. Try to remember if anybody saw you that night. Casner says they haven't charged you yet—they're still trying to decide if they have enough evidence to do it. Help them. He's a straight-up guy—I've known him a long time. He'll be fair, but he's gonna need something to go on."

Stone looked up and met his eyes. "You believe me, then?"

"Yeah, I do. Maybe I'm a damn fool, but I know Jason. He wouldn't think that highly of a guy who could stab a woman in the chest with a letter opener." He sighed again. "I've been in this business long enough to learn a few things, Dr. Stone. I'm pretty good at reading people, and I'm pretty good at looking at the way somebody acts and being able to tell if they're capable of that kind of thing."

"You barely know me, Sergeant."

"Yeah, but Jason does. And besides that, just talking to you, you don't strike me as a fit-of-passion kind of guy. Jason, yeah, maybe. You, no."

Stone nodded. "Has there been any news on Jason?"

"No." Lopez's tone was as flat as Stone's. "No sign of him."

That didn't surprise him, of course. And being stuck in here, he wasn't getting a damned thing done toward finding out where Jason was.

"So, anyway," Lopez said, "I'd better get going. But if I can help you, let me know. I know some good lawyers around here. I can hook you up if you want."

"Thank, you, Sergeant. I'll keep that in mind."

Time, Stone discovered, passed very slowly when you were confined to a small cell with nothing to occupy your mind but your own traitorous thoughts. When he was awake, he couldn't concentrate enough to think through the events of the past couple of days; mostly he dozed, his disjointed dreams haunted by a procession of bloody corpses: Lindsey's, Jason's, Verity's.

When Casner came in and called his name, he didn't even get up. He just lay there and watched the cop with dulled eyes, wondering what new bit of damning evidence the mysterious entity had managed to plant against him.

"Dr. Stone, you'll want to hear this," Casner said as he opened the cell door.

Stone sat up. "What is it now?"

"Please come with me."

He did as he was told, once again without protest or question. Casner took him into the interrogation room and motioned for him to sit down. When he did so, the detective opened his folder.

"We found the puncture in the mattress," he said. "It was right where you said it would be. But—this is, if you don't mind my saying so, Dr. Stone, the weirdest thing I've seen in all the years I've been on the force. I can't even begin to explain it."

Stone gave him a questioning look but otherwise remained silent.

"It seems a witness has turned up. Ms. Cole's next-door neighbor has a houseguest."

"A—witness? To what?" Could someone have seen the murder? Or—seen Lindsey Cole forced to kill herself?

"To you, Dr. Stone. Leaving." He glanced down at his papers. "The witness says he was on the front porch of the house across the street, having a cigarette because his host won't let him smoke inside the residence. He didn't come forward until now because he'd gotten up very early that morning and spent the day in Ventura surfing. He hadn't heard the news."

Stone stared at him. "What—does this mean?"

"He says he saw a tall, thin man in a long coat come out of the house, get into a dark-colored BMW sedan parked in Ms. Cole's driveway, and drive off at about 2:15 a.m."

Stone nodded. "That was about when I left," he said, raising up a bit from his slump. He wouldn't allow himself to hope—not yet. "But that doesn't prove that I didn't kill her, does it?"

"Not on its own, no. But when combined with one other thing the witness stated and the ME's declaration of time of death—" He pulled out another paper. "The witness states that after the car left, he remained on the porch finishing his cigarette for about five more minutes. In this time, he saw the door to Ms. Cole's house open, and a female figure in a robe appeared there. He says she stood there for a few seconds, then went back inside. Her porch light was on, so the witness got a good look at her. He IDed Lindsey Cole as the woman he saw."

Stone bowed his head. If this story was true, then Lindsey had come out right after he'd gone—perhaps to call him back inside? Now, he'd never know. But—"So...that proves she was alive when I left," he said softly.

Casner nodded. "That's correct. And after examining Ms. Cole's body, the ME has placed the time of death at some time between three and four a.m."

"Well after I left."

"Yes." Casner took a deep breath. "It appears, Dr. Stone, that your story holds up."

"So—you're satisfied that I didn't kill Ms. Cole? You aren't going to charge me with her murder?"

"We're not going to charge you," Casner said.

Stone took a deep breath, rubbing at his forehead. "And you don't think that I might have returned to her house later?"

"I might think that, except for two other bits of evidence we found. And one of them is where that weirdness that I mentioned comes in."

"Go on..." Stone said softly.

"First, we examined the scene, and found nothing to suggest that you killed her. Wounds like that bleed a lot, but there was no sign of anyone tracking blood across the carpeting, no sign of blood on your clothes—in fact, aside from the immediate area around Ms. Cole's body, we found no blood at all." Casner paused. "I shouldn't be telling you this, Dr. Stone. But when we examined the murder weapon, we did find your prints—but they were mostly obscured. By Ms. Cole's own."

And this is where it begins, Stone thought. "And this implies—"

"It implies that she touched the weapon after you did. And—" He looked down at his papers. Stone noticed that his breathing picked up a bit. He blew air through his teeth and met Stone's gaze. "As I said, I shouldn't be telling you this. I told you that my gut told me you didn't kill her before, and now I'm sure of it. I could get in a lot of trouble for sharing this information, so I hope you'll use your discretion."

"Of course," Stone said, leaning forward. He could see the effect this was having on Casner—something was seriously spooking the man. "You have my word, for whatever you might think that's worth."

For almost a full minute Casner was silent, his eyes on the papers in his folder. Then he looked up and spoke in a rush. "My guys examined the crime-scene photos and the weapon, Dr. Stone, and checked them against the ME's initial autopsy report. Lindsey Cole's cause of death was that letter opener, driven directly into her heart."

Stone frowned. "I'm not sure I see—"

"Let me put it to you this way," Casner said. "Unless she was unconscious when it was done, and there's no indication that she was, it would be nearly impossible for anyone to cleanly hit her heart in one shot. We'd expect to find multiple stab wounds, or the blade being diverted by the ribs, or a chip out of the nearest rib. No one conscious would simply sit still and allow such a thing without defending themselves, or at least flinching."

He stared at Stone, and there was something odd and disturbed in his eyes. "Dr. Stone—I was being a smartass when I asked you about it, but—unthinkable as it might be, all the evidence points to Ms. Cole stabbing *herself*."

| CHAPTER SIXTEEN

Two hours later, Stone sat in the chair in the living room of his rented house, gazing out the window into the street without seeing it. It was past five now; he hadn't eaten anything since dinner with Lindsey last night, and he didn't give a damn. The last thing on his mind right now was food. Alcohol maybe, and it was a good thing he didn't have any in the house, but not food. The best he'd managed was to shower, shave, and change into different clothes; that was mostly because he wanted to distance himself from last night and his day in custody as much as possible.

It wasn't working very well.

Casner had released him an hour ago, after having him sign a series of forms and extracting his promise that he would remain reachable if necessary. He walked out of the station as if in a dream, still unshaven and rumple-haired in his old jeans and faded black T-shirt. He didn't care about that either. He felt the cops' gazes on him as he left, sure that most of them still believed he'd been responsible for Lindsey's murder and thought Casner was insane for cutting him loose.

And why shouldn't they? The alternatives—that someone had broken into her home and murdered her after he left, or that she'd killed herself in some nigh-inconceivable way—were hardly as attractive as "jilted foreign lover snaps after being rejected." That was the kind of soap opera storyline small towns thrived on.

On an end table next to Stone's chair was a copy of the local paper. The headline across the front read *Local Realtor murdered in her home*. He'd forced himself to read the whole story carefully: his name was not mentioned, which was one tiny bit of this whole nightmarish affair that had gone in his favor. All it said was that the police were "questioning a person of interest" in the case, and that they hoped to make an arrest soon.

He sighed. Of course, it was the nature of small towns that it didn't matter that he wasn't mentioned in the article: everybody in town probably already knew the "person of interest" was the odd British visitor who'd been spotted around town over the past couple of days. And that, in turn, meant any anonymity he hoped to maintain while continuing his search for Jason had just gone right out the window. He could use his disregarding spell, of course, but he couldn't keep it going constantly, and it was less useful in any kind of crowd. He was sure that by now anyone who cared to do so had made the connection between the victim of the attempted strangling at Bart's yesterday (there was an article about that, too— Lindsey's murder had pushed it to a small area below the fold—and in that one he *was* mentioned by name) and the person of interest in Lindsey's murder case.

Hell, small-town busybodies were resourceful enough that Stone didn't doubt that some subset of them had already made the connection between those and the person who'd found the second victim of the town's *other* murderer.

This wasn't going to make anything easy.

And even worse than all of this was the chilling realization his oh-so-helpful brain had chosen to share with him while he was in the middle of shaving, nearly causing him to take a slice out of his jaw: he'd gotten very, very lucky. When he realized just *how* lucky, he'd actually felt faint and had to sit down on the edge of the bathtub for a moment to get his bearings.

There had been a witness to support his story. Someone who'd stated they'd seen him leaving Lindsey's house, and seen her alive after he'd left.

Whatever had taken over Lindsey had proven it could switch bodies with careless disregard. What if the thing had decided to take temporary residence inside the neighbor, and instead of telling the truth about what had happened, had told the police that he'd heard yelling and screams coming from inside Lindsey's house? Or that Stone hadn't left until much later?

Now, sitting in the chair looking at nothing, Stone continued pondering the implications of an opponent that could be anyone, and, unlike the Evil, wasn't confined to a single body. Sure, he could look for the aura. He'd have to get into the habit of doing that nearly constantly, even though maintaining his magical senses for such prolonged periods would take its toll on his endurance. That couldn't be helped. But he couldn't keep an eye on everyone who might call the police with lies about him, or speak to reporters, or even *be* reporters writing stories that *did* name names.

As Jason was fond of saying: Holy crap.

For a moment, a few seconds, Stone thought about simply calling it a day. Packing up and heading home, retaining a high-priced lawyer to deal with any leftover fallout, and just lying low until it all blew over. He could do that: he doubted that the powers that be at Stanford would sack him for anything that had happened thus far, and his students weren't likely to read any tiny articles about the situation that might find their way onto the back pages of the Bay Area newspapers.

Yeah, that would have been the easy thing to do.

But that left Jason still missing.

And it left a murderer running loose in this little town. One the mundane police had no hope of catching or stopping. If he left now, he was condemning an unknown number of people to death until the thing decided it had enough.

In Stone's experience, things like this rarely decided that they'd had enough. Usually, if something nasty from another dimension wanted revenge on a single person (perhaps someone who'd been audacious enough to summon it or attempt to enslave it) and it got the chance to achieve it, it would kill that person—often in some spectacularly messy way—and then depart back to its home plane.

If this one was killing multiple people, that probably meant it was more of an indiscriminate type that craved death for whatever reason: either because it somehow fed on the released energy, or because it simply liked killing. Either way, Stone had a pretty good idea there wasn't anyone else here who'd even gotten as far along the string of clues as he had, let alone who was powerful enough to have a chance of banishing or destroying it.

Brilliant. He had two choices, then: leave the town—and Jason—to their fates and live with the guilt for the rest of his life, or remain, endure whatever suspicion and anger the town's residents would doubtless throw at him and any further murder attempts the thing he was hunting wanted to try. That was assuming it didn't figure out a way to frame him for yet *another* murder. The first one had been relatively easy to get out of, since there was no way he could have committed it and that was clear to even the most casual examination. He'd dodged a much closer bullet with the second one. He had no doubt that whatever this thing was, it had the capacity to learn from its mistakes. If there was a third time, he might as well prepare himself for a very long stay in a very small room.

He couldn't allow it to get a third chance.

So that was his choice: he could leave, or he could stay.

And it wasn't a choice. Not at all.

This thing had Jason.

This thing had killed Lindsey Cole, an innocent bystander, simply because she'd been associated with him.

Both of those facts made it personal.

And that meant he might have to end up doing some things he didn't really want to do. Starting right now.

He shoved himself out of the chair, gathered up his books and notes, and reached for his coat. Five minutes and one phone call later he was back in the car and on the road.

| CHAPTER SEVENTEEN

S tan Lopez lived in a well-kept ranch-style home on a quiet side street in Oak View, a small community halfway between Ojai and Ventura. By the time Stone located it and knocked on the door, it was a little before six p.m. and the sun was just beginning its slow, late-summer descent.

Lopez answered at Stone's first knock. He was wearing the same clothes as when he'd visited Stone at the police station earlier that day, except the plaid overshirt was gone and he'd swapped the cowboy boots for slip-ons. He eyed Stone for a moment. "Pete told me they'd let you go," he said. "I'm glad. C'mon in."

Stone took a moment to scan Lopez with his magical senses, and was relieved to find no trace of the greenish aura. "Thank you," he said softly. He followed Lopez into a small living room dominated by a comfortable-looking brown leather recliner, an old sofa with a multicolored quilt thrown over the back, and a big-screen TV currently tuned to the news.

"You want a beer? This has to have been a bitch of a day for you. You look tired as hell."

"I've felt better," he admitted. "But no, thank you. Probably best if I avoid alcohol for a while."

Lopez nodded, waving toward the seating area. "Sit down. I was just about to figure out what to do for dinner. You like pizza? I could call out, so we can talk without having to go somewhere. Too hot to cook."

"Yes, that would be fine. Thank you." Now that he'd roused himself to action, the fact that he hadn't had anything to eat for nearly a day was making itself hard to ignore. He took a seat on the end of the sofa farthest from the TV.

Lopez headed to the kitchen to make the call, then returned a few minutes later carrying a Bud, a Coke, a stack of paper plates, and a roll of paper towels. He shrugged and grinned, putting everything but the beer down on the coffee table. "I'm not formal around here. Ever since the divorce, I've been reverting back to the bachelor lifestyle." He set the soda can on the coffee table in front of Stone, then settled into his recliner, popped the Bud, and took a long swig. "Now. What can I do for you, Dr. Stone? You said you had something you wanted to talk to me about. Is it about Jason?"

Stone took a deep breath. Even though he'd already made the decision to do this, it still wasn't anything like easy for him. "Indirectly it is," he said at last.

Lopez's gaze sharpened. "You found something about where he is?"

"No. Not yet. But I think in order to get any further in my search, I need to ask for your help. That's not something I'm terribly comfortable doing, but in light of recent events, I don't think I have a choice anymore."

Lopez frowned. "Why aren't you comfortable? I told you—Jason's like my own son. I'll do whatever it takes, whatever I can do to help find him. Why wouldn't you want me to do that?" His eyes narrowed. "Is it because you want to do something illegal?"

Stone shook his head. "No, that isn't it. Well—I don't think so, anyway. Please, Sergeant: let me explain it in my own way. After I'm finished, you can ask whatever questions you like and I promise to answer them to the best of my ability."

Lopez looked at him like he wasn't quite sure what to make of him. "If it helps Jason, I'll listen," he said. "But like I told you before: call me Stan. I'm only 'Sergeant' when I'm on duty."

Stone nodded. His gaze skimmed over the coffee table, which held a collection of newspapers and sports magazines. The topmost newspaper showed the headline about Lindsey's murder. He closed his eyes as the images rose again. With an effort, he forced them away.

Lopez followed his line of sight to the table. "Oh, shit, I'm sorry," he said, snatching the paper and shoving it under the stack. "Should've got rid of that before you got here."

"It's all right," he said without looking up. A full minute passed before he focused on Lopez again. He sighed, rubbing a hand over his face and up into his hair. "Sergeant—Stan—do you recall what I told you about the message Jason left for me before he disappeared?"

"Yeah. You said he told you he'd seen something weird down here, and thought you might be interested."

"Yes." He paused. "You said you would do anything to help Jason, correct?"

"Anything legal," Lopez said, frowning. "Anything else, I'm gonna need more details."

"Does that include being willing to give me your word that you'll keep the things I'm about to tell you between the two of us? Nothing illegal, I promise. Just—things I'd prefer not to have generally known."

Lopez looked hard at him, his eyes showing confusion and a hint of suspicion. After a moment, he nodded. "Dr. Stone, if whatever you tell me isn't about something illegal, and it'll help Jason for me to know it, then you have my word that I won't tell anyone else."

Stone's tense posture relaxed a bit. "All right, then." He took a deep breath, remembering back to the time when he'd had a similar conversation with Jason in the sitting room of his previous home in Palo Alto. It hadn't been easy then, either. Had it really only been less than three years ago? It seemed so much longer, now.

Casting about for the best way to begin, he finally said, "Jason left that message because he thought I'd be interested in what he found. But not because of what I do at the University."

"Why, then? I thought you said you taught that occult stuff."

"I don't just teach it, Stan," Stone said softly, his gaze fixed on Lopez's face. "I practice it."

Lopez stared at him. "What the hell does that mean?"

"I can show you. But I have to warn you: it will probably cause you some mental discomfort."

"Mental discomfort?"

"Accepting a new worldview is never easy. And from the conversations we've had thus far and what Jason's told me about you, I've got you pegged as a fairly pragmatic sort. But I can prove everything I tell you. Do you still want to see?"

Lopez continued to stare. Once again, Stone could see mental gears turning inside the older man's head. He wished he didn't have to do this; as uncomfortable as the whole thing was making Lopez, it was even harder on him. He was pretty sure that trusting someone—someone who was a virtual stranger to him, with only a close connection to Jason to convince him that the man was trustworthy—went against everything Lopez was.

If he'd miscalculated, if Lopez wasn't mentally capable of handling what he was about to show him, or if his need to tell the story of what he'd seen was stronger than his word, then Stone could be opening himself up to an extra-large helping of inconvenience. Sure, it was likely nobody would believe Lopez even if he did try to tell, but that would cause its own problems. A veteran cop who suddenly started spouting off about magic being real wouldn't last long on the force, at least not without some intensive psychological evaluation. Stone felt like he was standing on the brink of something huge, and his next step would change the course of two lives. Three, if you counted Jason.

No pressure.

Lopez swallowed. He hadn't taken his eyes off Stone the whole time. After another long pause, he nodded. "Yeah…yeah, I want to see."

Stone nodded. He saw how much those words had cost the man, and he could also see more clearly now why Jason held him in such high regard. He sensed that Stan Lopez was a man who would walk through hell for those who mattered to him, no matter how scared he was. Stone just hoped his courage would hold through the sort of thing that nobody unfamiliar with the magical world could ever be expected to deal with.

Taking a deep breath, he raised his hand, pointing it at the unopened can of Coke on the coffee table. It rose up and floated over to him. He plucked it from the air, popped the top, and took a long drink.

Lopez nearly dropped his beer. He bobbled it, lurching forward to stare at the can in Stone's hand. His eyes, normally crinkled in a deceptively easygoing squint, got so wide that Stone could see stark white all the way around. He struggled to speak, finally getting out: "What. In the *fuck*—?"

"Magic is real, Stan," Stone said in the same soft, calm tone. "It's real, and I can do it. Whatever Jason saw in Ojai, he called me because he thought it had something to do with the magical world. And judging from the fact that he disappeared soon after, he was probably correct."

Lopez's breath was coming fast. He swallowed a couple of times, then leaned farther forward and set his beer can on the table with exaggerated care, as if fearing it might explode. "You—" He pointed a shaking finger at Stone's Coke can. "You—" Another pause. "I didn't see that. Did I?"

In answer, Stone held up the can. This time he didn't even bother gesturing at it, but merely sent it levitating up with a flick of his mind. It did a couple of circuits around the table, and then floated neatly down onto the table next to Lopez's beer.

The doorbell rang.

Lopez didn't move. His gaze kept darting back and forth between Stone and the can on the table. His mouth moved, but no sound came out.

Stone rose. "I'll get that," he said, heading to the door. He came back a few moments later with a large pizza box, after scanning the deliveryman for greenish auras and finding none. With casual ease he gestured at the table, magically sweeping the papers and magazines out of the way, and set the box down. "This smells lovely," he said, levitating a paper plate over to Lopez. "Shall we?"

Lopez hadn't changed position except for his eyes, which continued tracking everything that had moved around the table. They settled on the plate hovering in front of him. Finally, after swallowing a couple more times, he said in a strangled tone, "Ja—Jason knows about this?"

Stone nodded. "He has since the first night we met. I actually used magic to get him out of a scrape, and then took him back to my home afterward. He'd only just arrived in the Bay Area recently, looking for Verity."

"Does—Verity know too?"

"She does, yes." He purposely didn't tell him that Verity could do magic as well; that was her secret to reveal if she chose, not his. Besides, Lopez was freaked out enough as it was.

Lopez reached up and gingerly took the hovering plate, as if he expected it to somehow zap him. He took a couple of long, slow breaths and let them out. "This…this isn't a trick, is it?"

"No. It's the real thing. I know it's hard to believe, but it's true."

"So you can—" He looked at the plate. "You can do—what else?"

"Quite a lot of things. You'll forgive me if I don't catalogue them for you right now—that's hardly the point, and it won't help us find Jason."

Moving with deliberate slowness, Lopez leaned forward and opened the pizza box, motioning for Stone to go first. He did so, nodding thanks. The enticing aroma was making him realize just how hungry he was. Lopez took a slice, reclaimed his beer, and leaned back in his recliner. "You'll have to forgive me, Dr. Stone," he said, his voice shaking. "This is all—pretty damn freaky."

"Quite all right," Stone said through a mouthful of pizza. He was already halfway through his current slice and eyeing his next one. "I didn't think it would be easy for you to accept. It wasn't easy for Jason, either. Some people are—shall we say—more predisposed toward disbelief. People who are strongly grounded in the so-called 'real world.'"

"Like cops," Lopez said.

"Like cops, yes." Stone liberated another slice of pizza from the box. "I do hate to do this to you, Stan—I know you really should have more time to process all of this. It's a lot to take in so quickly. But there's a fair bit more that I need to tell you before you'll be able to help me find Jason. Do you think you could—for Jason's sake—just accept that what I'm showing you is real, so we can go on from there? I promise I'll answer your questions when I've finished."

Lopez nodded slowly. "I—I'll try," he said. "But you got to give me a minute. This is a lot to swallow." He took a long swig of beer. "Go ahead—keep going. I'm listening. And believe me, you don't have to worry about me telling anybody else. They'd have me in a fuckin' straitjacket if I tried."

"Probably," Stone agreed. "I'm not worried, though. If Jason trusts you, I trust you. But now that you have the basics, let me tell you how they relate to our current problem."

Speaking in the same calm, professorial tone that he used for his classroom lectures at Stanford, Stone laid out the situation, beginning with the message Jason had left him and ending with what had happened with Lindsey. He paused several times to devour more pizza, and when he got to the part about Lindsey, his voice lost some of its cool objectivity and began to shake a bit. He forced himself to keep going—if Lopez was going to be of any help to him, he'd have to know what he was up against. He had to be able to decide for himself after hearing all the facts.

Lopez, for his part, didn't interrupt. He sat back in his chair, munching pizza and swigging beer with a kind of methodical lack of awareness, his eyes fixed on Stone. He neither nodded, made any sound, nor moved more than necessary to continue eating. His only change of expression came when Stone got to Lindsey, at which point he briefly closed his eyes, then opened them again.

When Stone finished his story, he waited, watching Lopez. He had no idea how the man was going to react: Lopez's poker face was as good as his own. The only sound in the room was the low drone of the TV, which had now switched to a game show.

Nearly two full minutes passed. Lopez leaned forward and dropped another slice of pizza onto his plate, then rose and picked up his empty beer can. He spoke in a quiet, even tone: "You want another Coke? Or something else?"

Stone nodded. "Another Coke is fine, thank you," he said in the same tone. He waited while Lopez left and returned, setting another can on the table next to the empty one. Without thinking about it Stone scanned him, but he remained thankfully free of green auras. The man's own aura was a clear, solid blue, shot through with jagged streaks of red: steadfast, but deeply disturbed. After another moment of silence, Stone ventured, "Are you all right?"

Lopez nodded. "Yeah." He took a deep breath. "This is—" His eyes came up and met Stone's. "Are there a lot of you—you—what do you call yourselves? Wizards? Warlocks?"

"The terms vary. In this part of the world, we usually use 'mage.'"

"Mage." He mulled that over. "So—are there a lot of—mages around?"

Stone realized that, no matter how much he wanted to move the process along and get started looking for Jason again, Lopez would need some time to work through this. He could speed things along somewhat, but there was no way he could bypass it. He leaned back on the sofa. "Quick answer: no. We're fairly rare. The biggest percentage are what we call minor talents: they have a few tricks they can do, but they haven't the innate ability or the desire to progress to the higher levels. Even those are rare, though. I doubt you've more than a few in the entire area."

"What about you? You're stronger than one of these—minor talents, right?"

Stone's eyebrow rose. "I get the job done."

"And—they—you, I mean—look just like regular people?"

Stone gave a mirthless chuckle. "You tell me. Do I look like 'regular people'?" When Lopez didn't reply, he continued, "They look like what they look like. I've met a couple who look like bankers, a few who go for the goth or hippie aesthetic, and most just look like your usual sort of person on the street. It just depends on the individual."

Lopez was silent again, obviously struggling with something. "Can you—kill people with magic?"

Stone saw where he was going, and didn't sugarcoat it. "Yes."

"Shit..." Lopez let out a long breath. "I'm just thinking about unsolved cases. How many of them could have been—" He looked up. "You think these murders in Ojai are related to this magic, don't you?"

Stone nodded.

"And Jason's disappearance."

Again he nodded.

Lopez shook his head, scrubbing his hand over his face. "Shit..." he said again, gaze rising to the ceiling. "I've got so many questions. I don't even know where to start. And we don't have *time* for me to ask them all." He turned back to Stone. "Okay. Questions later. Action now. What do you want me to do? How can I help find Jason, and find whatever did this to those people?"

Stone's answering expression held frank respect. He found himself suddenly reminded of a friend he hadn't thought of in a

156 |

long time—a mundane professor who had died helping him deal with another magical threat shortly after he'd arrived in America. Like Lopez, Tommy Langley had been scared to death, his whole world turned upside-down by the knowledge that the magical world existed, but both men had put aside that fear, squared their shoulders, and stepped up to fight for the people they loved. Stone didn't know if he himself would have been able to do that.

"Thank you, Stan," he said softly. "You don't know how much it means to me to have someone willing to help. I was beginning to feel very alone down here."

Lopez's face took on the resolute aspect of the career cop. "Jason's family, Dr. Stone. And you're his friend. That's good enough for me. Now what do you want me to do? I've got a bunch of vacation time banked—I can take a couple weeks off so I can focus on this completely. Just tell me what you need."

For the first time in what felt like days, Stone smiled. It was a small, brittle thing, but it was genuine. "The first thing I need is for you to stop calling me 'Dr. Stone.' If we're going to be working together, formality seems a bit—counterproductive."

| CHAPTER EIGHTEEN

"**O**kay," Lopez said. "So, where do we start?"

"Damn good question." Stone eyed the last slice of pizza and tried to decide whether he was still hungry. "I suppose I should start by asking you if you can do anything to help run a bit of interference with Casner and his lot. I assume I've managed to convince you that I didn't have anything to do with any of those murders, including Lindsey's?"

Lopez shrugged. "I already believed you when you said you didn't do it. But if you were anybody else, the whole magic thing would make me *less* inclined to believe you. I'm guessing some of the stuff you can do includes things like turning invisible and—what do they call it—teleporting?"

"Invisible, yes. Teleporting, no. Except by using carefully prepared gateways, and there aren't any around here."

"But you could have gotten out of custody if you'd wanted to?"

"Easily. Even more easily if I didn't care who I hurt."

"So why didn't you? Get out, I mean—not hurt anybody."

"Because I don't do things like that," Stone said. "They had perfectly legitimate reasons for assuming I might be involved, especially in Lindsey's case." He sighed. "Would I have let them put me in prison? No. Escaping would have caused me a significant amount of inconvenience, but being incarcerated for life for something I didn't do would have been worse. But as long as they were playing straight with me, I was willing to go along." He paused,

R. L. KING

remembering how close his last encounter with the police had been. "So, can you keep Casner off our backs without telling him anything he doesn't need to know?"

"I'm not sure," Lopez said. "But if you're with me, I can vouch for you. Might be a good idea to stick together. From what you're telling me, this thing wants to fuck you over hard. It's not a good idea for you to be alone with anybody else."

Stone bowed his head. If only he'd thought of that two days ago, Lindsey would still be alive.

Lopez frowned. "You're saying these things—what did you call them?"

"I didn't. I don't have a name for them yet."

"Whatever the hell they are—you said they can possess people? Take them over, like *Invasion of the Body Snatchers* or something?"

Stone had to give Lopez credit: like Jason, once he decided to accept the initial premise of magic, he seemed willing to at least make an attempt to work with the details. "Yes, and apparently with ease."

"Then how do you know they aren't possessing me right now?"

"Excellent question. I know because they have a telltale aura that, now that I know what I'm looking for, I can spot. I've been periodically scanning you for it."

Lopez frowned, obviously trying to decide how he felt about being "scanned" without his knowledge. "How do I know they aren't possessing *you*?"

"You don't. Though I can make a couple of educated guesses as to why they aren't: first, mages, especially ones of my power level, are extremely difficult to possess, mentally influence, or otherwise muck about with their minds. We learn mental defenses early in our training, and I've always been particularly strong in that regard. Second, I don't think if I were being possessed, I'd be able to do magic as easily as I can..." He trailed off, his gaze suddenly focusing on something far off in the distance.

"Something wrong?" Lopez asked.

Stone didn't answer for several seconds; when he finally did, he sounded distracted. "You may have just given me an idea." He switched back on. "So far, I've only interacted—at least that I know about—with two of these things when they were possessing a human being: Lindsey, and the boy at Bart's Books who tried to strangle me. I need to talk to him, by the way, if you can manage that. At any rate, they both had two things in common."

"What are those?" Lopez looked perplexed as he tried to keep up with Stone's careening train of thought.

"First, they either didn't speak at all, or else they sounded— odd. When Lindsey spoke to me while she was possessed, her voice didn't sound like her own." Stone made a deliberate effort to wall off both his feelings for and his guilt about Lindsey, focusing only on the facts. He could grieve later—and he would, no doubt to the accompaniment of copious amounts of alcohol, morose music, and days of solitary brooding. But now, he had to think clearly. "Second, neither of the victims remembered anything about what happened when they were possessed. Both of them, as soon as the entity vacated their bodies, acted as if they had no idea what they had been doing when they weren't driving."

"So—what's that mean?"

"It means I have a hypothesis that when they're possessing a human, they're fully in control, to the point where they can't access the human's mind or memories beyond some minimal comprehension of things like movement, speech, and spoken language."

"I still don't get it," Lopez said. "Sorry, I'm still pretty new at this."

"Quite all right," Stone said. He was already feeling his mind engaging with much greater clarity than when he'd been stuck with only his own thoughts for company. "You're helping me work it out as I go. What I'm trying to say is, I don't think these things are capable of using their hosts' higher mental processes. I've dealt with other similar entities that *are*—they can take over a human and create sort of a symbiotic relationship where they can pass

R. L. KING

flawlessly at whatever that human did in society. But these are different. They're more versatile in that they can hop from one body to another, but they have to be careful about who they interact with to avoid giving themselves away."

"And that helps us how?"

"I'm just wondering about something," Stone said. He rounded on Lopez, his eyes alight with purpose. "Tell me: when someone calls into the police department to report something, is the call recorded? Does it work like when someone calls 911?"

"It's recorded," Lopez said. "Why?"

"Is there any chance you could convince Casner to let you listen to the recording of whoever called in to report Lindsey's death?"

Finally the light dawned. "Ah, I get it. You want to hear if the voice sounded weird."

"Exactly. If it did, then that will fill in another piece in our puzzle."

"I'll give him a call tomorrow," he said. "I think he's off shift now, and I don't think we want to start dealing with somebody new at this point." He began gathering the pizza box and other dinner items to take them to the kitchen. "Anything else we can do tonight?"

Stone considered. "Yes, but you'll have to trust me a bit more if I'm to do it."

Lopez stopped. "Why's that?"

"I'd like to put up a—sort of block on your mind, to make you less attractive to anything that might fancy taking your body for a joyride."

"A block?" Lopez's eyes flashed fear and a little suspicion. "You mean like, mess with my mind?"

"Sort of," Stone said. His tone was understanding: he knew fully how much of a frightening thing it was to have anyone else—even someone you trusted with your life, and he didn't think he and Lopez had quite reached that point yet—poking around in your mind. "Not so much mess with it as put a wall around it to protect you from outside influence."

Lopez frowned. "Can you guys read minds?"

"No. That's one thing we can't do. Best we can do is get impressions, and any mundane who's skilled at reading facial expressions and body language can probably do it just as well."

"Mundane? Is that what you call us?"

"Sorry," Stone said, a little embarrassed. He normally didn't use that word around the uninitiated, since it tended to offend people. He realized just how tired he must be, despite his newfound surge of energy. "Non-magical people, then."

Lopez took a deep breath. "What would I have to do?"

"Nothing. Just let me concentrate for a few seconds, and don't resist. You won't feel anything."

"I can resist?"

Stone nodded, and didn't miss the trace of hope in Lopez's tone. "Probably not successfully, but mages can't just go around making changes to people's minds without expecting some resistance. I'd wager that as a veteran policeman, your mind is probably already at least somewhat resistant to influence."

Lopez didn't answer for several moments. "Okay," he finally said. "If it'll help, I'll do it."

The process didn't take long. Stone stood in front of Lopez, fixed an intense gaze on him, and brought one hand up to hover an inch or so away from Lopez's forehead. A few seconds later, he backed off. "There. That's done. And a relief: it means I don't have to re-scan you every time you leave the room. Though I probably still will, just to be completely sure."

Lopez touched his forehead. He blinked a couple of times, then shook his head. "Nope, don't feel a thing. You sure you did it?"

"Quite sure."

"I'll have to take your word for it, I guess." He went over and sat back down in his recliner. "Do you have a plan for what you want to do next, aside from me getting Pete to let me listen to that message?"

"Yes, but it's not something we can do tonight, since it's too close to dark." At Lopez's questioning look, he said, "I keep hearing things about Creek Road being the center of a lot of local urban legends of the supernatural variety. That's also where that first body was found. I want to take a look around there and see if I can find anything interesting."

"Creek Road?" He frowned. "You mean like Char Man and shit? Those are just stories that kids and stoners tell each other. I'm not even from Ojai and I've heard 'em for years."

Stone raised an eyebrow. "*Magic* is just a story that kids tell each other, remember? When you play in my world, you have to look at urban legends in a whole new light."

"Wait." Lopez leaned forward. "You mean Char Man might be…real?"

"No idea. I doubt it, honestly. But the fact that all those legends and stories center around there tells me there's quite likely *something* magically interesting in the area. And I want to see if I can find it."

He stood. "I don't think there's much else we can do tonight— I'll be honest with you, the last couple of days have taken quite a lot out of me. I'm trying to keep going, but I think I need a good night's sleep if I'm to be worth anything tomorrow. In the meantime, think of anything you might be aware of about odd stories in the area, unexplained crimes—anything you think could possibly be supernaturally related. You never know what might spark an idea."

Lopez nodded. "I'll do that. And yeah, you do look kinda like hell, if you don't mind my saying so." He started to say something else, then put a hand up. "Wait a sec. Where are you staying again?"

"I've got a small house I've rented for a week in Ojai. Why?"

"I'm just thinking, if we're going to be working together, it might be easier—and safer—to stick together, like I said before. I've got a spare bedroom—why don't you just stay here? Now that my ex is gone, I've got the place to myself."

Stone considered. On the one hand, he valued his privacy—but on the other, he'd had quite enough of his own company lately to satisfy him for the foreseeable future. And Lopez was right: even aside from the security angle (nobody could accuse him of murdering anyone in their sleep if Lopez could vouch for his whereabouts, and the wards he'd placed on the man's mind meant a repeat of the situation with Lindsey was unlikely), if they were going to be working together it made sense not to have to keep making the commute back and forth between Ojai and Oak View. It wasn't far by Stone's Bay Area standards, but it still took time that could be better spent. "I'll take you up on that," he said. "I'll pack up in the morning, settle up the house, and come over here after, if that's all right."

"Great. That'll give me some time to clean up a little." He grinned, but almost immediately looked serious again. "Do you think we're gonna find Jason alive? And find whatever it is that's doing these killings? Do you think you can deal with it if you *do* find it?"

Stone gave his answer careful consideration. "I think Jason is alive," he said at last. "And I think, given enough time, I'll be able to track down the thing that's responsible for the murders."

"And deal with it?"

"That part, I don't know. I don't know how powerful it is, and I don't know why it's here."

"Can you—call in more mages?"

"I wish I could," Stone said softly. "But as I said, there aren't that many around, and most of them aren't suited to this kind of work. Those I know who might be helpful aren't currently within my reach." That was true: aside from Verity being out of communication somewhere in Vermont with fellow mage Sharra, his old friend Madame Huan was in China hunting down magical ingredients. He'd had no contact with the enigmatic gray mage Harrison for over a year. And Stefan Kolinsky, the black mage with whom he traded useful tidbits of information and occasional favors, while he might prove somewhat helpful for research, wouldn't leave his spider's web in the Bay Area for anything short of a potential magical catastrophe. A few murders in a small town and a missing friend wouldn't even rate his notice.

"So we're on our own, is what you're saying."

"It very much appears that way." He sighed and stood. "But we will do this, and I will do everything in my power get Jason back and stop these killings. You have my word on that. I'll see you tomorrow, and we'll get started."

Lopez got up too. "You got it, Al. Get some rest."

Stone winced, but said nothing.

| CHAPTER NINETEEN

When Stone showed up at Lopez's house around ten the following morning, the cop was waiting for him. "You look better today," Lopez said. "You get some sleep and get moved out okay?"

Stone nodded. He had, in fact, gotten a reasonable night's sleep—he must have been truly exhausted, because he didn't even have any nightmares about Lindsey's bloody body. It was the part after he left the house that hadn't gone so well.

In retrospect, he should have simply surrendered the house over the telephone. Instead, he'd gone back to the real estate office to do it in person. The door had been locked, a hand-lettered sign tacked on it stating the office would be closed for the next couple days in observance of the tragic death of their friend and colleague.

Glancing inside, Stone had seen Lindsey Cole's older fellow agent, Florence, sitting at her desk looking miserable. She'd looked up, met Stone's eyes, and paled, quickly getting up and hurrying to the back. He hadn't waited to see if she'd return. He didn't know whether he was imagining the stares from passersby as he walked back to his car or if they were real, but either way they disturbed him.

"I got some good news and some bad news," Lopez was saying, his expression sober.

What now? "Oh?"

"The bad news is there's been another murder."

Stone stiffened. "When? Where?" He quickly scanned Lopez, but his blue aura (fewer angry red streaks now) was still free of any green interlopers.

"They found the body out on Rice Road, in the river bottom. Middle-aged lady named Linda Solis. She never came home from a trip to visit a friend, so her family got suspicious. Guy walking a dog found her body in some bushes. They think she was killed sometime yesterday afternoon."

"How was she killed?" Stone asked, irrationally relieved that there was no possible way they could suspect him of this one, since he'd been in a jail cell at the time.

"Stabbed several times in the chest and abdomen. Messy."

"And what's the good news?"

I went up to the station in Ojai this morning, and Pete let me listen to the call."

"And?"

"You were right. It was the freakiest thing: it was a woman, but the voice was raspy as hell, like maybe she'd just smoked a whole pack of cigarettes and followed it with a Drano chaser. And the phrasing was weird too: slow and kind of—*off*. Like the inflections were all wrong."

Stone nodded. "Good. Did Casner give you any trouble? Did you have to tell him you were working with me?"

"He didn't ask. I kinda think he doesn't want to know. He's spooked, Al. Like I told you, I've known him a long time. He's a good cop, but he's not too comfortable with the weird shit. He wants things to make sense."

"Don't we all?" Stone said with a raised eyebrow.

"Yeah, but I get the feeling your definition of 'sense' covers a lot more territory than Pete's does. Or mine, up until yesterday."

Something occurred to Stone. "Did you get any other details about this new murder?"

"Like what?"

"Was there a sort of—crude circle of blood around the body? It might have been hard to see if the investigators weren't specifically looking for it."

Lopez frowned, squinting. "I didn't ask. Is that important?"

"It could be. If you could find out—and also if there was one around the first victim—I'd appreciate it. What was her name, by the way? And did they ever identify the male victim on Creek Road?"

Lopez pulled a small leather-covered notebook from his back pocket and flipped through it. "First vic was the sixteen-year-old girl, Ashley Reed. Local kid, family's been in the valley forever. Good student, cheerleader, popular. Nobody had any good idea of what she was doing wandering around the Arbolada at that time of night. Second one—turns out he wasn't a drifter after all, which is what they thought originally. He was a twenty-seven-year-old male named Paul Gardo. Local lowlife, stoner type. Nobody called him in as missing because his roommates said he tended to wander off for days to 'find himself' in the wilderness. 'Finding himself' apparently being a euphemism for 'smoking lots of weed.'"

Stone nodded. "All right, then. Let me just bring a few things in and if you're ready, we'll get started."

An hour later, they were in Lopez's pickup, driving along Creek Road toward Ojai. "Anywhere in particular?" Lopez asked. "Or you just want me to drive around?"

"Just drive around for now," Stone said, only half-listening as he magically scanned the area.

Lopez had advised against taking Stone's BMW, and had, in fact, suggested that he put it in the garage. "People around town are definitely getting spooked over these murders," he said, "And a lot of 'em know you were a person of interest. Having a distinctive car parked out in the open might not be the wisest thing right now."

Before they'd left, Stone had insisted on spending the time it took to put up a ward around Lopez's house. Lopez had trailed behind him as he walked the perimeter muttering under his breath and pausing near each door and window to concentrate for several seconds before moving on. "This is just weird as hell," the cop had said.

Stone shrugged. "Just a precaution. It will keep most things from getting in—the ones it can't stop, it will at least take a reasonable bite out of. And I'll know if anybody tried to get in while we were away."

"Magic burglar alarms. What'll they think of next?"

It was a beautiful day, with a cloudless, bright blue sky overhead. Creek Road was two lanes wide, several miles long, and wound its tree-lined way past neatly kept homes and long stretches of unoccupied forest. They passed several bicyclists, a few walkers, and a couple of teenagers riding horses.

"Anything yet?" Lopez asked as he slowed down to go around a small knot of brightly-colored cyclists.

"Sort of. I'm getting some definite impressions of magic, but they're fleeting. I think we're going to need to park and hike around a bit. Too many people here. Is there a particular place the urban legends focus on more than any other? I remember reading something about a bridge—"

"Yeah, we're almost to that now. It's over by Hermosa Road. There's a bridge, and right near it is a campground. A lot of the folks who claim to have seen Char Man say it was near the campground."

"Let's start there, then."

They reached the campground in another five minutes. Lopez parked the truck in the large, mostly empty lot, and climbed out. He pulled two daypacks from the back seat and offered one to Stone.

"What's this?"

"You don't get outside much, do you?" Lopez asked, amused.

Stone raised an eyebrow. "Why do you ask?"

He looked the mage up and down, taking in his black Pink Floyd T-shirt, faded jeans, and black Doc Martens. "Well, first of all, you're so pale you look like you'll spontaneously combust in the sunlight. Even if you don't, you're gonna fry without a hat or sun protection. At least you brought sunglasses and left that coat home. That's a start, I guess." He waved the pack. "You've got sunscreen, water, and energy bars in there, along with a flashlight and a topo map of the area."

"You make it sound like we're setting out for a long journey, not just wandering about in the forest for a couple of hours." Stone protested, but he took the pack nonetheless. He removed his own black duffel from the truck, unzipped both, and transferred his magical paraphernalia to the backpack.

Lopez shrugged. "Better safe than sorry." He wore a long-sleeved blue chambray shirt, jeans, his cowboy boots, shades, and a wide-brimmed cowboy hat. His service pistol was attached to his belt in a holster. "Oh, right." He reached into the back seat and tossed Stone a hat much like his own.

"No. Thank you, that's quite all right. I'll take my chances," he said, tossing it back. He did, however, dig out the sunscreen and apply it liberally.

"Suit yourself." Lopez grinned and put the hat back in the truck. "Lead on, then. I'll follow and make sure you don't trip over any mountain lions while you're looking at magic butterflies or whatever."

Stone didn't even bother trying to defend his nonexistent woodsman skills—it would have been pointless, and they both knew it. Instead, he hoisted the pack onto one shoulder and set off toward the campground proper.

For the next hour, Stone tramped through the trees with Lopez a few steps behind him, looking for anything odd in the area's magical signature. It became a progression: pick a direction, walk for five minutes or so, stop and take bearings, and then re-orient and repeat. As was often the case when he was doing this kind of work, Stone lost track of both time and exactly where he was.

Finally, Lopez stopped. "Al?"

Stone paused, finishing the reading he was doing, and then turned back. "Yes?"

"You realize we've been out here for over an hour, right?"

He looked surprised, and glanced around at their unfamiliar surroundings. "Have we?"

Lopez shook his head, exasperated. "Are all mages like you? You're like a damn cat following a mouse or something. Do you even know where we are?"

"No idea," Stone said cheerfully.

"And how would you propose to find your way back to the truck?"

He shrugged. "Easy answer: follow you. Slightly more entertaining answer: turn invisible and levitate myself high enough until I can see the road, then go that way."

Lopez stared at him. "You're kidding, right?"

"Not at all. That's what I usually do when I get caught up in what I'm doing and forget to pay attention to where I am."

"Oo-kay," Lopez said in a long-suffering tone. "So, more to the point: have you found anything? Or are we just wandering around out here because we really like mosquitoes?"

Stone crouched down, his tone growing once more serious. "It's hard to say. There's definitely *something,* but it's not just here. I'm getting impressions of something more interesting—" He paused, closed his eyes, and turned himself around until he faced roughly southeast. "—that way," he finished, pointing. "But it's not close. I think it would be a considerable hike, judging from how weak the signal is." He opened his eyes and rose to his full height. "Is there anything over in that direction?"

Lopez pulled out his map without bothering to remind Stone that he had one in his own pack. He unfolded it and spread it out on a fallen log. "Gets pretty remote over there," he said, pointing. "See—there's a fire road, but mostly it's just a whole lot of trees."

Stone studied the map. "Can we go up there? Is the road accessible?"

"Should be. It'll take a while, though."

"Then we'd best get started."

They weren't as far from the truck as the amount of time they'd spent walking might have suggested, due to the winding, circuitous route Stone had taken while seeking magical traces. They got back to it in a half-hour, and Lopez pulled onto Creek Road again, continuing back toward Ojai. After about a mile, he turned right onto a small unmarked road.

"Keep an eye on that map," he told Stone. "I don't get out here very often, and these roads can get a little tricky."

Stone did as instructed, occasionally glancing up to get a quick magical look around. Lopez soon turned on to another road, and the truck jounced and shuddered along over the uneven, intermittent paving. "You sure about this?" he asked Stone.

"I'll let you know."

He grinned. "Good thing we *didn't* bring that fancy ride of yours, huh?"

Stone merely grimaced in reply.

They drove for another half-hour, making yet another turn onto yet another road. This one abandoned all pretense at pavement; it was little more than a wide, rutted dirt path occasionally overgrown with clumps of tall weeds.

"I hope we don't blunder into any freelance pot farms out here," Lopez said as one of the tires hit a pothole that nearly bounced both him and Stone into the headliner. "Most of the hippies around this area are pretty mellow, but occasionally you'll get your antisocial types who have an objection to anybody coming to visit."

Stone wasn't listening. He'd mostly given up on reading the map at this point. "We're getting closer," he said in a distracted tone. "It's getting stronger."

They reached a crossroads; the terrain ahead was growing more thickly forested in both directions. "Left, right, or straight?" Lopez asked.

Stone closed his eyes for a moment. "Right."

Lopez nodded, swinging the truck around. "I sure as hell hope you know what you're doing," he said. "And I'm really glad I filled up this morning."

The dirt road narrowed even more as it snaked through the thick trees on either side. Stone sat silent in the passenger seat, head bowed slightly, eyes closed. He paid no attention to the twists and turns as Lopez slowed down to keep the big vehicle on the road. It was barely wide enough for a single lane, the branches of the old trees forming a sun-dappled canopy over their heads.

"Here," Stone said suddenly, his head snapping up. They'd just negotiated a particularly sharp switchback and were heading down a gentle grade. "Stop here."

Lopez pulled the truck off the road as much as he could. There wasn't really room to park without more than half of the truck still poking out into the lane itself. "You sure?" he asked. "This isn't—"

Stone was already getting out. He stood for a moment, eyes closed, then grabbed his pack from the seat. "I can feel it," he said. "It's not too far from here. It's strong. I think we're near a ley line."

"A what?"

"A sort of—natural conduit of magical energy," he said, already heading into the trees. "Think of is as a power line, only magical."

Lopez hurried after him. "So, what's that mean? Are there a lot of these things around?"

"They're all over the earth," he said. "I don't think there are many around this area, but I don't have my map that shows them. And as for what it means: performing any sort of magic on or near a ley line gives it extra power. You can do things that you might normally not be able to do. And if you can find a place where two or more of them intersect, the power goes up considerably." He scrambled down a slope, struggling to stay upright as his boots slid on the carpet of dead leaves that covered the whole area, and plunged into a copse of trees. Lopez followed.

Stone kept up a quick pace for another ten minutes, moving unerringly through the forest. There was something here, he could tell. Without a ritual he wouldn't be able to get the exact nature of it, but he was certain it was related to the energy he'd picked up when he'd examined the site of Ashley Reed's murder—the same energy that had led him to the barn and Paul Gardo's body. He didn't even turn back to see if Lopez was still behind him, though he could hear the man crunching through the leaves a few yards back.

As he continued, the energy in the forest began to change. At first he didn't feel it: it was similar to what a person might feel if the ambient temperature around him was gradually increased a degree at a time. The fact that his breath was coming harder and his limbs felt heavier was probably just due to the fact that he'd been pushing himself too hard and his body was telling him to slow down. But Lopez's breathing sounded the same as before, and he hadn't slowed. It couldn't be—

Abruptly he stopped. Lopez nearly barreled into him from behind. "What?" the cop demanded. "Why are you—"

Stone held up a hand. "I need to check something." He pulled off his sunglasses and swiped a hand over his forehead. It came away wet, and his T-shirt was sticking to his shoulder blades. Something was going on here. He looked over at Lopez, who was watching him with concern. He looked a little tired, but he wasn't panting or sweating.

"You okay?" Lopez asked. "You look a little overheated."

"I'm all right." He pulled a water bottle from his pack and took a long drink, still breathing hard. "Can't you feel it?"

"Feel what?" He frowned. "You *sure* you're all right?"

Instead of answering, Stone shifted fully to magical senses. There was no doubt about it: something was wrong with the arcane energy in the area. Instead of the ordered patterns and bright, clear auras of the healthy earth and trees that normally characterized a natural area like this, the currents of magic were muddy, distorted, somehow *ill*. Something had happened here that had disrupted the very astral energy of the entire region. Just being in it was making Stone feel queasy.

"Al, buddy, tell me what's going on." Lopez's voice held concern and nervousness.

Stone took a deep breath. "There's something wrong here. Magically."

CHAPTER TWENTY

"What's that mean? Like somebody died here or something?" Lopez started looking around as if expecting to see dismembered body parts strewn across the mulch of dead leaves.

"No. It's far larger than that. A mere murder—or even more than one—wouldn't be enough to cause a disruption like this. Whatever happened here, it was either quite large, or it went on for a very long time." He took a couple deep breaths and let them out slowly. Normally, this kind of thing would be like catnip for his professional curiosity. He had never seen anything like this in all the years he'd been practicing magic. Now, though, he was having a hard time keeping his concentration straight.

"So it's—what—some kind of magical pollution?"

"That's a very good way to put it, yes." Stone took another drink from his water bottle and swiped sweat and damp hair off his forehead again. He forced himself to think. "I was right about a ley line running through here. That would explain why Ojai has been subjected to so many supernatural events: magical things have an affinity for ley lines, and tend to gravitate toward them."

"Is that bad?" Lopez asked.

"Not in and of itself. A lot of populated areas exist near ley lines. Usually the magical and mun—er—non-magical worlds don't interact much. A person would have to be at least somewhat magically aware to even notice anything at all, and even then most interactions are harmless. But this—" He made a wide, sweeping gesture to take in the area around them. "—this is different. This is—*corrupt.* That's the best way I can describe it."

"Is this what you were looking for?" The cop sounded dubious as he looked around. "I mean—everything looks fine to me. No weird, twisted trees or three-headed squirrels or anything like that—"

"I don't think this is new." Stone slowly turned around, scanning the area. "It feels like it's been here for a long time. I can't explain it, exactly, but it does. It feels like black magic, but not the kind that I'm familiar with."

"Wait—you know black magic?" Lopez's brows arched suspiciously.

Stone shook his head, holding up a hand to forestall his protests. "I don't practice it. But I'm familiar with its methods." With an obvious effort, he gathered himself. "Come on. I don't have time to explain it all now. I want to see if I can find the source of this."

Lopez eyed him. "You look like you're about to pass out. Are you sure you can do this?"

He nodded. "It's uncomfortable, but I don't think it's harmful. Like I said, it's old. I think it was very potent once, but magical power wanes over time."

"What are we looking for, then? At least let me help."

"I don't know. If I had to guess, I'd say—some sort of ceremonial area, or a graveyard, or—I've no idea, really. Something manmade, though, almost certainly."

"Okay. How about if we split up and look around a little? Keep each other in sight, but we can cover more ground that way."

Stone wasn't happy about that idea, but it made sense. "All right. But keep close. If there *is* something dangerous up here, I can't protect you if you're too far away. And if you see anything even the slightest bit odd, call me right away. Don't approach it or examine it too closely first."

Lopez nodded, looking apprehensive. After a moment, he picked a direction and moved off.

Stone paused for a few seconds, closing his eyes again to see if he could get even a slight sense of which direction he was looking for. He swallowed a couple of times, pushing back the growing nausea with an effort of will. *You're not ill,* he told himself firmly. *Just get on with it.* His head felt light and fuzzy, like he'd had a couple of strong drinks. *Just focus—*

There. Just a brief impression, but it was enough to give him a direction. He glanced back to make sure he could still see Lopez, then started off the other way.

The area was wild: he doubted that anyone, aside from the fire department crews that kept the roads passable, had been here in years. He thought about what Lopez had said about freelance pot farms—this would definitely be a good place to put one, if you didn't want it found. With grim amusement, he wondered what sort of experience one might get from smoking marijuana grown in the shadow of what was looking increasingly more like a corrupted section of a ley line. In his university days he had briefly experimented with hallucinogens (it wasn't uncommon for young mages to do so, to see what effect an "expanded consciousness" had on their magical abilities) but had long since sworn off them after a particularly vivid bad trip and had no desire to renew the acquaintance.

He kept moving forward. The feeling, whatever it was, was getting stronger. Even with only a fraction of his magical awareness active, he felt like the world was pressing in on him from all sides. He had never been scuba diving, but he imagined the feeling of constant pressure must be similar. It was making his skin crawl. He paused a moment to catch his breath.

Just go... The thought bubbled up in his head. *Just get out of here. Now. This is dangerous. Get out while you still can.*

An enormous oak tree loomed ten yards or so ahead of him, its trunk as big around as a small car. It was larger than the others around it, as if it had grown strong by sapping the vitality from them. Stone's unease increased with each step he took closer to it. "Stan!" he called. "I think I've found what I'm looking for!"

Run away...get away...it's coming for you...you'll die if you stay...

Lopez came hurrying back over, crunching through the carpet of leaves and dry twigs. He stopped next to Stone, who was standing still, staring at the tree. "What?"

"No..." he whispered. His heart was pounding; his voice shook. "No. We've got to get out of here—"

Lopez's eyes widened. "Al? You okay?"

He gripped Lopez's arm in a tight hold. "Come on. We need to go."

"Wait—you said you just found what you were looking for. What—"

"Come *on*." Somewhere on a deep level, Stone knew something had taken hold of him, but it was right: it wasn't safe to be here. It wasn't safe for either of them. Whatever was here needed to stay here, untouched and undiscovered.

He pulled hard on Lopez's arm, trying to lead him away. If the man refused to go, he'd have to just leave on his own. Lopez didn't understand, but—

His head rocked back as a sudden, sharp pain struck his face. Indignation rose, but then he realized that the sense of impending dread had ebbed away as if it had never come over him in the first place. He stared at Lopez, who was watching him with a fearful yet determined expression, his hand still raised.

Stone put a hand to his stinging cheek. "You slapped me."

"Yeah, and I'm gonna do it again if you don't get it together," he growled. "Something was eating at you. I could see it in your eyes. I thought you said you were hard to influence mentally."

Stone took a couple of experimental deep breaths. "Usually I am," he said slowly. Another breath. "Thank you."

"Sure, no problem. Now let's find whatever the hell this is and get out of here, okay?"

Stone nodded. Whatever the strange compulsion had been doing to him, it was no longer working. He still felt queasy and lightheaded and too hot, but the sense of panic was gone. After a moment of reinforcing his mental defenses, he pointed. "It's something about that tree there. See how it's much bigger than the others?" He moved forward slowly, ready to put up his shield if anything attacked them.

Nothing did. He approached the tree, taking in the enormous, ropy system of crisscrossing roots stretching out in all directions from its massive trunk. There was nothing particularly unusual or unnatural about its appearance, other than its size. It rose almost a hundred feet, easily dwarfing its neighbors, its branches spreading out in a vast, sweeping spread that blocked much of the sun.

"That thing's old," Lopez said in a low voice. "Looks like hundreds of years old. There's a lot of oaks around Ojai—the locals are passionate about them. I joke sometimes about how any year now they're gonna give 'em the vote. But I haven't seen too many *this* old."

Stone nodded, but he wasn't really listening. He edged closer to the tree, his magical senses fully active now, and examined it.

Oh, yes. This was the source of the corrupted energy, all right. Tendrils of it reached out from the roots and the earth beneath them, snaking sinuously through the air, around the other trees, and across the ground in every direction. He couldn't tell if it was the tree itself or something associated with it, but whatever it was, it started here.

Lopez put a hand on his shoulder and he jumped. "Just me," the cop said quickly. "You just went dead white. I thought you were gonna faint."

"No—just let me do this," he rasped.

"What are you trying to do?"

"There's something here," he said. He focused his arcane sight, trying to narrow down the source of the corrupt energy. "Look around the roots. See if you see anything." His voice came out rough through clenched teeth as he struggled against the nausea.

Lopez eyed him worriedly for a moment, but then crouched down and began examining the spaces between the enormous roots.

Stone did the same, moving in the opposite direction. He hoped to find what he was looking for soon—if there was even anything *to* find—because he knew he couldn't stay in the area for too much longer. The corruption—the pure unadulterated *wrongness* in the magical energy here—was reacting with his own magic like an insidious poison. Though he couldn't feel it doing him any actual harm beyond extreme discomfort, he had no idea if that would continue to be true. He could feel the psychic dread trying to worm its way back into his mind, but now that he knew it was there, it wasn't hard for him to block it. Small victories, at least.

"Hey!" Lopez called from the other side of the tree. "Al! Come over here! I think I found something."

Stone leaped up and hurried over to where he was kneeling near a particularly large confluence of roots. The cop had his flashlight out and was shining it into what looked like the space between two roots, each one as big around as a large man's thigh. Stone came up behind him, looked over his shoulder at what the beam had found, and then sagged, catching himself against Lopez's broad back.

"Whoa, whoa," Lopez caught him and lowered him down. "You okay?"

Stone was on his hands and knees, his back heaving as he struggled not to retch.

"Come on, lay down," Lopez said, trying to get him to roll over. "Just rest for a minute. Have some water."

Stone shook his head. This was it—what he'd been looking for. If he didn't examine it now, he wasn't sure he'd be able to later. He shoved himself back up to a kneeling position and leaned toward the opening. "Shine the light," he panted. "Hold it steady."

Lopez did as instructed, and Stone leaned in further until he was lying on his stomach, braced against the roots on either side of the hole. Lopez shifted the beam so it shone in over his shoulder.

The light illuminated a crevice carved into the earth, sheltered by the two large roots. It had smooth walls, suggesting that it might not have been created naturally, and measured around three feet from top to bottom and slightly less from side to side. The location of the tree, combined with the orientation of the crevice, the roots, and the upper branches of the tree, suggested it was well protected from weather and rain.

None of this, however, was what had captured Stone's attention. He held up his hand. "Let me have that flashlight," he said, distracted. He took it and shone it at a different angle, trying to get a better look at what he thought he'd seen.

At the back of the crevice was a wide earthen shelf that stretched about a foot out from the wall. Arrayed on it were a series of objects.

"What do you see?" Lopez asked. "I didn't get a good look."

Stone didn't reply. He moved the flashlight's beam around, sweeping it back and forth across the shelf. He blinked sweat out of his eyes, felt it dripping from his face into the crevice.

On the shelf was a series of what looked like large flat rocks, placed so they leaned against the back wall. There were three of them: two on the right and left, and a larger one in the center. They were all black, and all had some sort of strange writing on them in what looked like white paint. Just looking at the symbols increased Stone's growing unease.

In between them, like macabre table-setting decorations, were small piles of human bones, each one topped with a leering skull. These were surrounded by desiccated feathers and arrays of what looked like oddly-shaped beads. Taken as a whole, the tableau radiated corrupted magic like a tangible onslaught. Stone's entire body shook, a chill running through him despite the heat pouring off him.

R. L. KING

"Al, what the hell are you seeing down there?" Lopez demanded again, tapping his shoulder. When he still didn't answer, the cop grabbed him by the shoulders and pulled him up and back.

Stone didn't struggle. Lopez dragged him backward and lowered him to the leaf-covered ground. When he got a look at the mage's face, his own looked fearful. "Holy shit, man. I'm getting you out of here before you stroke out on me."

Stone shook his head. "No—just—I'll be all right." His words came out on a rush of air with no volume behind them.

Lopez pulled out a water bottle and offered it to him. "Here. Drink this. And tell me what you saw down there that freaked you out so bad."

"Wasn't—what I saw," Stone whispered. "Not entirely."

"What was in there? I saw some kind of shelf with some stuff on it—"

Stone fixed his gaze on Lopez. "You—don't feel it at all, do you?"

"Feel *what*?"

Stone closed his eyes, gathering his strength. He didn't like what he had to say next, but he didn't have a choice. "I need you to do something for me."

"Besides get you out of here, you mean?"

"No. I'm fine here. But—I can't get that close again. Do you have a notebook and a pen?"

"Yeah, but—"

"There are some—tablet sort of things in that space under the roots. Three of them. I want you to carefully—and I do mean *carefully*—transcribe what you see written on them. Please take as long as you need. It's vital that you get it right."

Lopez frowned. "There's writing in there? You mean like cave paintings or something, but on tablets?"

Stone nodded.

"Why don't we just get 'em out of there and take 'em with us?"

"No. Best to leave them here. I'm not sure I could be near them long enough to get them back to town. We'll just—mark where they are so we can find them again." He closed his eyes, then opened them. Now that he was away from the crevice, even just this short distance, he was feeling somewhat better.

"Why don't I just take some pictures of them?" He dug in his backpack and came up with a small camera.

Even as rotten as he felt right now, Stone had to grin. "Stan, my friend, remind me never to say another word about your over-preparedness thing." He considered. "I don't think I'd want to take these to be processed, though. Might be better to do the transcription."

"Wow," Lopez said, returning his grin. "You mages don't get with the times much, do you?" He held up the camera. "This is digital. It works with a home computer. You just plug it in and you can look at 'em on the screen."

Stone nodded. "Excellent. Take a few shots, but just to be safe, do the transcription, too. I've seen too many bits of electronic gear fail at inopportune times, and I don't fancy coming back here again right away without some preparation."

"Fine, fine. You just stay there and rest, and I'll—"

Suddenly, instantly, Stone sensed a flare of magical energy blooming behind Lopez. "Down!" he barked.

| CHAPTER TWENTY-ONE

L opez might no longer have been at the peak physical condition of his early days on the force, but his reflexes were still sharp as ever. He didn't question, just dropped to the ground, rolling onto his back in a single smooth motion. He was just in time to see something sail over him, though not to see what it was.

Stone, however, did see. A rock the size of a softball flew through the space occupied by Lopez's head a second earlier, slamming into a nearby tree trunk with enough force to carve a chunk out of its bark.

"What the hell—" Lopez shouted.

"Stay down!" Stone ordered. He had risen to a crouch next to Lopez and had already put up his shield around both of them, grateful that he'd remembered to charge up his focus rings last night. The odd thing about the corrupted energy emanating from the items under the big oak: they didn't seem to have caused any lessening of his power. He just had to use a lot more willpower to get to it. It was like trying to go to work when you had a raging case of the flu: it was doable, but it wasn't any fun.

Not that fun was any sort of consideration right now. Stone looked all around for more potential attacks. At the moment, no more rocks were forthcoming, but he didn't think that was going to last.

"What the hell is going *on*?" Lopez demanded again. He had obeyed Stone and stayed down, but had turned himself so he could look back toward where the rock had originated. "Is there somebody over there?"

"Technically, yes," Stone said grimly. "Hush! Let me concentrate."

Another rock flew from an unseen origin, this time off to his left, and slammed into the shield. Lopez's eyes widened. "How—" He had his hand on his gun, but hadn't drawn it yet.

"I'm shielding us," Stone said. "I can't do it for too long, though, so we're going to need to get out of here."

"Let's *go,* then!"

"Not yet. We need those photos. No time for the transcription. I'll keep you shielded—take the pictures. Quickly, but carefully. Make sure the writing is in focus."

Lopez sighed, but began crawling toward the roots, dragging his backpack with him. Stone followed him, rising to his feet as he moved. At least that way he'd make a better target, and as long as the shield was up they'd be safe. "Hurry," he urged as another rock struck the shield. It flared pink, then faded back to its normal nearly invisible contours.

Stone couldn't risk looking back at Lopez to follow his progress. He stood behind him, gaze scanning back and forth, magical senses at full awareness, trying to spot where the rocks were coming from. He couldn't. Either the invisible things at the barn had relocated here (which made sense—once the body was gone, any reason they would have to guard the place would be gone along with it), or something new was in play. Neither of these ideas filled him with confidence.

Something large and heavy crashed down on top of them with a loud cracking *THUD.* "*What was that?*" Lopez yelled, his head down in the crevice.

"Keep going!" Stone yelled back, staring at a branch the diameter of a child's torso that had smashed into the top of the shield. His hard, fast breathing wasn't coming entirely from the exertion of holding the shield: if it hadn't been protecting them, that branch likely would have crushed them both. These things, whatever they were, were getting serious.

As if the four murders so far weren't serious enough.

"Are you finished?" His voice shook a little. The power from one of the rings he was pumping into the shield to keep it up wouldn't last long; once it faded, he'd be forced to use his backup ring (which he didn't want to do) or his own power (which he *really* didn't want to do).

"Almost!"

Something rose up in Stone's peripheral vision, and he turned to face it. A section of the forest floor was moving. As he watched, a clump of dead leaves and twigs about three feet in diameter began whirling, rising up out of the ground to form a vaguely humanoid shape, a tiny tornado of viciously whipping leaves. It moved toward them, picking up more leaves as it went. It didn't get any larger, but with every foot closer it got thicker, denser. The wind rose to a shrill howl, the swirl of leaves crackling as it approached.

Stone shifted his concentration, struggling to form a spell past the distraction of the area's corruption. Behind him, he could sense Lopez backing slowly out of the crevice. Yelling something incomprehensible, like a martial artist about to break a stack of cinderblocks, he flung the spell at the leafy figure.

The magical energy tore the thing apart, scattering bits of leaves and twigs and pebbles in all directions. It screamed in indignation as what remained of its cohesion departed and the leaves fluttered back to the ground.

Stone roared in triumph—and realized a split second too late that the leaf-thing had been a diversion.

Another massive limb, this one even larger than the one that had slammed into the top of the shield, came barreling in from their right side. Stone flung out an arm and focused his power into shoring up that side of the shield to divert it, but even so it couldn't hold fully against a direct hit from something that heavy. It flared pink, then red, then disappeared. The branch, nearly all of its momentum expended in getting through the shield, crashed to the ground next to them with a force they could feel like a tiny earthquake.

"Holy *fuck!*" Lopez yelled.

Stone snatched up his pack. "Come on!" he ordered through his teeth. "We have to get out of here. Keep that camera safe and hold on tight!"

"What are we—" the cop began, but didn't have time to get the rest out as Stone grasped his arm and clamped on with far more strength than he should have been able to. A second later, they both rose off the ground.

Lopez, watching the carpet of leaves receding beneath his feet, tightened his own grip on Stone in near-panic. "What—"

"Shh!" he hissed, his face drawn from the effort of levitating them both and moving them away from the tree. They didn't have a shield now: if anything hit them hard enough to knock him out or even disrupt his concentration, they would fall. Maybe not to their deaths—not yet. But they had to go higher to get up over the trees.

"Look out!" Lopez yelled. "Three o'clock!"

Stone had no idea whose three o'clock he meant since they were facing different directions, but he took a chance and shifted them over to the left. Lopez's fingers dug into his arms as another chunk of tree limb arced up, missing them by scant feet, and fell gracefully back down to earth again.

They kept rising, tree branches and sharp prickly oak leaves tearing at their clothes and their exposed skin. The one positive in all this, Stone realized quickly, was that the farther they got away from the macabre tableau under the tree, the less he was affected by the nausea and disorientation caused by the corruption. Of course, now the exhaustion from maintaining the previous shield spell and levitating both himself and Lopez (who was no lightweight—like Jason, he was all muscle) was taking its place, but that would pass in time as soon as they got out of here.

If they got out of here.

"Go left!" Lopez called. He'd managed to clamp his right-hand grip onto Stone's shoulder instead of his arm, and was in the process of trying to do the same with his left.

"Your left or my left?" Stone rasped.

"The road's that way! I can see it!" Unable to free a hand to point, he jerked his head to his own left side.

Stone couldn't see where he was indicating, but once again he simply chose to trust him. He altered their direction, still scanning for any rocks or branches being flung their way. He couldn't see any. He wouldn't dare to hope that, as at the barn, the things were tethered to a particular site and couldn't move too far away from it. All he could do was keep concentrating.

"There's the truck!" Lopez called after a couple of minutes. "Go down!"

Stone, panting with exertion now, was only too happy to comply. His levitation spell was one of the easier for him to cast, but it was harder to carry others, and he'd never used it for such a long distance. Normally he employed it to get over walls or onto roofs, should the need arise—it had never been meant to serve as a means of transportation.

With another quick look around to make sure nothing was hurtling toward them, he began lowering them, and soon spotted Lopez's white truck parked halfway off the road. A moment later they touched ground, falling into a heap in the middle of the road about ten feet from the truck.

Lopez scrambled to his feet, scanning the skies for anything incoming. "Looks like we got away," he breathed. "Holy shit, what the hell have I gotten myself into?"

Stone hadn't bothered to get up. He lay in on his side, puffing like he'd just run all the way up here from Ojai. Like Lopez, his exposed skin was peppered with tiny scratches from the sharp little oak leaves they'd risen through; his black T-shirt had numerous small shredded holes. "Do you still have the camera?" he asked in a rough whisper.

"Right here." Lopez held it up from where it hung on a strap around his neck. He pulled it off, shoved it into his backpack, and tossed the pack into the back seat.

Then he stopped, stiffening.

As Stone watched in horror, Lopez turned back toward him, his shaking right hand inching toward the gun at his hip.

"Stan...?" With effort, he shifted to magical sight, and saw it instantly: a shifting green aura hovered around the cop's head. It didn't look quite like Lindsey's, though—instead of wreathing Lopez like a second aura, it moved and shifted as if trying to find its way inside.

If Stone hadn't been exhausted from his exertions, he would have cast some sort of spell—put up a shield, or telekinetically grabbed Lopez's arm to prevent him from reaching the gun. But his hesitation revealed something, something he wouldn't have noticed if he'd acted right away:

Lopez was fighting it.

The man's face was dotted with beads of sweat. His hand, which still hadn't reached the gun, shook as if he were straining against a nearly irresistible force. It stopped just above the weapon's grip, fingers twitching.

"Stan...?" Stone asked again. "Are you all right?" This was bad. Had he failed to put up a strong enough barrier around Lopez's mind? Or worse, was this thing simply potent enough to punch through his best effort? If the latter were true, they were both in trouble.

The green aura shifted again, and for a moment it seemed to settle more snugly around Lopez's head. His eyes flickered between their normal brown and the telltale red-orange glow.

His hand clamped spasmodically onto the gun's grip.

He pulled it halfway free of the holster.

Stone was struggling for the power to put up a shield when suddenly the green aura flashed and dissipated as if it had never been there at all.

Lopez's shoulders slumped. He loosened his grip on the gun and it dropped back into the holster.

"Are you all right?" Stone was still on the ground. He dropped the feeble shield, grateful he didn't have to keep it up any longer.

"I—" Lopez bent over, hands on his knees, panting. "What—the hell—*was* that?" His eyes flew open, and he stared at Stone in terror. "I felt something tryin' to get into my head! Did that thing—you said—" He paused to get his bearings. "It wanted me to—shoot you. I thought you said you put a block up—"

"I did." Stone let his breath out as he considered the implications. "I think it's more powerful up here. That's why it was able to get past my shielding. But Stan," he added, pushing himself up on an arm, "This is *good.*"

Lopez looked at him like he'd suddenly gone insane. "How the hell is this *good?* That thing almost made me shoot you!"

"The key word is '*almost,*'" Stone stated. "And that's why it's good. You threw it off."

"What? How?"

"If had to guess, probably because you're a cop. You've got a strong, trained mind. You're used to dealing with all sorts of mental influences. And—no offense—it's been my experience that most policemen are a bit...er...rigid in their thought processes. I think all of that helped you. At any rate, I'm glad you were able to do that. I'm not sure my shield would have been strong enough to stop you."

Lopez considered that a moment, then hauled Stone to his feet and slung the mage's arm around his neck. "Come on, let's get back home. And then you're gonna tell me what the hell all of that stuff up by the tree was about, right?"

Stone nodded, but didn't speak. Despite his confident words, Lopez's actions had spooked him. He'd have to keep a closer eye on the cop from now on. Just because the thing had failed once didn't mean it wouldn't try again.

He let Lopez drag him back to the truck and help him into the passenger seat, and spent most of the trip back to Lopez's house leaning against the window with his eyes closed and his head bowed.

| CHAPTER TWENTY-TWO

B y the time they got back to Oak View, Stone was starting to feel vaguely human again. He insisted on checking the wards he'd put up around Lopez's house before they went in, and was pleased to find that, at least as far as he could tell, nobody had tried to gain entry while they were away. He was also pleased to find no sign of green auras hovering around Lopez. He hoped his theory was correct.

A shower and fresh clothes mostly completed his transformation back from "half-dead cat" to "tired, sore, but otherwise mostly functional mage." When he emerged from his room and located Lopez, he found the cop in his office sitting at his home computer. He had the camera connected it to it with a cable and seemed to be waiting for something to finish.

"I really should get with the times," Stone said. "I suppose those things are useful in all sorts of ways."

Lopez nodded. "Yeah, for sure. They're getting more advanced every year. Though me, I mostly use mine to do my checkbook and play Solitaire. I just like gadgets."

"Please tell me you got something from the camera," Stone said. He wouldn't allow himself to hope: he'd been slapped upside the head too many times by Murphy's Law when he really needed something to go right, and the thought of making another trek up to the site of that malefic little shrine made his skin crawl. He knew they'd probably have to do it eventually, but not today.

"We'll know in a minute," Lopez said. "They're downloading." As if on cue, a little bell went off from the computer. "There we go." He hit a key and a progress bar began snaking its way across the screen.

"I must say," Stone said, pulling up another chair to take his place next to Lopez, "You're dealing with this whole business rather more calmly than I would have expected."

Lopez let out a long sigh. "You wouldn't say that if you could read my mind. Inside, I'm pretty much a little quivering ball of 'what the fuck just *happened* to me?'" He shrugged. "But you know, one of the things you learn in my line of work is that you have to roll with things, or you go crazy in a hurry. I've seen some pretty damn weird situations as a cop over the years. This is just another one in the series." He glanced up. "Okay, so this one's weirder than all the rest of them *combined,* but still. What good's it gonna do you or me or Jason if I lose it and can't be useful?"

Stone nodded. He could see why Jason respected this man so highly.

The progress bar went away, and a list of files popped up. "Okay, let's have a look," Lopez said, clicking on the first one in the list. "Fingers crossed."

For once, Murphy must have been on vacation. The first digital photo, of the leftmost of the three stone tablets, was perfect: well-lit and in focus, it showed the strange writing clearly. Stone hadn't realized he was holding his breath until now. He let it out. "Very nice," he said, nodding. "Well done."

They examined the rest of the photos in turn: there were twelve in total, and only three were unusable, probably blurred when Lopez had moved around while taking the picture. As it was, they had at least two clear shots of each of the tablets, and a couple that showed the whole tableau. Lopez grinned. "Not bad for being taken while scared shitless. I'll print these out for you." He stabbed a couple of keys and several minutes later handed Stone a stack of sheets with the images reproduced in neat grayscale. The mage spread them out on Lopez's desk and together they studied them.

"So—what the hell are we looking at here?" Lopez asked, squinting at the tiny pictographs on the black tablets.

"I have no idea," Stone said. "This isn't any sort of magical script I've ever seen before, and I'm not getting the uneasy feeling from the photos that I got from looking at the real thing. I was hoping it might look familiar to you."

Lopez shrugged. "It looks pretty old. If I had to make a totally wild-assed guess, I'd say maybe it's something from the Chumash. They were the local tribe that settled the area a long time ago. See the feathers and the beads? That looks kind of Indian, doesn't it?"

"How should I know?" Stone asked, raising an eyebrow. "You're the American."

Lopez gave him an indignant grin. "Hey, man, my people came from Mexico. And anyway, I spent the whole unit on the local Indians looking out the window and waiting for recess."

Stone chuckled. He studied another photo. "Is there anyone around here who might be able to give us more information?"

"Well, there's a museum in Ojai." Lopez glanced at the clock. "They might still be open, if you want to go today. Maybe somebody there knows, or can point us at somebody who does."

The museum, located downtown, was built in the same Spanish architectural style as the Arcade farther down Ojai Avenue. The main gallery area, featuring a series of photos and artifacts from the early days of the town, was empty as they entered save for a young woman wearing a name tag that read *Marcy—Guide*. "Welcome to the museum," she said with a smile.

"Thanks," Lopez said. Stone had suggested he do the talking, at least to start. "Kinda empty around here today."

She nodded ruefully. "It is. We were supposed to have a Cub Scout group this afternoon, but they canceled. Everybody's been a little nervous lately, what with—what's been happening." She glanced at Stone and her expression clouded, like she was trying to put something together in her mind.

Lopez quickly filled the silence. "Yeah, I can imagine. Hey, we were wondering if you could help us, though. We've got a little...project we were hoping somebody around here could shed some light on. Do you have anybody around who's familiar with old languages and cave paintings and that kind of thing?"

"Um—well, there's our director, Mr. Wheeler," she said.

"Is he here?"

"I think so, but he might be in a meeting right now—"

Lopez pulled out his badge wallet and flashed it. "We'd really appreciate it if he could spare us a few minutes," he said.

"Oh. Uh—of course. Just one moment, officer." With another sideways glance at Stone, she hurried out.

"I think we made the right choice," Stone murmured. "As soon as I open my mouth they're going to know who I am."

"Don't worry about it. The badge can get us past a lot of potential problems. And besides, this *is* relevant to an investigation, so we're not even lying to anybody."

A few moments later the young woman came back out and ushered them down a hall and into a cozily cluttered office. The man who sat behind the desk was about sixty, with thinning snow-white hair, a luxuriant mustache, and a weathered, tanned face. He smiled and motioned them to sit. "Welcome," he said. "Marcy said you had some questions for me. You're police officers?"

"I am," Lopez said, showing his badge. "This is Dr. Stone. He's the one with the questions."

"I'll do what I can to help, of course," Wheeler said.

"Thank you," Stone said. He opened the old briefcase Lopez had found and pulled out the sheaf of printouts. "What we're interested in is anything you might know about these. Who produced them, how old they might be, or anything else you think might be relevant."

Wheeler took the printouts, pulling a pair of reading glasses from his shirt pocket. He looked at the first one and Stone, watching him closely, saw him stiffen. "Where did you get these?" he asked, looking over the tops of his glasses at Stone.

Lopez answered. "That's not something we can discuss at this time, Mr. Wheeler." Stone didn't smile, but he wanted to. Lopez had been right: sometimes the badge *did* cut through a lot of difficulty. "Is there anything you can tell us?"

Wheeler returned his attention to the pages, studying each for several seconds before slipping them one after the other to the back of the stack. When he got to the end, he put them down. "I—don't know what to say."

Stone and Lopez both watched him silently, waiting.

He took a deep breath, shoving his glasses up to the top of his head. "I don't know where you got these, but I do hope that you'll be able to reveal their location when your investigation is complete. If these photos are genuine, they represent a significant find."

"What sort of find, Mr. Wheeler?" Stone asked. "Do you know who produced them?"

Wheeler took another breath, carefully considering his words. "That's the odd part." He put his glasses back on and shuffled through the stack, pulling out the best image of each of the three tablets. "This writing was obviously produced by the Chumash. It's consistent with the other examples of their written work."

"Why is that odd?" Stone asked. "Aren't they the major indigenous tribe for this area?"

"Yes, but—" he paused, his brow furrowing, and waved his hand over the images. "—this is all wrong for the Chumash. This looks positively—well—*sinister*. With the skulls and—are these human bones?" he asked as if he'd just noticed them.

"They're some kind of bones," Lopez said. "We didn't get a close enough look at them to tell if they were human, but I'm guessing since they were piled up under human skulls..." he let that trail off.

"You must contact the Native American authorities about this," Wheeler said. "This doesn't look like any Chumash burial site I've ever heard tell of, but if there are human bones there—"

"We will," Lopez assured him. "As soon as our investigation is complete. But for now, we need whatever answers you can give us."

"Can you read the writing?" Stone asked. "Do you have any idea what it's referring to?"

Wheeler shook his head. "I'm not familiar with the Chumash language, beyond a few words and being able to recognize it in written form. We have a few examples here at the museum, but mostly they're photographs of paintings on cave walls. I've never seen stone tablets like these." He peered at the pictures again. "This almost looks like some sort of shrine."

"That's what we thought too," Lopez said. "So if you can't read it, do you know of anyone who can?"

Wheeler thought about it, then nodded. "Let's see. I knew a couple who might, if anyone could. Unfortunately, one of them passed away last year, so she won't be able to help you. Sad, since she was one of the last known descendants of the Chumash in this area. The other is a retired anthropology professor from UC Santa Barbara named—uh—" he paused to leaf through a Rolodex on his desk "—ah! Here it is! His name is Dr. Matthew Garcia. He lives in Ventura now—I could give him a call for you if you like. I'm sure he'd be very interested in what you've got here."

"Thank you, Mr. Wheeler," Stone said. "We're grateful for your help."

"Wow," Lopez said. "That happened fast."

They were on the freeway headed toward Ventura in Lopez's truck. Stone had to chuckle. "Never underestimate the pathological curiosity of university professors when dealing with their subjects of interest," he said. "Trust me on that."

　　　　　　　　　　　　　　　　　R. L. KING

Dr. Matthew Garcia, once informed of a possible new specimen of Chumash rock writing, had nearly fallen over himself to invite the strangers to his home to discuss it. Even Wheeler had been surprised. "I guess it's a good thing Wheeler didn't connect you with the guy the police were questioning," Lopez said. "He might have been a little less willing to set up a meeting."

Garcia's home wasn't far from Downtown, a small green Victorian-style place on an older street. The door was answered by a plump, smiling woman in a housedress. "He's expecting you," she said, motioning them in and leading them down a narrow hall to a sitting area.

Dr. Matthew Garcia didn't rise when they came in; they could see from the folded wheelchair nearby that it wasn't a breach of etiquette. He looked to be in his mid-seventies, his thin body hinting at a more powerful frame in his youth. His eyes sparkled with anticipation. "Gentlemen. Come in," he urged, waving them toward a sofa. "Mrs. Teller, please bring our friends some refreshments."

"Pleasure to meet you, Dr. Garcia," Stone said, walking over to shake the old man's hand.

"You must be Dr. Stone," he said. "And this is Sergeant Lopez?" He chuckled. "I hope I'm not coming across as too over-eager, but if what Wheeler tells me is true, I am very excited to see what you have to show me. When you get to be my age, you can get away with a little impatience," he added, eyes twinkling.

Stone liked the man immediately. "Quite all right. We're eager to hear what you might be able to tell us about them." He pulled the printouts from the briefcase and handed them over.

Garcia took them with the care and anticipation of a child being handed a coveted but fragile new toy. He shifted the lamp next to his chair for better light, and immediately lowered his head to begin studying them.

Minutes passed in silence. Mrs. Teller returned with a tray bearing glasses of iced tea and some cookies; she placed it on the coffee table without a word, smiled, and departed. Lopez took a glass and a cookie, but Stone didn't move, his gaze still locked on Garcia.

Once, Lopez tapped Stone on the arm and made a wiggle-fingered gesture with both hands around his own head, followed by a questioning glance at Garcia. Stone, picking up his meaning, did a magical scan of the professor and then shook his head. Lopez looked relieved.

A full fifteen minutes passed before Garcia came up for air. For a second he looked startled to see that Stone and Lopez were still in the room, then he shook his head briefly. "Well…"

Stone leaned forward, waiting.

Another several seconds went by. "Well," Garcia said again. "This is…interesting. Interesting indeed. And very, very strange." He focused on Stone. "Where did you say these images came from?"

"We can't say right now, sir," Lopez said. "It's related to an ongoing investigation."

"That's a pity." Garcia shook his head. "I would give a great deal to be able to see these in person, if there's any chance of that."

"Can you tell us about them, Dr. Garcia?" Stone asked gently. "Can you read them?"

"I can read about half of what's here," Garcia said. "Enough to give me the basic idea of the meaning. But that's why it's strange. These were clearly produced by one or more members of one of the Chumash tribes, but—"

"But—?" Lopez asked.

"But," Garcia continued, "This is all wrong for the Chumash." He pointed at the first sheet, showing the leftmost tablet. "This appears to be some sort of—invocation. The first one here refers to a great wrong done to their people, and mentions something about frustration at their own people for failing to seek vengeance."

He slid that one to the back and pulled up printout showing the rightmost tablet. "These aren't in order. The two on the left and right appear to be sort of a—well, they seem to be explaining what they're doing, or perhaps justifying it. They call themselves something like "They Who Do What is Necessary."

He shuffled through the pages until he found one showing the middle, larger tablet. "This one is the actual invocation. They call upon—" he paused, squinting at the page "—something called 'He of Many Masks,' or 'He of Many Faces'—something like that. The pictographs are nonstandard, so I'm guessing a bit there." He looked up at Stone, and his eyes were very serious. "They call this 'He of Many Faces' and exhort him to seek vengeance upon the blood of those who have wronged them, for all of time. Blood and—" he squinted again "—something about entrails."

A chill ran through Stone. "This—He of Many Faces,'" he said softly. "Have you heard of him? Is he a Chumash deity, or some other supernatural being?"

Garcia shook his head. "No. Not that I'm aware of. That's what's so odd about this. You see, Dr. Stone, I don't know how much you know about the Chumash—"

"Almost nothing," Stone admitted.

"Well," he continued, "They were a very peaceful group. They weren't aggressive with other tribes in the area—mainly they were hunters, fishermen, and lived in harmony with each other and their surroundings." He shifted the papers again and held up the one showing a good shot of the skull-topped mound of bones. "This is not a Chumash construction. They wouldn't desecrate the bones of their people—or even their enemies—like this." Pointing at the base of the bone pile, he said, "It's hard to tell what this is on this printout: are these rocks?"

"They're some kind of beads," Lopez said. "Made out of shells, maybe, or polished stones."

Garcia nodded. "The Chumash people often buried their dead with ceremonial beads made from shells, so that part fits. But this is not a Chumash burial site. It looks as if the bones were brought here from somewhere else, and arranged for a particular purpose."

"Do you know what the purpose might be?" Stone asked.

"No. If it were another, more warlike tribe, I might suggest that it was some sort of medicine ceremony, with a focus of vengeance. The invocation on the tablet certainly suggests that they were trying to seek the favor of some sort of supernatural being and ask it to do their will by destroying their foes. I might almost say that the bones were part of a sacrifice. But none of that fits with the Chumash ways. They certainly never did human sacrifices. They were far too peaceful for something so brutal." He stared off into space for a moment, then started almost as if waking from a trance. "Oh!" he said, shuffling the papers. He pointed at one of the pictographs on the center tablet. "Very sorry, I misspoke before. See this here? This means 'blood,' all right, but not in the sense of what we have in our veins."

"What, then?" Lopez asked.

"Family," Garcia said, looking at each of them in turn. "Kin. Descendants." He took a deep breath, his excitement at what he was looking at warring with a clear disturbance about the subject matter. "In light of that, gentlemen, I would say that this is not only an invocation—it's a curse."

| CHAPTER TWENTY-THREE

"You want to stop for something to eat?" Lopez asked, glancing over.

Stone didn't reply. He'd been silent for the entire trip back to Oak View, his thousand-yard stare fixed on a point somewhere outside the truck's passenger window.

Lopez raised his voice a bit. "Hey! Earth calling Doctor Strange, Sorcerer Supreme."

Stone started. "Sorry. Just—thinking."

"Yeah, I figured that. Either that or you were ignoring me. What about?"

He sighed, running his hand through his hair. "What Dr. Garcia said."

"You mean the part about the curse? And you want to stop somewhere? I don't have much in the house, so it's either stop or order pizza again."

Stone shrugged. "Whatever you like." His gaze shifted back out the window. "And yes, the part about the curse."

"You think it's relevant somehow? I mean, come on—I can believe in magic now, because I've seen you do it and you saved my ass with it today. I can even believe that there's some kind of supernatural force that's taking over people and committing murders. But ancient Indian curses coming true? That stretches even *my* pretty flexible level of disbelief." He pulled the truck into the parking lot of a barbecue joint.

Stone didn't respond further until they'd found a seat in the back of the restaurant and placed their orders. "I don't know," he said at last. "Some of it fits surprisingly well."

"How so?"

"Do you remember what the professor called the entity they were trying to invoke?"

Lopez thought. "I don't remember, exactly...You with the Face or something like that, wasn't it?"

Stone raised an eyebrow. "He called it 'He of Many Masks' or 'He of Many Faces.'"

"So?"

"So," Stone said, "Doesn't that sound like a fairly accurate description of an extradimensional entity that can possess anyone it likes?"

Lopez stared at him. "*Day*-um," he said. "Shit, you're right."

Stone's mental wheels were turning again. "Stan—is there any way we could find out if the victims thus far were related in any way? Or at least if they had longtime ties to the area?"

"Maybe," he said. "Easiest way would be to check with Pete Casner and have him ask the families. I don't think he's going to be very forgiving if we start bothering the families of murder victims with questions about their ancestry."

"Can you do it without arousing too much suspicion?"

"Hell, at this point I can just tell him I'm working with you. I'll just spin it that you're a friend of Jason's, since he already knows that, and that I'm keeping an eye on you to make sure you don't do anything that'll get you in trouble."

"Lovely," Stone said archly. "Now I've got a minder."

"Speaking of Jason," Lopez said, frowning, "You had any brainwaves yet about where he might be? Do you still think he's alive?"

"I do think he's alive," Stone said with a sigh. "No new ideas, though, unfortunately. I was very much hoping that out little trip this morning would lead us to where he was being held."

"You sure it wouldn't have, somewhere? I mean, we had to get out of there pretty fast. What if he was there somewhere and we missed him?"

Stone didn't answer right away. The waitress came over with their orders and he sipped his Guinness thoughtfully, staring into its dark depths. There was something here he wasn't putting together. Something about Jason. "Bear with me a moment," he said. "Sometimes I think better when I bounce ideas off others, so you're the elected sounding board."

"Bounce away," Lopez said. "Listening is one of the first things they teach you in cop school. That, and how to hold your gun by the right end."

Stone nodded, once again lost in his own thoughts and not really hearing Lopez's words. "Let's assume," he said, "that Jason's alive, and this He of Many Faces—or one of his minions—is the one who has him." He took a deep breath. "With that assumed, let's look at our facts."

Lopez pulled out his notebook and pen, deftly managing his pulled-pork sandwich with his off hand. "Go for it."

"First," Stone said, "we know he saw something shortly before he disappeared—something he thought I would find interesting. That almost certainly means something supernatural."

Lopez jotted that down.

"Next, we know he was in the vicinity of the first murder, probably shortly after it occurred. The murder site was on the logical route he would take walking home from the party, and I detected traces of his aura at the scene."

Lopez nodded, still scribbling.

"We don't know for sure," Stone continued, "but I can be reasonably certain that he didn't have anything to do with the murder."

"How do you know that?" Lopez asked. "I mean, aside from the obvious fact that Jason isn't a murderer."

"Well, there's that, of course, but there's also the fact that the bits of his aura I could pick up near the murder site were not *at* the site *per se*, and didn't become nervous until a short distance down the road away from it. What it suggests to me is that he might have encountered the murderer—who was likely possessed at the time— after the murder had already been committed. And also that, aside from whatever bit of supernatural oddness he saw, he didn't connect it with a crime..." He paused, his gaze suddenly going unfocused. "Of *course!*"

"What?" Lopez demanded, pen poised over his notebook.

"I know what he must have seen now!" Stone leaned forward. "The night I was—with Lindsey—when I awoke to find her trying to stab me, I saw an odd light in her eyes. Sort of a yellowish-orange glow. The boy who strangled me probably had it too, but I wasn't in any position to see it. If he saw that—especially if it was coupled with that odd tone of voice the possession victims get—he certainly would have found it strange enough to warrant a call to me."

"That makes sense," Lopez said. "But why would it let him go, then? Why not just kill him?"

"My theory is, whoever it possessed and forced to commit the murder wasn't big or strong enough to overpower Jason. He's very difficult to possess—I've taught him a few mental techniques—and it would have been awkward to simply vacate the other body and hop into Jason in any case."

"So—they just let him go and then grabbed him later?"

"They've proven they can keep track of people," Stone said, nodding. "If he got back to his room at three or four in the morning, he probably passed out and woke up some time later. That's when he called me."

"Okay," Lopez said. "So far, so good. But then did he leave the room and go somewhere else?"

"I don't know," Stone said. "Let's go back to the facts. I am very good at tracking rituals. I performed one when I first got to Ojai, as soon as I moved into the house, since the motel room wasn't large enough to cast the circle." He paused, waiting for Lopez to ask, but the cop just made a 'go on' gesture. "I used something of Jason's as a tether, which makes it even more likely that if he was out there to find, I'd find him. Even if he was out of range of the spell, there would still be sort of an astral marker showing me the way to where he was. But all I got was faint flashes of his aura."

"What's that mean?"

"For one thing, it means he wasn't dead when I did the ritual," Stone said. "The fact that I got traces, and even a brief response from him to my call, indicates that he was within the range of the spell, but very difficult to track."

"How can that happen?"

"Usually it means the ritual subject is behind wards, or otherwise magically hidden," Stone said.

"So you think these things can do wards?" Lopez asked. "You mean like the ones you put on my house?"

Stone shrugged. "I have no idea what these things can do." He sighed loudly, frustrated. "Damn it, there's something I should be seeing here, and I'm missing it. I know it!"

"Well," Lopez said, "Let's think about the chain of events. You say Jason called you early on Saturday morning. Do you know he called from the motel? Do you know he got back there?"

"No," Stone said. "But it's a reasonable assumption. If he left the party sometime around two a.m. and didn't call me until seven, then where else would he have been in between? If he passed out somewhere along the way, then Faces or his minions would have had plenty of time to hop into a new body that could deal with him."

"Okay," Lopez agreed, nodding. "So he got back to the room and passed out, like you said. Then he woke up and called you. After that, he either had to stay there or go somewhere, right?"

Stone nodded. "I'd guess he probably waited at least a while in the room, since he wanted me to call him and the motel was the only way I had to reach him. Unless he popped out for breakfast or something. But judging by the amount he apparently had to drink, I'm doubting he would be interested in anything more than perhaps a cup of coffee. When I'm that hung over, the last thing I want is anything to eat."

"So, do you think somebody came to his room?" Lopez asked. "If one of those things came there and talked to him in that same weird voice, don't you think it would have freaked him out? He's sharp enough he wouldn't have gone with anybody like that. You said these things aren't very good at pretending to be people. So if they—" He stopped, staring at Stone. "What?"

The mage had stopped in the act of raising his glass. Once again, his eyes had gone strange. "Bloody hell, that's *it*," he whispered. "Stan, you're brilliant! That's how they did it! Oh, you *bastards*." He leaped up with such force that his chair nearly fell over, a wild look in his eyes. "Come on," he ordered, flinging a handful of cash onto the table. "We have to go!"

"Go where?" Lopez demanded, looking around. The restaurant's few other diners were eyeing Stone as if expecting him to pull out a gun and start shooting up the place.

"If I'm right—to find Jason."

| CHAPTER TWENTY-FOUR

"**A**re you sure about this?" Lopez asked. "This, what you're asking, is skating on pretty thin ice, legality-wise. If you're wrong—"

They were sitting in Lopez's truck in the parking lot of the Nest Motel. "Do you want to take the time to call Casner?" Stone asked. "Because if Faces gets wind of what we're up to, there's no telling what he might do. Even if I'm right, he might kill Jason just to keep us from getting him back."

Lopez thought about it, his face a mix of frustration and resolve. "Fuck it," he said at last. "I'm gonna retire soon anyway. I can live with a reprimand if it comes to that." He got out of the truck and slammed the door.

Stone followed him into the motel office, carrying the black leather duffel bag containing his magical gear. Behind the desk was a middle-aged woman in a neat floral blouse. "May I help you?" she asked.

Lopez flashed his badge. "Can you look up a record for us, please?"

She frowned. "A record?"

"We need to know which room one of your guests was staying in on Friday night, and we need to take a look around it if possible."

Behind him, Stone remained silent and used a minor version of his disregarding spell to fade into the background. This was not one of those instances when his memorable appearance would be helpful.

When Lopez told her the name he wanted her to look up, light dawned in her eyes. "Oh! That's the gentleman who's missing, right?"

"That's right," Lopez said.

She searched through her records. "Ah, here we are. Mr. Thayer. He was in room one forty-two. He was supposed to check out Sunday morning, but—" She consulted another book. "That room is booked for this evening, but the parties haven't arrived yet. They aren't due until after nine p.m."

"Can we take a look around?" Lopez asked. "It shouldn't be long."

She looked uncertain. "I'm not sure—"

"Please," he said. "I promise, we'll be out and gone before your guests arrive."

"All right," she said slowly. She pulled a key off a board and handed it to Lopez. "The room's been cleaned, so—"

"We won't mess anything up. Thank you, ma'am," Lopez said, and turned to go before she changed her mind or asked for his name. Stone followed him out, and they headed across the parking lot.

"This whole thing just keeps getting crazier," the cop said as he opened the door to room 142. "You're saying Jason is still *in* this room somewhere? How the hell can that even *be?*"

"I don't think you want a magical theory lecture right now," Stone said. "You're just going to have to trust me."

In fact was, he wasn't entirely sure himself, but he was convinced he was correct. It all fit: Jason was still in the area, but he couldn't find more than traces of him. He of Many Faces and his minions couldn't deal very well with human bodies beyond basic physical functions, which meant they sounded odd when they talked. It also meant that driving was likely beyond their capabilities, so they'd have to have possessed someone nearby and they had no way to get Jason out of the motel. As farfetched as it all sounded, everything Stone had deduced implied that he was still *at* the motel somewhere.

And when he started thinking along *those* lines, it was an easy leap of logic to consider the possibility that the reason he couldn't find Jason was that he either wasn't on this plane of existence, or was somehow out of phase with the material world. And that led to the idea that there had to still be some connection between Jason and *this* plane, otherwise Stone wouldn't have picked up the traces of him. The odd dream he'd had when he'd stayed here reinforced that idea further. As yet, he had no idea what that connection was, and why Faces and Co. were maintaining it, but that could come later, once they had Jason back.

The room was identical to the one he'd been staying in before, down to the photo of the pink-tinged mountain range and the tasteful Native American-print bedspread. He stepped into the center, sat down on the bed, and reached out with his magical senses. He used a bit of power from his second ring to augment his search, finding it perversely ironic that the whole thing would be much easier if he could have made use of Jason's odd innate ability to serve as a sort of "mana battery" for helping mages power spells.

"You getting anything?" Lopez said, moving over to close the door and drawing the curtains closed.

"Shh." Stone focused, carefully looking around the room. His theory was that if He of Many Faces had somehow managed to shift Jason's physical form to another plane or out of phase, there had to be at least a thread of magic connecting him to the material plane. They wanted him for something, otherwise they'd have killed him already. If he could find that thread, he'd be able to examine it and figure out how to shift Jason back.

He hoped.

If the thread existed at all, it was well hidden. Stone wasn't even sure what he was looking for, just that he was fairly sure he'd know it when he saw it. There weren't that many places it could be hidden: the room was only about fifteen feet square, and the only furniture aside from the bed was a table and chair, a dresser with a TV set on top of it, a tiny nightstand, and a mini-fridge. Rising from the bed, he began pacing around the room, peering into the dresser drawers and the nightstand, and even opening the mini-fridge. He could sense rather than see Lopez sidestepping to stay out of his way, confusion radiating from him like waves.

"What are you looking for?" he asked. "Anything I can do to help look?"

Stone shook his head without replying. Where was it? He was so sure he was right. If he wasn't, then they were back to square one, and he had no idea where to go from there. He stopped a moment, frustrated, and considered his options.

"You didn't look under the bed," Lopez pointed out. "Maybe it's there, whatever it is?"

It couldn't hurt. Again Stone didn't reply directly, but he dropped down to the floor and lay flat on his stomach, lifting the bedspread and peering into the shadows underneath. He had assumed that the bed, as in most hotels, was on a platform rather than on legs—but he was wrong.

The open space underneath was empty, with two exceptions: a large dust bunny that had apparently escaped the maid's vacuum cleaner—and a slender, reddish thread of energy that ran tight against the back wall of the room and disappeared into nothingness as it rose up alongside the mattress.

"Yes!" Stone said triumphantly, leaping to his feet.

"You found it?" came Lopez's eager voice from behind him.

"Under the bed," he said, pointing. "Brilliant idea."

"So—now what?"

"Now I'm going to need a bit of time—and probably to break the promise you made about not messing up the room. Can't be helped. Can you make sure to keep anyone out who might come to call?"

Lopez frowned."Uh—the motel clerk, yeah. Supernatural stuff, though, maybe not so much."

Stone waved him off. "This won't take long. Just watch the door and don't distract me."

He tossed his duffel bag on the chair, unzipped it, and began pulling out items: candles, chalk, crystals, bags of sand, bits of incense. He set them all on the table, then, moving quickly but methodically, sketched a circle directly on the bedspread with a thick piece of white chalk.

Lopez started to say something, then decided against it. He kept turning back and forth in place, watching the bed and the door in turn, his hand on his gun butt.

"This is a simple circle," Stone said as he placed crystals around its circumference. "It won't need to do much. The connection wasn't even meant to be noticed, let alone withstand any sort of strain. I think I'll be able to break it without much difficulty."

"What happens then?"

"We'll see, won't we?" Moving with a lot more grace than he'd have given himself credit for after everything his body had been through over the last couple days, Stone leaped neatly onto the bed without disturbing the circle, then lowered himself into the middle of it. "Might want to have that gun out, just to be safe. Just make sure you know what you're shooting at if you have to." Stone checked him quickly for green auras, but still found none. His theory about Faces' power relative to its base seemed to be holding, at least for now.

Lopez drew his pistol and took up a position near the door, his eyes never leaving Stone.

"All right, then: showtime," Stone said. "Standard disclaimer: please keep all arms and legs out of my circle at all times. Don't break it or otherwise disturb it. And stay quiet. I don't want to bugger this up."

Without turning to see if Lopez had any reply, he took a few centering breaths, closed his eyes, and fed power into his circle. It began to glow to his magical senses, a clear, pale blue that thrummed along his nerve endings like a low-grade electrical current.

Now that that he knew what he was looking for, the slender crimson thread was very obvious. He couldn't see all of it because it was obscured by the mattress, but all he needed to see was the tiny bit poking up from in front of the headboard. He focused his will on it, reaching out to examine it so he could figure out how to dismantle it.

It would be easiest if he could just break it: that he could do with a mere flick of his mind, but he saw right away that that wasn't possible. He could sense Jason's essence, very faint and distant, making up part of the thread like one strand in a woven rope, blue against the red of the rest of it. If he broke the whole thing cleanly, one of two things would happen, neither one desirable: either Jason would be stranded wherever he was being held with no way to return and no way for Stone to find him, or snapping the part of the cord that contained his essence would snuff out his life force. No, Stone realized, this was more like defusing a bomb than cutting a tether. He'd have to unravel the connection, separate Jason's thread from the others, and then break the remaining bits while keeping a tight hold on Jason's.

It was going to take longer than he thought.

Time passed, but he didn't notice it. Unraveling the glowing cord was delicate work, requiring all of his concentration; he had to trust Lopez to keep any potential distractions or threats away from him. *Hold on, Jason,* he sent, though he had no idea if Jason would hear him wherever he was.

The strand representing Jason's essence was tightly integrated into the rest of the cord. Stone sensed power coming through it, flowing from the unseen end to the one located in their own plane. This puzzled him: were they trying to power something on this side using energy from the other? That seemed odd—normally, once spirits manifested themselves here, they no longer needed supplemental power to keep them around. He didn't have time to examine the reasons for it, though. It required all his will and focus to keep his ethereal "hands" from shaking. With this new mysterious power source in play, he had to treat the operation as if one misstep might cause not only Jason's death, but a possible backlash that could take out him and Lopez and possibly a good portion of this motel.

Carefully, carefully—

At the periphery of his awareness he thought he heard Lopez say something, but he didn't have enough spare concentration to make it out. He risked a quick glance toward the door and saw only Lopez's glowing blue aura: it looked nervous, but not frightened or overly agitated.

Suddenly, something jerked in his grip. He spun his head back around and stiffened.

The red, multi-stranded cord with that single thread of blue had bucked, rearing up like some kind of glowing snake. It lunged toward him, the strands at the end snapping and seeking as if to latch onto him.

Stone pulled back, gripping the cord with one hand and holding it away from him. He sensed that if he dropped it now, all would be lost. *That's what it wants me to do. It's probably an illusion.*

It lunged again, sliding through his hand, and nipped his arm. Pain flared as it sunk its "teeth" into his ethereal form and held on. Stone set his jaw and kept going. He couldn't afford to stop now—he almost had the blue thread separated from the rest. Just a few more seconds—

Lopez's voice sounded again, louder this time. Stone ignored it. He didn't want to, but he couldn't do anything to help the cop right now.

The "snake" reared back and struck again, this time hitting his shoulder. Again, pain flared. He felt blood running, but wasn't sure if it was physical or merely ethereal. Not that it mattered: pain was pain.

He thought he felt something else—a pressure on his other shoulder. He snarled aloud and wrenched it forward as the blue, pulsing network of energy provided by the circle began to sputter. Someone or something had breached the circle! A crushing pain pressed in on him, centering on his head as the feedback built.

There was no more time. The circle was failing, its energy collapsing in on itself. He'd have to take the chance: no time to separate the strands further. Gripping the blue thread of Jason's essence in one hand and holding fast, he clamped his other hand on the bundle of red ones and wrenched with all his ethereal strength (which, being born of willpower rather than muscle and bone, was significantly more impressive than his physical strength), pulling the cord in a sharp jerk as if trying to yank a phone line out of a wall.

Dimly he heard a scream, but he didn't know if it was coming from himself, someone else, or both. Searing pain lanced up his arm as the cord ripped free, and then white-bright light flared. He felt his body go stiff and then crash backward. The last thing he felt before the room went to black was a vast frustration, and rage: pure, primal rage, all of it directed at him.

| CHAPTER TWENTY-FIVE

*T*ired...
    So tired...
    Muttered sounds, far away. Muddy voices filtered through multiple layers of cotton.

Shifting lights. Figures, moving. Looming.

"Al?"

Stone stirred.

"I think he's waking up."

He didn't want to wake up. Waking up took energy, and he didn't have any left. He just wanted to drift back off to the embrace of blessed, wonderful sleep, where he'd never have to do anything again. Ever. How lovely that would be.

"Al?"

Deep in the midst of the cotton wrapped tightly around his brain, one thought managed to get through: *That isn't Lopez's voice.*

That was important, somehow. He'd have to wake up to find out why.

Damn.

With great reluctance, he opened his eyes.

"Hey, Al," said a blurry form. "Welcome back."

He blinked, and the blurry form resolved itself into the familiar figure of—"Jason?"

"Yeah, it's me." He grinned. "Can't get rid of me that easy, I guess."

Stone blinked again. His brain didn't want to work right—it was as if all the myriad of questions he wanted to ask were backing up, and none of them could fight its way to the front of the line. "What—?" was all he could manage, and even in his brain-deprived state, he knew he sounded like an idiot.

"Wow, Jason, you told me he was a smart guy, but you didn't say he was *this* smart," came another voice. Lopez's face swam into view. He was grinning too.

"Yeah, college professor and all. Sharp as a bowling ball, Al is."

"Oh, sod off, both of you," Stone said sourly, mock indignation managing to finally begin piercing the layers of cotton. Everything was flooding back to him, which brought up even more questions. But right now, all he could do was stare at Jason. He was there, in the flesh, alive and well and safe, so clearly whatever Stone had been trying to do had worked. His expression grew serious. "Tell me what happened."

Jason pulled up a chair and sat down, and after a moment Lopez did the same. Stone realized he was lying on his bed in Lopez's spare room. "I take it no one got arrested, then?" His voice sounded so weak to him, and he was so tired. His shoulder hurt, along with his arm and his head. He didn't want to move, but he had to know what had happened.

"Took some fancy footwork," Lopez said. "I figure I'll be hearing from Casner soon, but we're okay for the moment."

Stone nodded. "What happened? Start at the beginning." He hunted around in his memory. "I heard you calling something—"

"Yeah. You want anything, by the way? Jason's eaten nearly everything that isn't nailed down, including a whole pizza all by himself, but I might have something—"

Stone looked at Jason, only now seeing the slight pallor under his friend's tan. There was more going on here than was immediately visible. "No. Thank you. Just tell me." He glanced around the room, looking for a clock. "What time is it?"

"About two thirty a.m. You've been out for a few hours, but we figured it'd be better just to let you sleep it off, since you didn't seem too hurt. Jase slept for some of that, too." Lopez took a deep breath. "That was some freaky shit tonight, Al. You said it would be simple, and it wouldn't take long."

"Apparently I don't always know what I'm talking about," Stone said.

"Yeah, I got that." He leaned back in his chair and took a moment to organize his thoughts. "So, there you were in the middle of that circle of yours on the bed, twitching your hands around. I don't know what the hell you were doing, but you sure were focused on it. That went on for a while, and then somebody knocked on the door. That's when I called you for the first time."

"I think I heard that," Stone said. "But I couldn't break my concentration. I assumed you would handle it."

Lopez nodded. "And I did. It was the desk clerk. Apparently the people who weren't supposed to get there till nine arrived early, and they wanted their room. I didn't open the door, just yelled that we'd be done soon. She left and I figured that was that. But then a few minutes later she came back, and she had the people with her. I yelled out that I'd let her know when we were done, but then she used the key and opened the door. She had those glowing eyes—and so did the other couple."

Stone stiffened. Three of them at once? "What did you do?"

"They shoved their way in. I didn't want to shoot them because I knew they weren't themselves, but it's damn hard to corral three different people when there's only one of me. While I had hold of two of them, the other one managed to slip past me and grab you. I thought the whole place was gonna go up. You stiffened up like somebody'd hit you with a hot wire. I grabbed 'em and threw 'em out into the parking lot—fortunately they weren't that strong—then slammed the door shut and braced it. That was about the time you screamed, and then there was this bright light everywhere. Next thing I know, Jason appeared outta nowhere on the bed, and you keeled over on the floor. Jason was pretty much out of it at that point, too." Lopez's breath was coming faster as he told the story.

Stone stared at him. "How did you get us out of there?"

"I knew I had to, before those things figured out a way to get us, or else the desk clerk called the police. So I flung open the door with my gun out. Weirdest thing—they weren't there anymore. I spotted them heading back toward the office, looking like they had no idea what the hell they were doing out in the parking lot. I got the truck over by the door and got you two into it. By that time Jason had come around a little, but he wasn't much use yet. I drove like a fuckin' choirboy back here. I figured if those things were out looking for us, better to be someplace with wards."

Stone smiled, shoving himself up a bit on the pillows. "Listen to you, Stan. You're an old hand at this already." Sobering, he looked at Jason. "And you," he said. "Tell me what happened to you."

Jason shuddered. "I don't remember a lot about it. I was drunk off my ass, walking back to the motel from the party. Then all of a sudden there was this guy in front of me. I said something to him and he answered, but his voice was weird. All gravelly, and like he didn't really understand English. And his eyes were—" Again, he shuddered.

"Glowing red-orange?" Stone asked.

"Yeah. I got outta there in a hurry. Went back to my room, slept it off for a while, then called you. Figured you'd bite my head off if I called you in the middle of the night." He grinned at Stan. "Al needs his beauty sleep, see?"

Lopez nodded gravely.

"Go on," Stone growled.

Jason turned the grin on Stone. "By the way, where were you? Why didn't you answer the phone?"

"I—wasn't home at the time."

"Ahhhh," he said knowingly, nodding. "Al, you dog."

R. L. KING

Stone glared at him. "Are we going to discuss my night life, or are you going to tell me what happened? Remember, we've still got a murderer out there."

That wiped the grin off Jason's face. "Murderer?"

"I haven't told him much about what's happened yet," Lopez told Stone. "I figured it'd make more sense to wait till you woke up, then compare notes. That way we don't have to repeat ourselves."

Stone nodded. "Please, Jason, continue. We'll get to the rest later. I need to know why they took you."

Jason sighed. "Okay. So I make the call and then a little bit later there's a knock on my door. I open it and the desk clerk guy is there. He's got another guy with him who looks like the janitor or something." He shrugged. "I don't remember much after that, until I showed up in the room again tonight."

"Anything?" Stone asked. "Everything you remember could be potentially helpful."

Jason thought about it. "It felt like I was kind of mostly asleep, you know? I was in a room with nothing in it. It was just white. No sense of time or anything. I had no idea I was there for several days until Stan told me."

"Did they speak to you at all?"

He shook his head. "No. Like I said, I was out of it. I think they might have drugged me or something. I was tired all the time. Not hungry, really, or thirsty—just so tired. I felt like something had drained all my energy, or—" He stopped, because Stone was staring hard at him. "What? You come up with something?"

"That could be it," Stone whispered. "That could be why they were holding you."

"What, draining my—" Again he stopped, his eyes getting wide. "Holy crap, Al."

"What?" Lopez demanded.

"You mean they could take my energy?" Jason said, ignoring Lopez's question. "I thought I had to be willing for that. I sure as hell wasn't willing."

"It's the only thing that makes sense," Stone said. "Perhaps they were using your energy to supplement their own—to allow them to do more on this plane than they normally would be able to." He sighed. "I don't know. I'm still not thinking too clearly yet. Perhaps we should continue this in the morning, after we've all had a chance to sleep for a while."

"No way," Jason said firmly. "You're gonna tell me what's been going on. What's this about a murderer?"

Stone looked at Lopez, and between the two of them they gave Jason the summary version of what had occurred over the past couple of days. Had it really only been a couple of days? So much had happened that it felt like much longer.

Jason listened with growing horror, especially during the part about Lindsey's murder and Stone's arrest, and then again when they got to what they'd discovered under the huge oak tree up above Creek Road. "Shit..." he breathed. "Just—*shit.*"

"I'll give you this, Jason," Stone said. "You don't discover *small* problems."

Lopez stood. "We really should get some sleep," he said. "We gotta figure out how to deal with some things tomorrow—like how we explain where Jason's been, for example. Remember, he's still wanted as a person of interest for Ashley Reed's murder. And we need to determine our next steps if we're going to find this Faces thing."

"We can think about all that tomorrow," Stone said. Already he could feel himself starting to fade again. He didn't think there was anything seriously wrong with him beyond exhaustion: his arm and shoulder hurt where the ethereal cord-snake had bitten him, but aside from angry red marks, there were no wounds. However, he knew his brain was operating in a fog right now, and that was no way to make life-or-death decisions. He'd just have to trust that the wards around the house would keep them safe. "Just—everybody stay inside. I'm not convinced that if you go out right now, that thing won't be waiting for you."

"No problem, Al," Jason said firmly. "Whatever happened to me, I don't ever want it to happen again."

| CHAPTER TWENTY-SIX

When Stone came out to the front room early the next morning, still bleary but feeling much more himself than the previous night, Jason was already up. He sat at the kitchen table with a cup of coffee, looking out into Lopez's small, neat backyard with a fair imitation of Stone's thousand-yard stare.

He looked up as Stone came in. "Hey, Al. Didn't think you'd be up yet."

"I could say the same thing. Are you all right?" He dropped into a chair across the table.

Jason rose, poured another cup of coffee, and set it in front of Stone. "Surprisingly, yeah. I was hungry as hell once I woke up last night. Stan wasn't kidding about me eating a whole pizza. But it was a weird feeling—not like I hadn't eaten for several days, but more like it just—switched back on after being turned off." He sipped his coffee, then looked at Stone with an odd expression, sober and thoughtful. "I didn't say thanks last night, Al," he said. "Thanks for coming for me, for getting me out of that. If you hadn't—"

Stone waved him off. "Think nothing of it. Rescuing people from magical threats is apparently becoming what I do."

"Still, I owe you big."

"We're not out of this yet," Stone pointed out. He looked down into his cup. "We—well, *I* anyway; you're not obligated—still need to track down He of Many Faces and figure out how to deal with him."

"We," Jason said firmly. "I'm in this till the end. I've got a score to settle with this thing anyway." He glanced up. "So you told Stan, huh? That was a surprise. I thought you wanted to keep the whole magic thing a secret. Did you tell him about me and Verity, by the way?"

"No. That's for you two to reveal if you wish." He shrugged. "As for why I told him—I didn't fancy getting arrested again, so I figured that having a law-enforcement officer on my side couldn't do me any harm. And you've told me you trust him. So far, it's proven to be one of my better decisions. He's been a valuable ally." He quirked an eyebrow at Jason. "And he tends to accept things much more easily than you do. It was quite refreshing not to have to deal with 'what the hell?' and 'holy crap' every five minutes."

"Hey, what can I say? I'm just skeptical like that." He paused, looking out the window again. "So, what's our next step? Do you think that thing will try to grab me again?"

Stone shook his head. "Probably not. I'm sure it knows that, now I know what I'm looking for, I could find you again much more easily. No, I think it's mostly focused on killing us now, along with whatever other plans it's pursuing."

"That's why I like you, Al: you're so comforting."

The phone rang before Stone could reply. After a single ring it stopped, as if it had been picked up in the other room. Five minutes after that, Lopez came down the hall in plaid boxers and under-shirt. He looked grim. "Bad news, guys. That was Casner calling. We got more murders."

"Murders plural?" Stone asked.

"Yeah. Three. Looks like a whole family this time. And Pete's pretty sure these are related to the others."

❖

"I don't like it," Stone said, "but I think we're going to have to try to get Casner to cooperate with us."

The three of them had reconvened at Lopez's kitchen table twenty minutes later, after showers and fresh clothes (fortunately, Jason was close enough in size to Lopez that he could borrow a shirt, though the Budweiser logo looked out of place on him). "You thinking of telling him about the magic thing?" Lopez asked, surprised.

"No. But I've already established myself as an expert on the occult. If these murders include the same odd circles that the others have, would we have any chance of convincing him that there might be occult involvement, at least enough to use me as a consultant? It would be easier if I could get access to the scene, especially when it's relatively fresh."

Lopez considered. "It'll be tough," he said at last. "Like I said, Casner's smart and he's a good cop, but he's not the kind to believe in ghoulies and ghosties and things that go bump in the night."

"Remember," Stone pointed out, "'Occult' doesn't necessarily mean real magic. The majority of occult-related crimes and people out there have nothing to do with the real thing. Satanists and whatnot, for example: sure, a few of them can be trouble if they have actual talent and genuinely *believe,* but ninety-nine percent of them are just fools in eyeliner."

Lopez nodded. "True. Even if the murderers were just cranks pretending to be spooks, I might be able to convince him that you could help."

"Does he know Jason is back yet?"

"Not yet. Apparently the people in the motel didn't call it in. Nobody did, which is weird considering how loud we were yelling."

"Probably just thought you were drunk or having an argument or something," Jason said. "Even around here, people don't always get involved." He looked at Lopez. "You have a lot of cred in the department, Stan. Can you make this Casner guy believe I didn't kill anybody and that Al could help with things?"

"I think I have to try. It's gonna come out pretty soon that you're back. It has to, since we can't let them keep devoting resources to finding you. I'll give him a call. I sure hope this doesn't blow up in our faces, though."

❖

"Make this fast, Stan," Peter Casner said, without looking up from a form he was filling out. "I need to get out to the crime scene. This one's going to take hours to process, even with help from Ventura." He tossed his pen down and glanced up—

—and stared.

Stone had to admit a bit of sympathy for the man. He thought he'd be talking to his old friend from another precinct, and instead he got the friend, the crackpot who'd been hauled in twice on suspicion of murder, and—

"Hey—aren't you the guy who's supposed to be missing?" Casner demanded, starting to rise from his chair. "Stan, what the hell—"

"Sit down, Pete, please," Lopez said, making a placating motion. "This is Jason Thayer, yeah."

"Come on, Stan, this is bullshit," Casner said, his brows furrowing in anger. "What hell's going on?" He did sit down, though.

"It's not bullshit," Lopez said. His tone was even, calm, steady. "Just hear us out, okay? Or are you so on top of seven murders now that you can afford to turn down help?"

Casner's gaze darted between the three of them. "Where'd you find him?" he asked, pointing at Jason. "You know he's wanted, right?"

"Now that *is* bullshit," Lopez growled. "You know as well as I do that this guy didn't do a damn thing but get smashed off his ass at a party in an unfamiliar area, wander off, and get himself lost."

Stone and Jason exchanged glances, but neither contradicted Lopez's words.

"For three days?" Casner demanded.

"Jason didn't kill anybody, Pete," Lopez said, shaking his head. "That's all that matters. You know it and I know it. Don't waste your time chasing useless leads. You don't have that kind of time or manpower right now."

Casner looked like he was going to protest, then let his breath out and subsided again. "Yeah," he said. "I know." He both looked and sounded very tired. "Right now I don't give a damn where he was, as long as he turned up safe and I can take him off my to-do list." He glared at Stone, who was leaning against the frame of the open office door. "What's *he* doing here?"

"He wants to help, Pete," Lopez said. "And I think maybe you oughta listen to him."

Casner rolled his eyes. "Come *on*. Get serious. You just said it: I'm dealing with seven murders here. And you want me to listen to some nutcase ghostbuster who can't even keep himself off the suspect list?" He started to rise again. "Thanks for coming by, Stan, but I've got to get out to the crime scene."

Stone stepped forward. When he spoke, his soft voice was every bit as chilled and intense as his gaze. "Lieutenant, Sergeant Lopez has been kind enough to bring me here, and as he's said, it would be best if you listen to what I have to say. You don't have the luxury of disbelief any longer. Whether you believe in genuine occult powers or not is irrelevant. Whoever has committed these murders *does* believe, and that's what matters. I can help you, if you're willing to put aside your literal-minded view of the world for a moment and let me."

Casner stared at him, and Stone could almost see the quick procession of thoughts running through the man's head. Sometimes you didn't need to be a mind reader to be able to follow the obvious. So far, the only sides of him the cop had seen were "concerned friend" and "grief-stricken suspect." Now, though, Stone had deliberately brought to bear a side of his personality that he didn't normally show, augmenting it with the full potent force of his magic. He'd never actually seen what he looked like when he let loose, but more formidable things than a harried, small-town police lieutenant had backed down when confronted with it. He didn't have time to waste in verbal sparring or posturing right now. Every hour they waited, more people would die.

Casner managed to hold the mage's unblinking gaze for another second or two, then looked back at Lopez again. "I got nothing, Stan," he said with an exhausted sigh. "I haven't got a fucking *clue* what's going on here. Seven people dead, no motive, no suspects."

He looked back at Stone warily. "I guess it couldn't hurt to see what you've got to say." His gaze hardened. "But on *my* terms, got it? I still don't trust you, Stone. I still think you know more about this situation than you're telling. But if Stan vouches for you, *and* you're willing to play it my way, I'll take a chance. For now."

Stone inclined his head. "Thank you, Lieutenant. What I'd like, if possible, is to see this latest crime scene while it's still fresh."

Casner looked suspicious. "Why?"

"Because if there are any impressions to be gathered, it will be easier than if we wait until later."

"Impressions? You mean like psychic readings or something?"

Stone made a small shrug. "Call it what you like. I'd also like to see if this scene includes the same crude circle I believe I mentioned to you before."

Casner rubbed the bridge of his nose. He sighed again, louder this time. "Fine, whatever. If you give me your word you'll follow my orders to the letter, you can come along. I don't want you getting in the way of the crime-scene guys or compromising the evidence."

"Of course, Lieutenant. You have my word."

The cop hooked a thumb at Jason. "What about him?"

"He's my assistant," Stone said.

"Don't worry about Jason, Pete," Lopez said. "He didn't get his fool ass expelled from the Academy until *after* the unit on how not to fuck up crime scenes."

Jason gave him a sour look, but didn't contradict him.

Casner stood. "This is turning into a fucking circus," he said. "Call me when the rest of the clowns get here. Come on. Let's go."

| CHAPTER TWENTY-SEVEN

The house that was the scene of the triple murder looked relentlessly suburban: a rambling, single story, peach-colored ranch with a shake roof, white shutters, and a large manicured lawn kept proudly green despite the late summer heat. The wooden sign hanging over the closed garage door read: *The Ayalas*. It looked like every other suburban ranch-style house in the neighborhood.

Except for the collection of squad cars, media vans, and other vehicles parked in its driveway and two deep along the curb in front, and the corresponding crowd of people milling around on the sidewalk. Stakes had been driven into the lawn and the flower-bed along the front walk and crime scene tape stretched out between them, cutting the front of the house off from everyone. Behind it, two cops stood on the porch, making notes and ignoring everything outside the tape.

Casner pulled his black SUV into a spot a short distance down the street. "Damn vultures," he muttered. "It's getting worse. They're sending them up from L.A. now."

He swung around in his seat to look at Stone and Jason, both sitting in the back. "Okay, I want you two to stay with Lopez. You do what he tells you, walk where he tells you, and don't walk where he tells you not to. You'll have to put on gloves and booties before you go in, but do *not* touch anything. You're not staying long. I don't have time to babysit you guys right now. If I see either of you anywhere but stapled to Stan's ass, you're outta there. Got it?"

Stone nodded. "Yes."

Casner started to get out, then stopped. "Oh—one more thing. Do *not* talk to the media. At all. They're gonna be barking at us as we go in. Just ignore them. You're a couple of deaf-mutes." He glared at Stone. "And for *God's* sake, don't tell them what you do." When Stone and Jason both nodded, he opened the door and got out, motioning for them and Lopez, who was in the shotgun spot, to do likewise.

As soon as they approached the house, they were accosted by a knot of reporters, photographers, and cameramen with large rigs on their shoulders. Stone shoved his hands deep into the pockets of his overcoat, bowed his head, and strode with Jason behind Casner and Lopez, who parted the sea of media with curt commands and hand gestures. They passed under the crime-scene tape and through the front door, which stood slightly ajar.

"I hope you guys have strong stomachs," Casner said as they all donned plastic gloves and slipped paper booties over their shoes in the tile-floored entry. "I hear this one's even worse than Creek Road."

Stone was sure he was right. Even out here, the stench of blood and the fainter tang of the beginning stages of decomposition were thick. He edged his magical senses open, not wanting to get hit with the solid wall of psychic feedback that would accompany such a scene, and followed Casner and the others into the rest of the house.

They passed through a living room that appeared undisturbed, mostly neat but cluttered with the items that made up the daily business of family living: newspapers, a stack of books on an end table, a boxed board game on a coffee table. A pair of technicians in coveralls were busy examining the scene. Casner didn't stop, but led them through and down a short hallway. He turned, gave them a stern *you'd better remember what I said* look, and then stepped inside to make room for them.

The hallway opened onto a large family room. On the right side was a breakfast bar with a cutaway leading into a kitchen. A pool table filled the left side, and the far wall was dominated by a large fireplace, its mantel covered with trophies and the photos of various smiling people, and a big-screen television set. An overstuffed sofa, strewn with a few stuffed toys, faced the television.

Right now, the room resembled some kind of hellish abattoir.

Stone stepped just into the room, moved aside so he wasn't blocking the doorway, and stared.

The bodies had been taken away by now, but the horrific aftermath of what had occurred was still clearly in evidence. Blood was everywhere: pooling on the floor, splattering the green felt of the pool table, drying on the backs of the chairs. Two more investigators in coveralls and booties moved carefully around the scene, taking photographs, placing small plastic markers with numbers on them, pausing to make notes.

Stone noticed the circle immediately. It was even less obvious this time: there was no "dome" effect to contain the blood, but it was there nonetheless, in the middle of the floor. He opened more of his magical sense and the circle lit up with arcane power. He swayed, paling a bit as the psychic energy from so much violent death in such a small place hit him like a wall. This fresh, it told him the story of what had occurred almost as clearly as if he'd watched it himself.

"You okay, Al?" Jason murmured. He was looking more than a bit pale himself.

"Don't you dare puke on my crime scene, Stone," Casner snapped. "Go outside if you're gonna do that."

Stone shook his head. "No," he said. "I'm not ill."

"Getting a vision?" Casner couldn't keep all the mocking from his tone, but to his credit he tried.

"They killed each other," he whispered.

All three of the others looked sharply at him. "What?" Lopez demanded.

"There were three of them," Stone said in the same soft tone. He didn't sound like he was answering them, but just speaking to the air in general. "Man, woman, and child. Girl." He glanced over at the mantel, noting that one of the larger photos showed a man, woman, and little girl about eight years old standing on a beach. All three had dark hair; they stood next to a blonde girl around the same age who must have been a friend of their daughter's. "The adults were sitting there—" he pointed at the sofa "—watching television."

"How the—" Casner began, but Lopez held up a hand to silence him.

Stone paused a moment, adjusting his mental barriers to attenuate some of the psychic onslaught while still allowing him to visualize the scene. "The little girl came out of her room. I'm not sure what time—that's not clear. She went to the kitchen and got those knives." He gestured at where three large bloodstained knives, including a meat cleaver, were scattered around the room, each with its own numbered tag. He took a deep breath. "She brought them to her parents."

"I'm sorry," Casner said firmly. "Maybe you believe this stuff, Stan, but this is fuckin' crazy. I don't have time for this." He started to turn away.

"Look at the circle, Lieutenant," Stone said, his voice soft. "There was one at the third murder too, wasn't there? The woman."

Casner stopped. "So you're telling me that this family killed *each other*. Just like that. The kid brought them the knives and they just started *carving*? Do you realize how goddamn *insane* that sounds?"

"I know," Stone said. "I do realize it. But I also realize that a woman stabbing herself with a letter opener looks quite insane as well." He pointed. "Look at the way the bodies fell. Look at the blood. You tell me, Lieutenant. I don't have any experience analyzing this sort of thing. I'm just giving you the impressions I'm getting."

Lopez's voice came, even and rational: "He's right, Pete. You know he is. If somebody showed me this scene and didn't tell me anything about it, I'd say they stood in the middle of the room and hacked at each other, crazy as that sounds to anyone with a shred of sanity."

"Pretty ferociously, too," Jason added. "Look at the spatter: it's all the way out to the walls in some spots."

Casner took a breath. "Even if that's true," he said, "what am I supposed to *do* with that information? What am I gonna tell people—that a suburban family hacked each other up with knives on a nice weeknight at home? Why would they do that?" He glared at Stone. "Even if you're giving me the what—and I still don't believe you, there's gotta be another explanation—that still doesn't give me the *why*. Where's the motive? Did they all go batshit at once? Is there something in the AC? Did they all eat a big helping of magic mushrooms for dinner?" He sighed. "I don't know. Maybe you guys should clear out now. I humored you—you had your look, but—" He paused, looking at Stone. "Hey, are you trancing out on

me again?"

"There's someone else here," Stone said, very quietly.

"What?" Casner frowned. "You mean a ghost or something?"

"No." He closed his eyes for a moment, focusing. Somewhere nearby, a tiny flare in the midst of the conflagration of violent astral energy, was— "That way," he said, pointing. "In the back yard, I think, or near it."

Casner sighed. "I don't have time for this. Stan, can you take him out and figure out what the hell he's talking about? I need to talk to the CSIs. And don't tromp through the scene."

There were no police or investigators in the back yard, which was large and included an above-ground pool, a shed that looked like it had been converted into a playhouse, a picnic table with a big gas barbecue, and a lot of outdoor toys spread across the area.

Either they hadn't deemed it interesting, or they hadn't gotten to it yet.

"Be careful," Lopez said when they arrived. "Let's not walk around too much. What are you picking up?"

Behind him, Stone paused again. The astral interference was somewhat less intense out here, blocked by the house's walls. "Over there," he said, nodding toward the playhouse.

Lopez put his hand on his gun in the holster, but Stone shook his head. "We're not looking for a murderer."

Moving carefully, the three of them crossed the back yard until they were standing outside the playhouse. Lopez motioned for them to stay put and he took a couple of steps forward until he could peer into one of the windows. He stiffened.

"Tell me it's not another body," Jason begged.

Lopez shook his head. He moved over and opened the door of the playhouse. "Come on out, honey," he said gently. "We won't hurt you."

Nothing happened. Stone came over next to him and looked inside. After a moment, so did Jason.

A small blonde girl, perhaps eight or nine years old, huddled in the back of the tiny house's shadowy interior, hidden behind some stacked boxes. Clad in lightweight pajamas with smiley faces on them, she had her knees drawn up under her chin and clutched a threadbare stuffed lion like it was the last anchor holding her to earth. Her eyes, big and scared, looked up at the three men from a tear-streaked face. She didn't speak.

"That's the girl in the picture on the fireplace," Jason whispered.

Stone nodded. He took a step forward and crouched down. "Hello," he said, keeping his voice soft.

She swallowed. "Are you a p'leeceman?" she asked in a shaking, barely audible voice.

"I'm a friend of policemen," he said. He nodded toward Lopez. "This nice man here is one of them. What's your name?"

"O-Olivia," she whispered.

"That's a very nice name," Stone said. He turned his head and whispered, "Someone should go get Casner."

"On it," Jason said, hurrying off.

To the girl, he said. "What are you doing out here, Olivia?"

She didn't answer.

"Does your friend live here?"

She shook her head.

"No?"

Again, she shook her head. "They hurted each other." Her small, scared voice sounded much younger than her apparent age.

Stone took a deep breath. He wished now that he'd let Lopez handle this; he had no idea how to relate to children, and usually limited his association with them on purpose. However, this one seemed to be responding to him, and he didn't want to jeopardize the fragile connection. He supposed Casner would have his head for talking to her at all, but he wasn't feeling too charitable toward the lieutenant at the moment. "They did?" he asked. "Your friend and her parents?"

She shook her head again. "They hurted each other. I thought they would hurt me, but they all just looked at me and then kept doing it." Tears sprang to her eyes again. "I want my mommy," she sobbed.

"Where's your mommy, honey?" Lopez asked. "I'm a policeman, like he said. If you tell me where to find her, we'll make sure you get back home."

"No!" she sobbed even louder. "I *am* home. My mommy and my daddy and my sister—they hurted each other!"

CHAPTER TWENTY-EIGHT

"Holy shit, this just keeps getting worse," Lopez said.

Stone didn't answer; he hadn't had much to say since they left the Ayala residence an hour ago, given a ride back to the station in one of Casner's men's cruisers. They'd reclaimed Jason's gear and his car from the police and headed back to Lopez's place after deciding there was too much chance somebody might recognize them from the crime scene if they went anywhere public. Currently, they sat in the living room, all looking some degree of shell-shocked.

"That poor kid," Jason agreed with a nod. "How the hell didn't they figure out there was another kid in the family and she was missing?"

"Give 'em a break, Jase," Lopez said. "The cops around here aren't like the big-city guys. Most of 'em won't see one scene like that in their whole career. They probably took a sweep of the area looking for the murderer, but the space she was hiding in was too small for an adult, so they let it go."

"What's gonna happen to her?" he asked.

"I'm sure they'll find somebody to look after her until they can find a relative." He sighed. "What I want to know, though, is why she was unharmed. Did you hear what she said? It was chilling: 'They looked at me and kept on hurting each other.' Can you imagine what that must have been like for a kid that age? Hell, for *anybody.* Kid's gonna be in therapy for years. But why did they kill each other and not her?"

Stone glanced up. "I wonder..." he murmured.

They both turned to him. "What?" Jason asked. "You got an idea?"

He nodded slowly. "I think I might. But I need to know something first. Stan, could you check something for me?"

"Maybe," Lopez said, his tone guarded.

"Can you find out if Olivia was the Ayalas' natural child?"

He frowned. "Natural? You mean like born to them?"

Stone nodded again.

Lopez looked reluctant, but he headed out to the kitchen and a moment later they heard him muttering into the phone. Jason shot Stone a quizzical look, but he didn't reply. After a moment Lopez came back in. "They found somebody who knew the family," he said. "You're right. Olivia was adopted. They didn't think they could have any kids, so they adopted her. Then a year later they got pregnant with Rose. That's the other girl, the one who—" He let that trail off and looked at Stone. "So what's that mean?"

Stone came up from where he was slouched into one corner of the sofa. "It means," he said, "that I think I might understand the motive now."

"You wanna share?" Jason asked.

The mage addressed Lopez. "Remember what Dr. Garcia said about the tablets? About the curse?"

Lopez looked confused for a moment, then light dawned and his eyes got wide. "This Faces guy—they wanted him to get revenge on the blood of those who'd wronged them."

"The blood," Stone said, nodding. He sat very still as the enormity of that sunk in. "He's hunting down the descendants of anyone that these people—whoever they were—thought had harmed them. With 'them' either being their own little group, which is bad enough, or the entire Chumash people." He turned to Lopez again. "Who would the Chumash believe harmed them?"

"I dunno—the white man?" Lopez shrugged. "I told you, that was a long time ago, and I didn't really pay that much attention in class."

But Jason was shaking his head. "You said this was a long time ago, right? Hundreds of years?"

"Almost certainly," Stone confirmed. "Why?"

"It'd be more specific than that," he said. "I *did* pay attention in class: we had to build Popsicle-stick Indian villages and all that stuff in grade school, and I actually thought it was pretty cool. It wasn't the generic white man who screwed over the Chumash. It was mostly the Spanish, with their European diseases. They wiped out a huge percentage of 'em when they first came here."

Stone was nodding. "Yes, it makes sense."

"So, you're saying it's killing the descendants of the Spanish explorers who came here?" Lopez asked, frowning. "From hundreds of years ago? That could be thousands of people, if you count anybody with a connection to any of those bloodlines." He paused. "You asked me before if we could find out if the victims were related in any way. But that's not it, is it? The only thing they have in common is that they were all descended from these Spanish settlers—or whatever other group those guys thought messed with 'em. So if both sides of the Ayala family were, but Olivia wasn't because she was adopted—" He let his breath out. "Casner's not gonna like this. And how are we supposed to protect these people, if we can't even figure out who they are? A lot of people don't even *know* who they're related to going back that far. Do we even need to? If this is a curse, is there a way to—I dunno—break it, so it can't affect them anymore? You know, like destroy that shrine thing?"

Stone shook his head, dropping back into his slouched position. "Breaking the curse is what we're trying to do, ultimately. But I wouldn't want to try destroying the shrine until we know more about it. It's too closely tied in with the area. I'm not even sure we *could,* but even so, destruction without knowledge can be dangerous."

"Anyway, that's not the only thing we need to figure out," Jason said suddenly. When Stone and Lopez both turned to him, he asked, "Where's this thing been all this time?"

"What do you mean?" Stone raised a questioning eyebrow.

He shrugged. "If you're right, and it's been running around killing these descendants, then how come there's not a huge trail of bodies going all the way back to however many hundreds of years ago it was first summoned?"

Stone's gaze locked on him. "That, Jason, is a *damned* good question."

"Maybe it only appears every so many years," Lopez said. "You know, like that creepy clown thing in that Stephen King book."

Jason shook his head. "Unless it's a pretty long interval, like every hundred years or even longer, somebody'll have noticed. I'd imagine if there was a bunch of people getting sliced up around here regularly, there'd at least be stories about it. That's a big deal. Ojai usually doesn't even have *one* murder in a year. This place is about as peaceful as it gets. We could check the newspaper archives, but—"

"He's got a point," Lopez said, sighing. "So that gets us back to the original question: if they called it up and told it to murder their enemies, and it actually *did* it, then why didn't it *keep* doing it? Did it off a bunch of people and sleep for three hundred years, and now it's woken up again?"

Stone shoved his hair back, his mind running fast as it examined possibilities. Nothing looked likely based on the facts as they knew them, or the speculations they had.

"If it got summoned, could it get sent back?" Jason asked.

"If it got sent back, though, wouldn't it be gone?" Lopez leaned forward. "I still can't believe I'm sitting here having this conversation."

But Stone sat up again. "Wait a moment," he said. "You might be on to something." He was silent for several seconds; nobody interrupted him. "This is obviously a reasonably powerful entity—if the magical corruption from the site of its summoning could persist even over this many years, it's not a lightweight. So to banish it would require a lot of power as well."

"So?" Jason asked.

"So," Stone said, "what if it isn't banished? What if it were—given a sort of astral 'time-out'? Sent away—or more likely, somehow had its power diminished. Or it just decided it had fulfilled its obligation and left on its own? Or—just let me ramble here, this is all speculation—someone bribed it to stay away."

"Spirits can be bribed?" Lopez asked, dubious.

"Sure, if you can find the thing they value. In this case, this one was summoned for vengeance and blood, so—" He shook his head. "I don't know. I think this line of reasoning might be valid, but I need to think about it a bit more."

"It's too bad there aren't any other mages around here," Jason said. "Could you maybe go talk to this Garcia guy again? Maybe he'll know more about this Faces thing."

"I doubt it," Stone said. "He didn't seem to recognize the name when he read it off the tablets. And as much as he was interested in the history of the Chumash, I'm fairly sure he doesn't believe in the supernatural aspect of it."

"So what do we do, then?" Jason sounded frustrated. "We can't just keep letting people die. It looks like it's started killing people in groups now. Why is it escalating?"

Stone was thinking again. "Stan, do you know if there were any other unusual murders around the area recently? Before Creek Road, I mean."

Lopez thought about it. "I don't recall any," he said. "That doesn't mean there weren't any, but I'd be surprised. That'd be easy enough to check with another phone call. I wouldn't even have to call Casner—I could check with somebody in Ventura. The records for the county are centralized." He frowned. "What are you thinking?"

"It just seems odd that these killings started so recently. Unless there are other bodies here that were killed before the man in the barn, then that places the first of the murders sometime last week."

"Yeah," Lopez said, nodding. "It doesn't seem like this thing is trying to hide the bodies very well. And the ME put Paul Gardo's— that's the guy in the barn—death somewhere around last Monday or Tuesday."

"Hmm," Stone murmured. "So if we assume Gardo was the first, that puts nearly a week between his death and Ashley Reed's. Leaving out Lindsey—I don't think she's part of the pattern here— it's another two days before the other woman's body was found." Again, he forced himself to submerge his vision of Lindsey's bloody body. She was every bit as much a victim as the others, even if she wasn't one of the descendants.

"Linda Solis," Lopez said.

"They're getting closer together," Jason said soberly.

Stone nodded. "Precisely my point. And then the Ayalas sometime last night or early this morning—three people at once."

"I don't see what you're getting at," Lopez said. "Aside from the fact that the killings are coming faster, which is bad enough."

"What does it imply to you that the killings started last week?"

"That this Faces thing just showed up on the scene again," Jason said.

"Exactly. Which, if you know about spirits, could mean any one of three things: either it's been dormant and re-awakened, it simply decided for whatever reason to start killing again, or it's been re-summoned." Stone shoved himself back to a more upright position. "There's also another thing to consider: why did it bother grabbing Jason?"

"I thought we agreed it wanted my power," Jason said.

"Yes, but why? It certainly wouldn't have reasonably expected someone like you to stray so enticingly into its path. Were you simply a target of opportunity, or did it see some advantage in taking time out from its primary mission to abduct you?"

Lopez looked confused. "You lost me. What's this power you're talking about?"

"Long story," Jason told him. "Short version: Mages like me because I have power they can use, if I let them. Sort of like a battery."

"Wait a second—you're snarled up in this whole magic thing, too?"

"Please," Stone cut in. "We don't have time for this right now. Stan, if you could make that call and verify that there haven't been any other unusual murders lately, that will help put another piece to our puzzle."

Lopez looked like he was going to push it, but then shrugged and headed back out to the kitchen. When he was gone, Jason turned toward Stone. "You've got an idea, don't you?"

"Possibly."

"Something crazy and probably dangerous, right?"

"Almost certainly, yes."

"You want to let me in on it?"

Stone shook his head. "Not yet. It's still baking. Let's see what Stan has to say. But I might need your help with it."

"You know you got it," Jason replied without hesitation.

Lopez came back a few minutes later. "Okay," he said. "I was right. No unusual murders in the county in the last six months. Nothing in Ojai, and even Ventura only had three: two gang drive-bys and one domestic violence case." He sat back down with a weary sigh. "This business is attracting a lot of attention. I mean, seven murders in a town that barely has one a year—Casner's guys are getting overwhelmed. And from what you say, it's only gonna get worse."

Stone nodded, his expression grim, and stood. "If you two will excuse me, I need to go think for a bit."

"But—" Lopez began.

Jason held up a hand. "Let him go, Stan. He does this. Hey, Al, is it safe for us to go out?"

Stone shrugged. "Probably. I'd stay together if I were you. Where were you planning to go?"

"Library. I want to check a couple of things, and if you're gonna be off meditating or something, it might be a good time to do it."

"Go," he said. "Give me an hour or two. I have some things I need to work through."

Alone in Lopez's house after the cop and Jason had departed, Stone lay on his back on his bed and stared up at the ceiling, at last letting his mind have its way with the cacophony of thoughts zooming around his head.

He still felt tired, more tired than he'd been since being in the thick of the Evil situation the previous year. The cumulative injuries he'd suffered over the past few days, none serious on their own, were more problematic when they all got together and linked arms. He'd tossed back a couple of ibuprofen before lying down; he still wished he could take something more potent, but now more than ever he couldn't afford to dull his mental processes.

He also couldn't afford to think too closely about the murder victims. About Ashley Reed, who'd been a good student and a cheerleader. About Linda Solis, who'd had a husband and children. About the Ayala family, slicing each other to ribbons in front of the television as a small girl looked on in horror.

About Lindsey Cole.

Thinking about them as people—people whose only crimes were being connected through ancient history to the enemies of an insane, vengeful group of long-dead Indians (or, in Lindsey's case, being connected to one very much alive, only slightly insane British mage)—wouldn't help him track down and deal with the entity that had caused their deaths. He couldn't help them now, no matter how much he wanted to turn back time and stop all of this from happening. Time travel wasn't something anyone had figured out how to do with magic yet, at least as far as Stone knew.

So the plan was to prevent any *further* deaths, including his own, Jason's, and Lopez's. Because he had no illusions about the fact that He of Many Faces had all three of them clearly in its bloodthirsty sights—and that he was right there at the top of its Most Wanted list.

He sighed, sitting up. None of this was helping. Even if he knew exactly what he needed to do to deal with the problem, once again he would certainly be fighting roadblocks that weren't even related to the situation. Roadblocks like Casner. Stone had no doubt that Lopez was right: Casner was a good cop and a good man. He only wanted to do the right thing. But he was also hopelessly mundane. When you combined "hopelessly mundane," "head of law enforcement for the relevant area," and "still half-suspects you of murder," it could only make for a significantly more difficult time getting anything accomplished.

He thought about Stan Lopez. A few days ago, he'd have thought of *him* as just as mundane as Casner. Perhaps he had been. Not for the first time, Stone considered what it might be like to be able to simply reveal what he was to people when he needed their help, or needed them to stay out of his way while he tried to get something done. It had a certain allure, sure, but so far he'd been very lucky. He didn't have any illusions about whether he'd keep up the streak if he got too indiscriminate about who he let in on the secret. The world of magic was definitely on a "need to know" basis, and Stone wasn't convinced yet that Casner needed to know. As long as Lopez could run interference, that would have to suffice.

The thing was, though, if he was being completely honest with himself, by Casner's reckoning Stone himself was every bit as much in the way of the investigation as he found Casner to be. Putting himself in the lieutenant's place, he wondered what he would think or how he'd react if some out-of-town nutter blew onto the scene and kept turning up at murder sites. That realization didn't make him feel any more charitable toward Casner and his stubbornness, but it did make him a bit more sympathetic. The man was just doing his job.

Unfortunately, however, no matter how hard Casner worked or how many mundane resources he brought to bear on the problem, he wouldn't be able to solve it. This wasn't the kind of thing you could solve with guns or smart police work. Despite their best efforts, Stone had no doubt that He of Many Faces would continue his campaign of revenge against his ancient enemies until he either killed them all or the sheer number of murders caught the attention of some other mage who decided it was worth his or her time to come to Ojai and investigate. That probably wouldn't happen until things were well past the point where anything short of a whole team of mages would be able to deal with it.

Which meant Stone was going to have to find a way to deal with it soon, whether he liked it or not.

He got up and headed for the living room. He only had one idea, and he hadn't been kidding when he'd told Jason it would be dangerous. He hoped Jason and Lopez would come back with some information from the library that would suggest another alternative, but he didn't think they would.

Usually things just didn't work that way.

❖

By the time Jason and Lopez got back a little over an hour later bearing fast-food bags and a small stack of papers, Stone was slouched on the sofa watching a news account of the latest murders. He shut off the television as they came in. "Find anything?"

Lopez went to the kitchen to get drinks while Jason dropped the bags on the coffee table. "Yeah. I think so, anyway."

When they were all seated, Jason held up the papers. "We got into the newspaper archives, starting ten years back and going from there. Just looking for anything that looked weird or unusual, especially murders or deaths. I was getting discouraged because we weren't finding anything, but then we got further back and found these." He passed the papers over to Stone. "Check it out and see what you think."

Stone glanced over the top sheet. It was a photocopy of a news story, dated twenty-seven years ago in late February. "Police have no suspects in murder of local woman," he read. He skimmed the rest of the article. "Name was Patricia Perez, age thirty. Throat slashed...no prints but hers on the weapon. Police thought it was a vengeful ex-husband, but never proved it." He raised an eyebrow. "I suppose it's possible, but—"

"Keep going," Jason said.

Stone slid that one behind the stack and looked at the next one. This one was dated in the same year, a month earlier. It described the attempted murder of a teenage boy in the locker room of the local high school. The coach had come in and caught another boy trying to stab him with a large pocket knife. Police could not find a motive for the attack: the boys barely knew each other, and no one, including the victim, could come up with any reason why the attacker would want to hurt him. More oddly, the attacker claimed not to remember committing the crime and seemed disoriented following discovery. The names of the victim and the attacker weren't mentioned in the article since they were both minors. Stone glanced up. "Interesting."

"One more," Lopez said, nodding toward the stack. "This one might not be relevant. It was a little different, but we made a copy of it just in case."

The third article, dated two weeks after the previous one, described the discovery of a 34-year-old local woman named Edna Soren by a group of hikers in a woody area off Creek Road. She had been severely injured and claimed not to remember what had happened to her. She was taken to a local hospital where at the time the article was written she was still being treated. "Creek Road again," Stone murmured. He glanced up. "Anything else?"

Jason shook his head. "Nothing after that one—the only other murders after that were all things like domestic violence, drunken brawls, gang stuff—all pretty normal."

"And nothing prior to these?"

"Not that we could find," Lopez said. "We went back through another twenty-five years or so to see if we could find a pattern, but there wasn't anything. Of course we only had time to check the Ojai paper—we might be able to turn up more in the Ventura one, but that would take a lot more research."

Stone nodded, thinking. "So we've got a murder and either one or two attempted murders that match the pattern of our current ones. Edna Soren didn't die, correct?"

Jason shrugged. "The papers didn't say anything else about her in the next few weeks, so I'm guessing not."

"What I want to know, though," Stone said as if talking to himself, "is if these are connected with the current ones, why so few, and so unsuccessful? One would think that if Faces went on another killing spree twenty-seven years ago, he wouldn't have stopped with one victim and two almosts."

"Yeah," Jason said. "That's a good point. But even so—especially the one with the kid that doesn't remember, that sounds like our guy, or thing, or whatever. It's like you said happened with the kid who tried to strangle you at Bart's."

"But why did it stop?" Lopez asked. "After seeing some of those bodies, I can't figure it just decided 'that's enough, I'll stop now.'"

"Good question," Stone said. "It's possible that someone stopped it."

"A mage, you mean?"

"Or more than one," Stone said. "It's possible. We don't exactly advertise our activities, generally. And if someone did stop it, they probably assumed it wouldn't be back, so there was no need to discuss it further."

"So, assuming you're right," Jason said, "the big questions are who stopped it, and why's it back now?"

"Yes," Stone agreed.

"Do you have any idea how to *answer* those questions?" Lopez asked.

"What about that plan you had, Al?" Jason added. "Did you work it out yet?"

"As well as I can—which isn't that well, I'm afraid." Stone stood. "I need to make a couple of phone calls. May I use your phone, Stan?"

"Sure, go for it."

"Hang on," Jason protested. "Don't leave us in suspense. What are you thinking of doing?"

"Trying to talk to it," Stone said, and disappeared into the kitchen.

| CHAPTER TWENTY-NINE

An hour later, Jason and Lopez were having an unspoken contest to see who looked more uncomfortable standing amid the doily-strewn tablecloths and gauzy decor of the Third Eye Bookstore and Mystic Emporium. As Stone studied the bookshelves, the two of them finally decided to declare the competition a tie.

"We'll be outside," Jason said as he turned sideways to fit past Stone in a narrow aisle. "You—uh—take all the time you need."

Stone nodded, flipping through a book.

On the other side of the store, the proprietress and her friend, the same woman who'd been here the last time Stone had visited, sipped tea and watched him while trying not to be obvious. After Jason and Lopez left, Stone headed toward them. He didn't miss the looks of apprehension on both their faces.

In truth, he didn't want to be here anymore than his two companions did. However, he needed some information, and the two phone calls he'd made—to Hubbard at the University and Stefan Kolinsky, his black-mage associate—had both gone unanswered. Since time was of the essence, he was forced to resort to plan B. "Ladies," he murmured with a nod.

"Oh! May I help you?" the proprietress asked. Her voice shook a little, and she never took her eyes off him.

Stone deliberately turned on the charm, wondering if the power of the cheery grin and the accent would trump what was no doubt a fear that he was going to murder them right there in the shop. "I hope so," he said. "Would you happen to have any reference material on this area's ley lines?"

In spite of herself, the proprietress's fearful look was replaced by one of surprise. "I don't get much call for that," she admitted.

Stone shrugged. "It's for a little project I'm working on. I'm down from the Bay Area, and I'm afraid I've left all my reference materials at home. I need to know where the ley lines run so I'll know where to get the best results."

"What—kind of results?" the woman asked.

He reached into the pocket of his overcoat—both women flinched a little—and pulled out one of his business cards. "Just getting an idea of the sort of mystical energy you have around here," he said. "Remember when I was in before, I was looking for information on local legends? Same project."

The woman stared at the card; her friend looked over her shoulder and did likewise. Then they both looked up at him. "You—*teach* the occult? At Stanford?"

Stone smiled inwardly. Hook baited, line cast, fish caught. Now all that was left was to reel them in. "I do," he said. "I'm always fascinated to find local shops like yours, and in this case yours was a godsend for my research." He amped up the smile a bit. "Who knows? You might even get a citation in the paper I'm working on."

The woman sighed. If Stone had been crueler, it would have been humorous: her expression looked like she couldn't decide whether to be awestruck or terrified by the thought that he was not only a potential murderer, but a potential murderer who was an expert on her own subject of interest. "I'm so sorry, Dr.—" she looked at the card again "—Stone. I wish I could help you, but I'm afraid I don't have anything about local ley lines. I might be able to order something, but—"

"Wait," the other woman spoke up. "I might have a map at home. In fact, I know I do. Do you have time? I could run home and get it. It would only take me fifteen minutes or so. I don't live far away."

Stone noticed that she didn't invite him home with her—the smile and the promise of her name in a real occult paper would only take him so far. "That would be lovely, Ms.—"

"Mrs. Washburn," she said. "Suzanne Washburn." She rose and grabbed her oversized purse. "You just wait here if you can, and I'll be right back." She waved and hurried out of the shop.

The proprietress smiled, still looking a little uncertain. "Suzanne has oodles of that sort of thing. She's bought a lot from me, and she haunts Bart's or sometimes even goes into Santa Barbara or L.A. to look for it. Like I said, one of my best customers ever since I opened the shop." She tilted her head, clearly gathering her courage. Finally, she ventured: "I saw you on the news, Dr. Stone."

He nodded. "I'm not surprised."

She glanced toward the door, suddenly realizing that she was alone in the shop with a potential murderer who had two large and intimidating-looking friends waiting outside. Swallowing, she said, "Is—is there anything else I can help you with while you wait?"

He shook his head. "No, thank you. If I'm making you uncomfortable, I could wait outside."

"No, no! I—" she dithered, trailing off.

He smiled. "It's no trouble. I'll just wait outside with my friends." He didn't miss the look of relief on her face as he turned to leave.

Suzanne Washburn returned as promised in about fifteen minutes, clutching a large book and a rolled-up map. She waved triumphantly at Stone and he followed her back inside.

"Here we are," she said, unrolling the map and spreading it across the counter. "Is this what you're looking for, Dr. Stone?"

He studied it. The map was quite detailed; it showed the western half of the United States and was crisscrossed with a series of familiar interconnected lines, along with others showing longitude and latitude. After checking to make sure that the ones he knew in the Bay Area were accurate, he focused his attention on the southern California area. "Yes, this will do nicely," he said. "Tell me: you ladies are obviously knowledgeable about the area's—mystical characteristics—"

"Oh, yes," Suzanne said proudly before the shop's proprietress could answer. "This valley has very good energy. It's known for it all over the world."

"I'm sure it is," he murmured, still examining the map. "But can you tell me if there are any specific areas that are known for being more mystically or spiritually active than usual?"

"There's quite a lot of them," the proprietress said. "Ojai's very spiritual. I think I've actually got a list somewhere. You know, for the tourists." She went off and in a couple of minutes came back with a small pamphlet titled *Your Gateway to Magical Ojai*, with a hand-drawn picture of a mountaintop and an oak tree under a large full moon. "This should help you."

"Thank you, he said, tucking the pamphlet into his coat. He indicated the map. "Do you happen to have a photocopier? I'll need to spend some time studying this."

"Why don't you keep it for now, Dr. Stone?" Suzanne said hastily. "As long as you need it. I use it to do astrological charts, but I have another one. You can just bring it back and leave it with Iris here when you're finished with it."

"Thank you both very much. I appreciate your help."

Once again, he didn't miss that both of them looked quite relieved to see him depart.

"About *time*," Jason said as Stone came out of the shop carrying the map and a large purple bag. "Stan and I have been out here discussing what a crazy-ass idea this is that you had. Are you sure you still want to go through with it?"

Stone kept going, headed back toward Lopez's truck. "I haven't been able to come up with anything better. Have you?"

Jason and Lopez fell into step behind him. "We've been trying," Jason said. "We got nothin'. But are you even gonna be able to do this? What makes you think it'll talk to you, or that you can handle it if it decides it would rather eat your face? Didn't you say it kicked you around like an old football at the barn out on Creek Road?"

"Yes, but I didn't have a secret weapon then," Stone said.

"And what's that?"

"You."

They reached the truck and climbed in. Jason stared at the mage, confused. "Me?"

"Faces won't expect me to have the kind of power I can toss around when I don't have to worry about what's driving it. I'm hoping that will give it a surprise if it tries anything. You *are* still willing to help, aren't you?"

"Sure," Jason said. "But—"

"I'll need an hour or so to study this map and compare it with the literature I've got," he said as if Jason hadn't spoken.

"What are you looking for?" Lopez asked, swinging the truck into a wide U-turn and heading back up Ojai Avenue.

"Someplace that might not exist—if it doesn't, I'll have to improvise. But if luck smiles on our efforts, there'll be somewhere around this area that combines a place of power, a ley line—or even two of them crossed, which is too much to ask—and few or no people likely to be nearby after dark."

"You realize," Lopez said, "that if you pull some kind of flashy stunt and get caught, you'll probably get hauled back into jail again. At some point they're gonna charge you with something just so they can sit on you."

"Yes, well, that's your contribution to our little party," Stone said. "If that should happen, it will be your job to talk our way out of whatever police trouble we find ourselves in."

Lopez grimaced. "Lucky me."

❖

Jason waited until they got back to Lopez's house and the cop was in the kitchen getting drinks before addressing Stone. "So you said you need my battery thing to help you with Faces," he said. "What about that other magic you were working on? The stuff from Harrison? I just realized you never mention it anymore. Did you give up on trying to learn it?"

Stone sighed. "Erm," he said. "That sort of thing's not really appropriate in this case. I haven't worked out yet how to do anything but open up the firehose and let fly, and that can be dangerous if I lose control of it." It wasn't the truth, and he hoped Jason didn't spot the fact that he was lying—or at least not telling the whole story. Apparently Verity had kept her word and never revealed to her brother what had happened the previous summer, when Stone had temporarily burned out his magical abilities while dealing with the Evil's ritual at Burning Man.

In truth, he'd put Harrison's research on the back burner after that. He didn't like to admit it, but the thought of permanently losing his magical abilities frightened him enough that every time he thought about resuming his experiments, he came up with an excuse for why it would be better to do it later.

Later hadn't come since he'd returned from Las Vegas, almost a year ago.

"You're not having second thoughts, are you?" he asked, to divert the subject.

"Nah," Jason said. "I told you I'm in, and I am. I just gotta say I don't think trying to talk to something that's murdered seven people so far is gonna work. It doesn't seem the talking type."

"You may be right," Stone said. "But I'm fresh out of other options."

| CHAPTER THIRTY

Stone took the map, along with his various books and pamphlets, and disappeared into his room. When he came back out an hour or so later carrying the map and a book with a marker sticking out of it, Jason and Lopez were watching another news account of the triple murder on the evening news.

"Anything new?" Stone asked, "or are they just repeating themselves for the dozenth time?"

"No suspects," Jason said. "They're asking for the public's help if they saw anybody near the house. There's speculation that it might be related to at least a couple of the other murders and they're telling everybody not to go anywhere alone, especially at night. Oh, and the little girl, Olivia, is in her grandparents' custody."

"Good, good." He sat on the couch and turned to Lopez. "Stan, are you familiar with a place called...Matilija Hot Springs?" He stumbled over the unfamiliar word.

"Sure," Lopez said. "It's a few miles outside Ojai, up Highway 33." He grinned. "And you totally mangled that name, Al. It's '*Ma-til-i-ha*.'"

"Whatever. Tell me about it."

Lopez shrugged. "It's kind of a local hippie hangout—hot springs, like the name says. There used to be a little resort thing, but it's been closed for the last couple of years. People still sneak up there sometimes to soak and smoke from what I hear, but they've got no-trespassing signs and a razor-wire fence around the whole thing to keep 'em out. I wouldn't be surprised if a few snuck in anyway, but it should be pretty private, especially on a weeknight. Is *that* where you want to go?"

Stone nodded. He indicated the rolled-up map and opened the book to the place he'd marked. "According to this, the Chumash considered it a sacred place of healing. It doesn't have intersecting ley lines, but it does have one running right through the middle of it. And I didn't realize it was closed—that makes it even better. Means we're less likely to encounter anyone, and if we do, you can just show them your badge and ask them to leave."

"You make it sound so easy," Jason said.

"Well, either it will work or it won't," Stone said. "It's not terribly complicated in theory."

"Theory isn't what usually tries to kill us."

Stone's expression grew serious. "I'm not forcing you to do this—either of you. There's a good chance it could be dangerous, especially if something goes wrong. If you want to back out, do it now."

Jason and Lopez exchanged glances. "Hell," Lopez said, "I didn't need to retire anyway."

"And I got nothing better to do," Jason said. "Looks like you're stuck with us, Al. When's this going down?"

"As soon as it gets dark. The sooner we do this, the sooner we have a chance of stopping the murders."

"What exactly are you going to do?" Lopez asked. "I'm not following this whole plan. You're gonna try to contact this thing and talk to it? And say what? 'Please, Mr. Ancient Evil Spirit of Vengeance, won't you stop killing people?' I know I'm pretty new at this whole supernatural gig, but somehow I don't think asking nicely and offering it a cookie are going to get you very far."

"I don't have a cookie," Stone pointed out. "So I'll have to make do with my natural charm, I guess."

"Al—" Jason started.

Stone shook his head. "Don't worry about it. I'm making this up as I go along, to be honest. But like I said before—what other alternative do we have? If you have other ideas, speak up now."

"If you get yourself killed, it's not gonna do anybody any good," Lopez said.

"I'm not planning to get myself—or anyone—killed. We'll be prepared before we go in, and that includes stronger mental protections and a much more elaborate circle."

"Great, except that thing got to you, even through your mental protections, remember?" Lopez pointed out. "And it almost made me shoot you."

"So far, though, he's shown no sign of being able to do that away from his nasty little shrine. As strong as he is, I don't think he's nearly as potent without being near a corrupted ley line combined with something that could hold its mystic charge over hundreds of years. If he could get to us out here, I think he'd have already done by now. I think he tried when I was getting Jason back, but he couldn't manage it."

Lopez got up. "Okay, then. Come on, Jason."

"Where are we going?"

"Hardware store, for some supplies. Al here has proven that he's great with the weird shit, but pretty much hopeless with anything practical. So it's up to us to be the practical ones."

Stone glared at them, but once again he didn't bother contradicting Lopez.

They waited until full dark before heading out of town. Stacked neatly in the truck's bed were three packs similar to the ones Lopez had prepared for their hike up to the shrine, along with a couple coils of rope, a first-aid kit, a fire extinguisher (Jason's idea, after pointing out that Stone's magical adventures often ended in something either catching fire or blowing up), a pack of glow sticks, a heavy blanket, a lantern, extra flashlights and batteries, two long-bladed machetes, and a flare gun. There was also a shotgun and a box of ammo in a locked box in the back of the cab, and Jason had convinced Lopez to lend him his spare pistol.

Stone had looked over all these preparations with amazement. "We're not going to war," he protested. "We're just going five miles outside town."

"Has one of these plans *ever* gone the way you expected, Al?" Jason asked, arms crossed. Despite the heat, he was carrying a leather jacket he'd borrowed from Lopez. The cop had one as well.

"With that kind of optimism, what can I do but assume everything will be fine?" Stone's voice dripped sarcasm as he tossed his black duffel bag, stuffed full of various ritual components supplemented by his purchases at the Third Eye and a few of his books, into the bed along with the rest of the gear. He had declined Lopez's offer of another leather jacket, preferring his own overcoat. It didn't have any armor, but he didn't think trying to do magic while flapping around in a jacket that fit someone who had forty pounds on him would be the best idea.

They had dinner at an Italian place Lopez suggested after Stone had quietly turned down the first suggestion of Don Armando's. Still, he barely touched his food, staring moodily into the table's candle as Lopez and Jason dug into their pasta and caught up on old news as if this were just a normal weeknight. If he noticed that their voices were a little unnaturally fast and bright, he didn't say anything.

The truth was, he had next to no idea how he was going to pull this off. He didn't even know if He of Many Faces would bother to answer his call, or what he would do if it did. His hope was that, like many things from the spirit world that liked to dress up as other people, it wasn't that powerful physically. That kind of being usually relied on subtlety rather than sheer power. The Evil were a good example: once you got them out of their stolen bodies, even the most powerful of them were vulnerable on this plane. The trick was getting them out, and hitting them once you did. Since he was reasonably sure now that Faces couldn't possess him or his friends, it would be forced to deal with him in a noncorporeal fashion. And further, if his theory about its minions requiring some connection (such the energy from a recently-killed victim) to be able to affect the material plane without possessing someone, then they, at least, might not be a factor in this.

There was also the possibility that Stone had deprived it of what might have been a significant power source when he rescued Jason from his extradimensional captivity. He still wasn't sure exactly what Faces had been doing with the power it had been pulling from Jason, but now it didn't have it anymore. That had to make *some* difference.

Hell, if he was being wildly optimistic about things (admittedly not a mental state he often enjoyed), perhaps the energy from Jason was why it had been so active this time, as opposed to twenty-seven years ago when it had barely managed to kill one person and make a go at another (or two) before disappearing again. Maybe it had a limited amount of energy, and could only be active for a short time before it was forced to go back home to recharge, and Jason's power had prolonged its shelf life. If that were true, then maybe the Ayalas were its last gasp as it had tried to do as much damage as possible before it had to go home.

As usual, it was all speculation, and probably wrong. That was the problem with dealing with the supernatural in real life: nothing was cut and dried, and almost nothing was simple. The whole thing would have been easier if it were more like the books, where things like vampires and werewolves and ghosts had their own laws and societies and physical rules that they followed. You know, like: *I'm facing a vampire. I'd better stock up on wooden stakes, holy water, and garlic bread.* Or: *Werewolf? Silver bullets, and done.* Instead, pretty much everything he'd faced so far in his magical career had been different from everything *else* he'd faced, to the point where it was impossible to be prepared for anything ahead of time. He was almost—*almost*—nostalgic for the Evil: at least they made sense once you figured them out.

He continued to be lost in his thoughts as they drove out of town, heading north up Highway 33. It was quite dark now; few cars passed them going the other way, and no one was behind them. Above, the night was nearly moonless.

"You ever been out here, Jason?" Lopez asked. He drove just a bit above the speed limit, the truck's smooth, powerful engine rumbling comfortingly.

"No, but some of my friends have. It was one of the good places to party and drink beer back in the day. The cops didn't bother you if you didn't make trouble. Not really my thing." He leaned forward from his spot in the back seat. "Hey, Al, you awake?"

Stone nodded, but didn't answer.

"Everything okay?" Lopez glanced over, then back at the road.

"Fine," he said without moving.

"Let him go, Stan. He's probably doing his magic preparation thing. Or else we're boring him. Or both." Jason grinned.

Stone still didn't reply. He didn't think there was anything to be gained from letting them in on what he was really doing: carefully watching the oncoming cars and preparing to shield the truck in case Faces or one of its minions decided to possess its driver and send it into an impromptu head-on collision.

The turnoff to Matilija Hot Springs was on their left, and not well marked. Lopez almost missed it before Jason jabbed a finger forward and called "There it is!" He hit the brakes and veered the truck off the road with only a small squeal of tires and a somewhat larger jostling of his passengers.

In front of them about fifty feet up, two metal posts rose on either side of the road. A chain stretched between them with a sign hanging from its center point: *NO TRESPASSING*. Lopez pulled the truck up to it and stopped. "We hike from here?"

"Is it far?"

"Another mile or so up the road."

Stone shook his head. "Too far, then. Give me a moment." He got out and went over to where the chain was connected to the pole. He stared at it for a moment, centering his will on one link. After a moment, it came loose with a small *pop*. He unhooked it and dropped it, then waved Lopez forward. After the truck rumbled past, he re-hooked the chain, but didn't repair the link. If they had to get out of here in a hurry it would be easier to break through the chain.

They continued on. Lopez drove slowly, the headlights' beams bouncing along a narrow road bounded by trees and rocks. Aside from the truck's lights, there were no others along the road, giving their approach a tunnel-like quality.

Stone kept a careful watch for any movement, his magical senses active. Aside from the occasional flash of a small animal darting across the road or between the trees, he saw nothing.

The road opened into a dirt parking lot. This too was chained off with another NO TRESPASSING sign, but this time Lopez could pull the truck around it. Beyond the lot, they could see the dark shapes of a few buildings and many trees.

"I think there's a path leading to the springs," Lopez said. And to Stone: "Do you need to go there specifically, or is this close enough?"

"Hold on." Stone got out of the truck and opened up his magical senses fully, taking in the energies of the area.

Immediately, a sense of peace and well-being flowed over him. The various small injuries he'd sustained over the past few days didn't fade, but it was as if they no longer mattered. As much as the tainted site of the grim shrine up above Creek Road had made him feel ill and uneasy, this place seemed to be its opposite. He felt the energies here moving in harmony, aspected toward health and healing instead of corruption and vengeance. Further, the ley line here thrummed with power—clean, untarnished power this time. It was the difference between a pool of sewage and a clear, fresh pond.

"Al?"

Stone started, reluctant to pull himself back from the area's pleasant embrace. "What? Oh—yes, this will do fine for what I need."

He grabbed his bag from the back of the truck; Jason and Lopez pulled out the lantern and flashlights, and Jason strapped Lopez's spare gun on and they both grabbed machetes. "Should I pull the truck around and leave the headlights on?" Lopez asked.

"No," Stone said. "You're fine there. Just bring the lantern, and a few of those glow sticks. I don't want to put the circle too close to the truck in case something goes wrong."

They got the lantern going and Stone began setting up. He slipped out of his coat and tossed it into the truck's passenger seat, then walked about twenty feet away. As Lopez and Jason watched, prowling the perimeter with their machetes and flashlights in hand, Stone drew a large circle with blue sand using a tool that looked ridiculously like what pastry chefs used for making icing curlicues on cupcakes. Then, using a smaller version of the same tool, he painstakingly began drawing smaller structures both fully inside it and intersecting its edges. He ignored everything but his work, trusting his friends to keep watch for any potential threats.

When he finished with the sand, he placed candles and crystals at strategic points, weaving the magic around and through them and the circle with utmost care. He focused on defense, protection, and clarity of mind: he wasn't trying to summon or imprison anything with this circle, but merely to make contact while preventing it from attacking him. He could feel the vast energy of the ley line flowing through him, augmenting his own not-inconsiderable powers, making the working both easier and stronger than it would have been in another location. The energy of the earth worked in harmony with his purpose—if he'd been trying to do harm or injury with his circle, he was sure, he would have met far more resistance and the ley line would prove a hindrance rather than a help.

When you got down to it, he realized, the people who had summoned He of Many Faces so many years ago had no doubt thought they were doing the right thing. They had seen their people decimated by these intruders' sicknesses and had only sought vengeance for the destruction of their way of life. Yes, they were twisted and bloodthirsty by the standards of their peaceful culture, but a small corner of Stone's mind could understand and sympathize with the desperate measures they'd taken.

The only problem was, those desperate measures were now causing untold injury to people who had nothing to do with their crusade. Killing the actual people who had brought the diseases to their tribe was perhaps understandable, if not entirely moral, but killing their descendants—innocent men, women, and children who harbored them no ill will—that was different. Stone hoped he'd have a chance of convincing He of Many Faces that it had fulfilled its purpose and could now go home permanently. Sometimes spirits from other dimensions could be reasonable.

Not too often, admittedly. But sometimes.

It took him nearly an hour to finish the circle, though he didn't realize it until he was done. He stopped in its center, swiping his hair off his forehead, and examined his handiwork. "There."

Jason and Lopez halted their sentry routes. "Done?" Jason asked. At Stone's nod, he said, "Okay, so what happens now?"

"Now we begin." He carefully stepped out of the circle. "This is going to get a bit tricky: I can't protect you unless you're actually inside the circle, but if anything physical should show up, you're going to need to deal with it."

"How does that work?" Lopez asked.

Stone pointed. "Notice I've left some gaps from the center out to the edge. If you step carefully, you can exit there, even in the middle of the ritual. I've allowed for that in the casting. The only important thing to remember is this: whatever you do, do *not* break the circle. Don't touch the sand. If you even smudge it a bit with your foot, all sorts of things I'd rather not think about could happen. Frying my brain with psychic backlash is probably the most pleasant one for you—and if anything is here, the rest won't be any fun either."

"Got it," Jason said. "He's not kidding, Stan. I remember one of these before—I tripped, and we both almost got eaten by a demon. So take this one seriously."

Lopez nodded. "Are you expecting anything to show up?"

"I *always* expect something to show up," Stone said. "As far as what, though, I have no idea. Just—be ready for anything."

Jason snorted. "Big help, Al."

Lopez frowned. "What if other people show up? You know, people this thing's possessed? We can't just shoot 'em, or slice 'em up with the machetes. That's murder."

"I know," Stone said. "I didn't say this would be easy. Just—do whatever you can to subdue them. Do you have your handcuffs? If you do, keep them close. Fortunately, it appears that even when possessed, the victims aren't any harder to deal with physically than a normal person. And I really don't expect to see any other people out here, do you? It seems fairly deserted."

Lopez nodded. "I hope you're right." He headed over to the truck and pulled out his handcuffs, along with a small bag which he handed to Jason. "Zip-ties. Just in case."

Jason stowed them in his pocket and let out a long sigh. "Okay, Al. Ready when you are." He shrugged into the leather jacket Lopez had lent him. "You do your thing, and we'll keep anything from jumping you."

"No." Stone shook his head. "That will have to be Stan's job. I need you to stay inside the circle. If anything goes wrong, I'll need you as a source of additional power."

"But I can help if—" he started to protest.

"No, Jason. I know you'd rather be tackling the bad guys than playing psychic battery, but I really need you to do this. I'm counting on the extra power to be able to manage this thing on my terms."

"Yeah, okay, fine," Jason grumbled. "Your show, your rules. Let's do this."

Stone ushered both men inside the circle and indicated where they should stand. This time he'd created a large center area, so they had room to move around. He himself took a position in the middle.

With one final glance at Jason and Lopez to make sure they were where they belonged, he took several deep, cleansing breaths, double-checked his mental defenses, and lit each of the candles in turn with quick gestures. Then, closing his eyes, he willed the circle into life, immediately feeling the power of the ley line once again augmenting his efforts. More than ever he felt like the center point of a conduit, the arcane energy running through his body and around the circle like some kind of mystic electrical circuit. For a moment, he allowed himself to revel in the sensation of holding this much power at his command. It had been a long time since he'd worked in a circle this large.

He only let himself do that for a few seconds, though: he knew he didn't have a lot of time to do what he needed to do. Even with the ley line's aid, his body could only handle the strain of channeling this kind of energy for maybe an hour at the maximum, and he didn't know how long it would take to reach He of Many Faces—if he could even reach it at all. "Look sharp," he murmured to Jason and Lopez, and reached out with his mind.

"Good evening, mageling," said a voice in his head.

As if it had been there waiting for him all along.

CHAPTER THIRTY-ONE

Without opening his eyes, Stone could see it in front of him. Its form was a shifting miasma of vaguely humanoid shape that flared a deep blood red. Encased in a darker red sheath that seemed barely capable of containing its various roiling patterns, it resembled a glowing, bloody body bag full of small, angry creatures struggling in vain to escape.

"I thought you would find me eventually," it continued. Its voice in Stone's head was smooth and mocking, but its strange cadence and unsettling tones made his mind want to reject it. *"It was amusing to watch you struggle. And now you have found me—or rather, I have allowed you to find me. It will do you no good, though. You should have left when I gave you the warning."*

Stone struggled to keep his mental "voice" even and calm. If he could keep it talking, perhaps if nothing else he could learn something. A chill ran through his body that had nothing to do with the magical energy coursing through him. *"I couldn't go,"* he said. *"I couldn't leave my friend."*

"You will suffer for that. He was mine."

"He was not *yours. He is not of your people. He is not why you were summoned. You wanted him only for the power you could steal from him."*

The figure seemed to shrug. *"It is no matter. I do not need him. He was a tasty trifle at best. You, however, will die for defying me. You and your friends. You will die like all the rest."*

Stone wasn't going to get into a pissing match with an ancient, extradimensional spirit of vengeance. He had things he needed to find out. *"What are you even doing here?"* he asked.

"You know my purpose," it said. *"I commend you. You are so young and you know so little, yet you found my source. You are the first to do that. It is unfortunate that I must kill you, but your power will feed me well."*

"Not if I get you first," Stone told it. *"You're an anachronism, Many Faces. You're out of your time. You succeeded in the purpose you were summoned for many years ago, did you not? Why are you still here?"*

"I am always here. I will always be here."

"I don't think so," Stone said, shaking his head. *"If you were, then why haven't you killed any others over the years? Why now? Why twenty-seven years ago—if you even have the concept of a 'year' wherever you come from?"*

"I have always been here," it repeated. *"Watching. Waiting. You think I have but one calling? I have many callings, in many places. I am everywhere."*

"Very impressive," Stone said, letting the sarcasm come through in his mind-voice. *"But do you know what I think? I think you were re-summoned. I think someone managed to pull your metaphysical arse back to this plane, and once you got here you set up shop and rediscovered your purpose in life. Tell me I'm wrong—if you can."* He grabbed hold of some of the energy from the ley line and fashioned it into a sort of mental amplifier. He didn't know if it would work, but it was worth a shot.

The thing made a sound that was sort of a derisive snort. *"Mageling, you know so little. Even with all your pride and all your power, you are by my reckoning barely less ignorant than the children who blundered into what they did not comprehend."*

"Children?" Stone asked.

"She of my masters' blood called me, but did not direct me. My connection to your world was weak then, because in their foolishness

she and her companions summoned me imperfectly, foolishly. Since then they have grown in age, if not in wisdom. This time they had an artifact of power to aid their summoning." Contempt came through in its tone. "*And still they do not know what they have done. Still, she of my masters' blood does not direct me, so I am left free to set my own path.*"

"*Oh?*" Stone matched its contempt. "*So 'left free to set your own path,' you simply continued blindly following your masters' orders? You're not very original, are you? Either that, or you're lying.*"

Anger flared, pressing against Stone's mental shields. "*Have a care, mageling. I can crush you where you stand.*"

"*I don't think you can,*" Stone told it. "*I think if you could do that, you'd have already done. I don't think anyone's ever gotten this close to you, have they?*"

It made an unwholesome laugh. "*And again your conceit shows, little one. Always you think you are the only one.*"

"*Someone else knows about you, then?*" That was news, unless it was talking about Jason and Lopez. Stone didn't think it was.

"*The woman will die as well,*" it said. "*She was fortunate to disperse me temporarily—as I said, the prior summoning was incomplete and inexpert. I nearly succeeded in destroying her in my weaker guise, even as she worked her medicine—this time, she will not survive, as you will not. Now I am in possession of my full power. There are many to feed my hunger, and the hunger of my children. And none who can stop us.*"

"*Go back where you came from,*" Stone told it, again drawing in power from the ley line. His mental voice was strong and steady, echoing across the astral space where they existed. "*Go back now. You've had enough vengeance. If you don't go, I'm warning you: I will find a way to send you back. If I can't do it on my own, I'll bring others. I know what you are now, so it's only a matter of time before I work out how to stop you, or one of the others I tell does. Your way is to work in secret—but I'll make sure you'll have no secrets. Even if you kill me, the others will hear, and they'll come. That's not a threat—it's a promise. Take your vile little pets and go while you still can.*"

He of Many Faces laughed. It too echoed through the space, full of scorn and amusement. "*Oh, mageling. Your voice is as the wolf pup yapping at the bear.*"

It struck without warning, so fast that Stone didn't have time to react. A solid wall of power slammed into his mental shields, staggering him backward. Only the ley line's additional potency prevented them from being shattered by the attack, but even so, the psychic assault that got through spiked into his head like someone had buried a cleaver in it. He felt his physical body drop to its knees, and faintly in the distance he could hear someone calling to him, though he couldn't make out what they were saying.

Gritting his teeth, he got back up. "Jason..." he muttered. "Are you there?" He risked shifting a portion of his attention to the material world.

"Right here, Al," came Jason's voice from behind him. He sounded concerned. "What's happening? Are you—"

Many Faces hit Stone with another blast of energy, powerful enough this time to knock him off his feet, somersaulting back out of the circle. He crashed to the ground in time to see Jason and Lopez flying backward as well. The circle flared brilliant blue and, with the source directing its power gone, died, leaving only the lantern Lopez had set up a short distance away and the feeble glows from the lightsticks as light sources.

Stone struggled back to his feet, fighting feedback from the circle's abrupt failure. It wasn't supposed to be able to do that. He glanced around, seeing Jason also scrambling back up. He looked dazed, but clearly Stone's shield had protected him from the brunt of it as well. There were a few advantages to being mundane, and one of the big ones was that you didn't take as much damage from psychic attacks as mages did.

Stone knew he only had one chance to hit the spirit hard, while it wasn't expecting him to be able to retaliate. He could still feel the comforting power of the ley line, though not as intimately as when he'd been plugged into it via the circle. Now it was a more diffuse, all-over sort of sense that it was there.

Staggering over to Jason, he dropped to his knees next to him. "Jason," he rasped, "I need power. Now." He wished he could risk using Harrison's magic, but if he couldn't take this thing down and his power cut out anyway, they'd all be dead.

"Do it," Jason growled.

Gathering magical energy first from within himself and his focus objects and then opening himself up to the ley line, he reached his left hand out and clamped it down on Jason's arm. He could see the shifting red form, fainter now since it was mostly in the astral realm.

One shot.

He was only going to get one shot.

Make it good.

He drew a deep breath, tightened his grip on Jason's arm, and flung his spell at the form at full strength. He held nothing back, waiting for the torrent of power from Jason's vast reservoir to flow into him.

Nothing happened.

| CHAPTER THIRTY-TWO

That wasn't technically true. The spell still went off—but crashed against He of Many Faces' bubbling, shifting carapace as ineffectually as a wave breaking against the side of a cliff.

Stone sank back, panting, his face drawn with the exertion of throwing around that kind of magic without being prepared—and without roughly half the power he'd expected to use.

"Jason!" he tried to yell, but it came out as more of a breathy shriek. "What are you doing?"

"I don't *know!*" Jason's voice came back, bright with panic. "I tried! I couldn't do it. I—"

An invisible missile slammed into him, carrying him halfway across the parking lot and into the side of Lopez's truck. He impacted with a loud *thud* and lay still.

Stone scrambled to his feet, swaying. This was not good. Whatever had happened with Jason, whatever had caused him not to be able to access his friend's power—none of that mattered if Jason was unconscious. "Stan!"

"Here!" came a voice somewhere to his right. "Al, what—"

"Get to the truck!" He looked around wildly, but didn't see Many Faces' glowing form on the astral or material plane. Where had it gone? Was it playing with them? Did it need to recharge its energy? This was going badly wrong. They needed to get out of here. "Grab Jason and get to the truck! I'll try to hold it off!"

Focusing his will, he struggled to rebuild his shield. It wasn't as strong as before, even with the ley line still providing part of its power, but he hoped it would prevent Many Faces' next attack from killing him outright. If they could make it to the truck and get away, it might let them go, as it had before.

It wasn't much of a hope, but it was all he had right now. This had been an ambush. Many Faces had known all along that he was coming. It had been ready for him.

In his peripheral vision, he glimpsed Lopez moving slowly toward the truck where Jason lay. He was limping, favoring his left leg. He made it about halfway before something picked him up in an invisible whirlwind, flung him several feet into the air, and dashed him back to the ground. He landed hard with an *oof* and he too lay unmoving.

Stone's gaze darted back and forth between his two downed friends and the shimmering form hovering over Lopez's prone body. If these things were here along with Many Faces, it could mean that it had killed someone—or more than one someone—recently. More death. Enraged, he drew power and hurled it at the form. "*No, damn you!*"

He was rewarded with the satisfying sight of the nearly invisible thing lighting up bright red and then flying to pieces. So the little ones didn't have the protection of the big one. That was something.

One down.

For a moment Stone could only stand there, panting, bent over with his hands on his knees. His gaze never stopped moving, though. He couldn't afford to get blindsided again. He heaved himself forward toward the truck.

Something slammed into him from behind, driving him forward to crash into the ground. He cried out as pain flared all over him, but once again his shield had absorbed most of the impact.

Stone rolled and came to his knees, flinging another spell with a roar without bothering to aim it. Another shimmering form sizzled and flared bright, then dark. Stone paused a moment to be glad he'd bothered to stage his mystical commando raid on favorable ground: if the ley line hadn't been here, even the small ones would have been too much for him after the psychic hit he'd taken from Many Faces' frighteningly potent attacks.

This thing was well and truly out of his league. He dragged himself up to his feet again and kept pushing toward the truck. Right now, his only chance was to take his friends and get the hell out of here, and then try to recruit more mages to help him deal with the problem.

Those, he realized, were two fairly remote possibilities. Many Faces had him now; he didn't think it was going to let him get away without a fight.

Let it try, then. At least if he could wake up Lopez or Jason, he could get them to leave while he covered their escape. He'd gotten them into this—he owed them getting them out.

His legs burned, heavy as lead as he trudged back toward the truck. He had nearly reached it when laughter echoed through the parking lot—or perhaps it was only through his mind. He was starting to have trouble telling the difference.

An invisible wall of force hit him again, shoving him across the lot. He fell over backward and hit the ground, but the shove had not been hard enough to injure him further. Blinking sweat (or was it blood?) from his eyes, he got back up again on shaking legs. *It's trying to keep me away from the truck.* Across the lot he thought he saw Lopez stir, but it was too dark to tell for sure.

The mocking laughter sounded again. *"Now, cub, see what happens when you push the bear too far."*

From the trees came an echoing, enraged roar.

Stone barely had time to spin to face it before a hulking, shadowy form hurtled out of the forest. Moving at frightening speed, it was on him before he could react, almost before his stunned mind could put the connection together:

Oh dear gods it's possessed a bear

He didn't have time to get a spell off before it leaped at him, forepaws spread wide, jaws gaping open, and slammed him back to the ground. It roared in his face, deafeningly loud, and he could hear the laughter behind the roar. Its hot breath, fetid and sour, washed over him. Its paws raked at his fading shield.

His mind spun uselessly. He couldn't think.

He had to think.

If he didn't do something *right now,* this creature was going to kill him.

"Jason! Stan!" he tried calling, with a desperate hope that one of them would wake up and shoot it. But there was no answering cry or gunshot: his voice had no strength behind it as the bear's massive weight pressed down on him. The shield held, but it was faltering. He had a few more seconds at most.

The bear roared again. It was an inhuman sound—hell, it was an un*bear*ish sound. There was something wild and primal and chaotic in that howl. And then he noticed its eyes: they glowed with a hellish red-orange light. It whipped its head back and forth as if fighting some inner compulsion—Stone realized this bear was every bit as much of a victim as he was. It didn't want to attack him.

That, right now, didn't matter. He'd worry about the majesty of the local wildlife later. Right now, if he had to kill the bear to save his life, then so be it.

The only problem was, he didn't think he could do it. He could hardly get a breath now. The shield was buckling. The bear raised a paw and took a mighty swipe at him. He shrank back, but not soon enough.

With a flare of red, the powerful blow breached the shield and his shoulder lit up in agony. He heard his thin T-shirt ripping under the bear's curved claws, and he screamed as they sunk into his shoulder and tore bloody furrows across his skin. In the midst of the white-hot pain, a tiny thought poked some back corner of his brain: *should have taken the leather jacket.*

It wouldn't have mattered, though. Not for long. The bear roared again, its right paw crushing down on Stone's injured shoulder as its left swiped another claw-studded blow at his chest, opening more furrows. Hot saliva dripped down from cavernous jaws, mixing with the blood that flowed freely from the wounds.

Nearly mad with pain and panic, Stone knew it might already be too late to do anything to save himself, even if he managed to drive the bear off. But that laughter—the mocking sound of Many Faces toying with him—

Rage rose to join the pain and the panic. If he was going to die, then damn it, he wasn't going to simply give up and let it happen. Barely able to see through the red haze, he glared into the bear's unnatural glowing eyes and formed a spell. He raised a shaking arm; he only needed a few seconds to pull the energy together. Only a few—

The bear's massive paw hit his upraised arm and he felt something snap. He screamed, the spell's energy dissipating harmlessly, uncast. A gray haze began to form over his thoughts.

I'm going to die. This is where it ends.

The bear roared, rearing back with both paws raised, its eyes glowing with the mad light, its shaggy dark form towering over Stone as he lay bleeding, desperately fighting to gather enough energy for one last spell—

He thought he heard someone yell something, but it had to be his mind playing tricks on him. The voice was—female? How could that be? There were no women here. Only Jason and Lopez, and they were both unconscious—

The bear faltered. It stood there, balanced on its hind legs, and suddenly it seemed confused as to why it was there. It dropped back to all fours with a vast *thud,* but it did not hit Stone again. In fact, its paws came down on either side of him.

The strange light was gone from its eyes.

Another sharp call that somehow managed to encapsulate both an order and a gentle command. Stone was too far gone to make out the words, but the intent came through. The bear, confused, backed off. It glanced around for a moment as if to say *what am I doing here?* and then trundled off at a lope into the forest.

The laughter died away.

Stone didn't move. He couldn't move, except to writhe feebly. He lay there in the dirt, blood running from his wounds and pooling beneath him. The pain was so intense that he didn't know how he could possibly still be conscious. He clamped his teeth down against a scream and waited for death to come. He wondered if Jason and Lopez would get out safely, and how they would explain all this.

Footsteps approached, hurrying toward him. A figure dropped down to its knees next to him, and a female voice spoke, harsh and rough with fear: "You idiot! What the hell do you think you're doing?"

| CHAPTER THIRTY-THREE

With great effort, Stone opened his eyes to see the blurred form of a woman hovering over him. The pain wouldn't let him concentrate enough to get any details, but he could tell she was a lot older than he was—at least sixty. She had long, steel-gray hair tied back in a ponytail, a tanned and weathered face, and wore a man's Native-American print shirt and jeans. She carried a lantern. Stone tried to say something, but couldn't do it. Instead he closed his eyes again and focused on not screaming. Despite the heat of the late-summer night, he began to shiver uncontrollably.

More footsteps. Familiar voices this time. "Oh, God. Al!" It was Jason. "Stan! Get over here!"

Still more footsteps, this time stumping as if their owner was having trouble walking. "Oh, man—" It was Lopez. "Jason. Get the blanket out of the truck, and the first-aid kit. We gotta get that bleeding under control and get him to a hospital." He seemed to notice the woman then. "Do you have a phone? We need to get an ambulance up here pronto."

Stone opened his eyes again. They were all huddled over him now, his friends' terrified faces gazing down at him like he was already dead. Was it that bad? He raised his head just a bit to get a look, and immediately wished he hadn't. His T-shirt was shredded, his chest and abdomen slick with blood and slashed with deep, ragged parallel furrows. They were still bleeding. He let his head fall wearily back to the ground.

The woman shook her head. "He won't survive if we wait for an ambulance. Bring him. I can help."

Jason glared. "Listen, lady, I don't know who you are, but *look* at him. He's gonna die if he doesn't get medical help!"

She glared right back. "No, boy. *You* listen. Your friend is a fool. He's messing with forces he doesn't understand. He has power, yes, but no wisdom to guide him. He's arrogant. This is the result. I can help him, but only if I do it soon."

Stone blinked. He felt his arms and legs growing cold even as sweat dotted his forehead and his chest, mingling with the blood. He knew what shock felt like, and this was it. The woman was right. He was dying. "You—" he whispered. "You're a—" His voice trailed off into a wracking half-sob, half-cough. Why couldn't he just pass out?

Again she glared. "Of course I am! I don't know who's the bigger idiot: you or your friends. Now tell them to shut up and listen to me if you want a chance to live!"

He looked at her. He didn't have the strength even to shift to magical sight, but even without it he could sense her power. Wearily, he looked at Jason and nodded. "Let her—" he whispered.

Jason and Lopez exchanged glances. It was clear they knew the mysterious woman was right: Stone wouldn't survive a trip back to Ojai, even if they gathered him up and took him in the truck instead of waiting for the ambulance. They nodded to the woman. "Okay," Lopez said. "Tell us what to do."

The woman bent over Stone. "You said you had a blanket. Get it. I need to get this bleeding stabilized before we can move him." To Stone, she said, "Try not to move around. You've lost a lot of blood with that idiotic stunt."

Stone nodded, his breathing fast and shallow. His body felt as if it couldn't decide whether to freeze or be on fire. The old woman's voice was harsh and matter-of-fact, but there was an undercurrent in it that was comforting on some primal level. Like he could trust her to know what she was doing. Still, his overworked mind kept trying to bring up things he needed to know: "Many—Faces—"

"Oh, he's rabbited for now," she said as if she understood exactly what he meant. Her deft hands tore away the shredded remains of his T-shirt and cast it aside. "He'll be back, but once I get you where we're going he won't be able to bother us for a while."

"How—did you—"

"Shush," she ordered. "This isn't as easy for me as it used to be. Let me work." She began probing his chest wounds with gentle pressure.

He gasped and must have passed out for a short time, because when he awakened, Jason was back. "Okay," the woman was saying. "Get him on the blanket. You two carry him and follow me. It's not far."

The next few minutes were agony. Jason and Lopez were as gentle as they could be as they lifted him onto the blanket and picked up the two ends, but as they followed the woman's bobbing lantern up the path out of the parking lot they couldn't help but jostle him—especially since Lopez's leg was clearly injured, forcing him to limp heavily. Stone kept his eyes closed and tried to will himself to pass out again, but he remained stubbornly conscious of every bump and misstep.

After a few minutes they reached some wooden stairs, illuminated by a line of graceful pole lights. "Where are we?" Jason asked, puffing.

"My house. I'm the caretaker up here. Hurry up—get him inside."

Stone began to lose the thread of the conversation. He slipped in and out of consciousness as every time the merciful blackness engulfed him, his carriers shifted him and jolted him awake again with waves of searing hot pain. He heard himself moaning, but couldn't stop it.

"Not much further," Lopez's voice came filtering through the haze. "Hang on, Al."

At last he felt himself lowered onto something soft, and the world stopped swaying back and forth. The pain didn't lessen, but it became more steady, throbbing at a regular pace instead of striking in short, sudden bursts. He tried to say something to the woman but he couldn't get it out.

"Okay, out," the woman ordered Jason and Lopez. "I need to work and you two will just be in the way. There's food in the kitchen, and you can fix yourself up with what you find in the bathroom cabinet. Go on."

A hand gripped his arm. "We'll be here, Al," Jason said, his voice rough. "You yell if you need us. And hold on, okay?"

Stone barely heard him. His body was on fire. He thrashed back and forth, feeling blood starting to trickle from his wounds again.

"Easy," the woman said, putting a hand on his uninjured shoulder. As before, her voice was harsh but soothing. She moved her hand up to swipe sweat-plastered hair off his forehead. "I'll be right back. I promise."

He didn't notice if she returned in five minutes or five hours, but at some point a cold cloth settled on his brow. It felt like a small oasis of bliss in the center of an inferno. "Mmm..." he murmured.

"All right," she said. "Can you hear me?"

"Mmhm..."

"You're going to need to help me, boy. Can you do that?"

He looked up into her lined face. Her eyes flickered deep brown in the firelight. "I—"

"It's been a long time since I've done this. I can't do it without your help. I know you've got the power. Will you help me?"

Again, he nodded. "I—I'll do—what I can." He wondered if she could even hear him.

"Good. You're a fighter. You'll need to be. What do I call you?"

"A—Alastair." Why did she keep talking to him? More to the point: why did she keep wanting him to *answer*? All he longed to do was drift away in a haze of darkness. If he woke up, great. If not—at least he wouldn't hurt anymore.

"Alastair. And I'm Edna. Good to meet you."

He heard the slosh of water in a basin, then felt another cool cloth on his chest and shoulders. Wherever it touched his wounds, the pain flared bright and sharp. Gasping, he tried feebly to roll away. He began to shake again.

A firm hand settled on his unwounded shoulder. "Stop," Edna ordered. "Now. Listen to me. I know you have the Talent, and you know what you're doing. You wouldn't have tried that fool stunt if you didn't."

It wasn't a question, but he felt he should respond anyway. He nodded weakly.

"Good. That means your mind is strong. I hope your body is as strong—it'll have to be to get through this." She snorted. "Getting yourself mauled by a bear. Who's that going to help?"

"Not—a bear," he whispered.

"It damn sure *was* a bear. I saw it. And I know what was driving it, too. I don't know what the hell ever gave you the idea you could stand up to that thing."

He had to gather himself before he could answer, but when he did there was an edge to his tone. "No one—else," he said through his teeth.

She rolled her eyes. "Yeah, yeah. Saving the world, you are. Damn kids." She sighed, and the water sloshed again in the basin. "So are you going to help me? Show me you're not a complete fool?"

He glared. "What—do I need to—do?"

She matched his glare, her eyes fierce. "Fight," she ordered. "Don't give in. Don't slip away from me. This is going to hurt like hell. Can you handle it, boy?"

"Do it," he whispered. His voice shook, but his eyes blazed.

"That's it," she said. Then she closed her eyes and began what sounded like a low, droning chant. Stone couldn't make out the words; he didn't think he could understand them if he could. He closed his own eyes and focused on her voice, letting his mind drift along the strange melody. She went on and on, for minutes or hours or perhaps days. At some deep level he could feel the power rising in the chant, strong and protective and comforting.

Then he heard the sound of water in the basin again, and something wet and scalding hot washed over his chest as the chant rose in volume once more.

He did scream then, and that was all he knew.

| CHAPTER THIRTY-FOUR

S he was still there when he awoke, sitting in a chair next to where he lay. "So, you're back," she said, marking her place in the book she was reading and setting it aside. "About time. Thought I was going to lose you there for a bit."

He blinked, taking inventory as best he could without moving. He was lying on what felt like a mattress, covered with some sort of heavy blanket. The ceiling was rough-hewn wood, as were the walls. A quick glance to his right showed him a large window with dappled sunlight shining in through a thick curtain of trees.

He turned to look at her. He hadn't really seen her before, not very well. She looked tired, her glittering eyes sunk far back in her lined face. Some of her iron-colored hair had escaped from her long ponytail and hovered in wisps at her forehead. She still wore the same man's shirt, its Native print now stained with dried blood.

My blood. He tried his voice, tentatively: "What—" When it came out sounding halfway like himself, he stared at her and continued: "You're—a mage."

"I'm a healer," she corrected in a sharp tone. "And an old woman." Her eyes narrowed. "I don't wrestle the world into submission like your type does—or tries to, anyway. How do you feel?"

"Tired."

"That's understandable. Your body's done a lot of work over the last few hours. I guess that's one good thing I can say about being that high on yourself: it gives you a good strong mind. You'd have died without it. You almost died anyway. News flash: bear claws aren't too sanitary."

He frowned. Clearly this woman, whoever she was, didn't think much of him—or perhaps of mages in general. Yet she had apparently saved his life. Moving carefully, he pushed down the blanket, fearful of what he was going to see. His eyes widened.

She had cleaned off the blood, so he got a clear view: except for a series of faint, interconnected scars running across his right shoulder and diagonally from his chest to his abdomen, the horrific, muscle-deep slashes the bear had inflicted on him were gone. He lifted his arm, which he remembered being broken by one of the bear's mighty paw swipes: it too was whole and uninjured. He still felt faint, distant echoes of his previous agony, but they were now more like dull aches, no worse than a muscle cramp. "How—?"

"I told you: I'm a healer. I'm out of practice, but some things you never lose." She gestured, encompassing the area around her. "It helped that you picked this place for your crazy-ass plan. Did you do that for a reason, or was it just dumb luck?"

He glared at her, wearily letting his arm drop back to the blanket. "Why do you keep saying that?"

"What? That you're a fool? Because you are. But I really do want to know: why did you pick this place? Are there going to be more of you coming?"

He shook his head, which was more like rolling it back and forth on the pillow. "No more," he said. "I—chose the location because of the ley line. And because it would likely be deserted. I didn't want anyone—happening by."

She snorted. "It's a damn good thing I did 'happen by,' or all three of you would be dead."

Stone stiffened as memories flooded back to him. "My friends—"

"They're fine. They're sleeping now. I couldn't get 'em to leave until you were out of danger. I fixed up the older one's leg, but they can deal with the rest of their bumps and bruises. Maybe it'll teach 'em to think a little harder about what they're doing."

He mulled that over for a while—his mind was still moving slower than usual. "Who—are you?" he asked. "I remember you told me your name, but—"

"Hold on," she said, rising. "I can see I'm not getting away without a long conversation, so let's get you something to eat first. You lost a lot of blood and used a lot of energy. You need to build yourself back up."

Stone didn't argue with her. He realized he was ravenous and his head felt woozy: she was probably right. He lay there, staring out the window and reveling in the relative absence of pain, until she returned a few minutes later with a tray, the sort used for serving breakfast in bed.

"Sit up a little," she ordered. She had the manner of a good nurse: brisk and efficient, benevolent without a shred of sentimentality. When he complied, she placed the tray across him. On it was a bowl of beef-vegetable soup and a tall glass of iced tea. "You eat, I'll talk," she said. "Not too fast, either. You made enough of a mess bleeding all over everything last night—no need to get sick too."

Once again he did as ordered. He took an experimental spoonful of the soup, and at that moment it tasted better than the finest meal he'd ever had in his life. "Thank you," he said, nodding.

She nodded back, once, in grudging acknowledgement. "So— you want to know who I am. My name is Edna Soren. I—" She stopped, because he was staring at her. "What?"

"Edna—Soren?" His gaze locked on her.

"That's what I said, boy." She sounded irritated. "Did that bear cuff your ears, too?"

He ignored her tone. "You're the woman who was found injured twenty-seven years ago—the last time Many Faces was active."

She looked surprised. "How do you know about that?"

"It attacked you, but failed to kill you."

"Damn right it failed," she growled.

Stone stared harder at her. "You sent it back, didn't you? Last time?"

She nodded, but this time she didn't meet his eyes. "That was a long time ago. I thought it might be back again now, but I didn't want to admit it."

"If you sent it back before, why don't you do it again?" Stone had forgotten about his soup.

She made a noise that was half-sigh, half-snort. "A lot of reasons. In case you hadn't noticed, boy, I'm an old woman. I haven't practiced my craft, aside from a little here and there to help me do my work, for over twenty years. I don't have anything like the strength I used to."

Stone gestured at his chest. "I don't know another mage who could have done this in his—or her—prime," he said softly. He doubted even Lamar, the old homeless man with one of the rarest of the Forgotten powers who had once saved his life after he'd been stabbed, could have dealt with these injuries.

Another snort. "Maybe so, but that's healing. And that's in a place that's *made* for healing. The waters here have always been known for their curative powers, and combined with the ley line…" She shrugged. "And besides that, you did a lot of the work. I just directed. If you hadn't been what you are, and we hadn't been *where* we are, I couldn't have saved you." She paused. "Anyway, I didn't exactly send it back. I just sort of—gave it a time-out. I ran it off. I hoped it was permanent, that it would find some other place to do its business. But either it found its own way back or else some idiot summoned it again."

Stone started to reply, but stopped when there was a knock on the doorframe. He looked up to see Jason standing there.

"Sorry to interrupt," Jason said. "I just wanted to see how Al was doing."

"I'm dead, thanks for asking," Stone said, but he managed a smile.

Jason nodded gravely; he couldn't pull it off, though. "Damn, man, it's good to see you awake."

"It's good to *be* awake. Being mostly free of debilitating injuries is quite nice, too. What time is it, by the way?" Stone asked.

"It's about four," Jason said. "You've been out a long time."

"You might as well come in," he said. "Bring Stan too, if he's awake. I think we all need to talk." He turned to Edna Soren. "They're involved in this as well. And I think they'll want to hear what you have to say."

Edna shrugged as if to say "whatever."

By the time Jason returned with Lopez, each of them dragging another chair into the room, Stone had finished the bowl of soup and was sitting up, propped against his pillows. He still felt tired and sore, but nowhere near as bad as he'd expect to feel after suffering such a grievous injury. He was beginning to believe Edna's claim that this place had actual restorative powers.

When the two newcomers were seated, Stone indicated Edna. "Has our hostess introduced herself to you yet?"

Lopez shook his head. "We didn't really have time for formalities. We were too busy trying to keep you from dying."

Stone nodded. "This," he said, "is Edna Soren."

Lopez and Jason exchanged glances. "From the paper?" Jason asked.

Stone wasn't surprised that they both remembered; he supposed that was one of the things policemen were trained to do. He filled them in on the conversation so far, then turned back to Edna. "Let me tell you the rest. Perhaps it will help you understand what we were doing here in the first place, and how we managed to blunder into the situation."

At her nod, he began to speak. He told her everything, starting with Jason's call and ending with their trip up to Matilija Hot Springs so he could try to communicate with Many Faces. She listened without comment until the end, then snorted. "Talk to him.

Honestly. And he wonders why I get nettled when he tries to call me a mage."

"You aren't a mage?" Jason asked, confused. "But—"

"Like I told him—I'm a healer. What I do is in harmony with the earth. What he does is impose his own will on the universe. Big difference."

"I think perhaps it might be best if we discussed philosophical differences some other time," Stone said gently. "For now—" he spread his hands "—I'm at a loss as to what to do. I don't have any other ideas on how to convince Many Faces to go back where it came from." He sighed. "I might—*might*—be able to pull off such a banishing if I had a team of mages to help, and time to build a proper circle. But even then, I doubt it." He looked at Jason, re-membering something. "Jason—"

Jason didn't return his gaze. "I...don't know, Al. I don't know what happened. That's never happened before."

"What are you talking about?" Edna demanded.

"Jason has an—ability—that allows him to channel power to mages if he desires it. We've used it before. With Jason's power added to mine, I can cast much more powerful spells with much less effort. But last night—I called for it, but for whatever reason it didn't work."

"I was *trying*," Jason said. He sounded miserable. "I don't know why it didn't work. It's never not worked before."

"Well," Stone said, "I don't know, either. Possibly it has some-thing to do with your captivity: perhaps Many Faces drained enough of your power that it will require time to recharge. I don't know. But it means that for now, any plans we make can't assume its availability."

Edna *harrumph*ed. "Listen to you—still planning. Still talking about power and tactics. Haven't you figured it out yet, boy? You might be strong, but it doesn't matter. This isn't about strength. No matter how strong you are, it's stronger. It's stronger than all of us."

"Then what do you suggest?" Stone asked, an edge to his tone. "That we give up? Allow this thing to march through and murder everyone it likes?"

"No," she said, shaking her head. "Right now, what I suggest is that we get some rest. I'm wiped out from the workings I did on you. And I can see that even though your pride's making you try to hide it, you still are, too. Your body still needs to heal. Rest until tonight, and then we'll talk some more."

"So you're going to help us?" Lopez asked.

"We'll talk tonight," she said again. She turned to him and Jason. "You two: I suggest that you go down and clean up the mess you left in the parking lot. You can bring your truck up here—I'll show you where the road is."

"What about Faces?" Jason asked.

She snorted. "No offense, but you two are small potatoes. I don't think it'll waste its time on you. It's your arrogant friend it wants. And in any case, you're under my protection here. Don't spend the day out there, but if anybody comes up here you don't want them to find that circle or the big patch of your friend's blood."

Stone wanted to protest, but he knew she was right—and even if he himself weren't tired from the effort of telling their story, he could see that Edna was badly in need of rest. In spite of her grumpy demeanor, Stone respected her for remaining with him until she was sure he would survive. "Go," he told her. "We can afford a few hours."

She nodded, rising with effort from her chair. At that moment, her lean, sinewy body looked every bit its age and more. She waved vaguely in their direction, then trudged out of the room.

Jason and Lopez rose too. "We'll let you rest," Jason said. "She's right: we should clear that stuff out of the parking lot before anybody comes up here and finds it."

Stone thought about telling them to hunt for bodies, since according to his theory Many Faces would have to have murdered more people to power his "associates," but he didn't. If there were any bodies, they could wait; despite Edna Soren's assurances, he didn't want his friends wandering around outside her wards any longer than they had to.

Right now, he had some thinking to do.

| CHAPTER THIRTY-FIVE

They made an unlikely war council when they reconvened a few hours later in Edna's rustic, comfortable living room: Jason and Lopez, bruised and battered and still wearing the same torn and dusty clothes from the previous night, sat in two of the chairs; Stone, pale and clad only in his bloodstained, shredded jeans since his T-shirt hadn't survived the bear attack, was propped on pillows on the sofa; and Edna, who had changed out of her bloody shirt into a blue denim one decorated with intricate embroidery, was settled in a carved wooden rocker. She had brought them all more soup, bread, and iced tea ("Sorry it's not fancy—it's usually just me, and I don't keep that much in the house.") and they now all sat facing each other and trying to decide where to begin.

Finally Stone spoke softly: "Tell us about what happened twenty-seven years ago, if you would, Ms. Soren." He sounded much better than he had earlier that day: he'd managed to organize his thoughts before dropping off to sleep again, but just barely. When he'd awakened the last vestiges of the pain were gone, though it appeared that he would carry the faint scars indefinitely.

She shrugged. "You might as well call me Edna. And there isn't that much to tell, really."

"How did you realize what was going on?"

"I sensed it, when the killings started. There was an unease in the general aura of the area. I was more active in those days: I've lived in Ojai all my life, and ever since I became aware I had my gifts, I felt they were given to me to protect the town."

"Was there really only one killing?" Lopez asked. "In the newspaper articles we found, it mentioned a woman whose throat was cut, and a high-school boy who tried to stab another, but was discovered before he could finish."

"There was another one that didn't make the papers. A transient. They hushed it up, because it was extremely violent and extremely strange, and they didn't want to disturb the public. They could get away with that a little more back then."

"Extremely violent and strange?" Jason asked. "How so?"

"The victim disemboweled himself," Edna said, her tone matter-of-fact. "Of course, they didn't know that—how could they? He managed to unzip his gut with a carving knife and rip out half his innards before he died. People don't *do* that to themselves."

"Unless they're possessed," Jason said. He looked a little green.

"You got it. And who believes that? Besides me, I mean. That one came after the two boys. When I heard *that* story, I suspected something was up. I didn't know what, but I've dealt with possession before. Naturally, they wrote it off as a bad drug trip and swept it under the rug."

"So you've no idea who summoned this one?" Stone asked.

She shook her head. "I didn't even know it had a name until you mentioned Many Faces. I knew who you were talking about, of course—I read the papers and listen to the news. I recognized the same motivations." She frowned at Stone, furrowing her wrinkled brow. "You said you found some sort of shrine, and a corrupted ley line section. I'd like to see that, if you could find it again."

"Are you sure?" Lopez asked. "Al practically couldn't function around it. It seems to have a thing against magic types."

"I'm not like him," she said, with some pride.

Stone didn't take offense at that; in fact, he was only half-listening. The other half of his mind was going over what Many Faces had said during their conversation the previous night. "I think the same people summoned it both times," he said suddenly. "And I'm not sure they had any idea what they were doing."

They all stared at him. "What?" Jason asked. "Why do you think that?"

Speaking slowly, pausing to go over the words to make sure he was getting them right, he told them about Many Faces' statements—about the "foolish children" and their "inexpert and imperfect" summoning, and about how they had "grown in age, if not in wisdom" and somehow obtained an "artifact of power." He shook his head, addressing Edna. "He spoke of *she of my masters' blood.* Am I wrong, or does that sound to you like someone who's related to the dissident group who summoned it all those years ago?"

Edna didn't answer for a long time. "It makes sense," she finally admitted. "More sense than anything else I've heard. If there are still descendants of the Spanish in the area, it's possible that the descendants of that group are still here, too. Of course, we don't know how many of them there were."

"So—a woman summoned it?" Jason asked. And to Edna: "Are there any other female magic types around here that you know of? Somebody who would have been here twenty-seven years ago and is still here?"

Edna shook her head. "Not that I'm aware of. There are people who claim to be magically talented, like that stupid woman who runs that ridiculous shop downtown, but all they do is put on a good show for the tourists."

Stone was thinking again. "It mentioned that whoever the summoner was—and it sounds like there were more than one—they didn't do it on purpose. That they didn't know what they'd done, and didn't direct it once it was here. I wonder—is it possible that they didn't *know* they summoned it?"

"How would that work?" Jason asked. "How do you summon something and not know it?"

But Edna was nodding. "It is possible," she said. "There are invocations that can summon things from other planes just by reading them aloud." She fixed her beady gaze on Stone. "You're sure it mentioned 'she of my masters' blood'?"

"Quite sure, yes."

She stared into her lap and was silent for a few seconds. "From what you've told me of the shrine, and what was written on the rock tablets—blood was integral to this summoning. It sounds like there was a sacrifice to bring it into initial being, so any descendants of the summoners would be connected with it, if even in a small way."

"But how would they summon it?" Stone asked. "Are you saying they had a formula? Or even its true name?"

"I don't know," she said, a little peevishly. "I don't make a habit of summoning spirits of vengeance. But they might not have needed one. If the summoner was a direct descendant of the original summoners, it might have been waiting for someone to call it. We don't know why it went away in the first place—that's got to be lost to history. But if it wasn't banished, but merely waiting for a new master to serve—"

"Right, right," Stone said, warming to the idea. "And that's how the summoning could have been 'imperfect.' It said its connection to the world was weak—that's consistent with a botched summoning. If the blood descendant called it without a proper invocation, they might have gotten *something*, but not *everything*."

"But what about the artifact?" Jason asked. "What's that supposed to be?"

"Who knows?" Stone said, shrugging. "Perhaps in the meantime she got hold of something that allowed her to do the summoning properly, but she still didn't know she was doing it."

Lopez sighed. "That's all well and good," he said, "But it still doesn't tell us who it is, or how to get rid of this thing."

"And," Jason said, "It doesn't explain *why* they'd do it. I mean, okay, maybe you can call up something without knowing you're doing it if you've got the right genetics, but think about it: how many people do you know who just sit around chanting things that even *might* be calls for ancient vengeance demons? You know: 'Hey, it's Saturday! Let's all hold hands and summon Satan! Then we'll have pie!' I'm not buying it."

Stone nodded, raising an eyebrow. "You've a point there. If there was more than one person involved, then they had to be doing *something* that approximated a summoning. Even with the blood connection, there's got to be more to it than looking in a mirror and saying 'Bloody Mary' three times."

Lopez leaned forward. "Okay, let's look at our evidence, or at least what we're pretty sure of. I can't help with any of this magic stuff, but evidence examination I know." He pulled out a notebook from his back pocket and began jotting things down as he spoke. "You're saying that whoever summoned this thing did it twenty-seven years ago, didn't know what they did, and they didn't do it right, yeah?"

"Right," Stone said, nodding.

Lopez finished writing that down. "You said at least one of the group is probably a blood descendant of one of the people who summoned it originally back hundreds of years ago."

"Yes," Stone said. "Though that probably isn't much help, since I doubt anyone's traced the lineage, and after all these years it could have drifted so much that we're not necessarily looking for someone Chumash. Hell, by now their family could be Polish or Mongolian or Japanese for all we know. We—" He stopped a moment.

Jason tilted his head. "Al?"

Stone held up a hand. Something he'd said had tripped a distant memory in his mind, but it was fleeting and every time he tried to chase it down, it flitted maddeningly away. "Never mind," he said at last, frustrated. "I thought I had something, but it's gone now. Please continue, Stan."

Lopez consulted his notebook. "Okay, so let's see. We also know that at least one of the group is female, because of the 'she of my master's blood' thing."

"Yeah," Jason said. "And if we make the assumption that both the old summoning and the recent one happened in Ojai, then we're looking for somebody who lived here back then and still does."

"Or someone who went away and came back," Lopez added.

Stone addressed Edna: "You said you didn't know of any female mages in the area. Is it possible they're simply keeping quiet about their power, like you do? Does anyone know about *you?*"

"Does it even *have* to be a mage?" Jason interrupted. Then, to Edna: "You said that there were ways to summon something by just reading something off a piece of paper, or out of a book. Do you have to be magically talented to do that? Could *I* do it, or Stan? Or does the power have to be there somewhere in the first place?"

Edna thought about that. She looked at Stone first. "Like I said, I don't know of any female practitioners in the valley, but I don't honestly go around checking that often. In fact, the only magical person of any power at all that I knew of in the valley died last year. He was a friend of mine. Cranky old bird, but I'm a cranky old bird too, so we got along. I got a fair bit of his library before his idiot heirs gave it all away to Bart's." To Jason, she added, "As far as I know, it's *possible* to do a summoning without any magical ability if it's written up properly by someone who *does* have some, but I've never seen or heard of a case where it's happened."

Lopez jotted all of this down in his notebook. He glanced up. "Al, you mentioned 'stupid children' or something, didn't you?"

"Foolish children," Stone confirmed. "Why?"

He shrugged. "Just thinking, wondering: do you think that meant *real* children? Or is he just so old that he'd think of all of us as children?"

"Wait," Jason protested. "You're saying it might have been *kids* who summoned it?"

"Age wouldn't matter," Edna said. "Even though most magical people don't come into their powers until around puberty or even later, that doesn't mean the potential isn't there. Especially if the child was related by blood to the original summoners. And teenagers, with all their passions and their emotions so close to the surface—it's definitely possible. Especially for this kind of summoning, which is all *about* passion. But that still doesn't help us—" Her gaze darted to her left. "Hey, are you sick?"

Stone had sat suddenly upright on the couch, swinging his legs around until he was leaning forward. His eyes burned with an odd intensity. "Teenagers," he whispered.

"Huh?" Jason stared at him, confused.

"Teenagers!" he said again, louder. And then more softly: "Japanese...I wonder..."

Edna glared at him. "Is your fever coming back? Maybe we should—"

He held up an abrupt hand. "Quiet, please. I'm trying to put something together." He closed his eyes and began tracing something in the air, like a schoolchild trying to solve a math problem. After a few seconds of this he opened his eyes again. "The numbers work, at least," he said triumphantly. "It's probably nothing, but at least it's a lead." He sounded like he was talking to himself, and no longer even seemed aware that the others were in the room.

"Al, what the *hell* are you talking about?" Jason demanded. "Want to pull into a station one of these days so we can board your train of thought?"

Stone paused to gather himself for a moment before answering. "The night I had dinner with Lindsey, she mentioned that when she was a little girl, she had a babysitter she quite liked because she belonged to some sort of 'witch club,' and she let Lindsey wear her green robe. I didn't think anything of it at the time—like I said, it's probably nothing—but what made me think of it was when I said the family could be Japanese by now. The babysitter was Japanese."

Jason frowned. "That's pretty sketchy. You think this girl is the summoner?"

"Not necessarily. But Lindsey said there was a group of them." He paused a moment, racking his brain to try to recall what she'd told him while not allowing himself to think too hard about anything else from that night. "She said it was all about fairies and magic wands and that sort of thing—and that they got together to cast spells and make love potions."

Edna looked skeptical. "If the girls were in high school at the time, then that would make them—"

"—Early to mid-forties now," Lopez said. "I agree with Jason: it's pretty sketchy. How would we even find out who they are? We can't exactly take out an ad in the classifieds: 'Wanted, Witch Club members from nearly thirty years ago.'" He turned toward Stone. "Did she tell you this babysitter's name?"

Stone pondered. "I don't think so. All she said was that her nickname was something like Nikki, or—no, it was Mickey. Lindsey said she used to call her 'Mickey Mouse.'"

"Let's check the yearbooks," Jason said. "They've got to have them at the library. This area's mostly white and Hispanic—I don't think you'll find a lot of Japanese kids, especially not that long ago. Shouldn't be too hard to at least narrow it down."

"Assuming you're even right," Lopez said, "What then?"

Stone shrugged. "I don't know. I'm still working this out as I go along." He settled back onto the sofa. "Edna—what do you think?"

"I think you're all crazy," she said frankly. "But you're right—it could be possible, and I'm not comin' up with anything else either. See where this goes, and if it pans out then we'll talk about what to do next."

"Do you think you can get rid of it again?" Lopez asked her. "Like you did last time?"

"No way," she said. "For one thing, I'm not anywhere near as strong as I was nearly thirty years ago. And for another—I didn't even get rid of it then. Like I said before, I just kind of gave it a time-out."

"What about if you two worked together?" Jason said, pointing at Stone.

She gave Stone a critical look and shrugged. "I don't know if we can. Our magic comes from completely different places. It's possible, though. I'll want to see those tablets if I can. I can't read 'em, of course, but maybe I can get something from them if I can get close."

"We can do that tomorrow," Stone said. "I warn you, though: it's a bit of a hike. Are you sure you're up to—"

"Don't you worry about me, boy," she said with pride in her tone. "I might be old, but like I said, I'm a tough old bird. Who do you think keeps things repaired around here, wood sprites?"

"I don't think we should split up," Lopez said. "I wouldn't want to go near those tablets without you around, Al, in case Faces gets nasty again. And I doubt you could find the place on your own anyway. Normally I'd say send Jason to look for the yearbooks, but—"

"No, we'll stay together," Stone said. To Edna, he said. "May we stay the night here?"

"I figured you would. Can't go out like that in the middle of the night."

He nodded, and his expression sobered. "After we're gone, you might want to look around a bit. I suspect you might find bodies somewhere near here. My working theory is that Faces requires them to summon or sustain his smaller minions, and those were definitely in evidence last night."

"Great," she said, letting out a loud sigh. "Sometimes I wonder why I didn't just move to Hawaii and get it over with."

| CHAPTER THIRTY-SIX

Early the next morning, Lopez brought the truck around, and they prepared to head back to Ojai. While he and Jason loaded up the gear, Stone took Edna aside.

"I realized I hadn't thanked you for what you did," he said. He'd reclaimed his black overcoat; he stood now with his hands in its pockets, looking out over the parking lot where he'd come so close to death only a short time ago. It was already shaping up to be a beautiful day, the sun rising above the trees into a brilliant blue sky without a single cloud.

Edna shrugged. "Too much death around here lately," she said. "If you can do something about it, least I can do is help by keeping your fool head alive long enough to figure it out."

He chuckled mirthlessly. "I know you don't think much of me, Edna, but I promise: I'll do whatever I can to deal with Many Faces and end this once and for all."

"It's not you personally I don't think much of," she said, looking out over the parking lot. "It's your kind. That attitude. Your type thinks magic is all about formulas and study and imposing your will. The type who thinks they *make* things happen."

She turned to him, and her expression was odd. "Your kind are the ones who cause the problems that my kind has to clean up. I haven't seen a damn one of you who has half the wisdom to steer all that power. You're like a mouse riding a runaway bull. Doesn't matter how smart that mouse is, or how much he thinks he can

R. L. KING

control that bull—maybe he can, for a while. But if he loses control, then things break. And whatever gets in the bull's way gets trampled."

Stone shrugged. "That's one way to look at it, I suppose. And you might be right. But sometimes we *do* make things happen for the better. Sometimes by sheer stubbornness, we manage to accomplish what we set out to do."

She nodded. "Maybe so. You're probably the strongest of your type I've ever met, and you're young—I don't think you're done growing yet. I just hope you learn before it's too late that sometimes strength isn't what's needed. Sometimes you have to work *with* the world instead of against it."

"Sometimes," he said. "But at the moment, the world doesn't seem terribly invested in sending this thing back to wherever it came from. That leaves me—and you as well, if you'll help—to figure out some way to sort this out."

"And I hope you do, this time," she said, nodding. "Because unlike you, I'm *not* convinced I can do anything I want to do. Why do you think I've been holed up in my house behind my wards ever since the first couple of murders? As soon as I figured out that the thing I nearly died just trying to divert all those years ago was back, and stronger than ever?" Her dark brown eyes met his from her tanned, wrinkled face. "I'm *scared*. There's *my* pride: I didn't want to admit it. I've been up here pretending that it's something else, or that somebody else will deal with it this time. Because I know what it can do. I saw what it did to you. I saw the kind of magic you put out trying to oppose it, and it meant *nothing*. So where does that leave me?"

Stone shook his head. "I don't think you're nearly as weak as you think you are, Edna." His voice grew gentle. "Perhaps you don't have the raw power anymore, but you said it yourself: your style isn't direct. You don't oppose things head-on. When you work indirectly, you don't need the same power level to get results. It's a lesson I need to learn myself." He chuckled. "I'm working on it."

He put a hand on her shoulder. "Come on—I think they're finished loading up. Let's go see what we can do, the four of us. We might surprise ourselves."

"Or we might die like four mice getting trampled by a bull," she grumbled, but didn't succeed in hiding the tiniest of smiles. "Splat."

❖

Their first stop was Lopez's house for showers, shaves, and fresh clothes. When Stone came out to the kitchen after spending far too long luxuriating under the hot water, he found Edna and Lopez seated at the table sipping coffee. The photos of the stone tablets were spread out on the table in front of them.

"There was another murder yesterday," Lopez said, looking up.

"Who?" Stone poured himself a cup and dropped down into a vacant chair.

"Farmer out in the east end threw himself headfirst into a wood chipper. Officially they're calling it a suicide."

Stone winced. "Ouch. Hardly a popular suicide method."

"Yeah, I don't think Casner's buying it anymore. They're bringing in a bunch more cops from Ventura—I'll probably get called back in soon."

"We'd better get going, then," Stone said as Jason came out tying back his damp hair. "If we hurry, we can get up to the site of the shrine and be back before the library opens. Many Faces seems to be escalating."

"Packs are already loaded in the truck. Let's just hope he doesn't stage a repeat performance of last time we were up there," Lopez said grimly.

❖

All four of them spent the entire trip up the fire road south of Creek Road and the subsequent hike up to the shrine on edge, constantly expecting something to attack them. However, to their surprise they reached the massive oak tree without any sign of He of Many Faces or his minions. True to her word, Edna Soren hiked along next to the others without slowing down or tiring in any visible way.

"Can you feel it?" Stone asked her shortly after they left the truck.

She nodded. "Oh, yeah. Hard to miss."

As they drew closer, Stone began experiencing the same unease as before: his heart rate quickened, and he began to feel warm and queasy.

Edna, however, seemed unaffected. "You all right?" she asked him at one point when he slowed.

He nodded. "I'll be fine. I'm surprised you aren't feeling the same thing."

"Here, let me see if I can fix that," she said. She took hold of both of his hands and faced him, peering up into his eyes and whispering something under her breath. After a moment, she let go and stepped back. "Is that better?"

Stone stared at her, astonished. "It is. Thank you. How did you do that?"

She grinned. "I might be over the hill, but I've still got a few tricks."

After that, it was a simple matter to follow the corrupted magical energy trails to the tree. Stone stood guard, his magical senses at full awareness, while Lopez and Jason helped Edna into the proper position to view the tablets. When she came back over to where Stone prowled a few minutes later, she was pale under her tan.

"I had no idea it was that bad," she said, her voice shaking.

"What did you get?"

"Those things have corrupted this entire area," she said. "The earth's aura is—disturbed here. And it's spreading. Not quickly—but this ley line is very slowly being corrupted by what's under that tree."

"Should we move it?" Stone asked.

She sighed, spreading her hands. "I don't know. I don't think I want to touch it, and I certainly wouldn't want it near where any people are. If it can do that to a ley line, I don't want to think about what it could do to humans. I think the shrine and the ley line are somehow feeding on each other." She glanced back at the tree; Lopez and Jason were gathering up the packs and coming back over. "What I really think is that it should be destroyed. And I don't say that lightly."

"That won't stop what's happening with Many Faces, though, will it?" Stone asked. "Destroying the shrine won't send it back?"

"I wish," she said. "If that were true, I'd say let's just destroy it now. Even if we did, though, I wouldn't want to do it without a lot of preparation. I'm sure it would fight back, worse than you described before. But even so, I doubt the more recent summoners ever got anywhere near this place. This is where it originated, but I don't think it's any kind of anchor for it." Again she glanced back at the tree. "I did get one impression, though. I don't know if it's right, but if it is it might help you. You aren't going to like it, though."

Stone made a 'go on' gesture.

"You'd better hope that whoever 'she of my masters' blood' is, she's still alive and willing to help us send Many Faces back."

"Why is that?"

"Because if I read those signs right, since the summoning is so closely tied to that bloodline, I don't think anybody else *can* send it back."

| CHAPTER THIRTY-SEVEN

W hen the Ojai Library opened at ten a.m., the librarian was surprised to see the group loitering in the court-yard. She gave them an odd look when Stone requested back issues of the local high school's yearbooks, but like all good librarians, she didn't ask questions. She merely directed them to the alcove where a collection that began more than seventy years ago and continued to a shiny copy from the current year was shelved.

Stone pulled a small stack centering on the one from twenty-seven years ago and commandeered a nearby table. "We're looking for a Japanese girl," he said. "And anything else that looks likely. I doubt this 'Witch Club' got a write-up in the yearbook, but stranger things have happened." He picked up one and began paging through it, motioning for the others to do the same.

It was Jason who found it. "Hey!" he exclaimed after about twenty minutes of searching, waving apology at a man at a nearby table who glared at him over his newspaper. Dropping his voice to a whisper, he added, "Look at this!" He shoved the open book into the middle of the table.

Stone studied the pages and immediately saw what Jason had found. Among the collection of black-and-white headshots of mostly white and Hispanic teenagers, the face of a pert, pretty Asian girl in a demure white blouse smiled up at them. The legend identified her as Michiko Isaka. "She might be the one."

"I only saw two other Asian kids," Jason said. "One's a Chinese freshman girl, and the other one's a boy."

Stone was idly glancing through the remainder of the junior class, looking for any other names that stood out. He didn't expect to see any, but was surprised as he neared the end of the list to spot one person he recognized. "This is interesting…" he murmured.

"What?" Lopez asked, still paging through his own volume.

He pointed. "Suzanne Washburn. She's in the same class as Michiko Isaka. It calls her 'Suzanne Proust' here, but it's obviously the same person."

"Who's Suzanne Washburn?" Jason asked.

"Remember when we were at the Third Eye? Not the woman who owned the place, but her friend. The one who brought the ley line map."

Edna's eyebrows rose. "That pair are a couple of charlatans. Not a shred of talent in either one of them."

"Still," Stone said, "if I'm remembering correctly, the owner said Mrs. Washburn has been interested in the occult for a long time. If that stretched back to high school, and there was some sort of witch club, it's possible she was a member."

"Maybe," Jason said. "But I think we should try to find Michiko first, since if she's the babysitter we know she was in the club."

Lopez was getting up. "Let me check the phone book." After a moment he came back carrying a slender book. "There's an Isaka here, but it's not Michiko. It's listed as 'S. Isaka.'"

"Let's try it," Jason said. "Whoever it is, they're probably related. They might be able to tell us where she is."

"I'll do it," Edna said. "If it's a man it won't matter, but if it's a woman, she'll be less suspicious if another woman calls." She too got up and headed outside to the pay phone.

Stone, Jason, and Lopez continued paging through the yearbooks while she was gone, but they didn't find anything else useful. She came back in five minutes and sat down. "S. Isaka is Satoko," she said. "She's Michiko's mother. She still lives in Ojai, but she said Michiko is up in the Bay Area now. San Francisco."

Stone frowned. "Hmm...well, that buggers part of my theory, then: if the group wasn't all here in town, they couldn't have gotten together to do the recent summoning."

"Wait a minute," Edna said. "You didn't let me finish. I told her I was an old friend trying to get hold of her, and she gave me her number—but she said it was too bad I hadn't called two weeks ago, when she was down here for their twenty-five-year class reunion."

They all stared at her. "When was that?" Stone asked. Then he held up a finger. "Wait a moment. I remember something—hold on." He hurried off and returned with a newspaper back issue, which he spread out. "I remember seeing this the first night I arrived in Ojai, when I was trying to find the names of Jason's friends who were getting married." He stabbed at an article on the social page. "Here it is: a Nordhoff High School twenty-five-year reunion was held at the Ojai Valley Inn a week ago last Saturday."

"Holy crap, that fits," Jason said. "Unless there are more bodies out there that they haven't found yet, the murders started just after that." He looked at Stone. "We need to call this Michiko, and soon."

Stone nodded. "Come on. Let's go back to Stan's place."

Back at Lopez's house, the others waited in the front room while Stone went to his room to make the call. He sat at the small desk with a legal pad in front of him, on which he'd jotted a few things he wanted to mention. Tense with anticipation, he hoped that Michiko Isaka could help them with another piece of their puzzle. There were too many murders, and they weren't showing any signs of stopping. He punched in the number and waited.

"Dr. Isaka's office," a pleasant female voice said. "How may I help you?"

This was unexpected. He wondered what sort of doctor Michiko was. "I'm trying to reach Michiko Isaka," he said. "Is she available?"

"I'm afraid she isn't at the moment," the woman said. "May I take a message?"

"Please," he said. "It's very important I reach her. Could you tell her that I'm an old friend and that it's related to something that happened at her recent reunion in Ojai?" He poured on every bit of charm he could.

There was a pause. "One moment, please, sir." The phone switched over to bouncy, soulless hold music.

When it picked up again five minutes later, a different voice spoke. "This is Dr. Isaka," she said. She sounded a little impatient. "Who is this? As far as I know I don't have any British men as friends, and I'm sure there weren't any at my reunion."

"I do apologize for the slight deception, Dr. Isaka," Stone said, keeping his voice deliberately soft and non-threatening. "My name is Alastair Stone, and in truth we've never met. But the other bit *was* true: it is related to your reunion—or at least I think it is. That's what I'm calling to try to find out."

She still sounded impatient. "I'm sorry, but I have no idea what you're talking about. I don't have a lot of time—could you get to the point, please?"

"All right, then: If you're who I believe you to be, I understand that you were a member of some sort of club or group during your school years. Something to do with magic and witches. Do I have the right person?"

Silence.

Stone let it drag out for a few seconds. "Dr. Isaka?"

"How—did you know that?" Her voice was different now— quieter, and a little strained.

"A lovely woman told me—she said you used to mind her when she was a little girl, and you let her wear your pretty green

R. L. KING

robe. She told me she called you 'Mickey Mouse.'" His tone, too, was soft as images of Lindsey Cole came unbidden to his mind.

"Oh, God," she whispered. "Lindsey..." Another long pause, and then she said, "I just heard about her recently. My mother called to tell me. She was—"

"Yes," Stone said gently. "I'm sorry."

There was another silence; Stone could almost see her gathering herself together before speaking again. "I don't understand—what does Lindsey have to do with—"

"It's not directly related to Lindsey," Stone told her. "But it's very important that I find out about this group. Tell me—did you by chance get together with the other members at your reunion two weeks ago? Did you perhaps stage some sort of ritual or ceremony, for nostalgia's sake?"

"How do you *know* this?" she demanded, voice rising. "Who *are* you?"

"I'm a friend, Dr. Isaka," he said. "I'm someone who's trying to sort something out, and this is where I think it's leading." He sighed. "I wish I could talk with you in person—this is more difficult over the phone."

"What's more difficult? What are you trying to sort out? I'm sorry, but you're confusing me. Why does some silly group my friends and I belonged to in school matter to you?"

Here goes, Stone thought. *This is where she either believes me, or hangs up on me and calls the police.* "I know this is going to sound absurd," he said, "But I've good reason to believe that something connected with your group might be associated with the recent murders in Ojai—and the ones that occurred twenty-seven years ago."

She didn't hang up on him. She didn't say anything, either. On the other end of the line was only silence, punctuated by the occasional squeak of a chair.

"Dr. Isaka?"

"You're crazy," she whispered. "You're insane. Who put you up to this?"

All right, time to get a little more forceful. "Listen to me, Dr. Isaka. I'm not insane. I'm not trying to intimidate you. As I said, I know it sounds farfetched, but believe me, I wouldn't be calling you if it wasn't important. If you want to check my credentials, call Stanford University—I'm a professor there, specializing in the occult. If you want to do it now, I'll give you my number here and wait. When you're convinced, call me back and we'll talk further."

She paused. When she spoke again, her voice was stronger, and angry. "I'm going to call your bluff, Mr. Stone or whatever your name is."

"Please do." He gave her Lopez's number. "I'm not lying to you. It's vital that you call me back."

"We'll see." She hung up.

Stone sat staring at the wall for several moments, then picked up the cordless phone and drifted back out to the front of the house, where the others were seated in the living room. The news droned in the background, but at least right now it wasn't covering the Ojai murders. "Any luck?" Jason asked.

"Possibly. We'll know shortly." He threw himself wearily down in the nearest empty seat and closed his eyes. He had to entertain the possibility that Michiko Isaka wouldn't call him back; if so, his next stop was to question Suzanne Washburn, on the chance that her interest in things odd and spooky extended all the way back to her days in school. He wasn't looking forward to making that call.

It was twenty minutes before the phone rang again. Stone, who had fallen into a light doze, snapped awake and grabbed it. "Lopez residence."

"Dr. Stone? It's Michiko Isaka." Her voice held a strange edge, nervous and contemplative.

He leaped up off the couch and hurried down the hall. "Dr. Isaka. So glad you called back. My credentials passed inspection, then, did they?"

"I called Stanford. They really do have an Occult Studies department. And you really are a professor there." She paused. "But I still don't understand why you're calling me. Why don't you explain it to me? I've cleared my next appointment, so I'm listening."

He sighed. "I'm calling you because I need information about your group. I can't explain it all right now—it would take too long, and we need to move fast if we've any hope of preventing more murders. The short version is, absurd as it might sound, it appears that one of the members of your group has a—connection—to something that caused a lot of trouble in this area many years ago. That connection allowed your group to bring it back, almost certainly accidentally, but now that it's back it's causing trouble again. Deadly trouble."

Silence. Stone was used to it by now; he simply waited while she digested everything he'd told her. He tried to remind himself that, unlike himself and his friends who had been immersed in the situation for days, this was her first taste of any of it. It was a lot to drop on a mundane all at once. If the stakes hadn't been so high, he'd have given her more time to get used to the idea, but time was something they didn't have.

After nearly a minute, she said, "You're telling me that a bunch of kids playing at being witches actually summoned something *real?* Come on, Dr. Stone: that sounds like a bad horror movie."

"Tell that to the eight people who are dead now," he said, his voice cold sober. "Including the little girl you minded. Not to mention the ones who died twenty-seven years ago the first time this happened."

This time when the silence came, Stone didn't wait for her to speak. If shock was what it took to motivate her, then so be it. "I need the names of the other people in the group, Dr. Isaka," he said. "It might be that you don't have to be involved further. I need to talk to all of them—or at least all of those who attended the ritual you conducted two weeks ago."

He could hear her breathing hard. "Okay," she said at last, her voice shaking. "I don't believe this..."

"Believe it," he said. "Please—you must help me. I'm not working alone—I've got friends helping me, including a police officer. If you can make it easier for us, you might prevent more deaths."

"Okay," she said again. She sounded reluctant. "There—there were five of us. Me, Debbie Margolis, Carly Rosales, Karen Butler, and Suzanne Proust. Karen is Karen Blanco now, and Suzanne is Suzanne Washburn." She paused. "Karen and Suzanne still live in Ojai. Debbie's in Colorado somewhere, and Carly's in—Santa Maria, I think."

"Do you know how to contact the out-of-town members?" he asked, inwardly trying to decide if he was pleased or dismayed that it was looking like his next step was going to be Suzanne Washburn after all.

"No, not really. We all kind of lost touch with each other after we left school. Suzanne has everybody's information, I think. She was the group's leader. She was the one who suggested we get back together for one last ritual. I can give you her address." She did so, then sighed. "It all seems so stupid now. We were just kids. We each had a 'magical' name in the group. Mine was 'Tsukiko,' which meant 'Child of the Moon.' Suzanne's was 'Elinaria.' Since the whole thing was her idea originally, we called ourselves 'The Sisterhood of Elinaria.' You know, this is embarrassing to even be telling you. I didn't even want to do it after a while, but they were my friends, so I went along. You know how kids are. I was pretty shy in those days, and I wanted them to like me. You know?"

"I understand," he said, his voice gentle as he jotted down the things she'd told him. "All right. Thank you for this. I think you're right: I need to talk to Suzanne. Fortunately, I've already met her, so it might be a bit easier. Would you mind if I asked you to be available should I need to contact you again?"

"I thought you said you wouldn't."

"I said I *might* not need to," he said. "It depends on what I find out."

"What do you expect to find out, Dr. Stone? We're not witches. We didn't know how to summon anything. We were just a bunch of teenage girls messing around with pretty robes and magic wands. Is that wrong?"

"Of course not. I'm sure whatever happened, no one intended it. And I know you don't believe me. I understand that. Most people don't."

Another pause, and when she spoke again her voice was a little stronger. "I've grown up, Dr. Stone. I have a successful dental practice. I have a partner, and we have two young children. Please—don't get me involved in this. You're right: I don't believe any of what you're telling me. I'm only answering your questions because it seems like you *do* believe it, and your story checks out. But I really don't want to be involved."

"I'll do my best to make sure you don't have to be, Dr. Isaka. Again, thank you for your help. Even if this ends your involvement, you might well have already helped save lives."

This time when Stone came out of the back room, he moved slowly. Once again he sank onto the couch.

"You okay?" Lopez asked. "Did she tell you what you needed to know?"

"She told me," he said. "She gave me the names of the rest of the group. We were right: they did get together and do rituals and ceremonies as part of their little club. And they did another one around the time of the reunion, for old time's sake."

"So, what's the problem?" Jason asked. "Isn't that what you were hoping for? It means we're on the right track, right?"

"We are," Stone confirmed. "But I'm not liking what I have to do next."

"Which is—?"

He glanced over at Edna, who was watching him as she idly leafed through an old copy of *Sports Illustrated*. "Only two of the group still live in Ojai. And one of them is Suzanne Washburn."

Edna tossed the magazine aside with a snort. "I told you before: that one's about as magical as a rock. I'd bet everything I own that she's not our descendant."

"I wouldn't take that bet," Stone said. "But the fact remains, she wasn't only in the group, she was its instigator. And that means we're going to have to talk to her."

"I don't see the problem yet," Lopez said. "Yeah, maybe she's not your favorite person, but if she can help—"

"It's more that *I'm* not *her* favorite person," Stone pointed out. "Remember, she thinks I'm a murderer? Also, she strikes me as quite the busybody type—both she and that friend of hers who runs the Third Eye. If we talk to her, we'll probably end up having to tell her more than I want to. And if we do tell her, she'll tell her friend. Before the day's out it will likely be all over the town. Which, aside from making things potentially very uncomfortable for me, will probably cause Casner to run us all out of town on a rail for impeding his investigation. That is, if he doesn't arrest me again."

"True," Lopez said soberly. "Though if I go along, show her my badge, and tell her you've been cleared of any suspicion, at least she won't think you're a murderer anymore. I hope."

"There's no helping it, I suppose. I can try playing up my credentials as an occult expert without letting her in on the existence of magic, but I doubt that will work once we actually have to start doing something, as opposed to just talking." He stood. "We'd best get going, then, before I change my mind."

Edna rolled her eyes. "You're a piece of work, Stone, I'll say that. You'll stand up to ancient spirits that try to rip you to pieces without even flinching, but a middle-aged lady scares the crap out of you."

He smiled tightly at her. "Guilty as charged."

| CHAPTER THIRTY-EIGHT

Suzanne Washburn's address was—as so many other things related to their current situation seemed to be—in the Arbolada, on a quiet, winding street peppered with venerable old oak trees. When she appeared at the door of her large, rambling home set back from the street, and saw Stone standing on her front porch, her eyes widened and she gasped.

"D-Dr. Stone," she stammered, her gaze darting nervously between him and Lopez. "How—uh—nice to see you again!" She didn't say *how did you find out where I live?* but Stone could see it right there on her face as clearly as if she were holding up a sign. He could also see that she was fighting very hard against a temptation to slam the door in his face and hide until he went away.

"Mrs. Washburn," he said, inclining his head in greeting. He held up her ley-line map, carefully rolled and secured with a wide rubber band. "I'm returning your map—thank you very much, by the way, it was quite helpful. And we'd like to talk with you briefly, if we may." He indicated Lopez. "This is Sergeant Stan Lopez of the Ventura Sheriff's Department."

"Pleased to meet you," Lopez said. He pulled out his wallet and showed her his badge and official identification.

She looked at it, then back up at him, a different sort of fear settling over her features. "Am I in some kind of trouble, officer?" She glanced sideways at Stone in suspicion, as if expecting him to be Lopez's prisoner or something.

"You're not in any trouble with the police, Mrs. Washburn," Stone said. "In fact, I asked Sergeant Lopez to accompany me today to prove to you that *I'm* not, either. I need to talk with you about something very important, and I couldn't do that if you were afraid I was still under some sort of suspicion for the murders."

"I didn't—" she began to protest.

"Yes, you did," Stone said gently. "I could see it in your face the other day. And I don't blame you—things have been rather chaotic for me the past couple of days. But I assure you, I've been cleared of any suspicion."

"It's true," Lopez confirmed. "He was questioned and released. Just routine. He's not wanted for anything at this time."

She swallowed, considered, and nodded once, her hand's death grip on the door loosening infinitesimally. "Well—all right, then. You can't blame me for being concerned. And thank you for returning my map. What else can I do for you, Dr. Stone?"

"May we come in?" he asked.

She looked back and forth between him and Lopez again, but finally nodded. "Yes, of course." She swung the door wide and motioned them inside.

Suzanne Washburn or her husband obviously had money: Stone and Lopez followed her down a tiled hallway lined with paintings and fine sculptures and into a large, elegant but comfortable living room. "Let's chat in the back yard," she said, moving through the living room to a set of French doors leading out to an equally elegant patio. "It's a lovely day." She motioned toward a group of chairs arranged around an umbrella-topped table next to a sparkling kidney-shaped pool. "Sit down," she said. "I'll bring us some refreshments."

They sat down and she hurried off. "She doesn't want us inside her home," Stone said.

"Sure looks that way," Lopez agreed. He glanced around at the large yard, which was surrounded by oak trees. "I don't think anyone's gonna hear us out here, though."

Suzanne returned a few minutes later bearing a tray with a pitcher of iced tea, three glasses, and a plate with a hunk of brie, assorted crackers, a knife, and some napkins. After pouring each of them a glass and settling herself down, she looked between Stone and Lopez. "Now—what can I help you with?"

Stone met her gaze and held it. "We'd like to talk to you about the Sisterhood of Elinaria, Mrs. Washburn," he said softly.

She nearly dropped her glass. "What did you say?" she whispered, setting it down with a shaking hand.

"The Sisterhood," he repeated. "We'd like you to tell us about it."

"Why? How did you find out about—"

"Michiko Isaka told us," he said. "Please don't hold it against her—she had good reason." He paused a moment, deciding how to proceed. "Mrs. Washburn—how long have you had your interest in the occult?"

She looked like she wasn't going to answer, but finally sighed. "Since I was a little girl, I guess. I've been interested in witches and fairies and astrology and that kind of thing since grade school." Her eyes came up. "What's this about, Dr. Stone?"

"Do you believe in spirits?"

She nodded. "I do. I've seen them. I think the spirit of my husband is still in this house. That's why I won't sell it, even though it's really too big for me now that the children are away at college."

"Tell us about the Sisterhood, Mrs. Washburn, please." Stone kept his voice soft and soothing. He didn't know if his powers of persuasion would overshadow the fact that he was still making her nervous, but he gave it his best shot. "When did you start it?"

"Junior high," she said. "Eighth grade." She plucked up a cracker and examined it before taking an experimental nibble. "It was just me and a couple of friends to start with. Like I said, I'd been interested for a long time, and I kind of rubbed off on them eventually. We'd go out to a quiet area of campus during lunchtime and have our little rituals. Another girl noticed, and she was interested, so she joined shortly after that."

"Where did you get these little rituals?" Stone asked.

"We—well, *I*, at least to start with—just made them up. I'd write them in my notebook during class, when I was supposed to be listening to the teacher." She giggled, but it was more an uneasy sound than a happy one. Then her expression clouded. "You're leading to something, Dr. Stone. I can tell. What is it?"

"I'll tell you, I promise. But first I'd very much like for you to continue."

She glanced at Lopez. "Are you sure I'm not in trouble, Sergeant Lopez? I don't need a lawyer, do I? He's not trying to get me to incriminate myself in anything, is he?"

Lopez shook his head. "No, ma'am. None of this is official. The only reason I'm here is because I've been working with Dr. Stone on this, and we figured you'd be more comfortable if a police officer could assure you that he's not wanted for anything."

Her eyes stayed on him for a long time, as if she were trying to decide if he was telling the truth. Then she nodded again. "We— kept it up for years. All through high school, too. It got more elaborate as we got older—Debbie liked to sew, so she made us all lovely satin robes. We'd collect pretty bottles to use for our 'potions,' and we each had a wand. Each of us also picked a special name that we used—I guess you know something about that, since you referred to the Sisterhood. I was Elinaria. Karen was Belladonna, Michiko was Tsukiko, and Debbie was Ariadne."

Stone frowned a little. "I thought there were five of you."

"Oh, there were, later. Carly didn't join until after we were in high school. She overheard us discussing getting together one evening, and asked if she could join. We thought she was making fun of us, since she was kind of an 'other side of the tracks' kind of girl and always seemed to be in trouble, but she seemed sincere so we let her come to one of the rituals. She loved it, and turned out to be very nice, so she joined us then. Her magical name was 'Tansy.'"

　　　　　　　　　　　　　　　　　　　　　　　　　　　　　　　　R. L. KING

Lopez looked troubled. "So you're saying you got together all through high school and put on robes and waved wands around and did magic spells? That seems—well, let's just say I've dealt with a lot of high-school girls, and it doesn't seem like the sort of thing that would survive that long after you all started dating."

She smiled wistfully. "Oh, we didn't do it all the time. By the time we got to high school our meetings were only once every couple of months, usually at my house since it was the biggest. They were as much about talking and laughing and eating pizza as they were about the rituals. But we were all good friends, Sergeant. We had a special bond, and we didn't want to lose that. I think the Sisterhood really got to just be a way for us to reconnect, as we all went our separate ways socially." She looked at Stone. "Does that make sense?"

"It does," Stone said gently. "I'm going to ask you what seems an odd question now, but if you could try to remember, it would be very helpful."

She looked worried. "All right..."

"Can you recall any rituals you did in your second year in high school—"

"Sophomore year," Lopez supplied with a grin. "Dr. Stone's not from around here, if you hadn't guessed."

Stone gave him a look, but didn't contradict him. "Sophomore year," he agreed. "Anything that might have been out of the ordinary in some way? Perhaps you got the source of the ritual from somewhere different, or it was for a different purpose than usual?"

"Why is this important?" she asked, frowning. "Why do you want to know?" She looked back and forth between them, her gaze sharpening. "Before I answer your question, Dr. Stone, I think you owe me an explanation about why you want it. I think I've told you quite a bit on faith so far, but now you need to give me something."

Stone was hoping to get a bit further along before arriving at this point, but it couldn't be helped. In truth, his grudging respect for Suzanne Washburn was increasing. She might be a magical fraud, but it wasn't a crime to be interested in the supernatural without having any talent for it.

"All right," he said. "Fair enough. You have a right to know." He took a deep breath, then spoke with care: "I have reason to believe that something in your rituals might be related to the recent murders, as well as a smaller number that occurred twenty-seven years ago."

She gaped at him, eyes wide, mouth open. Her hand closed convulsively around her iced-tea glass, making it rattle the table's glass top. She swallowed a couple of times. Clearly, whatever she'd been thinking he might say, this wasn't even in the same time zone. "You—think *we* had something to do with the murders?" Her gaze cut to Lopez and then back to Stone. "That's—that's *horrible,* Dr. Stone. How could you think we—"

He held up a hand to stop her. "I don't believe it was intentional," he said. "Not at all. You said you believed in spirits—I think what happened is that something in one of your rituals might have accidentally called a spirit. And that spirit is what's been doing the killing."

"A—spirit?" Her expression was still stunned, shocked. She seemed to be having trouble forming a thought.

Stone nodded. "Please, Mrs. Washburn. No one is accusing you or your friends of anything. These things happen sometimes, even when there wasn't any conscious intent behind them. But we need to know as much of the detail as we can."

"Why?" she whispered. "What—what are you going to do?"

"We're going to try to stop it, if we can."

She frowned; she'd barely blinked since Stone had dropped his bombshell. "You—can do that?" And to Lopez, she added, "The police know about this?"

"Not officially," Lopez replied. "Not formally. But the murders are increasing, and I'm convinced that Dr. Stone is on to something here. The evidence I've seen is too strong for me to doubt it."

"As for your other question: I don't know if we can stop it," Stone said softly. "But we're going to do everything we can. And I do know that if we're to have a chance at it, we'll need all the information you can give us."

She didn't move. Dropping her gaze down to her ring-bedecked hands, she wrung at one of the napkins.

"Mrs. Washburn?"

"No," she whispered. "This is—crazy." A tear trickled from one eye and wandered down her cheek, cutting a track through her perfect makeup. "We can't have—" She reached out and picked up the knife, scooping out some of the brie and spreading it on a cracker. Her hand shook, her shoulders stiffening.

Stone wasn't sure why he chose that exact moment to engage his magical senses: perhaps it was something odd in her movement, or just some sort of supernatural hunch. But in any case, he noticed the greenish aura only a second before Suzanne glanced back up.

"You are resourceful, mageling," He of Many Faces said using her voice, roughening it and adding its strange inflection. *"But you will not follow this avenue."*

Before Stone could lunge forward, Suzanne, her eyes now shining with an unearthly red-orange glow, leaped from her chair and danced several steps backward, still clutching the knife.

| CHAPTER THIRTY-NINE

"What the hell—?" Lopez demanded.

Stone was already standing, his chair clattering over behind him and nearly falling into the pool. "Let her go," he ordered, eyes blazing.

"*When I am ready,*" the Suzanne-thing said. "*You surprise me. I nearly ripped your flesh from your bones, and still you come after me. You are even more foolish than I thought.*"

In the periphery of his vision, Stone sensed Lopez moving up behind him. He held a hand out and back in a *wait* gesture. "I'm not going to give up. None of us are. We've got your little plan figured out now, and it's just a matter of time before we send you slinking back to wherever you came from. Now *let her go.*"

It laughed, a sound like gargling acid. "*I think not, mageling.*"

It raised the knife and plunged it toward Suzanne's chest.

Lopez yelled and dived forward, but Stone was expecting the move. As soon as Suzanne's arm lifted, he magically seized the knife in a telekinetic grip far stronger than he could have managed with his physical body. The Suzanne-thing only got it down a few inches before an invisible force stopped it in midair. A second later it wrenched free of her hand and flew over the pool, dropping in with a splash.

Lopez, still moving, grabbed her arm and held it, only loosening his grip when he realized that she was no longer holding the knife.

Suzanne sagged a bit as if she had lost her balance. She blinked and her eyes returned to normal, fixed first on Lopez and then on Stone in panic. "What are you doing?" she demanded. "Let go of me!" She yanked her arm from Lopez's grasp; he immediately let her go.

"Mrs. Washburn, wait. Please," Stone began, but Suzanne was already backing away toward the house.

"I don't know what you did to me," she said, voice shaking, "but I'm calling the police!"

"Wait!" Lopez called. "It's not like that!"

"Mrs. Washburn. Please hear us out," Stone said urgently, moving toward her. "You were just possessed by the spirit I was telling you about. That's what it *does*. It possesses people, and they don't remember anything it when it leaves them."

"Well, *that's* convenient, isn't it?" she snapped. "You must think I'm an idiot." She continued backing toward the house, her eyes darting between the two of them as if she expected them to jump her again.

"Stop!" Lopez ordered, his tone commanding—the sort of tone he would use on a suspect he was about to apprehend.

She stopped, briefly, looking like a cornered animal.

"What if we can prove it to you?" he asked.

"How can you do that?" she demanded, voice high with panic.

Stone was looking at him in astonishment. "Yes—how *can* you do that?"

He pointed up toward the roofline of the house. "That's a security camera, right? Does it work? Please tell me you don't have one of those fake ones."

Warily, she said, "It works. There are several of them around the house. I never used them much before, but since the murders started—"

"Go look at your tape," he told her. "We'll wait out here. See what it shows you. Just do it before you call the police. If you see what I think you'll see, you probably won't want to."

"Wait," Stone said. "Where do you keep the recorder for the cameras?"

She looked confused by his question. "In Lester's study," she said, waving toward one of the windows along the wall. "Why?"

"We want to be able to keep an eye on you," he said. "Isn't that right, Sergeant?"

Lopez looked almost as confused as Suzanne, but went with it. "Uh...yeah. Just to be safe."

She seemed uncertain, but finally she nodded. "All right," she said. "I'll go in and look. But you stay here. I'll open the curtains so you can see in, but I don't want you coming in with me. I've still got Lester's guns in the house—if you try to break in, I'll shoot you."

She backed the rest of the way to the French doors, opened them, slipped inside, and clicked the lock. After a moment, the curtains to the room she'd indicated opened. She began fiddling with something on a desk.

Stone let his breath out and walked over to station himself next to the window so he could keep watch. "Nicely done," he told Lopez. "I didn't even notice the cameras."

"It's one of the things you get used to looking for when you're a cop," Lopez said. He nodded at the window. "How did you know she was possessed?"

"Green aura, remember?" Stone kept his attention focused closely on Suzanne as his heart rate slowly returned to normal. He didn't have any intention of showing Many Faces (or even Lopez), but the encounter, the first since his too-close brush with death, had spooked him more than he cared to admit.

Lopez went back to the table, righted Stone's fallen chair, and sank into it. "I sure hope something shows on that tape," he said. "Otherwise we're up shit creek. If she calls the police, I'm not even sure *I* can convince Casner not to haul both our asses in." He glanced at Stone. "Why are you so concerned about keeping an eye on her, anyway? You don't really think she's going to shoot us, do you? Or run away?"

R. L. KING

Stone didn't turn away from the window. "I'm more worried about what she might do to herself. I haven't done anything to prevent Many Faces from reoccupying her."

"You know, you could have gone all day without saying that."

It was fifteen minutes before Suzanne finished what she was doing inside. She left the room, and a moment later the French doors opened again. Stone and Lopez both stiffened, but Suzanne came out slowly, empty-handed. She looked pale, shell-shocked. Stone shifted to magical sight to check her, but her own aura, a disturbed muddy gold that was probably much brighter when she wasn't agitated, showed no sign of Many Faces. "Are you all right, Mrs. Washburn?" Stone asked.

She shook her head. "No."

He and Lopez carefully approached her. They led her over to the table and helped her sit down; she didn't object. When they too were reseated, she looked at them with haunted eyes. "I—I watched the tape."

"Yes—?" Stone prompted.

She took a deep, shuddering breath. "I don't even know what to say," she said bleakly. "I don't know what to think. I don't even remember doing any of what I saw. I don't remember getting up, or grabbing that knife. And—it looked like I was going to stab myself if you hadn't stopped me, Sergeant."

Lopez started to say something, but Stone tapped his arm and shook his head. If Suzanne wanted to believe it was Lopez who'd stopped her, that was all the longer before Stone would have to explain anything inexplicable. Thank goodness for cameras that were sharp enough to see what was going on, but blurry enough not to show detail.

"How can that be?" she demanded, sounding like she was wanted to cry, or scream, or leap up from her chair and run away.

"That's what this spirit *does*, Mrs. Washburn," Stone said gently. "It possesses people and forces them to do things. Often it forces them to kill themselves, or other people. That's why the police don't have any suspects: because there *aren't* any suspects in most cases." He leaned forward, his gaze intense but kind. "Do you believe us now, at least that this could be possible?"

Her slow nod was reluctant. Her frightened eyes came up to meet his. "I've always been interested in the supernatural, Dr. Stone. I wasn't lying to you when I said I thought I felt Les's spirit in the house. But—this is something different. Something—horrible." Her eyes widened. "Oh, my God," she whispered. "This has something to do with what happened to that poor woman they thought you—" She trailed off, but didn't take her eyes off Stone.

He nodded, his jaw clenching. "Yes."

Once again tears began to run down her cheeks. "I just want to wake up and find out this was all a nightmare."

"I know," Stone said, his voice soothing as he tried to put the image of Lindsey out of his mind. "I know. I think we all wish that. But I still need your help, Mrs. Washburn. I need you to tell me what you know. That's the only way we can stop this nightmare."

Suzanne looked down at her hands for a long time. Then she drew a deep breath. "Ask your questions. I'll—I'll do my best."

"Thank you," Stone said. "What I need to know is anything you remember about rituals you did when you were in your sophomore year."

She thought about that. "I—I used to write them all up," she said. "All the rituals and meetings. I still have the write-ups. I could find them, if it would help—"

That was better than Stone could have hoped for. "That would be brilliant, Mrs. Washburn. Can you find those for us now?"

"I think so," she said, standing.

Stone stood too. "We'd best go with you, I think. Now that you believe us, it would be safer."

"Safer—why?"

"I'm concerned that the spirit might try to possess you again and make you do something to yourself when you're alone."

Her eyes widened and she went even more pale. "Oh, God," she moaned. "What about after you're gone? Will it—"

"I can help you with that," Stone said. "I can teach you a mental technique that's effective in keeping it out." He didn't tell her that what he really planned to do was put a block on her mind, as well as at least a minimal ward around her house. That was for later, as soon as he figured out how to tell her what he was doing without letting on that he was performing real magic.

She looked dubious, but nodded. "Come on," she said. "I'll find you those write-ups."

Twenty minutes later Stone and Lopez were seated in the living room, watching Suzanne leaf through spiral-bound notebooks whose covers were decorated with unicorns, rainbows, fairies, and other whimsical stickers. "Hardly the type you'd expect to be summoning spirits of vengeance," Stone muttered to Lopez, indicating the notebooks with a quick head gesture.

"Here it is," she announced. She held up one of the notebooks. "We only did a couple rituals that year. Like I told you before, the whole thing had started to wind down by then. Most of the time, we got together for a meeting but ended up watching movies and gossiping about boys instead." She pointed at the notebook. "I remember this one, though. It was right after Tansy joined the group. She wanted to do a curse."

Stone frowned. "A curse? I take it that wasn't your usual activity."

"Oh, no. Our spells were all 'good witch' stuff: health and happiness for us and our families, 'love potions,' that kind of thing."

"What sort of curse was it?"

"Something to do with a boy. I think he'd dumped her, and she wanted to get even with him."

"And you went along with it?" Lopez asked.

She shrugged. "Sure. It's not like we believed any of it was real. Although—" She gasped. "Oh, my God."

"What?" Stone leaned forward. "Are you all right?"

"How could I have forgotten about that?" she whispered. "At the time we thought it was just coincidence, but it still scared us enough that we never did another curse again."

"What are you talking about, Mrs. Washburn?"

She met his gaze. "The boy," she said, her voice shaking. "The one Carly wanted to put the curse on. A couple days later, he was attacked in the high school locker room by another boy who tried to stab him."

"Wait," Lopez said. "The kid who almost died was the one she put the curse on?"

Suzanne nodded. "We—we were all afraid that God was punishing us for doing something so awful, even though we knew it couldn't have been our fault. Even Carly was scared." She stiffened. "I remember—it was in the papers, of course. The boy who did it claimed he had no idea what he was doing, or why. They barely even knew who each other were." She stared at Stone. "It was the same thing, wasn't it? Like what just happened to me."

"Almost certainly," Stone said.

"Then—it *was* our fault!" She grasped the notebook in shaking hands, erupting into tears again. "Oh, God, it was our fault—"

"Mrs. Washburn, please. It wasn't anyone's fault. You didn't know."

"But—" she said in a trembling voice, "Why did it stop? You said it killed other people. You said it was back. We—summoned it again? After it was gone?" She looked utterly miserable, letting the notebook drop back into the box.

Stone nodded. "It appears so." He tried to keep his voice gentle, but he couldn't take the time to try to comfort her right now. He needed to get this information. "Mrs. Washburn—when you got together to do the ritual two weeks ago—what was the subject? What were you trying to accomplish with it?"

She shrugged without looking up. "Nothing special. It—it wasn't a curse or anything bad. Just wishing us all continued health and happiness."

"Did you have any sort of new materials to use?"

That time she did look up. "You know, I did," she said. "I had a book—I'd found it a few months ago, at Bart's. It had all these passages in Latin, and I thought it might make the ritual sound more—authentic."

Stone sighed. Mundanes. "Do you still have the book?"

"Of course. Do you want to see it?"

"Please. And—do you know Latin, Mrs. Washburn?"

She gave him a damp, wan smile. "Not a word. They didn't teach it in high school, and I didn't study it in college. It just seemed—magical." She stood. "It's in the library. Will you come with me?"

She led them down another hall and into a small room. All four walls were lined with bookshelves; the only other furnishings were a comfortable chair, a pole lamp near the window, and a desk in the middle of the room. Stone glanced around, scanning some of the titles; it was a highly eclectic collection dominated by swashbuckling adventures, romances, and 'pop-occult' volumes. Switching to magical senses, he wasn't surprised that he didn't immediately notice anything that glowed with an aura indicating it was more than it seemed.

Until he directed his gaze toward the area where Suzanne had headed.

He saw it before she plucked it off the shelf: an old, leatherbound tome larger than a modern hardcover, its cracking binding held together with a single, equally ancient leather strap. Several multicolored slips of paper poked out from between its pages. "Here it is," she said. "I find a lot of things at Bart's. Usually I just buy anything that looks interesting, especially if it's related to the supernatural. I got this one a few months ago, and it's always intrigued me even though I can't read anything in it. I just got a vibe from it, you know?" She held it out, offering it to Stone.

He wasn't surprised that she had gotten a 'vibe,' even despite her being completely mundane. The book fairly radiated magic, its aura glowing so brightly that it obscured the other books behind it. When he took it in his hands he felt a faint buzz, like an electrical current was running through it. "You got this at Bart's?"

She nodded. "The owner told me that a whole bunch of books had come in from an old man who died. I was there the day they came in, so he let me look through them before he put them out for sale. When I looked through that one, I got the idea for getting the Sisterhood back together at the reunion for one last ceremony."

Stone tore his attention from the book long enough to verify that nothing else magically interesting resided on the dark wooden shelves. "Is it all right if take a look inside?" he asked. His voice sounded a little oddly husky: aside from this book's potential for being the 'artifact' that Many Faces had spoken of, it was also a very old and highly magical tome. Alternative name, at least where Stone was concerned: 'mage catnip.' The temptation to take the book somewhere private and spend the next two or three days delving into its secrets was overwhelming, but they didn't have time for that right now.

"Of course." She waved him toward the desk.

Stone sat down after first glancing at Lopez and, with a subtle head movement toward Suzanne, indicated that he should keep an eye on her. Lopez nodded. Moving with deliberate care, Stone undid the leather strap around the book, opened it to a random page, and began to read.

It was a beautiful book, its age-brittle pages hand illustrated, its text set in flowery, elaborate type. The illustrations ran the gamut from the fascinating to the grotesque (though Stone had to allow that the grotesque ones were equally fascinating). His breath picked up as he continued reading. This was the real deal.

"Uh—Al?" came Lopez's soft voice.

He started. "Yes, what?"

"Find anything?" The cop sounded amused. "It's been twenty minutes and you haven't said a word."

Stone looked up to discover both Lopez and Suzanne watching him intently. "Er—sorry," he muttered. "Got a bit carried away."

"You can read that?" Suzanne asked.

He nodded. "It's intriguing. Do you remember which bit you used for your ceremony?"

"The pink bookmark there toward the back," she said, pointing.

Stone carefully turned to the page she indicated. The first thing he noticed was the illustration, which showed a small group of robed figures surrounding what looked like some sort of burning object. Smoke rose from the object and formed into a ghostly, humanoid shape, which appeared to be gazing down at the assembled group with approval. He switched his focus to the text, taking his time to make sure he was reading it correctly. He was fluent in Latin, but some of the vocabulary in the book was oddly archaic, as if someone had been trying to obscure the text's meaning. That was entirely possible: Stone had seen instances before where spells were written in a sort of skewed pseudo-version of an ancient language that only those who had created them or who worked with them could decipher.

"Anything?" Lopez asked.

"I picked that one because of the picture," Suzanne said. "Whatever that ghostly thing is, it looks happy. I thought it might be good for health and happiness."

Stone let his breath out. "Well," he said, running a hand back through his hair until it spiked. "You're right about that bit—it *is* happy. But not for the reason you think. It's happy to finally be summoned into the world." He pointed at the text. "This is an odd spell—I haven't seen too many like it. It's actually quite versatile, because it's not specific."

"What do you mean, 'not specific'?" Suzanne asked.

"I mean, it's not designed to summon a specific entity." He ran his finger over the lines of the spell. "See—there's no true name in here. Usually when you're summoning something, or trying to get rid of it, you'll want its true name. That gives you control over it."

"I remember reading that somewhere in one of my books," Suzanne said, nodding. "But—if it's not meant to summon something specific, then what *is* it meant for?"

Stone considered his words. "It's—sort of an all-purpose generic summoning spell," he said at last. "It's up to the people doing the summoning to imprint their will on it in order to get what they're looking for."

"Wait a minute," Suzanne protested. "If that was true, then why would we have gotten this horrible thing that's killing people? I told you—we were wishing for happiness. Health. Prosperity. Positive things. So why didn't we get a positive spirit?"

Stone turned a little to face her. "Here's the thing—I don't think everyone in your group actually influenced the summoning. In fact, I'm convinced that it was only one person. And I'm sorry, Mrs. Washburn, but it wasn't you."

She stared, wide-eyed. "Why—why not? I mean, I was the group leader. I read the words of the spell from the book—well, as well as I could since I didn't know if I was pronouncing them right. Why wouldn't I be the one to influence it?"

For a long time Stone was silent as he tried to find a way to explain it to her without revealing the existence of magic. "Well," he said, "The way this spell works, it's sort of like you're making a soup. If you've got a group who's all contributing to the recipe, the person who puts in, say, flour isn't going to change the taste as much as the one who drops in a lot of pepper." He raised an eyebrow with a faint smile. "Sorry, I'm rubbish at cooking so forgive me if that's a terrible metaphor, but you get the idea."

"So you're saying that there's someone else in the group who—put in the pepper?" She still looked confused. "What would affect that? Not that I would want to be the one responsible for that awful thing, but—"

This was getting more difficult to explain without going places Stone didn't want to go. Again, he took a long pause to think. "Please, Mrs. Washburn, don't be offended by this. I know you're very interested in this sort of thing and have spent quite a lot of time studying it, but—some people are more—innately connected to the spirit world than others." He took a breath. "Also—I suspect that someone in your group might have a specific connection to the spirit that was summoned."

Suzanne pondered that. "I'm not offended, Dr. Stone. In fact, after seeing those tapes, I'm not sure I really want anything to do with the supernatural anymore." She nodded toward the book. "Will you—take that? Get it away from here? I don't want to look at it anymore."

Stone tried his best to hide the fact that for a brief moment he felt like a kid on Christmas morning who'd just been handed the coolest, most-impossible-to-get toy ever, and he mostly succeeded. "Of course."

"So—what happens now? What are you going to do? Call the police?"

"The police already know about my theories. Aside from Sergeant Lopez here, they don't think much of them." He fixed what he hoped was a comforting gaze on Suzanne. "We might need your help, though. We might need the help of all of the Sisterhood."

She frowned. "How—can we help?"

"I have to do a bit more research, but it's possible that in order to send this spirit back where it came from, it will require another ceremony from the people who summoned it in the first place."

"But...isn't that dangerous?" she asked, paling. "Dr. Stone, if you're right and this spirit is killing people—"

"I'm hoping it won't come to that," he said. "I'm just letting you know it might, and asking if I can count on you. It might only require the person who did the actual imprinting. I don't know yet.

But if we need all of you, will you help? Will you help get the others together?"

He waited, watching her expression change as the thoughts flitted through her mind. She was scared—hell, she was *petrified*. Stone had seen this sort of thing before: mundanes with a strong interest in the occult who, when confronted with the real thing, couldn't cope with it. Sometimes inveterate skeptics like Lopez or Jason dealt with the odd and freaky better than the witches-and-horoscopes crowd, because they had fewer preconceived notions about the way it was supposed to work.

The one thing most of the hobbyists never even considered before they'd been tossed neck-deep into it was that the supernatural world was *dangerous*. They tended to look at it in benign terms: predicting the future, helping to find lost people, or being visited by the ghosts of long-dead loved ones. Most never expected to find a place full of more malevolent entities—or at least more that didn't give the tiniest damn about the sensibilities of the insignificant bags of meat crawling around on an insignificant dustball in an insignificant corner of the metaphysical cosmos—than friendly ones. A place filled with things that would kill you for your first misstep, and wouldn't even take enough notice to care. *That* was a major reason why even experienced practitioners like Stone didn't initiate contact with those realms unless he absolutely had to. He knew there were things out there, lots of them, that could gobble up He of Many Faces like a light snack. If you were smart, and if you wanted to see your next birthday, you left that kind of thing well the hell alone. Edna Soren might call him arrogant and conceited—and okay, there were times when he definitely qualified—but some things were best just avoided. If Suzanne hadn't been petrified after what she'd seen on that security tape, Stone would have wondered about her sanity.

She looked at him like a weary little girl would look at a trusted adult, someone she believed would keep the boogeyman away and the closet free of monsters. "If I get involved in this, Dr. Stone, could I get hurt? Could I even—die?"

He put a gentle hand on her arm. "Mrs. Washburn," he said softly, "You're already involved. I can't lie to you—you've been so brave already, I owe you the truth. This is dangerous. You could get hurt. Yes, it's possible you could even die. You saw what happened today. But I can promise you this: you'll be safer if you help us, and if you let us help you. Because regardless of whether you agree to help, I'm not going to stop. Sergeant Lopez and our other friends aren't going to stop. We can't. This thing is killing people, and *it* isn't going to stop."

Lopez took a step forward. "You know," he said in the sort of calm tone used to comfort lost children, "I know this all seems pretty freaky to you. It did to me, too, when he first dropped it on me. But he knows what he's doing." He nodded at Stone, who'd taken a step back. "If anybody's got a chance to get rid of this spirit, it's this guy, and the other folks he's working with. I've seen them in action, and I believe in them. Please—help us before anybody else is killed."

She swallowed and nodded. "Okay," she whispered, tears sparkling in the corners of her eyes. "What do I need to do?"

"We need to find which one of your group is associated with the spirit," Stone said. "Can you call the others, and ask them to talk with me? Don't tell them anything specific—let me do that. Just tell them you're working with me, and that they should answer my questions."

She nodded again, sniffing. "Okay. I—I guess it makes sense to call Karen first, since she's local." Pausing, she looked at Stone. "You said before—that you could teach me something that would make it so that thing couldn't get in my head and make me do things again."

"I can," he said.

"Will it take long? Because I'm really scared. I don't want to go anywhere alone now."

"Not long at all." He moved closer to her and reached out, hovering his hand near her forehead. He gave her a questioning look, and when she nodded, wide-eyed, he gently touched her with the tips of his fingers. "All right," he murmured. "I'm going to give you a phrase to repeat. Sort of a mantra. Just repeat it in your head when you're alone, periodically."

"That will work?" she asked, dubious.

"Trust him," Lopez said. "He did it to me, and I've been working with him for days. No sign of anything trying to get in my head."

Hardly any sign, Stone thought. But that was beside the point. It wasn't as if they'd be taking Suzanne Washburn anywhere near the shrine.

"Well...okay..."

Stone closed his eyes and concentrated for a moment, then stepped back. "Right, then," he said. "Now, I'll write the mantra down for you so you don't forget it." He took a pen and a piece of scratch paper from the desk, thought a moment, then jotted something down and handed it to her.

She studied it, then looked at him, head tilted. "'*Guard well the pips, and the fruit shall grow without let*'?"

He shrugged. "Very mystical."

She held his gaze for a moment longer, as if expecting him to burst out laughing. When he didn't, she gave a confused nod, mouthed the words again, and picked up the phone. "I'll call Karen."

Stone and Lopez backed off into the corner of the room. Turned away from Suzanne so she couldn't see him, Lopez gave Stone a look. "What the hell was that?" he whispered, trying to keep from chuckling. "Guard well the—what?"

Stone shrugged. "I saw it in a late-night horror movie about a charlatan mystic. It seemed apropos."

Lopez started to reply, but Stone's expression went suddenly from cynical amusement to sharp-eyed focus. "What?" he asked.

Stone was no longer paying him any attention. "What is it, Mrs. Washburn?" he asked, stepping toward her.

She had been murmuring into the phone when her expression had gone rigid. She hung up with a slow deliberate motion and stood very still in the middle of the room.

Then she looked up at Stone, her eyes once more haunted. "That—thing," she said. "I think it has Karen."

| CHAPTER FORTY

"What?" Stone demanded. He snatched up the phone and put it to his ear, but there was nothing now but the dial tone. "Why do you think so?"

"She—spoke to me in this...strange, growly voice," Suzanne said numbly. "It hardly even sounded like her. All—slow and creepy."

"What did she say?" Stone's heartbeat picked up again, and he struggled to keep his voice even.

"She said—" Tears crawled down her cheeks. "—she said I should—" She paused, recalling the words. "She said I should 'tell the mageling that the agony of the last time will be nothing compared to what I will visit upon him now,' and that I shouldn't help you, or she would kill me, too." She was shaking hard now, the tears flowing freely. "What does it mean? What's happened?"

Stone exchanged glances with Lopez. This wasn't good. "I think it means we'd best go check on Karen," he said, his tone grim.

"You know," Lopez said, "we're going to have to call Casner if we—"

Stone sighed. *If we find anything.* He didn't like it—especially getting Casner involved this close to the conversation with Suzanne—but there was no way around it. "Let's check first," he said. "If we get there soon enough—" He turned to Suzanne. "Can you tell us where Karen lives?"

"I'll go with you," she said.

"Mrs. Washburn—"

"No," she said, and there was a steel behind her tone that hadn't been there before. "Karen's my friend. If there's something—wrong with her, or any way I can help, I want to go." Her sudden bravado slipped just a bit as she addressed Stone. "You—you think that thing might make her hurt herself, don't you?"

"I don't know, Mrs. Washburn," he said softly. And to Lopez: "We should go."

"There it is," Suzanne said from the back seat of Lopez's truck, pointing. "The two-story yellow house there on the left."

Stone could already tell that something was wrong, even from out here. As soon as he switched to magical senses he could see the profound disturbance in the house's no-doubt normally peaceful aura. He glanced at Lopez and shook his head once, looking grim.

Jason's old Ford was parked outside; he and Edna got out as Lopez parked on the street. Stone had called them before they left Suzanne's place and asked them to meet at Karen's address, but not to go in until he, Lopez, and Suzanne arrived. Jason started to ask Stone something as he approached, but one look at the mage's expression silenced him. Edna, too, looked bleak: she had clearly noticed the aura as well.

"What are we waiting for?" Suzanne demanded. "Let's go."

Stone shook his head. "Mrs. Washburn—I think it would be best if you didn't."

"What do you mean?" Her voice pitched higher. "You think there's something wrong?"

"Call Casner," Stone said under his breath to Lopez.

"You sure?"

He nodded. "Do it."

As Lopez headed off, Suzanne looked back and forth between them. "What are you saying? Aren't you going into the house?"

When Stone didn't reply right away, her face set. "Well, if you're not, I am!" Before he could stop her, she took off at a quick stride.

Edna raised a hand, but Stone shook his head. "Let her go," he said, his voice full of all the exhaustion that was coming back to haunt him from the past few days. "She'll have to see for herself, I think."

All of them watched as she hurried up the drive and knocked on the door. When there was no answer, she moved over and peered in through a large picture window mostly covered by thick drapes.

Then she screamed.

Moving almost as one, Stone, Jason, and Edna hurried to her. Suzanne had dropped to her knees on the broad wooden deck surrounding the house; her shoulders heaved as she sobbed into her hands. Stone nodded at his companions, then at her, then went to the window and peered into the house.

What he saw was a large living room with a ceiling that clearly rose up to the second story, even though he couldn't see that far from his limited vantage point. He took in the comfortable, functional furniture, open stairway, fireplace, and series of family photos on the mantelpiece—but none of these held his attention.

What did hold it was a massive object near the stairway: it appeared to be some sort of welded sculpture made of various bits of mechanical detritus, and topped with a pointed spire that extended the sculpture's height to nearly eight feet tall.

The body of a woman was impaled face-down on the spire, as if she had taken a flying leap from the top of the stairs and crashed down on it, making no effort to twist or otherwise avoid it. Blood streaked the sculpture and ran down from the body, giving its lower half the grotesque appearance of something cobbled together in a demon's workshop. As Stone stared, the body twitched occasionally, but his magical senses told him that it no longer held any life.

"Al?" came Jason's voice. "What do you see?"

"Let's back up," Stone said in a monotone. He noticed Edna had an arm wrapped around Suzanne's shuddering shoulders, and was attempting to get her to her feet.

Jason mouthed, *"She dead?"*

Stone nodded. "Come on, Suzanne," he said. "Let's go—the police will be here soon." It was hard to keep his voice soothing in the face of yet another senseless death, but sometimes this job didn't give you the easy stuff. He put his hand on her other shoulder and helped Edna get her up. She allowed the two of them to lead her back out to the street.

The houses out here were far enough apart that no one had come running in response to the scream; the four of them stood there next to Jason's car until Lopez returned from his truck.

A couple minutes later, sirens could be heard in the distance. Shortly after that, two squad cars and an unmarked white sedan pulled up and parked behind Jason's and Lopez's vehicles.

Peter Casner got out of the white sedan. When he saw Lopez standing with Stone and Jason, he strode over. He looked pissed. "What the hell's going on, Stan?"

Stone spoke: "Check the house, Lieutenant," he said softly, nodding toward it. "We didn't go inside—just looked through the window."

Casner glared at him, but turned to his officers and ordered them to check out the house. Then he addressed the group. "You people just stay right here. Don't go anywhere. I'll get to you in a minute." He hurried off after the uniformed officers.

Suzanne, still sobbing, watched them go. "She—she's got a husband—kids—"

"I'm so sorry," Stone murmured.

"This is my fault. If I hadn't—"

"Shh...It's not your fault. You didn't cause this."

"What am I going to tell the police?" she whispered.

Stone thought about that. On the one hand, Suzanne clearly wasn't the type who'd be adept at lying, so asking her to do that, morality aside, would probably end up getting them all in trouble if she broke down and spilled everything—even more so if she let slip that Stone had told her to lie. Given his current reputation with Casner, that would probably be enough to get him tossed back in a cell again, if for no other charge than "obstructing justice."

On the other hand, though, if she did tell Casner about everything they'd discussed, including the Sisterhood, the security tape, and the magical tome, he might feel duty-bound to investigate. And having an avowed skeptic like Casner acting as the Sisterhood's first contact point to what was going on could be disastrous. Choosing his words with care, he said, "I can't tell you what to say, Mrs. Washburn. But I can tell you this: Lieutenant Casner and his officers are doing the best job they can trying to find what's behind these murders—but they won't be able to do it. Literally the only thing he can do if he knows all the details of what's going on is make things worse, and probably get others killed if he gets in the way of what we're trying to do." He indicated Lopez, Jason, and Edna.

"So—you want me to lie to the police?"

He shook his head. "Of course not. But if you believe me—if you want us to have a chance at ending this before more people are killed—I would try to avoid telling him about the Sisterhood, or the book you gave me. Or that security tape. I doubt he'll ask you about it. If he asks about why I was talking to you, tell him that my investigation led me to you because of your occult interests. That's actually the truth, though obviously not the entire truth. Do you think you can do that, Mrs. Washburn?"

She struggled not to start crying again. Her elegant makeup had run to the point where she looked like a well-coiffed raccoon. She met Stone's gaze. "Yes," she whispered. "I think so."

He patted her shoulder. "Thank you. As soon as they let us go here, please try to contact the others. I'll be wanting to talk to them now more than ever."

"Do you think they're in danger, too?"

"I've no way to know that," he said, shaking his head. "It's possible that the spirit is confined to this area. It seems to be heavily associated with Ojai, so if we're lucky, it will stay here. If we're not—" He shrugged. "We'll just have to wait and see."

Casner was coming back over. He pointed at Lopez and then at Stone, then made a sharp 'get over here' gesture. His expression was carved from rock.

When the two of them drew close, he said without preamble, "How did you know?"

Lopez spoke first. "Dr. Stone wanted to talk to Mrs. Washburn. He'd met her before at the Third Eye downtown—you know, the witchy shop. He's still checking into local legends and stories, and he thought she might know some."

"What's that got to do with our vic?" he asked, pointing toward the house.

"They were friends. Mrs. Washburn was worried about her, with the murders and all. When she couldn't reach her on the phone, she asked us to come over here with her to check, in case anybody dangerous was around."

Casner's eyes narrowed and he focused on Stone. "Just won't leave it alone, will you, Stone?"

Stone shook his head, not flinching in the slightest before Casner's obvious attempt at intimidation. When you'd nearly been ripped to shreds by a five-hundred-pound bear driven by an ancient psychopathic vengeance spirit less than two days ago, a grumpy detective lieutenant no longer even rated on the scale. "I can't, Lieutenant. I won't impede your investigation, and I won't interfere with your crime scenes. I'll even help when I can—just as I'm doing now. But don't ask me to stop. This is too big and too potentially deadly for me to do that."

Casner glared at him. "I said it before and I'm saying it again: if you know something you're not telling me, you'd better start talking. Because even if I can't get you for murder, withholding information from the police is a crime, too. Don't think I won't haul your ass in again in a heartbeat if I think that's what you're doing. I've got too damn much going on here and too many people getting killed to put up with you and your mystical bullshit."

By now a small crowd had gathered, drawn by the police cruisers outside Karen Blanco's house. Stone dropped his voice so only Casner and Lopez could hear him. His eyes were every bit as cold as Casner's. "Lieutenant, I *tried* to tell you before. Remember, at the Ayala house? I tried to help you. I told you what I knew. You didn't believe me. Tell me—did your men find any evidence of any other people inside that house? Did you talk to the little girl, Olivia? What did she tell you?"

Casner looked like he was gearing up to blow his top at Stone, but he took a moment to get control of himself, let out a long, frustrated breath, and said instead, "Screw it. I just want the world to make fucking sense again."

"What did she tell you, Lieutenant?" Stone asked again, softly.

"She said that she walked in on her family hacking each other up with knives." he said in a monotone. "That's what that little eight-year-old girl told us. And we can't find one *fucking* bit of evidence that shows she was wrong."

Suddenly he looked very tired, almost visibly deflating. He glanced over at where more cruisers and a crime-scene van were arriving, and three police officers were herding the crowd back across the street and away from the area. When he spoke again, he addressed Lopez. "Stan, I'm in way over my damn head here. We all are. None of this is making a fucking bit of sense. We're doing everything right—and God knows that's getting hard to do, since we're strapped to the wall with all these murders to process, and nothing's coming up like it's supposed to."

Lopez nodded, sympathetic but steady. "Pete, I'm telling you. You know me. You know I'm not about woo and fairy dust. I know it sounds insane, and I know your cop's brain doesn't want to accept anything you can't prove. I get that. I didn't either. But I'm telling you—as a colleague and an old friend—let Dr. Stone keep on

　　　　　　　　　　　　　　　　R. L. KING

doing what he's doing. I've *seen* him work, man. You can't do what he does, just like he can't do what we do. If we work together, we might just get through this without too many more people ending up dead."

A shadow of the old fire flashed in Casner's eyes. "What do you want me to do, Stan, make him an official consultant? You want me to put a *professor of the occult* on the payroll?"

"If that's what it takes, then yeah," Lopez said, crossing his arms.

"Do you realize what the press would do with that?" he snapped. "They'd rip us to shreds. The whole department would be laughingstocks. We wouldn't be able to do our jobs!"

Stone nodded. "Lieutenant, I understand. I'm not asking for any sort of official relationship; in fact, that would be as detrimental to me as it would be to you. All I need is for you to stop getting in my way. Stop making me have to concern myself with looking over my shoulder to make sure you're not hovering there, waiting to pack me back off to jail because you think I'm somehow involved in these murders." His icy gaze bored into Casner's. "Because I'll tell you this, Lieutenant: if it *were* me who was committing them, then doesn't that tell you something? You have no evidence. I have alibis for most of them, assuming you don't think Sergeant Lopez is in league with me. So if I'm committing them, then you'll *never* be able to stop me. But I'm not. I don't want to kill anyone. All I'm interested in is the same thing you are: stopping this, preferably before anyone else is killed."

He took a couple centering breaths, realizing that his voice had risen in volume. When he spoke again, his tone was quiet, even, and implacable. "Just as Sergeant Lopez said: you can't do what I do. You won't pursue the same leads that I will, because you won't know they exist. I won't be in your way. Please, if you want this to end—stay out of mine."

Casner was silent for a long time. His gaze flicked from Stone to Lopez, to Jason and Edna, to the house where Karen Blanco had impaled herself upon her own sculpture. When he spoke at last, he sounded like the words were being pulled from him with great reluctance, like a surrender. "I don't know what else I can do. Fine, Dr. Stone. You do your thing. If anybody gives you trouble, tell them to call me. I'm not going to condone what you're doing—whatever the hell it even *is*—but I won't stop you. But do *not* get in the way of official investigations. Go pursue whatever cockamamie supernatural leads you think might help, as long as Stan thinks you're accomplishing something. I've got no fucking idea what's going on, but Stan and I go way back, and I trust him not to have lost his mind. Don't make me regret it."

"You won't regret it, Lieutenant," Stone said softly.

Casner glanced over at the house. "Right now, though, I've got another crime scene to examine. So unless you've got anything useful to contribute, I'd appreciate it if you'd get out of here and take your goddamn Scooby gang with you."

| CHAPTER FORTY-ONE

They drove back to Suzanne's house in silence. She hadn't wanted to go with them, guilt-ridden and reluctant to leave her old friend, but Stone had gently convinced her that she would honor Karen's memory more by doing what she could to help them stop her killer.

"What are you going to do next?" she asked as they all trooped into her large living room. Her voice sounded bleak, heartbroken.

"We need to contact the others," Stone said. He'd introduced Jason to her, and she already knew Edna in passing from seeing her around town.

"Debbie and Carly," Suzanne said. "You said you'd already called Michiko?"

"Yes, but I'll want to call her again as well," Stone said. "After—what's happened, I want to make sure she's all right. If she is, then that will add to my theory that the spirit is operating in Ojai." He paused. "Which one did you say was the latecomer to the group? The one who wanted to do the curse?"

"Carly," Suzanne said. "Carly Rosales."

"And she's where, now?"

"Santa Maria, I think," she said. "That's up a little south of San Luis Obispo."

Stone nodded. "All right, then. What I'd like to do is call Debbie and Michiko, but not tell Debbie anything about this yet. Let's just do a welfare check on them—make sure they haven't experienced anything odd in the last day or two. But I want to focus on Carly first."

"Why? Because of the curse?"

"Partly. But mostly because it seems that things started to happen after she joined you. If you were doing these rituals since junior high school, but the spirit didn't appear until after she joined, that suggests that she might have been the catalyst."

"That, and the fact that the kid she wanted to put the curse on almost ended up as one of the victims," Lopez added. "Don't forget that."

"Good point," Stone said. "I should be taking notes." He turned back to Suzanne. "Tell me about Carly if you could, please." He kept his voice gentle; as focused as he was on moving his investigation along as quickly as possible to avoid further bloodshed, he reminded himself that this woman had just lost one of her lifelong friends in a particularly horrifying way. He could afford to do what he could to make his questions as easy as possible on her.

She dabbed at her mascara-streaked eyes with a tissue and made a little shrug. "She was always—different from the rest of us. Debbie and Michiko and Karen and I—we all came from nice homes. My parents were wealthy, and so were Michiko's, at least before her father died, but even after that they did all right. Debbie and Karen were typical middle-class suburban girls. Carly, though—I think I told you she was more of a 'wrong side of the tracks' type."

"How so?" Stone asked.

She shrugged again. "She came from a poorer part of town— lived in an apartment with her single mom. It seemed like she got in trouble a lot: you know, talking back to teachers, running with a crowd that was always in detention, that kind of thing. But she wasn't mean or anything. Everybody liked her fine. I think we kind of envied her a little, since she got away with things we'd never be brave enough to try."

Stone leaned forward. "And she asked if she could join your group?"

Suzanne nodded. "She—overheard us one day when we were planning our next ritual at lunchtime in the cafeteria. After school, she came up to me and asked about it. I remember thinking she was being sarcastic, making fun of us. I was kind of mortified that she'd heard. But she seemed sincere—she said she was interested in the supernatural and ghosts and witches, and told me some things to prove it. So I talked to the others, and we all agreed to invite her to the meeting."

"And how did that go?"

"Fine. She fit in with us like she'd always been there. I think we all sort of realized that the reason she was so wild is that she didn't really know what she wanted to do with herself. We figured if we were nice to her, got to be friends with her, she'd calm down."

"Did that happen?"

"Mostly. She still went out with the wrong kinds of boys, and stayed out too late. But her grades got better and she got fewer detentions. She even went to college for a while, though I don't think that worked out for her."

"You didn't talk about it when she was here recently?"

"No, we thought it was none of our business. We wanted to keep everything positive and upbeat. She did seem—distracted, though. Kind of out of sorts. We tried to be especially kind to her. But I think we were all a little glad to say goodbye. You know what they say: 'you can't go home again.' I think we'd decided that we wouldn't try getting the Sisterhood together again at the next reunion. Some things just need to come to an end, you know?"

Stone nodded. "I understand. Could you call them for us now, Mrs. Washburn? Remember—don't say anything to Debbie, and as little as possible to Michiko. And ask Carly if she'd be willing to talk to me."

"All right," she said, wiping her eyes again. She got up and went off toward the kitchen. "I'll be back in a few minutes."

After she was gone, Jason gestured toward where she'd headed. "She gonna be okay?"

Stone nodded. "I put a shield on her mind earlier." He settled back on the comfortable, overstuffed couch, closed his eyes, and let his breath out, allowing himself to rest for at least a short while. The constant adrenaline rollercoaster, coupled with his recent injuries, loss of blood, and near-nonstop mental stress, were all doing a number on his body. Usually, in constant motion, he wouldn't allow himself to notice it; however, any time he settled down to rest it all came crashing back, threatening to submerge him into a sleep that would last for days. He couldn't afford that. Not yet.

"So, you think this Carly is 'she of my masters' blood'?" Lopez asked.

Stone nodded without opening his eyes. "It makes sense. And I'd bet a lot of money she's got magical talent, even if she doesn't realize it."

"So if we can talk to her, maybe you can figure out how to set up a ritual to send Faces back?" Jason asked.

Edna snorted. "You've got them all trained, don't you, Stone?"

Stone cracked his eyes open. "Hmm?"

"You've got them all talking about 'power' and using it to force things. How many times do I have to tell you: that isn't going to get you anywhere this time."

"I'm not sure you're right about that, Edna," he murmured, trying to kick his brain back into gear again. It was getting harder to do. "Let's talk to this Carly, and see if my theory is correct. If it is, then we'll go from there."

"Dr. Stone?"

Suzanne's voice held an odd note. Stone sat up quickly to see her standing in the doorway to the kitchen. "What is it, Mrs. Washburn?"

"I think we have a problem."

He froze. "It's got Carly?"

"No, no," she said hastily, holding up her hands. "Not that—thing. But it is about Carly." He paused, taking a deep breath. "She won't talk to me. She won't talk to you. She says she wants nothing to do with any of us anymore." Another pause. "I think she was very drunk. Or worse."

CHAPTER FORTY-TWO

"Al?"

"Hmm?" Stone, slumped into the corner of the big black BMW's soft leather passenger seat, didn't stir. His reply was more a rumble than a word.

"You awake?"

"Must I be?"

They were cruising up Highway 101, Jason at the wheel because Stone hadn't trusted his concentration enough to make the two-hour drive, and he'd refused to ride in Jason's elderly Ford when more upscale alternatives were available. Jason hadn't objected in the slightest. Currently, they were on the open stretch between Santa Barbara and Santa Maria, and Stone had been asleep for most of the way so far.

"Just got a couple things I want to say. We haven't had much chance to talk since I—got back."

Stone shook his head to clear it, dragging himself to a more upright position in his seat. "I doubt I'm fit company right now, but if you don't mind monosyllabic replies, be my guest. Where are we, by the way?"

"About a half-hour north of Santa Barbara."

He nodded. That meant Santa Maria, their destination, was still another half-hour away. Glancing at the clock on the dash he saw that it was a little before eight. A bit late to be paying social calls, but this wasn't exactly your standard Emily Post sort of situation. He ran a hand through his hair, yawned, and made a "go on" motion at Jason. "Talk, then. If I drop back off, punch me or something."

Jason didn't take his eyes off the road. "I've been thinking about the fight up at the Hot Springs."

"What about it?"

"You nearly died up there, Al. And it was my fault."

Stone frowned. "Why was it your fault? You didn't hire that bear, did you?"

"You needed power, and I didn't have it to give you. I still don't know why it didn't work."

"I don't know either. But don't worry about it. I shouldn't be depending on your power anyway."

Jason continued to steadfastly avoid looking at Stone. He didn't reply.

"Jason?"

"Eh, never mind."

"There's something else going on here, isn't there?"

"What makes you think that?" Jason's tone was wary.

"Because I know you. Because I'm good at reading people. Because you're being evasive."

"You're half asleep. Sorry I woke you up. Just get some rest and I'll tell you when we get there."

Stone scrubbed his hand over his face and tried to clear some more cobwebs from his brain. He sensed this wasn't a discussion that could be improved by cobwebs. "Come on, Jason: out with it."

There was a very long pause. The scenery, an endless progression of scrubby brush punctuated periodically by trees, flashed by. "I had a lot of time to think while that thing had me," he said at last. His voice was inflectionless.

"About what?"

He shrugged. "About my power. About how that thing was just—*taking* it. I thought I could control it. I thought nobody could use it without my permission. That was what you said."

"It's what I thought," Stone said. "Even the Evil couldn't do it."

Jason's face twisted, and his voice came out harsh. "I couldn't stop it. I tried, but I couldn't do it. I felt like some kind of gas pump. Some kind of fucking *cow*."

"Jason—"

He shook his head. "Don't, Al. You can't fix it. I know that. This is all about me and my head."

Carefully, Stone said, "You think that's why you couldn't—"

"I don't *know*," he said. He did turn for a moment to look at Stone before returning his attention to the road, and his expression was hard. He sighed loudly. "I don't know what to think, Al. I don't even know what I bring to this party anymore. Not really."

Stone's eyes narrowed. "Why would—"

"I mean, look at me," he said, still in the same harsh tone. "You two can do *magic*. Even after all this time I still have a hard time getting my mind around that. My friend and my sister can shape the fucking *world* with their *brains*. And what can I do? I can stand in the back and give you the juice to help you do it better. Like you two are the varsity team, and I'm the fucking *waterboy*."

Stone sat up a little more, all vestiges of his mental cobwebs gone now. He stared at Jason, momentarily struck speechless by his friend's sudden ferocity. Clearly this wasn't something new—from the sound of Jason's words, it had been building up for a long time. Had he missed it? All those times when he'd relied on his friend for supplemental power, was this how Jason perceived it? "Is that what you think?"

"How can I *not* think it?" His hands gripped the steering wheel so hard his knuckles whitened. "Even Stan is a real cop, at least. I couldn't even make it through the academy without getting my ass expelled. And look at me now. I work at a restaurant. I dick around with my car. I lift weights. Meanwhile, my sister's learning more magic, and my friend, when he's not teaching college and portaling back and forth between here and England, is shooting lightning bolts out of his hands." He sighed loudly. "Ah, screw it. Don't worry about it, Al. Really. This is just something I gotta work through."

"Jason, if you don't want me to—"

"I said don't worry about it," he said in an *I'm done talking about it* tone.

Stone was silent, leaning back and looking out the window without seeing anything. He wanted to say more, because Jason had the wrong idea about how he, Stone, perceived him. Yes, all right, he had to admit that he might have been guilty of taking Jason's power for granted on occasion, especially when he needed an extra jolt to do a particularly difficult or power-intensive spell. Still, he didn't do that often, and usually it was only in life-or-death situations. He had begun to wonder if Jason's inability to provide the power that had always been there before was more psychological than physical, and his friend's current outburst all but confirmed it. If he had felt he was being used before, even subconsciously, then being kidnapped by an extradimensional being and held in near-suspended animation while being mined for the very thing he believed he had to consent to give could easily have pushed him over the edge and given him some sort of mental block about allowing *anyone*—even his closest friends—to make use of his ability.

He wished he'd spent a little more time studying psychology. He had no idea if he even *should* try to help Jason work through this—would any attempt at doing so just be seen as another effort to use him? For now, he decided to let it go. Maybe Jason would work through it on his own. If he brought it up again, Stone would take that as an indication that he might want some help dealing with it. Until then, however, he would simply have to rely on his own power. It wasn't as if that weren't usually enough anyway.

"You think Stan and Edna will be okay?" Jason asked into the silence. His tone was back to normal—mostly—but he still looked straight ahead.

"I think so," he said, taking the cue. They had decided it wouldn't make sense for all four of them to go to Santa Maria, so

Edna and Lopez had elected to remain in Ojai at Lopez's house. Stone had lent Edna the tome Suzanne had given him, asking her to take a look at it and see if she could identify anything useful in its pages. Lopez didn't say anything about it, but Stone could tell he was relieved to have a night off. Not everyone was used to the sort of pace he and Jason tended to keep while trying to deal with a problem.

Suzanne, after Stone had assured her that her "mantra" would keep the spirit out of her mind, had remained in her home, promising not to allow anyone except the four of them inside and to watch carefully for signs of possession in anyone around her.

"I just had a bad thought," Jason said suddenly after they had driven another ten miles or so.

"I suppose it can join the party," Stone said. "What is it?"

"This thing, and the little ones it summons, possess people to kill them. We figure it sometimes kills people just to get the power to spawn more little ones, so it's not limiting itself to killing descendants of the Spanish. Does that mean it can possess anybody?"

Stone shrugged. "I don't know. So far, everyone we know of that they've possessed has been to further their ends: either to generate more minions, to get something done like when they grabbed you at the motel, or to kill descendants. We're all but certain that they can't pass as human like the Evil could, so by necessity they're limited in what they can do."

"So you think that's why it hasn't possessed, say, the cops? Casner?"

"It tried it on Stan once—but that was up near the shrine, and he was able to throw it off."

"When were you gonna tell me about that?"

"I forgot about it—a lot's been going on, and there's been no sign of a repeat performance. My theory is that it's hard to possess police and other people with more disciplined minds, but I don't know." He scrubbed at his face. "What I *do* know is if we start going down that road, we'll paralyze ourselves until we can't act. For whatever reason it seems fairly focused even when it isn't directly killing victims. I hate to bring this up, but perhaps that's what it was using your stolen power for: to allow it to work outside its purview more than it normally would be able to. I don't know."

Jason nodded. "Just a thought." He paused. "What makes you think this Carly will talk to us after we come all the way up here? The way Suzanne sounded, she's pretty much done with the whole bit."

"We'll just have to persuade her," Stone said. "If I'm right, and she is the linchpin in this whole situation, I don't plan to let her get away with keeping her head in the sand because she's unhappy about her life."

"You can't exactly kidnap her and toss her in the trunk," Jason said. When Stone didn't answer, he glanced over. "You *can't*, right?"

"Of course not. But I can be very persuasive when I want to be. If that's necessary, then that's what I'll have to do."

They pulled into Santa Maria around 8:30. The sun was down now, the night warm with a sliver of a moon. Stone consulted the map, and soon the BMW was rolling down a narrow street populated mostly by apartment buildings along with a few small, older homes.

"This doesn't look like a great part of town," Jason said dubiously. "You sure you got the address right?"

"Quite sure. It should be right up ahead."

Carly Rosales's address was an upstairs unit in an older, two-story apartment building, set far back from the street behind two other similar structures. Jason opted to park down the street a bit; after they got out of the car, Stone put a disregarding spell on it and pulled on his overcoat, then the two of them hiked up the narrow driveway toward the rear of the complex.

The cars parked along one side were all older but well-maintained, the buildings in decent repair despite their age. The entire area had the look of a working-class neighborhood trying very hard not to slip into something more disreputable and so far mostly succeeding, though how long that would continue was up for debate. It was a far cry from the luxurious Arbolada digs of Suzanne Washburn, or even the comfortable two-story home of Karen Blanco. Stone and Jason exchanged glances, but neither spoke.

Each building in the small complex had four apartments: two on the first floor and two on the second. Carly's building was the farthest back, next to a chain-link fence bordering what looked like a large vacant lot. It was hard to tell for sure, because the street lights here were only sporadically functional, and the lot itself had no illumination. As Stone and Jason walked from the front of the complex to the back, the air was full of the noise of dueling stereos coming through open windows; somewhere nearby a couple was having a loud argument in one upstairs apartment, and a baby wailed in another.

There were no lights on in Carly's upstairs apartment. Even her porch light was off. Stone stood back while Jason knocked; they waited several minutes but no one answered. "I don't think she's home," Jason said. "Unless she's—"

Stone shifted to magical senses. The general aura of the area was muddy, disturbed, and uneasy, but it was nothing like he'd noticed outside Karen Blanco's place. As far as he could tell, no one had died violently here; it was simply that the complex's prevailing emotions were not positive ones. There were too many other conflicting signals for him to get anything else definitive. He shook his head.

"What do we do?" Jason asked. "You want to wait until she comes back?"

Stone supposed he should have expected this: though it would have been convenient to have Carly sitting at home waiting for them to arrive, things didn't generally work out that way. She could be anywhere—visiting a friend, out at a bar, on a date and not even planning to *come* home tonight. "Let's wait a short while," he said. "Perhaps she—"

"Shh!" Jason whispered, holding up a finger.

Stone raised a questioning eyebrow.

"I thought I heard something," he said, still in a whisper.

They both listened, but aside from the complex's ambient music and domestic discord, nothing else rose to catch their attention. After several minutes had passed, Stone pushed himself off the building where he'd been leaning. "Come on," he said. "We'll try back later." He headed back toward the stairs.

A window behind them shattered outward in a loud crash and a shower of tinkling glass shards.

| CHAPTER FORTY-THREE

tone and Jason whirled. In the scant illumination from the neighbor's porch light, they immediately spotted the area outside the far window at the end of Carly's apartment covered in sparkling bits of glass. Pale curtains wafted outward in the faint breeze.

They moved as one, rushing over to see what had happened. Stone expected to see some large item, or someone laid out in the space where the window was, after being tossed forcibly out or perhaps drunkenly staggering near the window and tripping to fall into it. But there was no sign of a person or object, just the glass.

As they drew closer, though, they could hear voices. "What the fuck—?" came a man's deep tones, followed by what sounded like a woman moaning in pain.

Jason poked his head in through the opening. "Carly? You okay?" he yelled.

Another moan, followed by a slap, and a harsh "Shut up, bitch!" from the man.

"In!" Stone ordered, moving behind Jason.

"Yeah." He was already clambering carefully over the blasted-out frame into the room.

Past him, Stone saw a figure rise in the darkened room, moving swiftly toward Jason as he was vulnerable. He pointed his hand at the figure, focused his will, and the man yelped as he was flung forcibly into the back wall.

Jason got the rest of the way in as the guy was recovering, and Stone hurried to join him. He spotted a lamp on the nightstand and flipped it on.

The tableau that presented itself in the newly lit room was obvious in its purpose. They were standing in a small bedroom, with a tousled double bed, single nightstand, and simple Ikea-style dresser. A woman lay sideways across the bed, sobbing and half aware as she struggled to pull her jeans back up. On the other side of the room, rising from where Stone had tossed him none too gently, a man was scrambling back to his feet. He was tall, wide, and bald, with colorful tattoos on both forearms. His jeans, too, were pulled down, and that was hindering his efforts to get up.

"Stay down, dirtbag," Jason growled.

"Who the fuck are you?" the man demanded, glaring first at Jason, then at Stone. "What the fuck happened?" His voice was slurred; the tang of alcohol in the room was strong.

"I'd listen to him if I were you," Stone said with a raised eyebrow. "I suspect if you try to get up, he'll have something to say about it. And if he doesn't, I will."

The man clearly didn't consider Stone's words to be a threat. He continued trying to push himself up the wall with one arm while dragging his pants up with the other hand. "What the *fuck?*" he roared. "Get the fuck outta here, faggot!"

"Suppose we ask the lady who she'd like to stay," Stone said, as Jason moved in and loomed over the drunken would-be rapist. Stone himself backed up toward the bed. "Ms. Rosales, are you all right?"

"Yeah," she sobbed. She, too, sounded very drunk. "He—" She gestured vaguely toward the man. "We were drinking, and—"

"Hey, she *asked* for it, " the man yelled. He'd succeeded in getting his pants up, but couldn't quite manage "standing upright" yet. "Fuckin' bitch led me on!"

"Al, lemme hit him. Just one," Jason growled. "I'll make it count."

"Call the police, Jason. Much as I share your desire to teach this man a bit about modern-day dating etiquette, we don't have time for you to get thrown in jail for assault right now."

For a moment Jason looked like he would argue, then he sighed and headed to the phone on the nightstand. Like Stone, he didn't take his eyes off the man.

Carly had gotten her jeans pulled back up, and she sat up, trying to get herself under control. She swayed for a moment and then leaped up, bolting for the bathroom. In a moment, they could all hear her being loudly sick.

The bald man switched his glare back and forth between Stone and Jason, then at the smashed window. Clearly he was trying to decide if it would be a good idea to make a run for it. Jason, still on the phone, casually walked over until he was standing in front of the opening.

"Just settle down," Stone advised the man. "You're not going anywhere until the police arrive."

Drunken rage suffused his face. "Shut up, you skinny fag!" he yelled, and surged forward in a head-down charge toward Stone. Stone flung him back into the wall with a casual gesture before Jason, who'd just hung up the phone, could get there. He landed on his ass against the same wall as before. This time he stayed down, glaring ineffectual fury at his captors.

"Damn it, Al," Jason said in mock frustration. "Stop hogging the dirtbag. I want a shot at him."

The man was far too drunk to have any chance of figuring out what had just happened to him. He remained where he was, muttering obscenities under his breath.

Carly Rosales came back out of the bathroom. She looked a mess: her hair hung in strings over her face, her shirt was in disarray, and she had the slack, unhappy expression of someone who was far too drunk and didn't want to be anymore. "Who are you guys?" she slurred. "Thanks for helping me, but—"

"We'll talk after this little matter is taken care of," Stone said, nodding toward the man. "We've come from Ojai. We'd like to talk with you, if you wouldn't mind. Jason, perhaps you could get her a cup of coffee—"

"Yeah," Carly agreed, nodding. "Coffee's good." She started to wander back out of the bedroom and Jason followed her. Stone remained with the bald man. Once, the guy eyed him speculatively, and his thought processes were obvious: *the big guy's gone. All that's left is the skinny guy. I can get past him. Or—can I?* Stone raised an eyebrow at him and shrugged as if to say *try it,* but apparently two of his alcoholically challenged brain cells managed to find each other and initiate a connection, because he elected to stay put.

The police arrived in ten minutes. Jason and Carly ushered them into the bedroom, and the next fifteen minutes were taken up by exchanges of identification, the snapping of photographs inside the bedroom and outside along the walk, and the collection of statements from everyone concerned.

"What were you guys doing here?" one of the cops asked Stone and Jason after the bald man was cuffed and safely locked in the back of the squad car.

"We're friends of Ms. Rosales's," Stone said smoothly, with a quick glance at Carly. "We were in the area and coming by to visit, when we heard something from inside the apartment that made us suspicious."

"So you broke the glass?" The other cop looked dubiously at the glass on the outside walk.

"No, obviously that was from the inside," Stone said with a raised eyebrow. "I'm not sure how it happened, but it was right after we heard the noise from inside."

"So you don't know what broke it?" The first cop was looking around outside, as if expecting to find something that had been tossed through the window. He directed the question at Carly.

She shook her head. "I dunno," she said. "Maybe Bill ran into it and broke it. He was pretty drunk."

The cop's expression as he looked her over suggested that he wasn't feeling terribly sympathetic toward either of the two participants in this crime, but he dutifully recorded her statement in his notebook. "I assume you want to press charges."

"Damn right I do!" Her voice sounded less slurred now. "Bastard tried to rape me!"

"Do you need an ambulance?" he asked.

She shook her head. "Nah, I'm okay now. Jus' drunk. These guys showed up before Bill could do anything much. He did slap me, though," she added, touching an angry red patch on her face. "That's assault, yeah?"

"Yes, ma'am," the cop said. "Do you want to come down to the station now? We've got your statement, so you can come in tonight or tomorrow if you want, to file formal charges."

She glanced at Stone and Jason. "I'll come in tomorrow," she said. "I want to talk to my friends here first, since they're only in town for tonight."

"Yes, ma'am," the cop said again. He gathered up his gear and departed.

Carly faced Stone and Jason across the living room. "Okay," she said. She still sounded drunk, clutching her cup of coffee like a lifeline. "You helped me out of a bad scene, so I owe you for that. Now what do you want?"

Stone noticed her hands were shaking, and she looked very pale. The red spot on her cheek where Bill had slapped her stood out like a flag. "Sit down, Ms. Rosales, please," he said. "That must have been quite traumatic for you. We can wait."

She shrugged. "Call me Carly. And yeah, it sucked. Not the first time I dodged a bullet, though. Man, what am I gonna do about my window?" She sank down into the nearest chair with a loud sigh. "What do you want?" she asked again. "You said you were from Ojai." Something dawned on her. "Did that bitch Suzanne send you?"

Stone shook his head. "No, she didn't send us. We've been talking with her, though."

Her eyes narrowed and she frowned. "Look," she said. "I'm done with that whole scene. I tried going back, but you know what? It just ain't for me. I shoulda realized it a long time ago."

"This isn't about your friends, Carly. Not exactly."

"They're not my friends," she said with some heat. "Oh, sure, they were all nice to me and everything, but it's not like I ever fit in with their little suburban American-dream lives. I could just tell they were all laughing at me when I wasn't around."

Stone took a deep breath. "Carly, we don't have a lot of time, so I'll get right to it. We need your help."

Her gaze came up. Her eyes were brown, wide and bloodshot. "My help? Why?" Again she frowned. "Who are you, anyway?" She eyed Stone, then Jason. "'Cause I know I'd remember guys who looked like you two." She nodded toward Jason first: "You maybe could be from Ojai, but you—" she nodded toward Stone "—no fucking way."

"We're not *from* Ojai," Stone said. "Well, I'm not, anyway. Jason here is originally from the area. But we're visiting. And we've run into a bit of a problem that it appears only you can help with."

"I told you, I don't want *anything* do to with those bitches back in Ojai," she said, more forcefully this time. "If that's all you're here about—thanks a lot for helping me out. I really do appreciate it. But you might as well go now. We're done."

Stone shook his head, his expression grim. "I'm sorry, Carly, but that's not an option." Very slowly, as he watched her grow more frustrated, he was formulating a hunch. "Tell me," he said, seemingly at random, "how *did* the window get broken in your bedroom?"

She blinked. "W-what?"

Jason looked at him sideways, questioning.

"A simple question: How did it get broken? You said Bill didn't blunder into it. The police found nothing tossed through, and in any case, the damage is far too extensive for that unless you'd used something large enough that it would be impossible to miss. Clearly the break was from the inside. So how did it happen?"

Carly hesitated, her confused gaze going to the hall leading toward the bedroom. "I—I guess I don't know."

Stone nodded as if that was the answer he was expecting. "Carly," he said, in a very soft, gentle voice, "Have things ever— happened around you? Odd things? Especially when you were angry, or agitated in some way?"

She stared at him. "What—are you talking about?" But there was something in her voice, a little quiver, that told him that she knew exactly what he was talking about.

Jason's eyes widened as he caught on. "Al—"

"A moment, Jason," he murmured. "Actually, Carly, could we use your phone?"

"Uh...sure." She seemed completely flummoxed by his careening train of thought.

"Jason, could you please call Stan and make sure all is well?"

Jason nodded and headed to the kitchen.

Stone directed his attention back to Carly. "I think you do know what I'm talking about," he said in the same soft, even voice. "About things happening, I mean."

She swallowed. "What—kinds of things?"

"Hard to say," he said, shrugging. "Things falling off shelves, perhaps. Unexplained mechanical failures. Or—windows breaking," he added, leaning forward to pin her with his gaze.

Carly gaped at him. "How...how did you know that?" she whispered. "How *could* you know it? I've never—"

"—told anyone?" he finished. "No, of course not. Because they'd think you'd gone mad, or perhaps had too much to drink. You can't control it, can you? It just happens sometimes, when you're emotional."

"Sometimes..." she agreed, looking down into her coffee. Then her eyes came up to meet his. "How did you know, though?"

Stone paused, formulating the best way to answer without going into a long discussion that they didn't have time for. He was about to say something when Jason came back into the room. "Uh, Al?"

Stone looked up, stiffening when he caught the grim look on Jason's face. "What's wrong?"

"I think we need to get our asses back down there. Stan's being called back to duty. They've had five new murders *tonight.* And he doesn't think it's over. Edna thinks something big's going down."

| CHAPTER FORTY-FOUR

"**A**l?"

Stone froze. "Bloody hell," he murmured. Leaping to his feet, he stood over Carly, who was staring at him and Jason in shock. "Listen, Carly: I'd like very much to be able to ease you into this, but we don't have that luxury. Here's the bottom line: There's something in Ojai that's killing people. It's here because of the ritual you and the rest of the Sisterhood performed a couple of weeks ago. And the only person who has a chance of sending it back is you."

As might have been expected, Carly's reaction to his words was to gape at him as if he had just announced that the Space Alien Armada had arrived on earth with the ghost of Elvis Presley at its helm.

Stone took a deep breath and let it out slowly, visibly forcing himself to calm. "It's true. Counting the five who died tonight—so far—I believe we're up to thirteen now. Including Karen Blanco, one of the Sisterhood. And if what our friend back in Ojai says is true, that's only the beginning. You have to come with us. We have to stop this."

"Karen's—dead?" She was still gaping. "And you want me to come...with you? Look, I don't know what you're talking about, but I don't have anything to do with any killings! I've been up here since I left the reunion. I heard there were some murders in Ojai, but—"

"It's not you, Carly. It's what you helped to summon." Another deep breath. Stone hated doing this to her, especially after what she'd already been through tonight, but in the back of his mind he could feel the minutes ticking away and almost hear Many Faces laughing at them as it touched off its massacre—the massacre it had waited until the mage who'd gotten its number had left town to orchestrate. "You've got magical talent. That's what's causing things to happen when you get emotional. That's what's broken your window: the manifestation of your magic that you can't control yet coming out in any way it can." He spread his hands. "I know it all sounds preposterous, but it's true. The fact that you've got this magical talent was what took a ceremony staged by a group of school friends for fun and allowed it to summon a being from another plane. And it happened before, Carly. Do you remember when you were a teenager, and you joined the Sisterhood? You wanted to do a curse, because you were angry at a boy who'd dumped you? Do you remember what happened to that boy?" His voice picked up speed again, despite his efforts to stay calm.

Her eyes were steadily growing more huge as he spoke. "Oh, my God..." she whispered. "Dean..."

"Dean?" Jason asked. Like Stone, he nearly thrummed with pent-up energy, stalking back and forth across the floor.

"He almost got killed..." Her voice sounded dead. "Jerry Bekin tried to stab him...But he said he didn't know what he was doing..."

"That's because he was possessed by the thing that was summoned in your ceremony," Stone said. "Carly, you've got to believe me. Come with us back to Ojai. You're the only one who can stop this. If you won't come with us, countless more people could die tonight."

Her eyes got wild. "Why me?" she demanded, high and brittle and shrieky. "How the hell can I stop it? I was only one part of that ceremony! Even if you're telling the truth, Suzanne was in charge of it. Get her to help you!"

"She's already helping," Stone said. "She's already given us the book where she got the latest ritual. But she can't stop it. Only you can do that, Carly. Only you are the descendant of the people who originally summoned it, hundreds of years ago. You're the only one who has a chance."

Carly looked like she couldn't decide whether to scream or cry or vomit. Her face was dead pale, her eyes wide and terrified. Across the room, two books and a small figurine teetered and crashed to the carpeting with small *thumps*. She jumped. "Oh, my God! Was that me?"

Stone nodded. "I can help you," he said, leaning forward. "I can help you deal with your powers, Carly. I promise, I will. But you have to help us first. Please. I beg you—come with us. If you've ever wanted to make a difference in your life, now is the time to do it."

Without trying to, he'd hit on the right words. He could see it in the change to her face. She still looked terrified, but something in her eyes hardened and her jaw tightened. "Okay," she said. "Okay. I'll go. But we have to figure out something to do with my window first. If I leave it open like that I'll come home and all my stuff will be gone."

"I'll do that," Jason said, and hurried out in search of something to board up the window with.

Carly started to rise; Stone took her hand and helped her up. "Thank you," he said softly.

"I'm not doing it for you," she said. "I'm still not sure I believe you. Let me get some stuff together." She started down the hall, but turned back. "Uh—what's your name, anyway?"

"Alastair Stone. My friend is Jason Thayer."

She nodded. "So—you can really help me with my—problem?"

"I can," he said. "Absolutely."

"Guys lie to me all the time. You know that, right? So maybe I don't believe them very often anymore."

Stone held up a hand, making light flicker and dance around it. "I can help you, Carly, and I will. I promise."

She swallowed hard, her eyes fixed on the glimmering light, and backed up toward the hall. "I'll—get my stuff."

❖

Fifteen minutes later, they were on the road and flying back toward Ojai under Stone's disregarding spell. Jason, who had found some plywood around the back of the neighboring building and nailed it over Carly's window, was driving. Despite the gravity of the situation he couldn't help looking a bit like a kid in a candy shop as he piloted the powerful car at over a hundred miles per hour down the nearly deserted freeway.

Carly sat in the back seat, clutching the small bag she'd packed. She still looked shell-shocked by everything that had happened, and had said nothing as Stone had guided her to the car and got her settled.

She didn't speak again until they'd been on the freeway for several miles. "So—" she started, her voice still shaking. "We've got time now, right? You can explain a little better about what's going on?"

Stone nodded, still focused on the road ahead to watch for anything that might get in their way. Trying to make it as clear and simple as possible, he told her about the renegade group of Chumash exiles who'd summoned He of Many Faces to get vengeance on the Spanish interlopers, and how it had reappeared as a result of the Sisterhood's ceremonies years ago and again recently.

"Where's it been?" she asked. "If this is real, why wasn't it killing people all along?"

"No one knows where it was for the intervening years. And the first time it was summoned back by the Sisterhood, they didn't have a proper invocation," Stone told her. "Essentially, you didn't summon it properly, which was a good thing. It was still able to react to your bloodline, though. That's why you got it at all."

"Man..." she breathed, looking down into her lap. "I've always been kind of a screw-up, but now you're saying this is my fault, too..." Her voice was bleak, beaten.

Stone got the impression that she'd experienced a lot of similar feelings throughout her life. "Carly," he said softly. "It *isn't* your fault. It tells me much more about you that you're willing to take the word of two strangers and try to set this right than it does that an accident of birth made it possible to bring it here in the first place. There's no possible way you could have known."

She nodded, but her expression suggested she didn't believe it. "So—how are we gonna get rid of it? I still don't get how I'm gonna be able to help. Even if what you said about—magic—is right, I don't know anything about it. I'm still pretty sure you're just trying to put something over on me."

Stone did turn around then, his eyes grave. "Carly. Do I look like I'm trying to deceive you? Can you possibly believe that we're not sincere about this? I'm a decent actor, but I'm not *that* good."

She took a breath. "I think something's going on in Ojai," she said. "That part I believe. But magic—" She shook her head. "I just don't know."

"Well," he said, turning back to face front. "It doesn't matter anyway, fortunately. You don't have to do very much, and nothing magic-related. All you need to do is be present, and focus as hard as you can on sending the spirit back where it came from. Just keep thinking 'go home' to it. I and a colleague will do the rest."

"That's—all? That's *crazy,*" she protested. "You know that, right? This whole thing just sounds insane."

"That's a good word for it," Jason agreed without taking his eyes off the road. "The whole thing's fucking insane. But every bit of it's true. We've seen it."

Carly subsided into silence then, and after a couple of minutes Jason turned on the car's radio. "See if you can get the news," he said to Stone. "If something this big is going down in Ojai, they might be talking about it."

Stone fiddled with the tuner until he got a local news channel. They listened for a few moments as the reporter finished a national story; then the dispassionate voice of the newsman announced: "Switching to local news: additional police officers from the Ventura County Sheriff's Department are being deployed to Ojai following a series of grisly murders occurring within the last two hours in the small town. These bring the total over the last two weeks to thirteen. Ojai police chief Marilyn Darnell has asked the public to avoid the town at this time—unless you're a resident or you have urgent business there, you're urged to stay away. Police have their hands full tonight with the murders, which have struck in apparently unrelated locations, including a local concert being held at Libbey Park. More news updates as we receive them. Now, to weather—"

Stone snapped the radio off and stared at it. "It waited until we were away," he said in a monotone.

"What?" Jason asked.

"It waited. It knows Edna can't deal with it on her own, which means that with me out of town, there's nobody there who can stop it. It knows we went after Carly. It waited until we left to do this."

"We couldn't stay there forever, Al," Jason said. "You know that. If it was gonna happen, it was gonna happen eventually. We'll just have to get there as fast as we can and do what we can to deal with it." He nudged the car a bit faster. "Just watch the road and get ready to take off the spell if you see any cars."

Normally, it would have taken them almost two hours to get from Santa Maria to Ojai. Between the dearth of traffic on the highway, Jason's reflexes, Stone's spell, and the BMW's comfort at one-hundred-mile-per-hour plus cruising speeds, they managed to cut almost an hour off that time. They only had to slow down when they got off 101 in Ventura, and both Stone and Jason were visibly impatient as they continued at what seemed like a relative standstill toward Oak View and Lopez's house. Carly, exhausted by her evening's ordeal, an incipient hangover, and all the information she'd had to process in a short time, had dozed off around Santa Barbara, and was now snoring softly in the back seat.

The lights were off in Lopez's house as they pulled up in the driveway. "He must have had to report in already," Jason said, getting out.

"Let's see if Edna's here," Stone said. He hurried up to the front door and knocked. "Edna? Are you in there?"

He began growing concerned when no one answered, but after almost a full minute a light switched on and the door opened a crack. "That you?" came a familiar voice. "About time!"

"We got here as fast as we could," Stone protested. "I assume Stan has already gone?"

"Yeah, about an hour ago. They're calling in all the police they can get their hands on." She pushed the door open further; she was wearing her usual outfit of jeans and Native-print shirt, with a thin leather jacket over it. "Did you bring Carly?"

"She's in the car," Jason said, coming up behind Stone. "We'd better get going."

"Did you find anything in the book?" Stone asked. "Please tell me you did."

"I did," she said. "Tell you on the way. Let's take Stan's truck, though. He told me to. I've got the keys."

"Why?" Jason asked.

"In case we need to go anywhere that overpriced land-yacht of yours can't manage," she snapped. "Plus, Stan seems to think yours might be recognized—some people still think you were connected with the murders, and that's not good tonight. Come on, we're wasting time." She closed and locked the door behind her.

Stone noticed she was carrying a bag over her shoulder. "Is the book in there?"

She nodded. "Be careful driving," she told Jason. "It's a madhouse out there. I've been listening to Stan's police radio. There've been two more murders since you talked to him, including another one at the concert downtown. The police are trying to control the situation, but people are scared and they're having a hell of a time. They're worried about a riot."

Stone quickly gathered his magical gear, which he'd stowed in the BMW's trunk, then they pulled it into Stan's garage. Jason woke up Carly and all of them got in the truck.

Jason, who was driving, switched on the police radio as he got moving back toward Ojai. "Holy crap, Al," he said under his breath. "This was a bad scene before—now it's turning into a nightmare. If people get scared and start trashing the town—"

"We'll do what we can, Jason," he said grimly. "Just get us there."

The chatter on the radio wasn't encouraging . Apparently it was taking some time to deploy the police from Ventura, so they were still coming in and getting their briefings. Nobody was saying where the murders had taken place, except that there were now at least three of them at the concert at the downtown park. The police and other emergency personnel that were already on the scene were trying to disperse the crowd and deal with the bodies, but the people were scared and uncooperative, and some were acting erratically.

"Where you want to start?" Jason asked Stone.

"Let's get downtown if we can," he said. "We won't have time to set up more than a rudimentary circle, but with Carly on hand that might be all we need. If it's killing people to make more minions, then I'm hoping if we can get rid of it, the minions will just leave on their own." He twisted in his seat to face Edna, who was in the back. "Do you concur?"

She shrugged. "Sounds like it might work. I don't know, though. I never had to deal with anything but the main guy."

"Uh—" Jason interrupted. "Al? Problem."

Stone turned back. Up ahead of them, a line of red brake lights loomed in the road. Beyond that they could make out the flashing blue-and-reds of a police car. "Bugger," he snapped. "They're blocking the road. Probably don't want any more people than necessary coming in to play tourist."

"What do we do?"

Stone noticed the roadblock extended out on both sides, which meant nobody was leaving town and the road going out was clear. "Drive up to them on the other side," he directed.

Jason stared at him. "You sure?"

"Wait!" Edna said. "Can you turn around?"

There were already cars behind them, but there was no traffic on the other side. Some of the others were already getting the same idea, pulling out and changing direction to head back the way they'd come. "Yeah, but—"

"Do it," she said. "If we go back, we can catch Villanova Road and get in from there."

"Won't they have that blocked, too?" Stone asked, as Jason began turning the truck around.

"Not likely," Jason said. "They don't have that many cops in Ojai, and the radio said the Ventura guys are just getting their orders. Things are gonna be a clusterfuck. They don't have enough men to block all the ways in and out."

"Should we go pick up Suzanne?" Jason asked.

"No time," Stone said. "We've got her book and we've got Carly—I think that's all we need." He turned around to Carly. "Are you all right back there?"

"Scared shitless," she said in a shaky voice. "But I'm starting to think you might be telling the truth."

"Well, that's something. Don't worry, we'll keep you safe." He hoped he could keep that promise.

They drove a short distance back toward Ventura when Edna pointed. "There. Turn left."

Jason did as instructed. Stone noticed that none of the other cars were doing the same thing: either they weren't familiar with the local roads or else the police presence had dissuaded them from trying to get closer to the action. Someone had set up cones across the road to stop anyone from going further, but it was easy to drive around them.

Villanova Road was narrow, tree-lined, and twisty, but it didn't go on very far. In less than ten minutes they'd reached its end and made a right back onto the road that would become Ojai Avenue. As they drove past the junction of highways 150 and 33, no more flashing lights greeted them. "Good," Jason said. "No more blocks. Like I said, I doubt they have the manpower to block everything off."

They soon had another problem, though: traffic. Ojai Avenue, they discovered, was considerably more choked with vehicles than one would expect on a sleepy late-summer Sunday night. "Left here," Edna ordered. "I can get us there on back roads."

Stone, grateful that they had someone who could navigate the town without having to resort to map-reading, nodded. "Tell me what you found in the book," he said, as Jason turned the truck in the direction Edna had indicated.

She reached in her bag and pulled it out. A new bookmark poked out of it, about halfway through. "It's not much," she said, "but it looks like a pretty good banishment spell. Similar to the summoning spell you found: it's not specific to a particular entity. The magic in here is more your style than mine, though, and my Latin's rusty." She passed it forward. "Take a look."

Stone flipped on the dome light, took the book and opened it to the page Edna had indicated, bowing his head low over the scribblings.

"Is that a magic book?" Carly asked from the back seat.

"The real thing," Edna said.

"Oh, wow..." she murmured. She was still looking very much like something large and heavy had smacked her hard between the eyes. "I think I need a drink."

"Extradimensional vengeance spirit first," Stone said without looking up. "Drink after."

Following Edna's directions, Jason got the truck the rest of the way downtown until they were one street over from Ojai Avenue near Libbey Park. Sirens sounded in the distance, and even with the truck's windows up they could hear yells, the occasional crash of glass breaking, and general pandemonium.

"Pull in here," Edna ordered, pointing at a narrow drive that looked like it led back behind a small, closed business. "Can't guarantee the truck'll be safe, but I don't think people will look here."

Jason again did as directed. He grabbed a walkie-talkie and they piled out of the truck. Stone closed the book, stowed it in his leather bag, and slung the bag over his shoulder.

"Anything?" Edna asked him.

"You were right," he said. "This should do just fine, assuming we can pin it down long enough. Can you get any sense of where it is?"

Edna paused a moment, leaning against the back of the truck and closing her eyes. "It's close," she said. "I'm guessing it's right in the middle of the action, wherever that is."

"Sounds like Libbey Park," Jason said. When everybody started to move, he said, "Hold on one sec."

"Jason," Stone protested. "We don't have time—"

"No, listen. This is important." His expression was serious. "We gotta be careful. This isn't just about magic. This is about panicked people, and they can be every bit as dangerous as magic when you get enough of 'em together. They're like herd animals when they're spooked."

"We'll be careful, Jason," Stone said. "Now let's—"

"No, I don't think you get it, Al," Jason said, continuing to stand his ground. "It'll be tough for you to shield all of us with all this shit going on. When people get in mobs, they do things they'd never do normally. When you add in people who could be possessed—including cops—"

Stone took a deep breath. "Point taken," he said. "All right. You're the expert in this situation. Get us as close as you can to the park, so we can find out if Many Faces is there. Once we locate him, we'll work out the next stage of the plan."

Jason nodded. "Okay, got it. C'mon."

"Don't forget—even if they're possessed, they're still just people. We'll have to be careful. We don't want to kill anyone."

"That's the plan," Jason said. "But a lot more people will die if we don't stop this thing, yeah?"

Stone and Edna both nodded soberly.

"Wait," Carly said. "I'm not gonna *kill* anybody!"

"We'll be careful," Stone said. "None of us want to do that. Jason: let's go."

"Stay close together," he said, and started off.

They crossed the street and moved around the back of a row of small shops that backed up the more picturesque Arcade. "This way," Edna said, pointing at an arch to their left. "We can get through to the other side of the Arcade here."

As they headed through the arch and out to Ojai Avenue, they passed several people going the other way, their faces wreathed in fright bordering on panic. They moved fast and, aside from jostling them as they went by, paid Stone and the others no attention. Ahead, yells, screams, and the amplified voices of police on bullhorns split what would normally have been a peaceful night.

When they reached the Arcade, they saw instantly that whatever they wanted to do, it wasn't going to be easy. The sidewalks and streets near Libbey Park across the street teemed with people—there had to be at least two or three hundred of them milling around, shoving their way past, and shrieking in fear. A broken bottle flew past them and crashed into the side of the building in a shower of broken glass.

Stone paused a moment to switch to magical senses, and what he saw made him stiffen. Several of the people in the crowd were suffused with the sickish green aura that indicated possession by Faces or one of his minions. "Edna—?" he said grimly.

"I see it," she replied in the same tone.

"What?" Carly demanded.

"Several of them are possessed already," Stone said. "That's probably why Faces committed all the murders tonight—to get himself more minions."

"Are they just killing people indiscriminately?" Jason asked. "I thought they were mostly only killing descendants, unless they needed more forces."

"Looks like they need more forces," Stone said. "That means everybody we meet is going to be potentially possessed—and trying to kill others."

"Try not to get surrounded," Jason said. "Come on—let's go." He held up the walkie-talkie. "I want to see if I can find Stan."

They worked their way around the periphery of the crowd, crossing the street and moving east up Ojai Avenue until the crowd began to thin. Several more improvised missiles sailed past them, including rocks, bottles, and full soda cans; none hit, but one flew uncomfortably close to Edna's head.

Behind them, a scream rose up, followed by a collective shriek of fear. Stone whirled just in time to see a figure plummet from the town's iconic post office tower and crash to the street, where it was immediately surrounded by people.

Jason had the radio turned on, and a series of ordered but somehow still urgent voices crackled out of its tiny speaker. He listened for a moment, then pointed back toward Libbey Park. "Sounds like they've set up a command post in the gazebo in the park. Come on. Let's go check in with them and maybe we can find Stan."

"Don't we have to find what we're looking for?" Carly asked. She was staying close to Jason and looking terrified.

"We will," Stone said. "We've got another friend we want to try to locate, but if we can't do it soon, we'll just have to move on without him."

They were about to slip into the park when a voice called, "Hey!" All of them looked up to see two men heading toward them.

Their expressions were angry, and one of them carried a long, thick tree branch. "Possessed," Stone said, raising his hands to prepare a spell.

"Wait," Edna said. "Let me see if I can divert them."

She concentrated for a moment, standing still as the two men approached. The one with the tree branch drew it back in a mighty windup, preparing to charge the group, but then he stopped, branch in mid-swing, and suddenly looked confused. So did his friend. As the others watched, the man dropped the branch and the two of them wandered off into the crowd as if nothing had happened.

"Nice job," Stone said. "They're still possessed—what did you do?"

"Just gave them a new purpose," she said. "See? It's not all about direct power."

Stone glanced sideways at her. "Yes, point taken. Come on."

Behind them, someone yelled. Jason spun in time to see another man, this one with a large pocketknife, lunging toward their group. Stone turned a second later to see him grab the man's arm, twist it to make him drop the knife, and fling him into the low wall separating the sidewalk from the park. He snatched up the knife, folded it, and stuck it in his pocket, letting his breath out. "This is fucking insane," he announced to nobody in particular.

They could see as soon as they entered the park that the police had indeed set up their command post in a large wooden gazebo that was one of Libbey Park's centerpieces. Two squad cars, lights whirling, were parked between the gazebo and the street, and three bright spotlights on stands had been set up next to them, shining harsh illumination over a large area nearby. Several cops were inside the gazebo, a couple talking on police radios. They all wore helmets and what looked like riot gear.

"There's Casner," Stone said, pointing. "Give me a moment—let's not all go in at once."

Jason and Edna, hyper-vigilant, steered Carly over near—but not too close to—the squad cars while Stone moved toward the gazebo. When he got about ten feet away, a voice boomed over a speaker: "Back off, sir."

"Casner!" Stone yelled. "It's Alastair Stone. I need to talk to you." He didn't stop moving: once he'd identified himself, he didn't think Casner would shoot him. The cop had too many *real* threats to deal with. The other cop, now recognizable as Aguirre, had has gun in one hand and was yelling something into a mic he held in the other, but he didn't seem to be paying any attention to Stone.

"Stone, what the *hell* are you doing here?" Casner demanded. "Take your little crew and get the hell out of the area. We've got enough problems—"

"Yes, exactly," Stone said, mounting the gazebo's steps. "We might be able to help you with your problem. Where's Stan Lopez?"

"How the hell should I know?" He made a sweeping gesture to encompass the park and the street. "In case you haven't noticed, I'm trying to coordinate this mess so we don't end up with a massacre. Lopez is doing whatever he was told to do."

"Look, Lieutenant," Stone said. "I haven't got time to spoon-feed you this time. You've got a full-blown supernatural situation here. Some of these people are possessed, and they're going to do their best to kill other people so they can bring over more of the things that are possessing them. If we don't stop this very soon, it will grow exponentially to the point where you'll have to mow down crowds of civilians to have a chance of stemming it. Now are you going to listen to me or not?"

"Stone," Casner growled, "I'm only gonna tell you this one more time, and then I'm going to arrest you and shove your ass in the back of a squad car until we get this under control. I don't have time for your supernatural *bullshit* right now! Get. The hell. Out of here. Now. Do you understand?"

Stone clenched his fists. Normally it didn't bother him that most mundanes' minds were truly breathtaking in their refusal to accept what was going on right under their noses. It meant that even when he was forced to use magic in front of them, they never believed that was what they'd seen after everything was over. They were masters at coming up with "logical" explanations for why the skinny guy in the long black coat was flinging lightning bolts out of his hands, or throwing people through the air with a gesture. Right now, though, it was going to get a lot of people killed, and that wasn't something Stone wanted to deal with.

"Casner, you idiot," he snarled, preparing to turn toward the crowd and do something showy and magical that the man *couldn't* deny.

Until he realized that Aguirre wasn't yelling into his mic anymore.

He spun, and froze. "Casner! Down!" he yelled, already putting up a shield between Casner and Aguirre, who was pointing his gun at his boss. Aguirre's eyes glowed red-orange.

CHAPTER FORTY-FIVE

The gun went off with a deafening roar. The round bounced off the shield and ricocheted into the night. Aguirre's expression went from enraged to dumbfounded, and he let the gun slip from his nerveless fingers.

"Holy *shit!*" Casner's gaze cut back and forth between Stone, the glowing shield that was still up, and the confused cop. He drew his own gun and pointed it at Aguirre. "Holy shit—Aguirre, you just tried to shoot me!"

"Put the gun down, Lieutenant," Stone ordered, shifting to magical senses and seeing that the green aura had left Aguirre. "He's all right now." He made a show of letting the shield drop as Jason, Edna, and Carly came running over. Despite the potential lethality of the situation he'd just defused, he had to give Faces credit: he couldn't have asked for a better demonstration that something weird was going on. "*Now* do you believe me?"

Casner was staring at Aguirre. "You tried to *shoot* me." His gaze switched to Stone. "And you—"

"Put up a shield to prevent it," Stone said, nodding. "Casner, we don't have time for this. We're looking for someone, and we need to find him fast."

"Lopez—" Casner's voice sounded strange—stunned and confused, nothing like his normal confident and authoritative tones.

"Not Lopez, though we'd like to find him as well. The one who's responsible for this whole mess."

Casner looked at Aguirre again, then at Stone. Then he took a deep breath. His expression went through a series of changes that Stone was very familiar with: they were the progression of a mundane who had finally been forced to accept that the supernatural really *did* exist and whose mind was steadfastly trying to shield him from this acceptance. Usually it stopped there: the person simply shut down and began the process of rationalization. This time, though, Stone could tell that after everything Peter Casner had seen over the last few days, he'd finally seen something that had broken through his self-imposed wall of ignorance. It was not a pleasant sight, nor, did Stone expect, was it a pleasant experience for Casner. But that didn't matter now.

The radio squawked, but both Casner and the thoroughly flummoxed Aguirre ignored it. "What do you want?" Casner asked Stone in a quiet monotone.

"Call Lopez. Tell him to meet us here if he's close."

"And then what?"

Stone shrugged. "Then we try to find the source of all this. We—"

Casner's expression suddenly changed. His mouth worked, and a voice came out—flat, dead, but somehow amused. "*I'm not hiding, mageling,*"

Stone and all the rest of them, including Aguirre, stared at him. "Well," Stone said. "Nice of you to show up and talk to us." So much for his theory about Faces' inability to possess cops away from its shrine. Maybe it was growing more powerful. Still, though, as long as it was talking, it wasn't out killing anyone else. Small victories.

"*I have nothing more to say to you,*" Casner's body said in the weird voice. "*You will die like the rest. All of you will.*" He turned his head, and settled his eerie red-orange gaze on Carly. "*Not all of you. Why are you here, little sister of my blood?*"

Carly was shaking, her eyes huge and terrified. "M-me?" She tried to duck behind Jason.

"What the hell is going *on*?" Aguirre demanded, backing away, his voice high and bright with near-panic.

Everyone ignored him. He of Many Faces was still watching Carly. "*I have no quarrel with you, little sister. Why do you aid these fools?*"

"I—" Carly's voice shook. She seemed to gather a bit of courage from being behind Jason. She swallowed. "You have to stop killing people! Go home! Go away!"

Casner/Faces laughed: an unsettling sound, like the creak of old hinges. "*Oh, little sister. Your foolish friends have convinced you that you can command me. None can command me. I will fulfill the purpose for which I was called, and you can do nothing to stop it.*"

"Like hell she can't," Stone said, eyes blazing. "She summoned you. She can send you back." He unzipped his leather bag and pulled out the book. He didn't think they'd be able to do it here—that would have been too much to ask—but he wasn't going to turn down an opportunity to give it a shot.

Faces laughed again. "*She has power, but she doesn't know how to use it. She summoned me, true, but she did not give me direction. She is weak. She is nothing like those of her bloodline who called me into being and set my purpose so long ago. She will do nothing to stop me. She did not make me—she cannot unmake me.*"

Stone opened the book to the page where the ritual that Edna had found was printed. Doing this without a circle would be difficult and risky, if it were even possible at all. "Edna?"

"Here," Edna said, coming up next to him.

"Carly, you too," Stone said.

"Al?" Jason called.

"What?" Stone sounded impatient. He didn't have time to deal with distractions right now.

"They're coming! A bunch of them are coming this way!"

"Fuck!" Aguirre said. Behind them, he was finally getting himself back together, and he too had turned toward the park. "What are they—"

Stone spared a glance in the same direction. A good half-dozen men and women, including one policewoman awkwardly carrying a gun, were moving in their direction. A quick magical glance told him all he needed to know: these were Faces' minions, and the spirit wasn't taking any chances that he and his group might be able to get their banishing spell off.

"*Fools,*" Faces said again, and then the light left Casner's eyes and he stood there, swaying and confused. "Fine," he said, reaching for the mic as if nothing had happened. "I'll call Lopez, and then—"

The armed group was approaching. The policewoman raised her gun and fired into the gazebo—everyone hit the deck except Stone and Edna, who both summoned shields, and Casner, who hadn't clued in yet that he'd just lost a couple of minutes of his life. The bullets bounced harmlessly off the shield.

"Hold that shield," Stone told Edna. He let his own drop, shoved the book back in the bag, and spread both hands to point at the oncoming group. A wave of force issued from them, catching the possessed group at around chest level and bowling them over like tenpins. With his magical sight active, he saw the small insubstantial forms dart upward from the falling people, and flung a ball of magical energy at the two closest to him. They flared red and flew to pieces. Next to them, another one simply faded out of existence. He glanced sideways at Edna, and saw that she had dropped her own shield now that the gunwoman was down and was pointing her hand in a different direction. "Casner! Call Lopez!"

Aguirre had recovered enough that he was back on his own radio. "I've got him here. He's at the park, on the other side over by Signal."

"Tell him to come here," Stone said, without taking his eyes off the group. One glowing-eyed young man wielded a baseball bat near the fountain; he'd already knocked down two people and was winding up on a third. Stone sent another bolt of magical energy at him, and he overbalanced backward and landed in the fountain with a splash. Next to him, Edna was using her more subtle magic to defuse tense situations, sending confused would-be rioters wandering off in random directions.

"I can't do this for long," she told Stone through gritted teeth. Sweat stood out on her tanned forehead. "I need more preparation these days to be able to do anything big."

"We can't keep doing this in any case," Stone said. He wasn't tiring yet: even though combat spells weren't his strongest suit, the practice he'd gotten over the last couple years and the methods he'd studied meant he had more endurance with them than he used to. Adrenaline was helping. "Every time one of those things kills someone, it brings another minion into the physical world. We'll be overrun."

"What else can we do?" Jason demanded. His gaze scanned the crowd, watching for anyone who might be coming closer or aiming a gun at them.

Out in the park, the cops were struggling to contain the crowd, but there were so many that it was difficult: as soon as they pinned down one or two, another five ran off. Naturally, it was impossible for them to tell which ones were possessed and which ones were simply drunk and taking advantage of the mob situation to let loose. Stone scanned the area, and with just a quick glance spotted two dead bodies, one nearly decapitated, the other with gaping bloody slashes in its abdomen. The crowd was giving both of them a wide berth. Fire and emergency personnel were hurrying among the chaos, trying to aid victims who were still alive as the police tried to get the situation under control.

"Here comes Lopez," Edna said, pointing. Sure enough, his familiar form was approaching through the crowd toward the command post. He had his nightstick in hand, and was clad in uniform, bulletproof vest, and helmet. His face was grim, but he looked relieved when he spotted Stone, Edna, and Jason.

"Thank God," he said. "It's been like hell here tonight. It's like the whole town's gone insane."

"I think that's pretty much what's happened," Jason said. He ducked as another bottle flew through the air and smashed into the side of one of the police radios.

Stone was staring out over the scene, his mind obviously elsewhere.

"Al?" Lopez ventured.

"I know what we have to do," Stone said, snapping back on.

"What?"

"We can't fight it here. It's too easy for it to switch from one body to another, like it did with Casner. That, and there's too much chaos here. We'd never be able to get any kind of circle going."

"Where, then?" Jason asked.

But Lopez had already caught on. "At the tree," he stated. And to Stone: "Right?"

He nodded. "We need to take it to the source. That's where it came into being—that's where we'll have to send it back."

Edna, too, nodded. "Yes," she said. "It will be strong there, but with Carly along we should be able to do it. If it doesn't kill us first."

"If we get moving, we might be able to get up there before it catches on what we're planning," Stone said. "Not likely, but it's got a lot to be dealing with here. It might be distracted. Come on."

He turned back to Casner, who was on the radio again. "We're leaving," he said. "We'll be in Stan's truck. If you've got any road-blocks over near Creek Road, tell your men to let us through."

Casner, still looking dubious but a lot less so than before, nodded. "Where are you going?"

"Best if we don't say. Just tell them to leave us alone." Without waiting for a response, he waved for the others to follow him out of the park.

| CHAPTER FORTY-SIX

They got back to the truck without major incident. Twice they had to deal with groups of drunken rioters trying to hassle them, but both times a combination of Stone's and Edna's magic, Jason's muscle, and Lopez's police uniform got them through without any injuries on either side. They didn't encounter any more possessed individuals once they got clear of Ojai Avenue. "I think they're still focusing on killing descendants," Edna said. "It's the only explanation I can think of why there isn't more of a bloodbath than there is. They can get their reinforcements while still fulfilling their orders."

"Whatever they're doing, we need to get away from it," Jason said. They piled into the truck, shifting around to make room for Lopez, who took the wheel.

"Look sharp," Stone said from the shotgun seat as Lopez took off back down the back street away from the Arcade. "If Faces figures out what we're up to, he's going to try to stop us."

All five of them were on edge as the truck headed toward Creek Road. Lopez drove quickly but carefully, scanning the road for anyone who might dart out in front of them. Fortunately, most of the action seemed to be downtown. Lopez left the police radio on, so they were able to keep track of the chatter as more reinforcements from the Ventura Sheriff's Department arrived and were deployed. It sounded like they were beginning to get the panic under control, but there were still dozens of civilians and the police were confused by the unexplained behavior of some of the crowd. As Stone and the others listened, a report came in of another death as someone had scaled to the top of Libbey Bowl and jumped off headfirst into the concrete below.

"This is unreal," Lopez muttered. "This town's never gonna be the same after this. And the worst part is that they're not gonna know what the hell hit them."

Stone nodded. "I don't doubt that as soon as this is over, Casner will find some way to rationalize what happened. Aguirre didn't really shoot at him—he was shooting at something over his shoulder. Something like that. You lot are masters at coming up with convoluted explanations instead of just accepting what *is*."

They paralleled Ojai Avenue until they got out of the downtown area, then Lopez took the first left and headed south. Stone recognized it as the route he'd taken on his first trip out to Creek Road what seemed like several lifetimes ago.

"Jason," Lopez said, "Dig around back there under the seat. There's a portable light down there. I want this traffic to get the hell out of our way."

Jason found it and passed it forward; Lopez turned it on, lowered the truck's window, and stuck it to the roof. "Might not help," he said, "but won't hurt."

It was a good idea: Ojai Avenue, even out this far, was still at a standstill with traffic in both directions. Lopez blasted the horn a few times and the cars shuffled themselves around, barely making room for him to squeeze the big vehicle through. He cruised along half on the road and half off, then turned onto Country Club Drive as soon as he could, still mirroring Stone's route.

Fortunately the traffic seemed confined to the main drag; this road was deserted, and when they reached the intersection with Creek Road, it was as well. Lopez opened up the truck a bit more, and in only a couple of minutes he'd turned onto the fire road leading up to the area containing the shrine.

"I hope you've got some gear in here somewhere," Jason said. "How are we gonna find the place without light?"

"Flashlights in the toolbox," Lopez said.

"We can provide light if necessary," Stone said, indicating himself and Edna. "But I don't want to use too much magic until we get there. Don't want to give Faces anything to notice."

"Keep your eyes open," Edna said, looking out the front window. "I'd be surprised if it hasn't already noticed."

The truck jounced along the narrow dirt road, the light from its headlights bouncing eerily into the thickly growing trees on either side. Stone shifted to magical senses, on the watch for the glowing forms of Faces' minions approaching. Thus far, though, he saw nothing. "Maybe not," he said. "Do you see anything, Edna?"

"No, but I don't think it'll show its hand yet," she said. "It knows this is going to be the end—it's saving its energy. I can sense the area, though—we're getting close to where we need to stop."

"Just let me know," Lopez said. "This all looks the same in the dark."

Stone glanced around at the back seat. Carly was huddled in a corner, staring down into her lap. "You all right, Carly?"

"No," she said in a small voice. "I'm really scared. Those people were—killing each other. That guy jumped off the post office tower—" She took a deep, shuddering breath. "I can't do this. I'm gonna fuck it up, I just know it."

Stone was about to answer her when Edna reached out and gripped her shoulder. "Enough of that," she ordered, her voice full of that same stern but kind tone she'd used on Stone when he was injured. She fixed her gaze on Carly, tilting the other woman's chin up. "You listen to me. Look at me."

Carly's reluctant gaze came up.

"Of course you're scared," the older woman said. "You'd be an idiot if you weren't. Only idiots would walk into something like this and not feel like they're gonna piss themselves any minute. The trick is that you have to do it *anyway*."

Carly took another ragged breath. "But what if I *do* screw up? It's not like I don't have a lot of practice screwing things up. What if you depend on me and I can't do it?"

Edna shrugged. "Then you can't do it, and we aren't any worse off than we started." She shook her head. "You want to know something?"

"What?"

"I'm scared to death *I'm* not going to be able to do it." She waved around at the rutted dirt road, the trees, and the black, star-dappled sky up above them. "I'm an old woman. I haven't done any serious magic in twenty years. This isn't even the kind of magic I *do*." She hooked a thumb at Stone. "He's the one that thinks you deal with problems by kicking their asses. I'm hoping that isn't what we'll have to do, but I'm afraid it is, so I'm here. It's either go up there and give it my best shot, or let that thing run around killing people until it decides it's had enough."

Carly nodded, looking down into her lap again. "I hope you're right."

"You can do it, Carly," Stone said from the front seat. "You and Edna aren't the only ones who are scared. I think it's a safe bet to say all of us are. This doesn't get any easier just because you've done things like it before."

"Here," Edna broke in, pointing. "This is close. Let's stop here."

Lopez pulled the truck off the road and shut off the engine and the headlights. For a moment, they all sat there, unmoving, each alone with his or her own thoughts. The darkness out here was crushing, almost a physical thing, and the only sounds were crickets and the occasional creak of a tree branch or the rustle of a small animal running through the carpet of dead leaves.

"Well," Stone said softly after a few seconds. "Shall we do this?"

In answer, Lopez opened the truck door, bathing the immediate area in light again.

They all got out and stood in the road. Stone held up a glowing hand as Jason and Lopez hunted around in the bed's toolbox for flashlights. They found three; Lopez and Jason each took one, and gave the last one to Carly. She clutched it like an anchor.

"No packs this time," Lopez said. "Didn't have time to throw them in when I got called in. We'll just have to go with what we have." He rummaged around and came up with the two machetes he and Stone had had on their first trip. "Still got these, though, if they'll do any good." He handed one to Jason.

They set off into the forest. Lopez took point, with Jason trailing behind to watch for anything sneaking up on them. Stone, Edna, and Carly walked in the middle; Stone shifted every few seconds from mundane to magical sight, and noticed that Edna appeared to be doing the same thing. It was a mild night; not quite hot but pleasantly warm, and the walk wasn't difficult.

"Where are they?" Jason asked under his breath. "I can't believe they haven't figured it out yet."

Nobody answered. They kept moving, each of them tense, expecting someone or something to come crashing out of the trees at them at any moment. Lopez kept glancing up, and Stone knew why: he was no doubt remembering the thick tree branch that nearly crushed him when they'd first discovered the tablets. Stone himself focused on the spaces between the trees, trying not to think too hard about the fact that more than one bear probably called this forest home.

"I feel weird," Carly whispered after they'd been walking for several minutes.

"Queasy?" Stone asked. He was beginning to feel that way too, and was just about to ask Edna to do whatever she'd done last time to alleviate it. He couldn't afford to have his concentration compromised by even mild nausea—the various aches and pains from the last few days' leftover injuries were hard enough to work through without adding extras.

"No. Just—weird. I can't explain it. Like—everything's *humming*. Kind of like when you hold onto the gas-pump hose when it's pumping."

Stone glanced at Edna. "She's sensing the ley line already?" he murmured.

"Sounds like—or else the energy from the shrine. Makes sense, since it's tied to her."

"Is that bad?" Carly asked, sounding fearful.

Stone shook his head. "Actually, it might be good. It could mean you're attuned, which is what we wanted. Say something if it gets worse, but I don't think it will. Edna, speaking of bad, could you—?"

She nodded, pausing a moment to put her fingers on Stone's forehead. "Better?"

"Yes, thank you."

They kept moving, and eventually the enormous twisted oak tree loomed up ahead of them. As soon as Carly saw it, she stopped, staring wide-eyed.

"Carly?" Edna moved next to her. "Something wrong?"

She shook her head. "Not...wrong," she said slowly. "I—feel like I've been here before. But that's crazy. I don't even know where we are anymore."

"Not surprised," Stone said. He dropped down near the roots and unzipped his duffel bag. "Let's get this circle up. We won't have time for anything complex, but even a basic protective ward will help if we can manage it before anything shows up. Edna, do you want to help me, or watch for anything approaching?"

"I'll watch," she said. "Our circles probably aren't compatible, and I haven't done one in years anyway. You set it up, and I'll see if I can add anything to it."

Stone nodded. "Jason and Stan, stay close to Edna. If anything physical shows up, you'll have to keep her safe. She'll handle the magical threats."

Lopez unsnapped the strap holding his gun in its holster and loosened it, and Jason slid his machete out of its sheath.

"What about me?" Carly asked. She was looking around, trying to take everything in at once in the shifting beams of the three flashlights.

"Stay with Edna," Stone told her. "If you sense anything odd or unusual, let her know. You might be more sensitive to it than any of us are."

"Everything *around* here is odd or unusual," she protested, but she did as directed and headed over toward Edna.

Stone, holding up a light spell so he could see what he was doing, quickly hunted around in his bag and pulled out the components he would need. He didn't have everything for a perfectly made circle, but that didn't matter because he didn't have time to make one. Circles weren't about their components anyway, not really. Their effectiveness had more to do with the skill of the mage who cast them than with the materials used: a highly skilled mage could make a circle using only chalk or sand, or even just lines scratched into dirt with a stick, while an inexperienced one could be given access to a stockpile of perfectly prepared components but wouldn't be able to summon a fraction of the power.

Stone hoped he was skilled enough to pull this off, because you couldn't draw a circle with chalk on ground covered in inches of dried leaves and mulch. Ideally, he would have liked to enclose the entire tree, but he had neither enough components nor enough time to have any chance of doing that—it would have taken hours. Instead, he settled for using his bags of sand to sketch a circle around ten feet in diameter next to the tree, on the same side as the tablets' alcove. It wouldn't enclose the alcove itself, because there wouldn't have been any way to close it with the roots in the way. Its purpose would have to be, as he'd said, simple protection: something that would—with luck—be able to hold off the worst of Many Faces' assault long enough for him, Edna, and Carly to complete the ritual to send it back.

He forced himself to move deliberately; even though his breath was coming faster and sweat ran down his back, he couldn't afford to make a mistake because something in the back of his mind couldn't stop picturing the massive form of a bear stalking stealthily through the forest, getting ready to leap out when his back was turned. *There's no bear,* he told himself, frustrated. *Pull yourself together. They're counting on you!*

Even so, he couldn't help raising his head. "Anything out there?"

"Clear so far," Edna replied.

"I don't see anything either," Jason said, sweeping the flashlight's beam out into the trees again. "It's making me nervous."

You and me both, Stone thought as he continued drawing the circle. He couldn't even use candles out here: candles and dry ground covered in leaves were rarely a desirable combination under the best of circumstances, and he was all but certain there would be enough chaos flying around when they started the banishment that he couldn't risk something getting knocked over and starting a forest fire. They might still get rid of Faces, but burning down half the forest and killing themselves in the process seemed counterproductive to their overall purpose.

Are you sure *that bear isn't out there somewhere?* a small voice asked in his mind. He shook his head to clear it, unsure of whether the voice was coming from somewhere else or from his own overworked subconscious.

It nearly killed you, the little voice reminded him. *Do you remember how it felt when those claws ripped into your chest? Into your stomach? Do you remember how big its teeth were as they were about to sink into you? Do you remember what its breath smelled like? Do you remember what your* blood *smelled like? There's a bear out there now. It's close. It's bigger this time. It's coming for you. Edna won't be able to help you.*

"Stop it!" he hissed aloud.

"Was that you, Al?" Lopez called. "You okay?"

"Fine," he got out between his teeth. He closed his eyes for a moment and then forced himself to continue with the circle, even though he was sure he had heard leaves rustling out beyond the reach of the flashlight beam—rustling as if something heavy was making its careful way through them—

It will kill you. It will rip your skin from your body. It will gut you like the helpless prey you are, and it will kill all your friends—

Above him, the tree creaked ominously, almost as if it were groaning.

Something cracked.

Stone didn't hesitate. Summoning his shield over his head, he leaped to his feet and dived out of the circle toward clear ground.

The limb, at least a foot in diameter and six feet long, crashed into the center of the circle.

On the other side of the circle, someone cried out in pain and surprise, and one of the flashlights spun to the ground.

And then the clearing was full of whirling forms.

| CHAPTER FORTY-SEVEN

S tone rolled back to his feet. "Get over here!" he called. "All of you! And don't drop your lights!" He hurried back to the circle and snatched up his bag. The branch had destroyed his work—there was no way he'd be able to re-do it now—but he wasn't about to let the magic tome containing the banishment ritual go.

Jason, apparently the one who'd dropped his light, cursed and yelped in pain as he darted toward it just in time for another branch to come crashing down onto his shoulder. It wasn't nearly as big as the one that had landed in the circle, but it was big enough.

Carly, meanwhile was screaming in fright. All around them, whirls of leaves rose up like little tornadoes, circling them as they moved closer to Stone.

"Hush!" Edna admonished Carly sharply.

"Jason? You all right?" Lopez was backing up, keeping his flashlight beam focused on as many of the mini-tornadoes as he could.

"Might have broken something," came his tight voice through the darkness. "Fuck!"

"Get over here!" Stone yelled again. "Hurry!" One of the tornadoes surged forward and tried to rip the bag from his grasp, but he put his arm through the straps and held on with both arms until it subsided, concentrating hard on keeping the shield he'd summoned above himself going.

Carly shrieked again as another tornado knocked her off her feet. The things weren't large—most of them were no more than five feet tall—but they whipped the leaves around with a mad intensity far in excess of their dimensions. As the others watched, it lifted her from the ground and began to move away from the circle.

"No!" Edna snarled, pointing her hand at the tornado. It seemed to hesitate for a moment, then let Carly down and joined its fellows. Stone used another spell to levitate the terrified woman and bring her back over to their group.

"What do we do now?" Lopez demanded. "The circle's shot, isn't it?"

"Yes," Stone confirmed. "We'll have to do it without the circle. It will be harder, but we have no choice."

From the forest, a low, growling roar sounded. Stone stiffened, staring in the direction it had come from. *It's out there. It's coming. It's coming for me.*

"Al?" Lopez looked away from where he was trying to get a quick examination of Jason's arm. "Hey, man, what's wrong?"

Carly was having a meltdown. She sank to her knees, shaking and sobbing. "I can't do this! Oh, fuck, I can't *do* this!"

"Al?" Lopez shook Stone's shoulder hard.

Stone didn't move. His gaze was locked on the section of dark forest where he'd heard the growl. "It's out there..." he whispered as Edna dropped to her knees and tried to deal with Carly.

"What's out there?" Lopez shone the flashlight around in the direction where Stone was looking, but it only picked out more trees.

"It's coming...don't you hear it?" Stone couldn't believe Lopez couldn't hear it. The rumbling growl rose and fell, as if the bear were prowling back and forth, biding its time.

"I don't hear anything except those tornado things. What is it?"

"The bear...I hear it growling..."

"There's no bear out there," Edna said. "Stone, pull yourself to-gether! If you lose it, we're all dead!" She was still on her knees next to Carly, but she glared up at him with harsh, glittering eyes. "There's *no bear* out there! And keep that damn shield up!"

Stone gathered himself. He didn't believe Lopez, didn't believe Edna: it *was* out there. And it was coming. But something in Edna's tone got through to him enough that he realized he'd let his con-centration on the shield slip. He got it powered back up an instant before something flew through the darkness and hit it hard, making a red flaring *crack* before crashing to the leaves.

"Holy fuck!" Jason said through his teeth. "That rock's the size of my *head!*" He was still clutching his left arm, holding the machete with his right hand. "Al, you'd better get to it soon."

Edna stood up and got in Stone's face. "Listen to me, Mr. 'I Shape the Universe With My Will'! You'd damn well *better* get to it, or we're all screwed. Faces knows we can't hold it off forever."

Stone drew a deep breath, trying to look past her. "Edna—"

She slapped him, hard, rocking his head back. "*Listen!* Even if there *is* a bear, which there *isn't*, which you'd know if you bothered to check magically—I can *deal* with bears. I dealt with the last one, remember? Now damn you, live up to your hype and *do this!*"

He glared at her, but her words sunk in. "Right then," he growled. "Help me hold this shield." The little voice was still there, still trying to serve up grotesque images of massive, snarling bears, but he forced himself to ignore it. He didn't have time for it. If there was a bear out there, then there was a bear out there. That wasn't his problem right now. He pointed his hand at one of the mini-tornadoes and blew it apart with a blast of energy, then raised the book and opened it to the page with the ritual.

"What do we do?" Lopez yelled. The rest of the tornadoes were spinning faster now, moving closer, the leaves and twigs and wind providing constant background noise.

"Just—don't let anything get too close," Stone said, distracted. "If any of those things get within reach, hit them with your machetes. It should at least drive them back." He reached down and put a hand on the still-kneeling Carly's shoulder. "Carly, it's time."

She looked up at him with big, haunted, tear-filled eyes. "I can't—I can't do it..." she whispered, voice shaking.

"You *can* do it," he said firmly. "Come on—just stand up. All you have to do is concentrate. Tell it to go home. Tell it to go back where it came from. If you need to do it out loud, then do that."

She stumbled to her feet, with Edna helping her up. "You can do it, Carly," the older woman said, gripping her shoulder. "You can make it all go away."

Stone held up the book and began reading the words of the banishing ritual in a loud, commanding voice that easily carried over the whooshing leaves in the mini-tornadoes. He gathered his will, forcing himself to focus on nothing but what he was doing: he couldn't pay attention to the tornadoes, or his friends, or the shield. This whole operation depended on three things: his spell, Edna's shield, and Carly's ability to order He of Many Faces to return to its home plane. If any of those three things failed, Faces would kill them. He knew it. He'd rarely been more sure of anything in his life.

The invocation was not a long one, but he was careful to read each word precisely. It was almost never safe to get even one word of a spell wrong, especially when you were dealing with things this potentially dangerous. At best, and most likely, the spell simply wouldn't work if he misspoke any of the words. However, there were other possibilities—ones he didn't want to think about be-cause most of them involved horrific and violent deaths for all of them. Avoiding that kind of distraction was one of the things that mages' masters spent a lot of time drilling into them during their apprenticeships, and fortunately Stone had learned those lessons well.

He reached the part of the invocation where Carly would have to insert her command to send Faces back. He paused a moment, reaching out to grip her shoulder again. "Carly! Now!"

Nothing happened.

"Carly! Do it!" He turned to face her, finally taking notice of what was going on around him.

And he froze.

Carly was not standing slumped and dejected in the middle of the group anymore. Instead, she stood tall, shoulders thrown back, an expression of confidence and wonder on her plain features. "It's so beautiful..." she whispered.

Harsh laughter echoed through the clearing.

| CHAPTER FORTY-EIGHT

S tone reacted quickly: he grabbed Carly by her upper arms and spun her to face him. "Carly! Snap out of it!"

She smiled at him. "Why didn't you tell me?" she murmured. "Why didn't you tell me what I could be?"

The remaining mini-tornadoes sank back into the ground in a hail of spinning leaves.

"What the hell is going on?" Jason demanded.

But Edna was catching on as well. She stared at Carly in horror, but didn't drop the shield she was maintaining.

The laughter continued. "*Mageling, did you truly think that it would be so easy to rid yourself of me before I've completed my purpose?*"

Something slammed into the side of Edna's shield.

"Al, damn it, what's happening?" Jason yelled.

Edna answered, her tone grim. "Faces is trying to get into her head."

Carly, meanwhile, was holding her hands up and looking at them as if she'd never seen them before. Moving as though in a daze, she pointed one at a small nearby tree and closed her eyes for a second. Energy shot from her hand and hit the tree with a sound like thunder. It swayed, though it did not fall. When her eyes opened again, they were shining with amazement. "That's what magic's like?" she said in wonder. "That's what I can do? Why didn't you tell me?"

"*Carly!*" Stone said urgently. "Faces is lying to you. That power isn't yours. It's his. He's—infusing you with it somehow."

She concentrated for a moment, then her expression clouded. She frowned. "You're jealous," she stated. "You're just jealous because I've got more power than you do now. You were never going to show me how to use this, were you?"

"Oh, holy crap..." Lopez said under his breath as he realized what was happening. He raised his hand, clearly preparing to slap Carly. "Al, should I—?"

"No!" Stone snapped, holding up his own hand to block Lopez's. "If it doesn't work, she could kill you. She doesn't know how to handle that kind of power."

The laughter came again. *"She will learn."*

Something else slammed into the shield, and another hefty tree branch came crashing down atop it. "I can't hold this forever," Edna said, strain in her voice.

Stone gripped Carly's arms again. "Carly, listen to me. He's not going to let you keep that power. He *lies.* Now come on—do what you came here for. Order him to go back where he came from. Do that and this will all be over. No one else has to die." He could hear the shake in his own voice; even as he said the words, he knew that they were having little effect on Carly. Her face was not twisted or evil or vengeful—she simply looked like someone who had been given an amazing new toy.

"I told you that you were a fool, mageling. No one else has to die? How did you plan to banish me without death? I was born in death."

Stone started to reply, but then stopped. He knew Faces's voice was only in his mind, that the others couldn't hear it. And it was only now that he realized Faces was right: he *had* been a fool.

He'd forgotten the most important component of the ritual.

"Bloody hell..." he said aloud.

"What?" Jason called. "Al, what's going on? What's up with Carly?"

The laughter again. *"Now you see, don't you? You can't send me back. You don't have the stomach for it. None of you do."*

Something, some kind of force, exploded inside the shield. The sound was deafening, the unseen force blowing them outward—all but Carly—like they'd been at ground zero of a bomb detonation. Not quite a bomb, though, or all of them would have been blown to pieces since neither Stone nor Edna had anticipated the blast. Instead, they were blown around as if by a huge gust of wind, propelled into various trees. Stone managed to get his shield up before he hit, which probably saved his life. Around him he could hear the thuds and grunts of his friends' similar impacts. One of the flashlights dropped to the ground.

"Stan? Jason? Edna?" Stone called, scrambling to his feet and summoning a light spell to illuminate the area.

"Here," came Edna's voice from his right. She sounded pained, but still strong.

"I'm—mostly okay," Jason rasped. He was struggling up, clutching his injured arm. He picked up his machete from where it had landed near him.

"Lopez?"

No response.

From the center of where the circle had been, Carly was watching them with interest, but the faintest bit of uncertainty flashed across her face. "I didn't do that," she said. "That wasn't me!"

"What was the 'bloody hell' for?" Edna asked Stone as she came up next to him. She moved slowly, never taking her eyes off Carly.

"Faces," Stone said. "It's right—I forgot something."

"How is it right?" Jason demanded. He was shining his flashlight around, trying to spot Lopez.

Stone's voice sounded beaten. "We can't banish it."

"What do you mean, we can't banish it?" Jason glared at him. "You mean because it's got Carly?"

"No. Because—"

"Because it took a sacrifice to summon it," Edna said, getting a look at Stone's expression and putting two and two together. "Right?"

Stone nodded wearily. "It took a sacrifice to summon it, and it will take one to get rid of it, even *with* Carly's help." He half-expected Faces to chime in about then, but it was strangely silent.

Oddly, so was Carly. Her face had lost some of its enraptured wonder, and now looked like she was wrestling with some kind of dilemma. Maybe the two of them were chatting—Stone wasn't sure. He shifted to magical senses again and blew away another of Faces' minions that was preparing to take another pass at them.

"You mean we gotta *kill* somebody?" Jason stared. "We can't get rid of it without doing that?"

Stone sighed. "I don't know if it will take a death, but that's what it took to bring it here in the first place." He bowed his head. He was out of ideas. If he was right—and he was certain he was—then either he or one of his friends would have to die to send Faces back. They could try using blood, but because it had taken not just blood but the energy of death to bring it across from whatever plane it had come from, he doubted that anything less than that—even when directed by one bound by blood with its original summoners—would provide sufficient power to send it back. The energies of birth and death were some of the most powerful forces known to magic: they could provide the kind of energy that could sustain massively powerful workings. And when a mage was sacrificed—Stone's mind flashed back to several years ago, when his own apprentice had nearly died in the same sort of sacrifice, used to power another summoning ritual. The destruction when it had failed had been incredible.

"Al?" Jason grabbed his shoulder. "What do we do?"

"Look at Carly," Edna murmured.

Stone's gaze came up and locked on Carly. She still stood in the middle of what had been the circle, and she still had an expression of stubborn confusion on her face. "No!" she said loudly, shaking her head. "I won't do that!"

Stone took a step forward. "What does it want you to do, Carly?" he called. "Kill us?"

She focused on him, but didn't answer, not right away. Nearly a minute passed, during which she appeared to be grappling with some difficult inner struggle. Her body shook, sweat breaking out on her forehead. "It says you can't send it back. It says someone would have to die for that. Is that right? Does somebody have to die?"

"Carly," Stone said, taking another step toward her. "Even if it's true, we still need you. We can't send it back without you. You know it has to go back. Think of all the people who have died. Think of Karen, Carly. Your friend. This thing killed your friend. It's lying to you about the power. It isn't going to let you keep it."

"No!" she cried. She lashed out again, but it was obvious she wasn't aiming at anyone. "You're—you're jealous!" She didn't sound so sure this time, though.

"Why isn't it attacking us?" Jason whispered.

"I think it's focusing on her," Edna replied in the same tone. "It's giving her its power, but that means it doesn't have much left to use on its own."

"Carly, you know I'm right," Stone said, forcing himself to keep his voice even, calm, sane. "You know I'm right, don't you? We can't let this thing stay here. Think of how many more people it will kill. Men, women, children—people whose only crime is their bloodline."

"But—" She hesitated. "Somebody has to die. Are you going to kill somebody? Is one of you going to die?"

Stone took a deep breath. "If that's what it takes," he said softly, "if you'll help us, then—yes."

She swallowed. "Really? Who? Which one of you is going to die?"

"I am."

The words came from three of them at once: Jason, Edna, and Stone. They looked at each other; something passed between them, and they turned as one back to Carly. "We're ready, Carly. If that's what it takes. If you'll help us." Stone took a step forward. "Do it. You said you didn't want to mess this one up. You won't. You know you can do it. Do the right thing, Carly Rosales. End this thing you started."

Carly stared at him for a long moment. She swallowed again, appeared to be listening to something, and shook her head hard, like she was trying to clear away gnats. Then she took a deep breath. "I've been a screwup all my life," she said. "Maybe now, at least, I can do something right."

She pointed her hand at Stone. He stiffened, squaring his shoulders and waiting for the blow.

It never came. Instead, he heard Jason yelp. For a moment he thought she had hit his friend instead, but then something sailed past his head so fast he couldn't even tell what it was.

"What the—?" Jason started.

"Carly! *No!*" Stone cried, surging forward.

Carly still stood where she had been, but obviously wouldn't be for long. She swayed, her hands going to her chest, where Jason's machete had hit her so hard its blade had passed through her body and out the other side. Blood welled up around the wound.

As Stone ran to her, her knees buckled and she collapsed in slow motion to the leaf-carpeted ground. He dropped down next to her, grabbing her shoulders. "Carly!"

"Not...gonna be a screwup...again," she whispered. Blood bubbled up around her lips. Stone, shifting to magical senses, could see her radiating power like a small sun.

Carly took a deep shuddering breath, coughed more blood, and then yelled, "*Go home! Go home now!*"

Stone still seeing the world magically, saw the power begin to coalesce. He heard a shriek that would have split the whole clearing if it had been physical, and saw something try to rush toward Carly.

He raised his head and screamed out the final words of the spell that would banish the spirit.

Later, he wouldn't quite be able to reconstruct what happened next. The power of his words joined with the vast glowing pulse that was Carly, forming into some sort of mystical battering ram that shot out like a cannonball, cleaved the dark energy in two, and slammed into the enormous tree under which He of Many Faces's shrine had resided for hundreds of years. The tree rumbled ominously as a glowing rift appeared in front of it. The dark energy, which had flowed back together into one piece again, was sucked inexorably toward the rift.

Many Faces screamed as it disappeared inside, the psychic feedback from its cry nearly deafening Stone. It fought, flinging tree branches, leaves, anything it could reach, but it had no aim. The rift flared bright, then began to shrink. Stone looked down at Carly.

Her eyes were closed. Her chest, with the wicked hilt of the machete protruding from it, was still.

She was smiling.

The tree rumbled again. The glowing rift was getting smaller, collapsing inward on itself.

Stone leaped to his feet, snatching up the magic book, and ran toward Jason and Edna. They had located Lopez, lying up against another tree. He was unconscious. "Come on!" he cried. "We have to go!" But even as he said it, he knew they weren't going to make it. He grabbed Edna's shoulder and shoved her down next to the tree where Lopez lay. "No. Never mind. Edna, we have to put up a shield. That thing's going to blow any second!" Already he was forming his own, and already he was afraid it wouldn't be enough. He was sure that when things went up, they would go up big.

Edna gritted her teeth, sweat pouring from her brow. "I'll try," she said. "Almost out of power, though—" She raised her own shield, but almost immediately it sputtered and died. She looked every bit her age at that moment, and then some; deep, furrowed lines stood out on her ashen-gray face. "Sorry—"

Stone didn't answer. He closed his eyes, breathing hard, and focused everything he had on keeping them protected. "Get in close," he said. "I don't know if it's got enough power—"

He felt Jason pull him in on one side, Edna on the other, and they all huddled in a protective ball over Lopez's unconscious body.

"Al—" Jason rasped.

"Not now, Jason." Stone's voice shook with the effort. He could feel the magic building. They might have run, but he knew there was no way they'd have gotten far enough. Not having to carry Lopez. Not tired as they were. They would have to make their stand here, and that was the best they could do.

"Al. Take my power."

Stone stared. "No, Jason. I can't—" *I can't count on you. I can't split my concentration on a gamble. If you don't come through, we're all dead for sure.*

"Al!" Jason's voice was harsh but strong. "Do it, damn it! If you trust me, *do it!*"

For only a second, Stone wavered. Then he clamped his hand on Jason's shoulder and called for power, as he'd done many times before.

For only a second more, he felt hesitation. *It's not going to work! He can't—*

But then it was there, flowing in, filling him with energy, lighting up his body with more power than he'd used in months.

And it wanted out.

Stone yelled something inarticulate and triumphant, flinging his hands to the sky. The shield flared brighter, forming a radiant, glowing white dome over them all.

The rift collapsed.

The tree exploded.

Everything was white.

And then it was black.

| CHAPTER FORTY-NINE

Two days later

"So, it's over," Peter Casner said.

Stone nodded.

"You aren't going to give me the details, are you?"

"Do you want to hear them?"

Long pause. "Do I need to?"

Stone shrugged. "I doubt it will do any good. No one will believe them."

"No, probably not." Casner shifted in his chair, glancing out his office window. "I suppose you want to know why I asked you to come down here."

"I hope it wasn't to arrest me again."

Casner made a sound that might have been meant as a laugh, but it came out more like a cynical snort. "Somehow, Dr. Stone, I doubt I could keep you on ice if I tried. But no."

"Why, then?"

"I'm not sure," Casner said, shrugging, not meeting Stone's eyes. "Maybe just because I wanted somebody to tell me it really happened."

"How many people died over the past few days, Lieutenant?" Stone asked softly.

Casner paused for a long moment. "Thirty-two, total. That's assuming we've found them all."

"Does that count Carly Rosales?"

"Who's that?"

"The woman who was with us when we came to the park."

"She's dead?" Casner jotted something on his pad. "How? Where is she?"

"You won't find her body. Vaporized, I expect. I can show you where if you like, but there's nothing left to find. Just a crater."

Casner considered. "So...whatever happened to...end this—it happened there?"

Stone nodded.

"But we won't find anything we can make sense of."

"No. Not likely." He paused, then sighed. "We might run into a bit of trouble from the police in Santa Maria, since they saw us with her the night she died. If you could deal with that situation, I'd appreciate it."

Casner nodded. "If they ask, I'll tell them that you had nothing to do with her disappearance."

Now it was Stone's turn for a mirthless laugh. "We had *everything* to do with her disappearance. But I want you to know something, Lieutenant."

"What's that?"

"Carly Rosales died a heroine. She's the one who ended this. We just made it possible for her to do it. If there's some way she could be memorialized—"

Casner looked like this was the last place he wanted to be right now, or the last thing he wanted to be thinking about, but he nodded. "I'll see what I can do."

"Thank you, Lieutenant." Stone rose. "Now, if you'll excuse me, I've a bus to meet."

As he turned to leave, Casner spoke. "Dr. Stone?"

Stone stopped without turning back. "Yes?"

Casner didn't respond for several seconds. "You know—I still want to figure out how to explain this all away. To pretend it didn't happen the way it did. To make some kind of sense out of it. Truth is, as time goes by, I probably will do that. But right now, I want to say—thanks. Because right now, I still believe it happened. And that maybe if you hadn't come down here looking for your friend, it would still be happening. And none of us could have done a fucking thing about it."

Stone shrugged. "You'd have found a way, Lieutenant. You wouldn't have had a choice."

"Maybe. But even so—thanks."

Stone nodded and left the office.

| CHAPTER FIFTY

Verity Thayer's eyes grew wide as she listened to the news reports on the radio from the back seat of Stone's BMW. The newscaster was talking about the aftermath and the cleanup efforts still going on downtown after what was being referred to as the "Ojai Valley Massacre."

"Holy shit," she breathed. "You weren't kidding. This was huge."

Stone nodded. "You're lucky you missed it. But I'd be lying if I said I hadn't wished you were there."

They were driving back to Lopez's house from the bus station in Ventura, where Verity had arrived earlier after returning home from her retreat and getting Stone's phone message the previous night. She nodded. "Yeah, I might have been able to help." She looked at Jason, who was in the shotgun seat. "Nice cast, by the way. You gonna let me sign it?"

He glared at her, but it didn't have much fire behind it. "Yeah, you can sign it—if you wait on me back at Stan's. I'm an invalid now, you know."

She snorted. "Yeah, some invalid. I'll cook for you, but no way am I giving you sponge baths." Her expression grew more serious. "You guys all could have been killed. How's Stan doing?"

"He's all right," Stone said. "Quite a few bumps and bruises, some fractured ribs, and a concussion—he's on medical leave for a few days, but he'll be fine."

"He was damned lucky," Jason said. "If he hadn't been fast enough to deflect himself a little when he got tossed into that tree, he'd be dead."

Verity sighed. "Well, since I missed all the excitement, I guess the least I can do is stick around for a few days and help you guys out till Stan's up and around, especially since Dr. Stone's gonna have to go back home for his classes soon. I already cleared it with Marta at the restaurant."

"Well," Jason said, "I'm not gonna say no to some of your cooking, given that between Stan, Al, and me we might be able to boil water. And that's if Stan's doing the cooking."

They reached Lopez's house and headed inside, Verity carrying her bag. Stone took her aside as Jason went on ahead. "Verity, there's someone else here—someone I'd like you to meet."

She looked puzzled. "Uh—sure. Who?"

"Another practitioner we met down here. She's got—a very different approach to mine. I want to see how the two of you get on. Talk with her for a while, and let me know what you think."

Verity still looked confused, but she'd been studying under Stone long enough to know not to ask too many questions until she'd done what he asked. She nodded and went on inside.

Stone paused inside the door. He'd been thinking about this for a while now, in the back of his mind, and after all of them had recovered as much as they were going to from the events of the last few days, he'd found some time last night to discuss it with Edna. She'd been hesitant at first, protesting that she was too old and out of practice to have anything of value to offer, but Stone had asked her to consider the possibility, and she'd agreed to at least talk with Verity.

It might not work out—there were many ways it could go wrong. Verity might not like Edna, or vice versa, though he suspected the older woman's irascible kindness and Verity's quick-witted cynicism would quickly find common ground. In a way, Stone felt as if he was stepping away from a responsibility, but he also felt like he wasn't doing Verity any favors if he didn't give her access to resources that were more in line with her talents. His apprentice was capable with everything he'd given her, though she didn't have the patience for the bits that involved a large amount of detailed study. What she excelled at, though, was healing magic, both physical and mental. He'd noticed it from the beginning of her time studying with him, and had done his best to incorporate it into her training. She had taken to it like she was born for it, while he, who had never spent much time on anything beyond a few simple healing spells, had improved in teaching her but struggled with the sort of empathic connection needed to truly master it.

He smiled a bit, wryly; Edna was probably right: he *was* too self-centered and arrogant to be more than passably good at other-centered magic like healing. He was a scholar and an innovator: Verity had the latter, but balked at the former. She would probably flourish under Edna's more organic, less book-focused tutelage, if the old woman would agree to take her on. It might be good for Edna, too: mages tended to live a fair bit longer than mundanes (if their work didn't kill them), which meant that Edna, despite her protests about being "old," probably wasn't much more than middle-aged for a magical practitioner. Stone believed the power she'd commanded when she was younger would come back to her in spades if she had to focus it to train someone else.

He sighed again, and reminded himself that he wasn't passing Verity off to a new master, but simply offering her the equivalent of a "visiting semester" where she could learn from another teacher with different skills. And if she didn't want to do it, that was fine, too. He was just glad that things had worked out so he *could* make the offer.

| CHAPTER FIFTY-ONE

I t was late the next afternoon when Jason knocked on the door of Stone's bedroom. "Al? Got a minute?"

"Come on in," Stone said, turning away from his packing. He planned to leave the next morning, which would give him a few days to rest at home before starting his new quarter at Stanford, and wanted to get the packing done before all of them went out for one final dinner together that evening.

Jason came in and sat down in the chair by the window without saying anything.

"How's the arm?" Stone asked.

He shrugged. "Doesn't hurt much. Shouldn't have to wear this thing for long—it's not a bad break."

Stone nodded. "What can I do for you?"

Jason hesitated, looking like he wasn't sure how to say what he had come to say. Finally, he started: "I talked to V this afternoon."

"Yes?"

"She and Edna are getting along great. She told me you want her to come down here and study with her for a while."

"Yes."

"And she says she's gonna do it."

"Yes," Stone said again.

Jason took a breath. "I think it's a good idea," he said. "I guess she's gonna live with Edna out there at her place by the Hot

Springs. I think she might be happy to come back down here for a while. I think she's missed it."

Stone sat down on the edge of the bed and fixed Jason with a probing gaze. "Jason, you didn't come in here to talk about Verity, did you?"

He shook his head. "No."

"What, then?"

"I've been thinking a lot over the last few days," he said after a pause.

"About—?"

"Life. What I want to do with myself. That whole thing with Faces kidnapping me spooked me, but it also got me thinking. I don't want to go through life being a battery. That's not what I'm about. I need to be *doing* things, not just—you know—making it easier for other people to do them." He looked down into his lap. "Does that make any sense?"

Stone nodded. "Of course it does. It can't have been easy for you, spending so much time with Verity and me. I understand that now. I guess I didn't really see it before, but your outburst in the car the other night didn't go unheard." He paused. "So what do you want to do?"

"I've been talking to Stan. I can't really go back to the Academy—I think that ship has sailed, and it doesn't make sense to try to make it work. But there is something else I can do."

"What's that?"

"I can get my PI license and become a private investigator."

Stone raised an eyebrow. "You mean following cheating spouses around and investigating insurance claims?"

"That's some of it," he admitted, "but there's a lot more than that. I can get my firearm carry permit, maybe set up my own little business." He sighed. "Al, all my life I dreamed of being a cop like my dad. I never even considered that it wouldn't work out for me. I can't go through life being an assistant manager at a restaurant—or a gas pump for a guy who can throw lightning bolts with his brain."

"Jason—"

Jason held up his hands. "No, that didn't come out right. I didn't mean it that way. It felt good to be able to help out. I think that's why I got it back there at the end—because I really did want to help. I wasn't conflicted about it anymore. And I don't want to stop doing it forever. But I need to get my head on straight and figure out what *I* want to do. Kinda like V does, you know?"

Stone nodded. "So how are you going to do this? When will you start?"

He took a deep breath. "That's the hard part. That's why I was talking to Stan. It takes classes, and also a lot of hours of working under a licensed PI, or the equivalent. My time at the Academy will count toward it, but Stan said he can talk to some friends and see about putting in a good word."

"I see," Stone said softly. "So what you're telling me is that you've decided to remain here."

"Yeah. At least for a while." He shook his head. "Stan said I could stay at his place for not too much rent, since he's got the extra bedrooms. The apartment up north is month-to-month, so I wouldn't lose too much there. And Marta—I think she'll understand. I think she's been expecting me to do something like this for a long time." He picked up a magazine from a nearby table and leafed through it. "Having V down here was kind of the final thing that made me decide to go for it. That way I can kinda look out for her too, you know?"

"And she, you," Stone said with a small, faraway smile. "Jason, what can I say? I wish you the best of luck, of course I do. I hope you'll make it back up to the Bay Area every now and then—both of you, in fact."

Jason grinned. "Hey, you're not getting rid of us that easily, Al. Besides—once I get my license and V finishes training with Edna, what's to say I can't come back up there and start my agency? And if I get any cases that seem like they're on your side of the street, maybe we can get together and play Ghostbusters again."

"I'll hold you to that," Stone said.

He stood up, still grinning. "Count on it." He paused, then looked hard at Stone. "You take care of yourself, Al. You're not gonna have us around to look after you and remind you to take time for boring stuff like food and sleep."

Stone raised an eyebrow. "I managed before I met you, Jason. I think I'll be all right."

| CHAPTER FIFTY-TWO

The Ojai cemetery was small, rustic, and very beautiful: rather than the typical design of a vast lawn and ordered rows of headstones, its haphazard randomness reminded Stone a bit of an English garden. Dotted by old trees, bounded by a low rock wall, and bisected by a single-lane road, it was nearly deserted at this hour of the morning.

Stone didn't hurry as he walked through, glancing at the headstones here and there as he went. Many of them were old, at least by American standards (Stone, who'd grown up in and around London, had his own ideas about what constituted 'old'), some no more than planks of wood with inscriptions so faint as to be illegible. A few of them sported flowers, some faded and brittle, some so fresh they must have been placed within the last day or two.

There were also several fresh graves, their mounded piles of dirt and lack of headstones paying silent testament to the horrors that had visited this small, peaceful town over the last few days. Stone headed toward one of these, his hair and his black overcoat whipping gently in the late-summer breeze.

He'd made a point of reading the local papers when they came out: there was no official explanation for what had happened. The press, both local and wider, treated the incidents as some sort of aberration—something in the water, perhaps, or in the air, or maybe some kind of bizarre sickness that had flashed through the town and left murder in its wake. None of the explanations made any sense, and Stone didn't think they fooled anyone; even Casner had been quoted in a couple places as being mystified about what had caused the horrors, though he did say he was confident that they were over now and that the citizens of the town could rest easy. Nobody believed that either, even though it was true. Stone supposed it would take a lot of time before people around here went back to leaving their doors unlocked and passing strangers on the street without suspicion.

There was no mention in any of the newspapers about the crater in the forest off a remote fire road a few miles from Creek Road. Stone wondered how long it would take anyone to even find it, or if the ley line in the area would return it to its normal healthy state now that the tablets had been vaporized along with the tree.

Along with Carly.

The grave he was looking for was on the far side of the cemetery, near the back. Like the other new ones it had no headstone, but he had checked with the authorities and been given the location. So many people had died that they were backed up on setting up niceties like headstones. They didn't even have room for all the bodies; the families of many of the victims would have to settle for final resting places in other nearby cities.

Stone raised the large bouquet of flowers, brightly colored in reds, oranges, and yellows, and placed it on the grave. Others were already there: a fading wreath that read *Beloved Daughter*, another smaller one that included a photograph enclosed in plastic to keep it safe from the elements. He crouched down, looking into the merry brown eyes of a woman he'd only had the chance to know a couple days, and thought about what might have been.

"Goodbye, Lindsey," he said softly, and rose again.

"I feel terrible that I ever suspected you of anything," said a gentle voice behind him.

He turned to see Suzanne Washburn standing there, dressed as usual in a bohemian-chic ensemble topped with a colorful headscarf. Her eyes were subdued, her face aged five years since he had last seen her only a short time ago.

"I didn't expect to see you here," he said softly. "In truth, I didn't expect to see anyone this early."

"I came to visit Karen," she said, nodding at another nearby unmarked grave awash in a riot of colorful arrangements. "It's really a shame that it's taking them so long to get the markers up."

"They've been a bit busy."

For a while she only stared at her feet, but then her eyes came up to meet his. "You stopped it, didn't you?"

He nodded. "It's over. I didn't do it alone, though. Mostly you can thank your friend Carly."

"Carly..." she whispered. "She's—gone, isn't she?"

He didn't reply. He didn't have to.

"I hope she found some peace," she said at last. "I always liked Carly, but I always felt like there were things going on in her life that the rest of us would never understand."

"I think that's true of all of us," Stone said.

"I guess it is at that," she agreed. She paused, looking out over the cemetery. A white hearse was coming in, followed by a half-dozen cars. She watched them silently for several moments, then turned back to him. "I don't want to intrude, Dr. Stone. I'll let you go. I just wanted to—" She spread her hands as if to say, *I don't know what I wanted.*

He thought he knew what she meant, even if she didn't. "I understand. Thank you, Mrs. Washburn."

He paused for several moments, taking in the area as if he were committing it to memory. Then he nodded farewell to her and started back toward the small parking area where he'd left the BMW, all packed up and ready to go.

He'd already said his goodbyes that morning to Lopez, Jason, Edna, and Verity. Jason and Verity would be returning to the Bay Area in the next few days to finish their affairs and pack their stuff, but this morning had been no less of a farewell.

He took a last look at Lindsey's grave, and thought about Carly Rodriguez. He thought about what Suzanne had just said, and the last expression on Carly's face.

All was not yet well in this small town, but he thought it was, at least, in the process of getting there. And that would have to be enough for now.

Alastair Stone will return in

HEART OF STONE

Book 7 of the Alastair Stone Chronicles

Coming soon!

AUTHOR'S NOTE

I spent the first eighteen years of my life in the Ojai Valley. *Blood and Stone* is a work of fiction, obviously, but a lot of the details are based on fact. Bart's Books is a real (and very cool) place, where I used to spend a lot of time when I lived there. The Nest Motel, Don Armando's Restaurant, and The Third Eye aren't real, but they're based on real Ojai locations. Matilija Hot Springs exists, though I took so much literary license with it that those familiar with the actual place probably won't recognize it. The Arcade, the Arbolada, Libbey Park, and Creek Road are all real, and almost all of the urban legends I described in the story (such as Char Man and the headless motorcyclist) are based on tales I heard throughout my childhood. You can even buy Char Man hot sauce around the area.

None of the characters in the story are real, nor are they based on real people, living or dead. The "witch club" is very loosely based on something I did myself, but it was in grade school and it was far less elaborate than anything the Sisterhood ever got involved in.

If you're ever visiting southern California, I highly recommend stopping by for a day. Ojai's a beautiful place with a lot of quaint shopping boutiques, great restaurants, and wonderful scenery.

I'm really sorry I broke the town. Nothing personal, I promise.

ABOUT THE AUTHOR

R. L. King is an award-winning author and game freelancer for Catalyst Game Labs, publisher of the popular roleplaying game *Shadowrun*. She has contributed fiction and game material to numerous sourcebooks, as well as one full-length adventure, "On the Run," included as part of the 2012 Origins-Award-winning "Runners' Toolkit." Her first novel in the *Shadowrun* universe, *Borrowed Time*, was published in Spring 2015.

When not doing her best to make life difficult for her characters, King is a software technical writer for a large Silicon Valley database company. In her spare time (*hah!*) she enjoys hanging out with her very understanding spouse and her small herd of cats, watching way too much *Doctor Who*, and attending conventions when she can. She is an Active member of the Horror Writers' Association and the Science Fiction and Fantasy Writers of America, and a member of the International Association of Media Tie-In Writers.

You can find her at *rlkingwriting.com* and *magespacepress.com*, on Facebook at https://www.facebook.com/AlastairStoneChronicles, or on Twitter at *@Dragonwriter11*.

To get a copy of the free novella *Shadows and Stone,* available only to mailing list subscribers, sign up at *rlkingwriting.com*.

Did you enjoy *Blood and Stone?* If you did, please consider posting a review on Amazon or Goodreads letting folks know what you thought!

Thank you so much, and I hope to see you back again for *Heart of Stone,* book #7 of the Alastair Stone Chronicles!

Made in the USA
Las Vegas, NV
11 October 2021